School Library

D0903490

IC HAV

Central High School Library Media Center
116 Rebel Drive
Park Hills, MO 63601

DISCARDED

point
OF
origin

.THE SURVIVORS.
2

point
OF
origin

AMANDA
HAVARD

CHAFIE PRESS · DALLAS, TX

THE SURVIVIORS
Point of Origin

© 2012 Amanda Havard

Published by:
CHAFIE PRESS
7557 Rambler Road, Suite 626
Dallas TX 75231
www.thesurvivorsseries.com

Cover and interior design by TLC Graphics, *www.TLCGraphics.com*
Cover: Tamara Dever; Interior: Erin Stark
Raven, grass, background art ©iStockphoto.com/bulentgultek
Vintage Mexican Skull art ©iStockphoto.com/Man Half-tube

Anonymous. *Beowulf.* Trans.
    Seamus Heany. New York: W.
    W. Norton & Co., 2000. Print.

Hesiod. *Theogony and Works & Days.*
    Trans. Schlegel, Catherine M.,
    and Henry Weinfield.

All rights reserved. No part of this book may be reproduced or transmitted in any form or by any means, electronic or mechanical, including photocopying, recording, or by any information storage and retrieval system, without permission in writing from the publisher, except for the inclusion of brief quotations in a review.

Printed in the U.S.A.

ISBN: 978-0-9833190-4-7

Library of Congress Control Number: 2012930279

To the music-makers for giving me life,
passion, and this story.

contents

Thou shalt not suffer a witch to live.
EXODUS 22:18

What if there was no light?
Nothing wrong, nothing right?
What if there was no time
And no reason or rhyme?
What if you should decide
That you don't want me there by your side
That you don't want me there in your life?

What if I got it wrong
And no poem or song
Could put right what I got wrong
Or make you feel I belong?
What if you should decide
That you don't want me there by your side
That you don't want me there in your life?

"What If?"
COLDPLAY

prologue

November 2, 2011
Suceava, Bukovina, Romania

PEOPLE WERE STARING.

The tall man towered over everyone else as he entered the café. His slick, black-walnut hair hung straight from his pale temples and fell in line with his jawbone. There were deep lines etched into his skin, which looked very much like someone had slashed lines out of wax to create his face. His skin had the sheen of wax, too, and his eyes were a glassy obsidian color. He wore a thick mink coat over a crisp black business suit. Only, somehow, his appearance was still youthful. His presence was so outwardly cold and intimidating that it visibly rattled the patrons of the small café. No one dared look him in the eye.

He took a seat at the table where Sam was waiting for him, reading a newspaper.

"Four thousand years on this planet, and you still can't manage to tell time," Sam said, neither meeting the newcomer's eyes nor putting down the newspaper.

"Come now, Sam, you know better than that. I can tell it. I just don't abide by it," he joked, his smile refulgent despite his severe appearance.

"That's fair. You abide by nothing," Sam said, still eyeing the copy of the *London Times*. "Did you do this, by the way?" Sam asked, flipping to the headline.

"A subway bombing?" he asked incredulously. "What on earth do you think I am?"

"A question I ask myself every day," Sam said with a sigh.

The man took the paper from Sam's hands and set it on the table, then leaned back in his chair and folded his hands across his stomach. His movements were stiff, and his eyes were menacing. "You don't look British. Have you always had that accent? Or did you pick it up along the way?"

"I'm sorry I don't look the part. My mother is from India, but I was born in London. I even went to Oxford for a few years before control became an issue," Sam said. "And I'm not you. I haven't spent my life moving around and taking on a new persona whenever I feel like it," Sam laughed.

The harrowing man across the table did not. "You neglect to acknowledge that adapting new personas is more a requirement than a whim when you're immortal," he said coolly. He was tired of small talk. He switched to Greek, which he sensed no one in the café would understand, preferring a certain privacy. "So you think you've found them?" he asked, his cold demeanor not conveying his excitement.

"Not all of them. I've found one," Sam said quietly, switching languages to match.

Sam's companion scoffed at this, creasing his brow. The lines on his face became so deep, it looked like his skin had cracked. "Impossible. They'd all be in one place. I made it clear they had to remain together," he said.

"What makes you think they listened to you?" Sam asked defiantly, overstepping bounds. "They didn't stay where you told them to go, did they? If they had, we wouldn't be having this conversation."

Sam's friend considered this. "How do you know this is the one I am looking for?"

"She's not a witch, not a vampire, not a shape-shifter — but she's immortal, a mind-reader, superhuman…yet not invincible. And, my god, she's got your hair and skin," Sam recounted almost nostalgically.

Sam's sentiment made the man uncomfortable. He loathed emotion of any kind. So he ignored it. "How do you know she's not invincible?" he asked. "Did you test it?" he asked, his eyes glinting.

"I did, in fact," Sam smiled. "But she also has scars."

"None of them have had scars. It would be impossible."

"And yet I saw them," Sam said coolly.

He was doubtful. "A beating heart?"

Sam looked away from him. "No."

He sighed. "They have had beating hearts."

"Not all of them! Not the ones who had changed already," Sam argued.

"But you said she wasn't a vampire or a shape-shifter. By definition, she hasn't changed!" he hissed.

"I think it's worth tracking," Sam said quietly, carefully.

He narrowed his eyes, penetrating Sam's light eyes with his own gaze. "Fine. Get on it. I'm sure you can handle this promptly, right?"

Sam deflected his gaze.

"You know where to find me when you've got her. I'll be waiting," he said. He was clearly angry that Sam seemed so confident when he was so doubtful.

Sam was hurt that he didn't want to stay. "Are you going there *now*? It's madness. They'll still be celebrating!" Sam said.

"Are you questioning my judgment?" he said. Sam said nothing. He rose to his feet. "I hope you're not wrong," he said flatly. It was a threat.

"I'm not," Sam said quietly. The tall man walked out the door and into the icy streets of Suceava.

the cave

I HAD BEGUN TO STIR. I COULD HEAR YOUNG SURVIVORS IN THE DIS-tance, laughing, running. The sound of chopping wood from a few houses down reverberated in my ears. I knew that, like every morning for the last 320 years, since their forgotten exile from Salem, Massachusetts, the 14 original Survivors were gathered in their chapel, holding a service. Andrew, our patriarch, would be standing in front of them, murmuring their Puritan prayers. And they'd all be following him, by habit if not by faith. They attended these services more often than they would have done in Salem — as if the accusation of witchcraft had stalked them for all these centuries and remained a cause for repentance. The morning ran routinely as it always did. I heard the youngest Survivors scurry past our door, a mixture of bare feet and boots crunching hard snow, reciting passages from their ancient Bible. It was as if I'd never left at all.

I rolled to my side, not wanting to wake up just yet. Eyes still closed tight, I sent one hand out to feel the other side of the bed. It was empty.

It was empty most mornings. In recent months, Everett had lain with me until I'd fallen asleep, but then he'd slip from bed. The Winters and I had spent the last three months living with the Survivors in their city, and though it wasn't my favorite arrangement, they loved being here. For one, Everett and his younger siblings, Mark and Ginny, had strong-armed their mother into allowing them to forgo their usual human routine now that they lived in a community full of immortals — none of whom needed sleep, many of whom couldn't — and so the nighttime had become their playground. They sometimes used it for making practical preparations for our dismal future, but based on the number of mornings one or more of them came back with eyes brighter and redder than when they had left, I was sure they indulged, during their darker waking hours, in activities they were still keeping secret from the Survivors.

I hadn't pushed to determine if this was the case exactly. I was still learning how to carefully balance loving someone and hating a part of him — a defining, integral part — at the same time. Asking Everett and his siblings fewer questions about midnight murders helped me walk this tightrope more effectively.

I finally opened my eyes. From the light, I could tell it was still very early. In the six months I had gone without sleep, I had forgotten the significance of mornings. I hadn't remembered what it felt like to exist in human-length days. There was peace at night, then welcome morning sun filtering through the bedroom windows and a bit of newness each day. I had fallen in love with these things in Moscow, just before I had come here, to the Survivors' city, and I had been sleeping ever since. I could only fall asleep, of course, if Everett Winter's arms hugged me close to his cool core. Honestly, I did not like that I depended on him like this. I didn't like to depend on anyone for anything.

The Winters had realized they would need a place of their own in the Survivors' City if we were to spend a long time here. So one day not long after we had come back to tell the Survivors of their grim fate, they had brought supplies for a house, and, in days, they had one built. It was modest by their standards, but it was still out of place here. It sat at the end of a row dilapidated houses off the main square of my family's city, taller than the others and certainly newer, its fresh layer of commercial paint taunting the old cabins that made up the place I once called home. I was embarrassed that we were living in a home nicer than the other Survivors'. It made it apparent to them that there were classes — that some people in this world were more privileged or had more resources than others. This had never been made known to Survivors before because no one from the outside had ever invaded, as the Winters were doing now. And I had brought them.

It was just one more thing to feel guilty about.

And, so, I didn't spend much of my free time among my Survivor peers. This morning, like every morning, when I climbed out of bed and sensed that no one else was in our house, I sank into an antique armchair I bought in Bigfork that stood in the corner of the room Everett and I shared. I put my feet up on the rickety ottoman and reached for a book from the stacks of them scattered on the floor. I was hopeful when Andrew had promised me that they — that the Survivors — would make peace with the Winters if it meant I would help them. I ignorantly assumed this meant that my family as a whole would accept the Winters and, more importantly, would accept my return.

And they did accept the Winters, to an extent. I could read it off of them. Young girls had crushes on each of the Winter brothers, and young men longed to be like them. Patriarchs respected Anthony's ferocity and firm hand. Many women and men alike revered Adelaide for all she could teach them about witchcraft. Every boy lusted after Ginny, even after Madeline when she came; they became symbols of glamour, of femininity. Of the beauty of the world outside.

But they hated me.

This was easier to forget when I was alone in this room, in a chair from the outside, with books from the outside. But I could not forget it entirely. I could, after all, feel every emotion, hear every thought of every Survivor inside the city walls.

So, as a distraction, I continued my research as if this were any other room I'd lived in anywhere in the world, ignoring the fact that my entire family lived just yards outside my window. And hated me.

I had purchased nearly every book on modern interpretations of supernatural creatures I could find — from an early edition of *Dracula* to textbooks dissecting the myths, and even every book off the teen section's "supernatural table" at a bookstore in Kalispell — and I had read them over and over again. I picked up one whose spine had already cracked and reread sections of it. I was always struck by how these fictional creatures who so closely mirrored the Winter children were characterized with such romance. When my boyfriend returned to me with glowing crimson eyes and a fresh vigor that I knew only came from consuming human blood, there was no romance in it. There was only pain in it. Only disgust. Only the gut-wrenching truth that we were not alike as immortals but rather so unalike as creatures. He could kill. I could not.

I shook my head to break the thought process. I could not dwell on this about him, about the Winters. This I learned. So I pretended not to notice.

Then I heard noises outside and below me, and I was grateful for the distraction. I rose from the chair and crossed the cool wood floors to the window overlooking the expansive backyard, a picturesque winter wonderland. Mark and Everett were wrestling in the snow. I heard Ginny rustling in the kitchen downstairs, making food of some kind at her supernatural pace. I knocked gently on the window, and both boys froze instantly, turning around to see me in the window. In seconds, Everett was in the house and up the stairs.

The door to our room flung open. He was disheveled, his dark chocolate hair was windblown, and his ivory skin was absolutely cold as ice, but Everett Winter was still as beautiful as the moment I'd met him. Only now, he was mine.

"Morning, gorgeous," he said, putting his icy hands on my cheeks as he kissed me. I shivered a little, from the cold or kiss I couldn't be sure. He pulled me closer.

"Mmm," I said softly, "Good morning to you." I had already seen from across the room that his eyes were a deep burgundy today and not the bright, glowing red they would be if he'd eaten overnight. I learned that the burgundy color was almost as bright as his eyes got in the wintertime, especially in weather this cold. No amount of green vegetables could turn them green — photosynthesis in the eyes, his father had once called it — in the tundra of winter in northwest Montana. "What have you crazy kids been up to?" I asked. I unbuttoned his thick coat and slid it off his arms, and then I put my arms around his neck and began to relax. It was a signal. A fraction of a second later, he had swooped me up into his arms, his favorite thing to do. I would only let him when I was feeling particularly lazy or lovable, or, like now, just wanted to be close to him.

"Where to, mademoiselle?" he smiled.

"Bed, perhaps," I said. I wouldn't mind dozing for a little while longer, held tight against him. "Or we could go see what Ginny's making if you want some food," I said, stroking his smooth face. He grinned at me, a little sideways. I sighed. "Okay, food it is." He was such a boy. "But we can't get too engrossed. We do have a plane to catch!" I said. He grinned again and sped quickly down the stairs and into the kitchen with me tucked close to his chest.

"Morning," Ginny said. She didn't turn around as we entered the small kitchen.

"Morning," I responded. "Down, please," I said to Everett. He always looked a little disappointed when I said this. I pretended not to notice.

"Sleep well?" Ginny asked, flipping pancakes.

"Would have slept better if you didn't steal Everett in the middle of the night," I joked.

"Don't blame me," she said. "It was all Polly."

"What was all Polly?" a voice from outside echoed. It was Mark. Polly was their affectionate — read: emasculating — nickname for him, supposedly because his middle name was Apollo. I tend to believe they just liked calling him Polly.

Ginny responded in a normal tone of voice, and then Mark spoke quietly again, his words too soft for me to make out. I could hear things from far away, but the Winters could hear everything. It never ceased to amaze me.

"Order up," Ginny said, sliding the pancakes onto a plate and handing it to Everett. Suddenly Mark swooped into the room, taking the plate from an unsuspecting Everett's hands.

"Hey!" he barked, and smacked the back of Mark's head. Mark slapped back at him, laughing.

Ginny and I leaned against the countertop, watching their antics. "They're five-year-olds," she breathed. I laughed. I adored them like this. I looked around the room at three of my favorite people in the world and was suddenly much happier.

I put my arm around Ginny and rested my head on her shoulder. "I love being a part of this," I said.

"Too bad. We hate you being a part of this," she joked, her arm around my waist. "You all packed and ready to abandon us for those human friends of yours?" she asked.

"Of course. I can't wait to get away from you, naturally," I kidded, nudging her.

Gin? I said in my mind.

Yeah?

Were you the one who told him I wanted to see Corrina for her birthday? I asked.

Actually, it was all him, she answered. I smiled. That made me love him even more.

The boys eventually stopped scuffling and sat down to eat. Mark had narrowly escaped a crushing blow from his big brother. This is how it would always end: in a draw. Everett was stronger; Mark was faster. Or maybe it was just a draw because neither would actually hurt the other.

"Mmm," Mark said. "Sis, you've outdone yourself." He leaned over and kissed Ginny's cheek. He turned to me and kissed my cheek, too. It was the first time I was close enough to see that his eyes were a glaring crimson red. "Morning, little one," he said.

"I hear you're to blame for stealing Everett," I said, nibbling on a few berries to distract myself from Mark's eyes.

"Guilty always," he smiled.

"She's going to fight you for that one of these days," Everett joked.

Mark was smug. "I'd like to see her try." I shoved him and he made a grand gesture of falling backward, but then he snapped himself up off the ground when he was only inches away from it. It was a very inhuman movement.

"Where is everyone else?" I asked.

"Mom and Madeline are at Lizzie's, I think," Ginny said. "Crazy how Mom and Lizzie have bonded, isn't it?"

I shrugged, thinking it wasn't that odd to me. I quite enjoyed that they liked each other. "What about Anthony and Patrick?" I asked.

"Dad and Pat are at the Canada house," Mark said, now tackling a basket of green vegetables to fade his eyes.

"Will I ever get to see this place?" I asked.

"Maybe," Everett said. "Depends on if we like you enough to keep you around." I stuck out my tongue at him. I blamed Mark for my newly acquired unceremonious tendencies.

"When do you guys have to get out of here?" Ginny asked. I drank some hot tea to warm myself.

"Our first flight leaves from Kalispell at 1:40," Everett said. "It will take about an hour to drive up there, I think. We'll leave around 11:30, maybe?"

"You're driving to the airport? You could run so much faster," Mark said.

"Oh, believe me, brother, I know. But I'm just guessing the princess won't want to run in couture, and I can only imagine how dressed she'll be to see her fashionista partner-in-crime," Everett said. A good guess. I had already laid out a newly ordered outfit delivered to a post office box I'd procured in Kalispell: Carolina Herrera cowl-neck fur, Alexander McQueen stiletto booties, and a knee-length Derek Lam leather skirt. No running for me.

"You know, you only get to call me princess if you say it in a loving way," I chided.

"Okay, *princess*," Mark chimed in, his voice high-pitched and mocking. I smacked him.

"We're going to miss you!" Ginny squealed. "We haven't been apart for this long in months!" The boys rolled their eyes. "Are you excited to see Corrina?"

"I am, but that doesn't hold a candle to how excited she is that I'm bringing a boy with me," I said, imagining Corrina's tendency to bounce when she was happy.

Everett laughed. "I'm excited to meet the ginger cheerleader," he admitted. Everett had formed a bond with Corrina and Felix though they've never met. They'd been speaking for months on Twitter after I'd once let it slip that I was no longer traveling alone. "Think she and Fefe are upset you're not skipping home hand-in-hand with the fair-haired boy?" he asked, winking at me. He was asking about Cole Hardwick, whose face I had last seen as I walked out on him at a Thai restaurant in London almost four months ago. I had left him heartbroken, and I felt miserably guilty for it. It was not my favorite topic of discussion, something Everett definitely knew. I narrowed my eyes at him and didn't respond.

So Ginny did, always looking to squash our tension. "I think she's more upset about 'getting so old,'" she said. Each of us laughed, the youngest among us was Mark, who'd be 100 in just a few short days.

But Corrina was upset at "aging." She frequently talked about it on Twitter. She was turning 24, which seemed impossible since I'd met her when she was only 21. She was aging so fast, and in that short time that I had known her, it appeared she had actually grown up. She graduated from college. She got married. I was 145, and though some days I felt 1,000, I usually felt sixteen for how little I'd done, for how little I'd learned about myself. I couldn't understand how Corrina had surpassed me in this way. How she'd figured out so much about herself, her life, and what she wanted when I had figured out so little.

"Think we have time for another round?" Mark goaded, punching Everett in the ribs.

"Hey!" Everett snapped.

"You can only have him if he's already packed, and if he will be clean and pretty and ready to go in two and a half hours," I said.

The boys were already on their feet, racing toward the door. "Done packing. I'll be pretty!" I heard Everett call as he tailed after Mark. I crossed my arms and frowned. Then Everett ran back in. "Forgot something," he smiled. Ginny rolled her eyes as Everett leaned in and kissed me. I kissed him back.

I put my hands on either side of his eyes. "If you two do anything that turns them red, you better come back here and eat your weight in vegetables. Deal?" I said as sternly as I could.

He laughed. "Deal." Then he flew out the door.

——◆——

IT DIDN'T TAKE US QUITE AN HOUR TO GET TO KALISPELL, BUT IT WAS CLOSE. We absolutely could have run faster, but I wanted to drive. The highway to the airport was clear enough for me to drive my CL 63, which I had missed, having been forced to drive one of the modified (or "tricked out," as I was coached to say) Toyota Land Cruisers in the snow for the last three months. Mark had commissioned the tricking-out of these when we were in Moscow, and the pair of them had become quite useful in getting us all around. But now I was transitioning to human Sadie. CL-63-AMG-driving, McQueen-heel-wearing Sadie. And I did want to look nice to see Corrina. Everett wanted to drive, having found a spot in his heart for the AMG engine and perhaps feeling a deep pang of separation from his Maserati from his experiences with the Land Cruisers too, but I refused. My car. My drive.

On the plane, Everett held my hand while he read a book at a human pace, a method he practiced to enjoy the literature and also to look inconspicuous. I closed my eyes and tried to focus. Having spent a good deal of time with my family over the last three weeks, my sensing abilities were growing. I was now able to sense minds from a distance with better accuracy, even read the thoughts of minds I knew from great distances. This was turning into a very useful talent, albeit disconcerting to quite literally hear voices in my head all the time.

But despite the increase in my powers, I had been unable to do the one thing I was trying to do lately: find the missing members of my family. It was mid-October when Everett and the rest of the Winter family followed me to a hillside in Romania to help fight the *nosferatu* shape-shifters I'd met there. And it was then that everything changed for me. That's when Anthony told me of his vision of a war between supernatural creatures — in fact, a war between Survivors. He'd seen the rogue members of my family bounding over the city walls, attacking the Survivors they'd left behind. The Winters believed that nothing could prevent what Anthony saw in a vision once he had it, but they thought we should find the dangerous rogues anyway. In early November, Andrew had asked me to track down the twenty-eight Survivors who had gone AWOL. Andrew just wanted to find his family, but my motives ran deeper. I believed that if we could find them, then we could stop the war before it began — even if it meant killing them to protect the rest of the family.

But this was proving to be difficult. Being a skilled tracker with unique senses, it should have been easy for me. I could find almost anyone, anywhere, but these twenty-eight were off my radar entirely.

It was now the last days of January, and I was frustrated I had made so little progress. In the air, in a quiet first class cabin with Everett's presence to soothe me, I centered my mind and filtered through all the humming and buzzing and voices in my head, scanning every mind I came across on the ground below. I did this for the entire plane ride from Kalispell to Seattle, then for the first two hours of our flight from Seattle to Dallas. Frustrated, I found nothing.

Abandoning this, I began flipping through books on my electronic reader. In addition to my foray into supernatural literature, I had also bought many classics. Plato's *The Republic*. Sun Tzu's *The Art of War*. Machiavelli's *The Prince*. Karl Marx's *Communist Manifesto*. Histories of the early American colonies, and philosophies from Hobbes, Locke, Payne, Calvin, Rousseau. Every one of Shakespeare's histories. Any works on world mythology I could find.

In my life, there were always questions I was researching. I wanted to know where we came from, and I wanted to know how and why the Survivors were the way they were. And, however shamefully, I searched because I wanted to learn how we could die. But my desire for my own mortality could no longer be at the forefront of my quest. Now that 28 of my siblings had evolved into violent *vieczy* versions of themselves who were undoubtedly roaming the earth murdering humans at an alarming rate, I needed to know — we all needed to know — how to

kill a Survivor. We were simultaneously searching for them and searching for a way to kill them. Everett hated this. He knew that if we found
a way to kill one of them, I'd have a way to kill myself, too — if I wanted
to. And for 128 years of my life, I'd wanted to. I just wanted one, normal
life. That would be enough for me.

I settled on Plato's *The Republic*. His famous depiction of Utopia
scarily mirrored the Survivors' society, right down to a description of
how the community could be stronger if loyalty was to the Republic
as a whole instead of to the individual family. Clearly, the fourteen original Survivors believed this to be a necessity: They pointed to it as the
reason that none of us knew who our parents were. It made me feel
less like a freak that there had already been theories of cultures like
my family's in place for thousands of years, but it angered me that Plato
would call our world a Utopia. But the Survivors, too, had always called
paradise what I had called a prison.

I reread the Allegory of the Cave. It had happened to me just the
way Plato said it would. I had first broken free of the chains my family
placed on me. I ventured into the world outside and saw the enlightened existence. And then I had come back to my family, who had lived
in such isolation, who had spent their existence in the proverbial cave,
and tried to show them the virtue of the outside world.

But they resisted. They couldn't see the outside world the way I had.
They had never known it, and so how could they understand it?

Plato had no rhetoric for what to do when you finally got the Unen-
lightened to turn their heads long enough to see the outside world at
precisely the moment it proved itself unworthy, but that's just what
happened here. My family knew now that Survivors who left our world
and ventured into the unknown turned into something terrible, something evil — even though I had been able to escape this evil for reasons
unknown to us all. So the other Survivors could remain forever inside

these walls, condemning all those who tried to show them the light outside as heretics.

And so they hated me, their conduit to the outside. There was merit to their hatred, though. They blamed me for the 28 rogue Survivors leaving. They were, after all, only following my example. They hated that I threatened that world, that the Winters, too, threatened their world because we had each experienced a world they pretended never existed. Until I came back. They could live on, satisfied that their world was better than the world outside. But it wasn't better. It just seemed safer. They could never understand the distinction. (What's the old parable? Ignorance is bliss?)

And then in the twist of all twists, going against everything Plato wrote, I, the enlightened one, wandered back into the cave and resumed my spot in the darkness, lined up among those in chains. And I'd hated every minute of it. The closer I got to Corrina — and to my nearly human life — the lighter I began to feel.

But it didn't change anything. I let the book reader fall on my chest. My throat felt tight and the bridge of my nose stung. My breathing was ragged and hiccuppy. Though no tears fell, I was crying.

"Princess?" Everett asked, having sensed my tension.

"I'm fine," I said.

"What..."

"Why did we come back?" I sobbed. "They hate me so much!"

He sighed heavily, as if he'd known this conversation would come. "They'll never understand the sacrifices you've made to go back. They'll never understand what it means for you to give up your freedom, to risk your life for your family. They're taking you for granted, but you know you're doing the right thing," he said.

"I wish none of this had happened. Just last year I was existing as a human. Living in that world. Doing stupid human things like being a bridesmaid. When did this happen, Everett? When did I give it all up?" I asked.

"You didn't," he said. "It's just on hold right now. We'll get back to normal some day." He pulled me close to him. I didn't want it to be on hold. I didn't want any of this.

Everett took *The Republic* out of my lap. "Rereading this will not help," he said.

"I didn't think it would," I admitted, unable to look him in the eye. Instantly, I was uneasy. I rose to my feet quickly, startling him. "I'm going to go touch up. We'll be landing soon, I'm sure," I said.

"Okay," he said. He looked worried. Really, I just needed to be alone.

I fumbled down the aisle and into the tiny airplane lavatory, and looked at my inhumanly perfect espresso hair and that glowing isabelline skin with resentment. I stared into those violet eyes, more tired now than they'd looked in 145 years.

I'd ruined my life.

CHAPTER TWO

visionary

WHEN WE WALKED OFF THE PLANE IN DALLAS THAT MONDAY NIGHT, I could hear Corrina's excitement all the way down the corridor. She was screaming in her head, *Sadie has a boyfriend! Sadie has a BOYFRIEND!* Then, seeing the scene through her eyes, I watched as the world in front of her began to shake violently. She was jumping up and down. I laughed out loud.

"What's funny?" Everett asked, nudging me as we walked down the corridor at the super-busy DFW airport. This was my first trip to Texas. From Corrina's love of the place, I was excited to see it.

"Corrina's freaking out," I said. "Like, a lot."

He smiled. "What's she saying?"

I rolled my eyes and let my voice take on Corrina's enthusiastic pitch. "Sadie's got a boyfriend! Sadie's got a boyfriend!" I mused. "Over and over and over again," I said, returning to my normal voice. "I think it's really more of a squeal than actual speech."

Everett laughed, too. "This is going to be great. I can already tell how much fun it is to be around someone who calls me your boyfriend," he said.

"How's that?" I asked. As we got closer to baggage claim, Corrina's mental screams grew deafening.

He paused and turned toward me. "Have you ever even once called me your boyfriend?" he asked.

"Out loud?" I asked. I thought about it. "Maybe when I told Corrina about you?"

"You did no such thing!" he said, jokingly offended. "I was there, Sadie. On Twitter, remember? You specifically said 'Oh, yeah… I've been traveling with this guy, Everett. He's…cool.' It was so romantic."

I rolled my eyes again. We had come to a stop in front of the giant revolving door that would take us out to baggage claim and toward the bouncy Corrina. "Okay, *boyfriend*," I said, dragging out the emphasis. "You ready for this?"

He smiled his most devious smile and grabbed me by the waist so my feet just skimmed the ground and kissed me. I realized too late he was pushing through the revolving door so that Corrina got a full view of this. She screamed out loud.

"Eeeeee! Sadie!"

"Oh, I'm sorry…" Everett said, pretending he hadn't realized she'd see us.

I shot him an icy stare. *Couldn't resist,* he said in his mind. Then he smiled again, flashing his beautiful teeth. I could not resist that smile. Everett had acquired the ability to shield me from his mind — a bulwark, he had called it — but over the past few weeks, he had learned how to push specific thoughts outside his mental armor so I could hear him when he wanted me to. Conversely, I had learned to crawl over the top of the mental rampart and graze a few things — sometimes thoughts but, more commonly, feelings and strong emotions — from his mind. He didn't know that, though. I knew he would not like me doing this. I even knew it was sort of…wrong. But I was making so much progress with my powers! I was beginning to have faith that one day I'd be able to dance back and forth across the bulwark at will.

"Corrina!" I said. She jumped into my arms just the way she had the last time I had met up with her days before her wedding in Tupelo, Mississippi. That was just over six months ago, but my entire world had shifted, shaken, and reshaped since then. The clearest evidence of this was the striking presence of my supernatural *boyfriend* being introduced to my only human friends.

"You're here! You're here!" she said, clapping her hands together. "And *you*!" she said, directing her gaze at Everett. An awestruck expression quickly appeared on her face. Her eyes went soft, and the sides of her mouth curled up into a syrupy smile. "Hello, there," she said. I got the impression she was trying to refrain from whistling at him. As Everett smiled back at her, she had only one clear thought: *Oh. My. God.*

Everett ate it up. "Corrina, it's so good to meet you. I feel like I already know you from everything Sadie's told me!" he said enthusiastically as he reached out and hugged her tight. She blushed furiously. I elbowed him. Hard. *So much fun*, he said in his mind.

"Honey," I said, my voice light but with an edge only Everett would pick up on, "Why don't you get our bags?"

"Sure, babe," he said, matching my game. We had never called each other "honey" or "babe" before. He sauntered away toward the conveyor belt but not before he had time to run one hand through his soft brown locks and wink over his shoulder as he went. Corrina swooned.

"Sadie," she said urgently, "Where did you find him?"

"California," I said. "Epic, isn't he?" I grinned. The comment was more than a little uncharacteristic.

"Epic," she agreed, dazed. She hadn't taken her eyes off him.

"Where's Felix?" I asked.

Oh no! she thought. She closed her eyes and exhaled through her teeth. "Right, Felix," she said. I laughed. "He's in the car," she said.

"Well, looks like Everett's got the bags, so let's not keep Felix waiting," I said.

Corrina had lost her focus again, and stared at Everett from across the room, even though he wasn't facing us.

She's still checking me out, isn't she? Everett asked me.

"Of course," I whispered low. He'd hear me.

"You know, I'm not sure which is getting me more," Corrina said. "That he's the most beautiful man I've ever met in person, that he's wearing a Roberto Cavalli red velvet sport coat and can actually pull it off, or that he is so madly in love with you that it like radiates out of his skin," she said. I smiled sheepishly. "I cannot believe you didn't tell me about him sooner," she said, smacking my arm.

"Let's go find Felix," I said as Everett walked up with the bags.

CORRINA, FELIX, EVERETT, AND I SPENT THE EVENING TOURING DALLAS. EVERY place we drove, Corrina gave us an extensive social rundown of who lived where and what sort of shopping could be done there. I was giddy when, in one of Dallas' nicest neighborhoods, Corrina pointed out Highland Park Village — which was essentially a glorified strip mall — and from the road I could see Chanel, Tory Burch, Prada, and about a dozen other places I could get lost in for hours.

"Can we go shopping here?" I asked, my voice cracking with excitement.

"Of course!" Corrina said. "We'll have to abandon the boys first, though. I'm assuming they won't swoon over a Birkin bag the way we might."

My ears perked at Birkin bag. "Hermès…" I whispered, so soft only Everett could hear.

He watched as I took all of this in, my excitement growing exponentially. He seemed thoroughly amused as he kissed my hand. "Princess," he breathed, winking at me out of the corner of his eye.

"Felix," I asked, "what will you boys do while we shop?" I hadn't considered that we might split up, but I should have seen it coming. I was instantly grateful for the unseasonably mild Dallas January weather — 64 degrees, even at eight o'clock at night. It would not go well if Corrina and Felix discovered Everett's...predatory tendencies. At least, not on this trip. I looked at Everett's eyes — a cool hazel with obvious green highlights coming out in the slivers of city light. It was the greenest I'd seen his eyes since he arrived in Moscow months before. I breathed a sigh of relief.

"Not sure," Felix said. "It depends on what your man is into. Do you golf, Everett?"

"Absolutely!" Everett enthused. I looked at him dumbfounded. I had never heard this before. "But I don't have my sticks with me, man."

"Not a problem. I've got a spare set if you don't mind playing with borrowed clubs," Felix said. There was testosterone-tainted excitement flowing through the air. The boys had connected.

I turned to Everett. "Golf?" I mouthed.

Sadie, I live 500 yards from Pebble Beach — the *golf destination of the U.S.* — *and it never crossed your mind that we might be into golf?* he asked. I shook my head. He smirked. *You know, before we got mixed in with you and the crazy Survivors and all this impending war nonsense, we were pretty typical — golfing and all.*

Even in his thoughts, I heard the tinge of regret in his words. He wasn't like his brothers and his father. He didn't have brutality pulsing through his venomous veins. I sensed that Everett wanted nothing more than the two of us to be together in a world unclouded by blood-lust and violence; all he wanted was for us to end up together in a peaceful existence. He was waiting for Anthony's vision of the two of us on the beach — happy and relaxed and uncomplicatedly in love — to come to fruition. He would do whatever it took to get us there.

"All right, it's settled," Corrina exclaimed. "Tomorrow morning, we'll go our separate ways. Felix, you get a tee time at the club so you boys can have your fun, and I'll show Sadie why I call Dallas a shopping mecca."

"Sounds like a plan," Everett said. He squeezed my hand. I smiled. This trip was the first time since I'd met him that we'd had a chance to act like a normal couple. I realized that our Dallas vacation was exactly what we needed to counteract months of stagnation in the Survivors' City, preparing for a battle we knew little about, and trying to track members of my family we couldn't find. For just these few days with Corrina and Felix we were allowed to feel like normal people. Like humans.

—◆—

THE NEXT DAY WITH CORRINA WAS BEYOND ENJOYABLE. THOUGH I WAS GROW-ing just as close to Ginny as I was with her, Corrina had a special place in my life. She'd taken me under her wing when I needed it most. She had nothing to do with anything negative or stressful in my life. So as we flipped through racks at Prada or perused the tables of scarves at Hermès, she was blissfully unaware of danger and complication, of all the things in my supernatural world. And it showed. We had so much fun together, our biggest concerns debating Tory Burch continuing the coral trend into winter or the acceptability of brightly colored Rag & Bone skinny jeans in January (we came out favorable on both counts). The most intense conversation we had was wondering whether Cor-rina's loving husband would notice that she spent more on a pair of Louboutins than their mortgage payment (less favorable on this one). And we laughed all day long. I had missed her. I had missed passing for a human.

Near the end of the day, Corrina and I made it back to her Uptown condo to get dressed for her birthday dinner. I used this opportunity to wear my newly-purchased long-sleeved Rebecca Minkoff dress that cut halfway up my thigh and hugged close to my body. It was a daring number for me, even with the opaque tights I had on underneath it. I slipped into an adventurous pair of red Fendi heels that made me Everett's height. I would not need to fit into the crook of his neck — my favorite place to be — sitting at the dinner table with Corrina and Felix.

When Everett saw me, his eyes widened. "You look beautiful," he said, a little stunned. As he leaned in to kiss my cheek, in his mind he added, *Anyone ever tell you that you make it hard to be a gentleman?*

My breath caught; my stomach tingled. Everett Winter was starting to affect me in ways I had never experienced.

We drove in Felix's Audi S5 convertible to Nobu in downtown Dallas. I loved the feel of the mild air as it spun around us. Having spent all my time in the wilderness lately, I was dazzled by the city lights. I missed the pace and even the plastic pretense of the city.

We had knocked out four courses and two bottles of wine when our dinner was winding down to the perfect mellow place. Everett and Felix were talking about playing a few courses in Southern California together. Corrina was leaning into Felix as he talked across the table, her own thoughts quiet. I held Everett's hand, but I was leaning back and quiet too. I idly wondered if Felix had planned it so that a birthday cake for Corrina would arrive at the end of dinner.

It was right then that the buzzing in my head erupted into violent screams, faintly familiar voices, and terror.

I heard Felix ask, "If you're used to ocean courses, have you played Trump National yet?" as my vision moved from the subdued ambience of Nobu and into a different kind of darkness. It was the last thing I heard before all five of my senses were immersed in a different place.

I was moving and turning and talking like I was a player instead of an onlooker.

I was unaware, at first, of who was talking around me. But the familiar voices matched faces I knew like my own. They were the faces of eight Survivors from my generation, all men, scattered in appearance as each of them had stopped aging anywhere between 15 and 50 years of age. They hissed at each other in low, cold voices. Their eyes were blood red, their skin paler and smoother than it had been the last time I had seen them. Their brows were tightly creased into venomous stares.

I couldn't read the minds around me, but I understood what was happening. They had herded a group of four young women into a dark, damp place. I tried to look around, tried to see where I was standing, but I couldn't move. I could only watch helplessly.

"Noah, you get this one's legs. Make her stop kicking," Derek, one of my gruff brothers barked.

"I can't," Noah's voice said. But the words had come out of my mouth. "Hurry up and finish her off. The venom's what's making her thrash like that." I understood then. I was inside Noah's body. Inside his mind.

In horror, I watched as Derek's mouth moved back to the flailing girl's throat. The other three terrified girls were sobbing hysterically, screaming, watching my deformed brother drink the life out of her. Unable to contain himself, another brother, Peter, snarled and latched onto the other side of the girl on the ground, sinking sharp white teeth into her leg to drink from another artery. I could feel a desire building inside me, one I couldn't explain or empathize with. I swallowed — Noah swallowed — hard as a white-hot searing pain built up in my throat. The longer we watched this happen, the hotter the burn became. It began to feel like swallowing knives. Or fire.

The others must have felt it, too. The remaining brothers pounced on the three girls. Despite his greatest efforts, Noah gave in too, and I felt helpless as he — as I — jumped toward one of the dying girls. In seconds, their bodies were limp as greedy mouths — my own included — sucked warm blood out of each of them, quieting their cries of terror. The part of me that was still *me* was physically sick, tormented by an image I already knew I'd never be able to erase. But a part of me was fully immersed in Noah's head, feeling what he was feeling, ignited by the hot human blood cooling the burn in my throat. His whole body reacted in a lusty mixture of relief and stimulation. The blood was warm on my tongue.

Then it all went black.

—◆—

I HEARD VOICES CALLING. "SADIE! SADIE!" EVERETT'S COLD HANDS CRADLED MY face. Corrina's screams were desperate.

I gasped for breath and tried to bite back the screams in my own throat. My body shook. I felt a pointed burn at the base of my skull, exactly the same burn I had felt in my throat while I was lost in Noah's mind.

My eyes unsealed themselves. I was splayed out on the ground, and a crowd hovered over me, including waiters and other diners. Felix was holding a terrified Corrina, and Everett's face was shrouded in fear and pain.

"Everett," I breathed, grinding my teeth, as the pain in my head throbbed. "I found them. I saw them!" I gasped. "I saw them kill. I tasted the blood," I cried. I was hysterical, not thinking at all who could hear me, or what they would think. Everett's face went even whiter as his eyes widened in horror. I began to seize violently.

"Call an ambulance!" a waiter screamed.

I grabbed Everett's shirt. "No!"

"Way ahead of you," he said, scooping me up into his arms. He was on his feet and pushing through the crowd in no time. I could only imagine the restraint it took him to move at a slow, human pace. "It's fine. She's fine. She'll be okay," he said. "Excuse me, please. Yes, she'll be okay." I let my head hang backward. The pain was so much more intense than any other pain I'd ever felt. "Felix, Corrina," Everett said. "Come on. We have to get her home." I could hear the questions and serious concern in their thoughts. Why weren't we going to the hospital? What the *hell* was that?

But they obliged anyway. I knew it was hard not to listen to Everett Winter when he told you to do something. It was a struggle I felt often.

In Felix's car, Everett held me against his cold chest. "Please get us home," he pleaded.

"Everett…" Corrina began.

"She's fine," he interrupted, his patience wearing thin.

"Maybe we should get her checked out, man," Felix tried.

"She's fine!" Everett snapped, harsher this time.

I found my voice again. "No doctors," I said hoarsely.

Corrina and Felix exchanged glances. They were terrified. *What are you not telling me, Sadie?* Corrina asked in her mind.

Once we were back at the condo, Everett laid me down on the couch. The pain in my skull had subsided, but a low fire in the spot still burned. I was certain it would be hot to the touch. I wanted desperately to flush the violent images from my mind, but I kept re-examining them, trying to find clues about where the attack had happened, where we would find at least these eight of my missing family. I tried to stop the gruesome scene in my mind before the metallic taste of blood filled my mouth again, but I could not stop it in time. My stomach lurched with each revolting echo.

Corrina hovered over me while Everett knelt at my side, his face close to mine. "What can we do for her?" Corrina asked.

"Can you just give us a minute?" Everett asked. Corrina arched an eyebrow at him. "Please," he said. Corrina's eyes met mine. I nodded, signaling it okay for her to leave. Defeated, she backed out of the room.

Everett's voice was low and hurried as he spoke directly into my ear. "What happened? What did you see?"

"Eight of my family attacking four girls. Drinking their blood," I said.
Everett winced.

His phone rang. "Ginny," he said.

"She might have seen it, too, if she was watching my mind," I said.

Everett stood up and answered his phone. "Hey," he said to Ginny, as
he paced. "She's okay, I think. Just shaken. Did you see it? Was it that
bad? Yeah…she mentioned that," he said as he glanced at me apologetically, his hand in his hair. Ginny had just said, *You could taste the blood.*"

Corrina heard Everett on the phone, so she took the opportunity to
come back in and see me. Everett stared her down, but I shooed him
off. He stepped out on the balcony to finish his call with Ginny.

"Your birthday…I'm sorry…" I began.

"Are you kidding? Forget my birthday. Are you okay?"

I tried my best to smile. I was still very disoriented, but I realized
the effects of my episode might have been more detrimental psycho-
logically than physically. "Yeah, I promise, Rina," I said, pulling myself
to a sitting position.

"Are you sure you don't want to go to the hospital? Just to make
sure?" she asked. Her thoughts were racing. Most of her was worried
about me, but part of her was morbidly curious. She had heard my
comment about tasting blood.

"I'm really okay. I just fainted. I'm sure it's nothing." As I said this, I
began to be slightly concerned for myself. I had never experienced
mind-reading in such a twisted way before. It was so vivid, and it was
so uncontrolled. I hadn't even been searching for Noah's mind when I
was thrown into the middle of it, and saw what he saw, felt what he
felt, as it was happening. And I had certainly never seized or passed
out in the process.

Corrina sat next to me now, her eyes downcast. We were quiet for
a while. She was growing more nervous, and her tension permeated
my skin. I tried to ignore it.

"You're going to leave now, aren't you?" she asked. I looked at her, wide-eyed. "Don't look so shocked," she said. "I have been paying attention for a few years now. This is how it goes. You seem normal for a while. We have a great time. And then something happens — like tonight — and you take off for a while, like these little tragedies are calling you to do something. And so you go."

"When has it happened before?" I asked.

"The first time was when you got that grisly cut on your arm," she said. She was referring to what was now a wide, thick scar on my left bicep. It had happened when I first read a legend about a spell you could put on poison-tipped arrows to make them break the skin of sorcerers. I tested it out by stabbing my arm with an arrow tipped in arsenic that I had cursed. It was my first scar. "You left the next day. Do you remember?" she asked. I nodded helplessly. "And then you came back with more and more of them over time. Eventually, of course, you got better at covering them up."

Corrina had apparently watched silently, in horror, as my body grew more and more mangled. She'd never mentioned the scars before. I wondered if this was the hand she had been waiting to play, her one shot to talk about them. I was trying to call her bluff, but even the bubbly and sweet Corrina had one hell of a poker face.

"That's only once," I said.

She shrugged this time. "I think something happened right after the wedding, too," she said. Perceptive. It had been the night of her wedding when I first met Mark Winter who, at the time, seemed like the greatest threat in the world to me. That encounter had started this entire journey — the one that led me to Everett and all that came with him.

"How do you figure?" I asked, again playing dumb.

"I leave my wedding reception and you are fine in the arms of Cole Hardwick. I get back from my honeymoon and you're living in Seattle, alone, depressed, spending your time on Twitter, and refusing to explain what took you there. At first, I thought it was because of Cole, that maybe something bad happened. So, I asked him, and he said you ran off as soon as we left the reception. That he had nothing to do with you running off to Seattle," she said. "I knew it was just another Sadie secret — just you being you."

Just me being me. Did I do that? Take off so often, so predictably, that it came across as a personality trait?

Corrina continued, "So now I know you'll leave. I know there is some strange subplot of your life that you've kept from me over the years. And you'll likely never tell me about it. I don't expect you to, though I wish you would. I've tried really hard not to ask questions and just to help when I could. But I'm not stupid, Sadie. Tell me you know me better than that. It's not like I didn't realize how weird your life was. No family. The money. The travel. Living in hotels like you're some kind of rock star or a damned nomad."

I didn't answer. What could I say? I couldn't defend myself. Corrina had me pegged, and I had been too smug, too content with my own performance as a human, to realize it.

And we would leave, of course. No doubt Everett was asking Ginny to book the tickets right now.

"Sadie, say something," Corrina said, looking directly at me this time.

I chose my words carefully. "Corrina, I appreciate everything you've ever done for me — more than you can know. And I'm sorry my life is strange and secretive. I only keep it from you in an attempt to keep you out of it," I said. Rethinking my words, I added, "To keep you safe." But was that really true?

"I suppose I understand," she said, her voice a little defeated. I was surprised she gave in so easily. "I mean, I used to think crazy things about Swiss bank accounts or crime syndicates. A part of me thought you were running from the law or maybe from something lawless, like you were in a self-imposed witness protection — a cowboy version of it, anyway. But at the restaurant, when you came to, you said that thing about tasting the blood, and I got a little freaked out. Your secret world might be a littler darker than I imagined."

"It is," I said. We were quiet then. I watched as strange images of Hollywood versions of monsters — beautiful vampires, grisly zombies, strange Pagan witches ritually sacrificing humans — flipped through Corrina's mind.

I wondered idly when I had started *looking* more into people's minds rather than feeling my way through them. Regardless of when it had happened, I used this strategy now. It was the rule rather than the exception.

From outside, in his mind, Everett said, *I'm coming in.* I hadn't been paying attention to him. Had he been listening to us? I wondered if his entrance was timed so that I would not reveal our secrets to Corrina in a moment of human-like weakness.

"Hey, princess," he said. "You're looking better."

I smiled weakly. "Feeling better," I said. Half-true.

He crossed the room to me and kissed my forehead, his cool lips soothing. "You know," he began, "I was just talking to Ginny, and she is really worried about you. Maybe we should cut this trip a little short. We can plan another one soon," he said. Corrina scoffed beside me.

I can't believe she found a guy who's in on her madness, Corrina thought. *Maybe that's why she never went for Cole. He's too normal.* I ignored her, or tried to anyway. But somehow that accusation cut at me, and I wasn't sure why. "Leaving in the morning?" she asked.

"Actually..." Everett began.

"Wait, let me guess," Corrina interrupted. Her voice was sarcastic. "There's a red-eye you want to take tonight and you can *just* make it if you leave now."

"So it seems," Everett said.

"No time to waste then. Y'all pack, and I'll tell Felix plans have changed," Corrina said.

Everett headed off to the guest room to pack our things. He'd be done by the time I got into the room behind him.

I grabbed Corrina on her way out. "I'm sorry," I said, my voice thick like I was going to cry. I hated this.

She shrugged. "Just you being you."

CHAPTER THREE

damages

I WAS INCONSOLABLE AT THE AIRPORT AND ON THE PLANE. WHEN Corrina hugged me goodbye, in her mind she said, *I love you so much, but I don't know how much longer I can play your games.*

I guess any human I'd ever love would always think it was just a game. Cole had thought it in London. Corrina thought it now. And I hated it. I didn't mean to do these things. Really, all I wanted was a life without all the secrecy, without complications, without…all of this. When I tucked my head against Everett's shoulder on the plane, I feared I had reached the end of an era. I had finally gotten good at passing as a human when this mess with the Winters and my family had begun. I had convinced the few humans I knew that I was one of them. But now it was obvious to all of them what a freak I was, and it was painfully obvious to me that, with each step I took toward my supernatural world — toward my family, toward the Winters, toward Everett — I took a step away from humanity.

Absentmindedly, I straightened up in my seat, lifting my head off Everett's marble shoulder.

I fixed my eyes straight out in front of me, and my mind idly wandered to the time that Cole Hardwick and I danced at Corrina and Felix's wedding.

"Sadie," Everett said softly, removing me from the daydream, "can we talk about what happened? Can you tell me more about what it felt like?"

"What's to tell?" I whispered. It may have been my imagination, but I shivered when I looked at him, as if Everett's coldness radiated off of him, the way Cole's warmth had in the reception hall at the June wedding. "I watched my family murder four girls, and I tasted the blood in my mouth when Noah did. There's not much else," I answered.

I could feel he badly wanted to say more, but he didn't know what he could say to make me tell him what I'd experienced or what I was thinking now. Though he could be persuasive, I made it abundantly clear when I didn't want to be charmed by him. Any charming or soothing he might do in an attempt to lessen the blow of the reality of my siblings becoming monsters — like him — would just upset me. He sometimes obliged.

But I couldn't see it in any other way. All the violence, the blood, the terror…that's what Everett and his siblings did almost every day. But look at how apathetic I'd become! My pretending that what they did wasn't all that bad was just a way of condoning it. Not to mention, the closer I got to him, the more at risk I was for becoming like him. Becoming a monster.

So I wouldn't ask what I desperately wanted to: Was it like that every time? Was it that horrific every time he drank someone's blood, every time he killed? Was there so much fear? So much tension? So much…blood?

"I think I've lost Corrina," I finally said.

He sighed, but he did not disagree with me. "Maybe it's not that you've lost her. I do think it will take her some time to figure out how to adjust. It might be shaky for a little while," he admitted.

"God, Everett, don't you see?" I sat up straighter. "I don't want there to have to be an adjustment. I want my friend. I want the life I had before all this began," I said.

"Before me," he said quietly. I knew this was his greatest insecurity.

"That's not what I meant," I said.

"But it's true," he countered.

"Don't make this any harder than it is," I said, unable or perhaps unwilling to lie to him just then. "You're the only redeeming thing that has come out of this."

"I'll be sure to tell Ginny and Mark that," he laughed, signaling he wasn't looking for a fight. He was still upset, but he was willing to let it go, for which I was grateful. "But in all seriousness," he added, "you've got us. We're going to get through this together."

Somehow, that didn't comfort me. Not the way it should have.

———◆———

I TRIED TO SLEEP. BUT EVERY TIME I CLOSED MY EYES, I SAW THAT SAME HORRIBLE image and heard those poor girls' screams. So, when we landed in Canada at 5 a.m., I was exhausted. Frustrated. Tense.

But then I saw Adelaide Winter's smiling face and open arms, and I relaxed. Adelaide — the matriarch — had stopped aging early enough in her life that she still looked youthful. She was a striking blonde just like Ginny. She had warm hazel eyes and her creamy, porcelain skin had the same flawless texture as mine. She dressed like a young, wealthy, well-bred Californian mother — a Nanette Lepore maxi dress perusing the Monterey Bay, or high-waisted, vintage-feeling Joe Jeans with a Catherine Malandrino fur vest like she was wearing now — and she didn't look a day over thirty-five, even though she was a 500-year-old witch.

Still, to me, she was the face of comfort. From the moment I'd met her, she had taken me in and cared for me as if I was her own child. Unofficially lacking a mother of my own, she had become mine. I needed her.

"My baby," she said, wrapping her arms around me tight. Every member of the family had come up with a moniker for me, all alluding to me being the baby of the family. I was, of course, neither family nor the youngest. But, as Mark had once put it, I was the newest, and that's what counted.

Everett kissed her on the cheek. "Missed you," he said.

"I'm glad to see you two," she said.

"Glad to see you, too, Mom," he said. As we walked outside, the cold Calgary air penetrated my skin, and I watched Everett's eyes instantly lose their green in the subzero temperature. I couldn't understand how his craving could be so instantaneously worsened anywhere that even felt like winter. But he was immediately tense. He was holding my hand, though I saw him repeatedly clenching and unclenching his other fist. His jaw was taut. He had been so much more relaxed in Dallas, away from the cold. I understood why the Winter family spent their time in warm places. They had told me that the weather intensified their urges on an instinctual level, but I hadn't imagined the extent of it. Abstaining under these circumstances was excruciating. Even feeding only took the need for it from excruciating down to painful.

It was always painful. And not just for him.

Adelaide picked us up in one of the two Land Cruisers Mark had been responsible for procuring while Everett and I returned from Moscow months earlier. I had told him we needed vehicles that would get us up and down the mountain through the winter, but it would be nice if they weren't also a pain to ride in. The Toyota Land Cruiser had been his choice. It was the interior of a Lexus mixed with the body of a truck he could alter to his heart's desire. I don't know what I was expecting, but this hadn't been it. When I went to pay for them in Seattle when we returned from Moscow, I'd nearly choked on the bill for the two. I'd dragged Mark down there to explain the invoice to me, since there were enough aftermarket modifications added to each one that we could have bought a third car.

He was crushed at my disappointment at the time. He gave this stately speech, and I replayed it in my head as we started the long drive to distract myself. He'd put his hands on the hood of one while we stood in the shop, and said, "Sadie, Sadie, Sadie. You don't understand! I've bought you the perfect utility vehicle. The Toyota Land Cruiser, even in stock form, has long had a reputation for being near indestructible making it the first choice for NGOs and warlords everywhere. Sure, no one's going to mistake you for a mom making a carpool run in them, but isn't that the point? Whatever weakness Toyota had left in them has been expertly removed with no expense spared."

"I can see that," I snarled.

He shook his head. "Look, just let me show you. The front bumper had been replaced with a solid ARB Bull Bar with integrated fog lights. Mounted in the bumper is a Warn 16.5 Ti, the most advanced winch on the market, capable of pulling more than twice the weight of even these modified behemoths. ARB's Old Man Emu suspension system raised the vehicle enough to clear a set 305/60R18E BF Goodrich Mud Terrain KM2s, which we absolutely could not have lived without. The already formidable locking center differential now houses a full ARB air locker system being powered by a compressor also used to keep the tires full. An ARB Safari snorkel here for anything that could come our way, and a ARB Roof Rack holding the ubiquitous High Lift Jack and 40 inches of Rigid Industries best LED Lights facing forward. The factory running boards have been swapped out in favor of ARB Side Rails, the rear stock bumper has been replaced by ARB's Modular Rear Bumper holding another meaty KM2. And that's just what you can see!"

"Is this supposed to be making me feel better?" I'd asked, massaging my temple.

"You're a *car* girl, Sadie. Now appreciate the truck too! Look, I've even made sure your engine is as powerful and Sadie-like as it can be. Just look. Under the hood we have an AirAid intake system replacing the factory intake, the ECU had been upgraded by the wizards at Jet and the engine exhaled freer through the MagnaFlow exhaust system and awesomely badass muffler. This lovely, dual core Optima Yellow-Top battery now powers all of the added accessories because they need a lot of juice. The extra power and weight taxed the factory brakes so they had to be replaced by this StopTech Big Brake Kit. And look, inside is still a car you and my sister won't mind riding in. I mean, the only things I had to add in there were the switches for the extra lights and the air locker, the Cobra Remote Mount CB, the Pelican case in the back holding the snow chains and recovery and emergency supplies, and then a small addition of WeatherTech liners to keep the dirt and snow off the carpet. All in all, little one, if this pair won't get us wherever the hell you drag us, not much with four wheels will. I built you a pair of tanks that look like they've been forced to endure six years of ballet and a double dose of finishing school. What more could you ask for?"

He had a point. What more could I ask for? I'd cut the man a check for the two, and we were on our way.

And so as I sat in the backseat of one now, I appreciated his additions, not only because they had in fact put up with the first part of a Montana winter without seeming to even break a sweat but also because I had memorized that entire conversation, and now I could replay it in moments like this. When I wanted to be distracted. When I wanted to forget.

I let my head slide back on the leather seat and tried to replay the next meaningless conversation I'd had, movie I'd watched, moment I'd live. I did anything to keep from remembering who I was.

It was a two-hour drive from Calgary to the Winters' home. We'd driven on big highways for a while, but then we turned off a main road and traveled off into a heavily wooded area. Initially, I could hear thoughts all around us, but the farther we drove into the woods, the farther away the voices seemed until I heard almost no sounds inside my head.

Adelaide turned onto a cleared path in the forest that was just the width of the car. All I could see, in every direction, were snow-covered trees. It was a winter wonderland.

Then I saw the house atop a rise in a clearing. It took me a moment to really see it, its architecture blended so well into the landscape around it. It was camouflaged. It was a beautiful, towering home three stories high. It was nothing like the glorified log cabin I expected in a home in rural Canada. The house was extremely contemporary, and its majestic façade was a smooth, silvery-white metal, and it was very uniquely shaped. As we got closer, I could see how wide and deep it was. At least twenty big windows dotted the front and sides of the house. Huge picture windows filled out the front, free of any window dressings. The double front doors were at least twice my height, and they were painted a striking blood red, the only color on the façade. There was a tower on one side, like a thick chimney, and smoke came out the top of it. There were giant fallen trees closely surrounding parts of the oddly shaped house. I couldn't understand the placement of them until I realized that the house was literally built within them, so that several trees four feet in diameter pierced the house on one side and came out the other, some on the ground and others up close to the roofline.

"This is the Canada house?" I asked in disbelief.

"No, sweetheart," Everett said. "We call the house in the Bahamas the Canada house just to screw with people." I elbowed him hard in the ribs and laughed.

I wondered, but did not ask, if there were really a house in the Bahamas.

"This is giant!" I said. "It has to be three times the size of your house in Pacific Grove."

"Actually, it's four times, but who's counting?" Adelaide joked. She sounded like Ginny when she said it. "Real estate doesn't exactly come cheap in California. But up here? We can afford to be a little more extravagant."

"A little? I would hate to see what a *lot* more extravagant looks like," I said under my breath. Truthfully, I wouldn't hate to see it. My own taste was absurdly and impractically extravagant — and exactly matched to the Winters'.

"Why do you think I can't hear you when you say these things?" Everett laughed. "And a *lot* more extravagant would be the house in the South of France. Just you wait till you see that one!"

I raised one eyebrow. "What else don't I know about you people?"

Everett kissed my forehead. "All in due time, my love," he said, deliberately not answering my question. I had noticed that they all did this quite frequently. I had surmised it was because none of them had it in them to outright lie to me, so they sidestepped the truth instead.

When we parked, Ginny and Mark came out to the car. "Thank you for coming home. I really was worried about you," Ginny said as she threw her arms around my neck. *I'm so sorry you had to see that,* she said to me in her mind.

Not as sorry as I am, I replied.

Mark kissed me on the cheek and grabbed my bags, a foreign look of sadness in his eyes. Ignoring it, I followed the others inside. The tall tower I'd seen from the drive was the entryway into their magnificent home. Against one wall, there was a fireplace with a slate-fronted chimney that extended from the floor up the tall tower. As we walked farther into the home, we arrived in a giant family room that spanned all three floors of the house with open railings from the upper floors overlooking it. It was at least fifty feet long. All the surfaces were greyish woods and shiny whites. The furniture was very contemporary, and the walls were dotted with modern art. The tall windows poured light into all the rooms, and offered panoramic views of the snow-covered landscape. The fallen trees I'd seen from the car literally extended through the house so that in some places there were thick tree trunks criss-crossing overhead and in other places they were obstructions in the middle of large rooms. It only took Mark hopping up on the trees once as if they were monkey bars on a giant playground to understand why they had left them there.

Anthony and Patrick were waiting here in the living room. Walking into this room was like the first time I had entered the Winters' California home when they had all been waiting for me to arrive.

Anthony's deep voice carried across the room. "Sadie, thank goodness you're okay," he said earnestly. When I reached him, he put one long arm around my shoulders and pulled me toward him. Patrick only nodded.

"I'm still a little freaked out," I admitted.

"I can imagine," Anthony said. "Ginny told me what you saw, but it was much fuzzier for her since you were so far away. I'd like to hear the details from you."

I took a deep breath and began, not even thinking to sit down. "We were at dinner with Corrina and Felix, and suddenly the buzzing and voices in my head changed drastically. First, I heard the girls screaming, and then I saw the scene and tuned out of our dinner completely. I have no idea what happened to my physical being after that, but in my mind, I watched the whole god-awful scene play out. I saw it all through my brother, Noah's, eyes," I explained. Saying this out loud made it more real, which in turn made it more twisted.

"And all of your senses were intact in the vision?" Anthony asked.

"My regular senses were, but my extra senses weren't. I couldn't read minds or pick up feelings from anyone there. My vision, smell and hearing were hyperfocused and felt really different, though. I think that was a result of being in Noah's mind, now that he's a…" I stopped myself. I couldn't say it.

"Like us," Patrick offered.

I winced. Making the comparison between the Winters and what I had seen was awful, much worse than just calling him what he was. I forced myself to say it. "Now that he's a *vieczy*," I said. "I didn't realize the difference between our senses was so great. His sight, sense, and smell were all much sharper than mine," I realized now that my glimpse into Noah's mind had been a glimpse into the mind of each of the Winters. I saw what they saw, felt the gut-wrenching urges they felt. It was, to say the least, eye-opening.

"Were you at all in control of your actions?" Anthony asked urgently.

"No," I said. Anthony looked disappointed. "I would have done something if I could have."

"Like what?" Patrick scoffed. In moments like this, where his disdain for my presence was so acute, I always found it odd how much he looked like his brothers. To me, that Winter hair and eyes and skin was beginning to signal a kind of love. But then Patrick would speak. He felt like an impostor.

So I ignored him. "I was helpless," I explained. "I could only see in his mind the way that I can see in the average person's mind, but it was much more vivid than readings usually are. And as I've never been able to control anyone, I wasn't able to do anything. I couldn't save them."

"Were you looking for Noah's mind specifically?" Anthony asked.

"No, not at all," I said. "It just came to me."

"The vision *found* you?" he asked incredulously. Everett stiffened beside me. I wasn't sure why.

"I guess you could say it that way," I said. "But was it a vision, Anthony? Wasn't I tapping into someone's mind like I always do, only this time I got all his senses, too?"

"That depends," he said.

"On?" I asked.

He hesitated, Patrick looked away, and Everett bit his lower lip, a tiny drop of gold seeped onto it — his venom. He was angry. I was, all of the sudden, on the defensive, knowing that whatever made Everett angry wouldn't please me. Anthony shifted his weight, another unnecessary movement, stalling, and finally spoke. "On whether four girls actually died somewhere last night or whether it hasn't happened yet," he said.

"Hasn't happened?" I asked incredulously. "You think I can see the future now?"

"We don't know yet," Anthony said. "But if you can, it's an entirely new power," he said eyeing me cautiously. I narrowed my eyes and tried in vain to read his mind. I may have been able to get tiny bits from the other side of Everett's bulwark, but I had no such success with the other Winters. I hadn't been practicing with them.

But I did know this: New powers didn't just develop. At best, they evolved from an existing power, but for the most part, they were acquired. And acquiring them meant killing whoever had the power in the first place. "Is there something you want to say?" I asked Anthony.

"No," Everett answered for him. "He doesn't have anything to say." Everett and Anthony stared each other down. I crossed my arms and looked back and forth between them, unsure of what was going on. "Come on, Sadie. Let's get settled in. I'm sure you'd like to sleep," he said.

"I'm fine," I said. "I want to talk about whatever it is you're keeping from me."

"No, he's right," Anthony said, breaking Everett's gaze but not looking at me. "Rest up. I'm sure you've had a tough night." He backed away from us and bounded out of the room over the giant fallen trees.

"What the hell was that?" I asked Everett.

"Nothing," he mustered, feigning a smile.

"You can't win that easily," I said, frustrated he was trying to charm his way out of this.

"Later?" he asked. I nodded. "Come on, let me show you our room." I obliged and followed him up the stairs.

EVERETT'S "ROOM" WAS REALLY MORE LIKE AN ENTIRE APARTMENT OF ITS OWN, complete with bedroom, bath, living area, game room with vintage arcade games I'd only seen in movies, a card table, a pool table, a foosball table, and who knows how many other tables. I didn't see the other bedrooms to know if they were like this, but the sheer size of all of it was starting to seem ridiculous. Even for me.

I still couldn't sleep, but I tried for a little while. Then I talked with Ginny and Mark about what had happened. All of the Winters looked in pain as I described the taste of the blood to them, the feel of the kill. It was partly because they pitied me, and partly because it fueled their desires, which made it so clear to me what I was really struggling with: How I could love them when I knew what they were capable of. It was one thing to know in theory, like I had for months. It was another thing to have experienced it.

Everett had quickly become stir crazy in the cold Canadian air, so he and his siblings left at midday to feed. They never told me this was what they were doing, but I could always tell. I hadn't figured out how often it had to happen because it seemed to depend on several variables. I did know, though, that Everett never went alone.

I wandered around outside, and eventually I dropped to the ground. I lay in the snow for several hours. Adelaide came to lay with me.

"Do you want to talk?" she asked softly, her eyes fixed up at the bright white sky like mine were. I think she knew what I was going through. Didn't she have the same struggle I did?

"I don't know," I admitted. "I feel like I've talked enough."

"I understand. I used to think it would be nice to have someone to vent to, someone who could understand, or who could at least just hear me out. But as time passes, I'm grateful for the silence I must keep. I've realized that saying it all out loud may actually make it worse," she said.

"It certainly makes it more real," I said.

"Is that what you're struggling with? That until now you could deny it in a way?" she asked.

I thought it over. "Probably," I said. I didn't know what I was struggling with. It was everything I had always struggled with, just amplified.

"You know, when he fell for you, I remembered thinking that you may be able to overlook what he does, what he *is* because you don't value life very highly," she said. This hit me in an odd way.

"I must be an awful person if that's how I come off," I said.

"That's not it. I just thought that maybe someone who regarded death and life in such a strange way would maybe be able not to think about what he does. What they all do," she said.

"Can you keep from thinking about it?" I asked.

A long pause floated on the frigid wind as Adelaide chewed on my question. Or how to respond to it. "No," she said. "And yes." She sighed. "It's complicated."

"Well, right now all I've got is 'no' and 'complicated' so tell me more about the 'yes' part," I implored, pushing myself up to a sitting position.

Adelaide sat up too. "I guess I think of it like this: In our supernatural world, there are powers and there are weaknesses. There are individual or specialized powers that only some of us have. Like your mind-reading. Ginny's mirroring. Or all these other powers Anthony finds for Mark to acquire. But there are specialized weaknesses too. *Vieczy* and other vampires, they have a weakness you and I don't have. Their lives are only sustained by taking life from others. Is it awful? Yes. Justified? Never. But that's how they were born. I'm not going to love my children any less for being that than if they were born with a disability, a terrible illness, or something that made them different in some way. I'm going to love my children unconditionally. I always have. I always will. And I can understand that this family isn't your God-given family, but I feel like God gave you to us. So I hope you can find a way to cope with what Everett is, with his weakness. He can look past your lesser qualities. Maybe you can look past his."

"The only person I've ever tried to kill is myself," I said quietly. "It's different."

Adelaide laughed a kind of sad, frustrated laugh. "What do you want me to say, Sadie? That you're a better person than he is, than all my children are?"

"I didn't mean it that way," I said apologetically. I traced circles in the snow around my feet. "What about Anthony? Can he look past what they do?"

"Anthony's view on it is a little different than mine, as you can imagine," she said.

"He thinks he's one of them," I said. "Or pretends he is."

Adelaide narrowed her eyes a bit. "What do you mean?"

I shrugged. "That night at the bonfire in Romania, when you all told me what was going to happen — his vision of Mark, the war, the beach and all — when he finally started answering my questions, he said things like 'our eyes' and 'our venom' and 'we need' and such. I didn't think of it until weeks later, and I don't even know why I thought of it then. But he acts like he is one of them even though he's not. He's a shape-shifter. He doesn't have to feed. He doesn't have to kill people. He's not venomous. He's not one of them."

"But he feels responsible for them," she said. "He has spent his entire time as a father, all century and a half of it, feeling guilty for fathering children he could never fully understand. It kills him, I think. Sometimes a little more each day. And so somewhere along the line, he just started acting as if he were just like them. Pretending, I guess, like you say. Maybe it helps him."

"He's said this to you?" I asked incredulously. I didn't imagine Anthony to be the type to talk about his feelings or deeply seeded fears.

"Never out loud, but I know," she said.

"If that's what kills him, why did he have children with you anyway? If he knew what they'd become when your kind mated with his?" I asked.

Adelaide nodded her head sadly, staring at the ground. "You've never done the math, have you?" she asked. I must have looked perplexed because she said, "Ginny was born the year Patrick stopped aging. The year he had to start killing. I had three children before I knew what I'd created from my womb. You think I would have gotten past one if I had known, if *we* had known?"

She was right. I hadn't done the math. "Oh, Adelaide…" she was crying now. Tears streaming down her pink cheeks, eyes reddening, so unlike her *vieczy* children. "You didn't know the legends?"

She shook her head. By the time she spoke again, the tears were freezing to her face. "The *vieczy* legend was so rare. We didn't hear of it until just before Mark was born. We didn't even know that's what they were. And at that time, in the late 18th century? The concept of any kind of creature close to what our children were was just so foreign. Dracula-like creatures who were bitten at the neck and turned into wild, terrible things. My children were just children. They displayed natural powers, but that was expected because they were magical. I didn't know they'd been born with the dormant *vieczy* disease," she cried, her words bitter, "until it was too late."

Except for Mark, I thought. She knew what Mark was going to be. But Anthony had had a vision that he would come, and so, like all the Winters, she didn't doubt that it would happen and that it was beyond her control.

"Besides," she said, "Anthony isn't exactly a regular shape-shifter. Even when we first heard of the *vieczy* legend, I didn't even think that's what our children were because Anthony wasn't actually shifting anymore." I wanted to bang my head against a wall. How hadn't I noticed *that*? Four months with the man, and I'd never once seen him shift forms in the slightest bit. And the shape-shifters we encountered — the nosferatu in Romania — they'd been mortal. Anthony was over a thousand years old. Then what kind of shape-shifter was he? It was stupid of me to assume he'd be a nosferatu. Just because Narcisa and Valentin were, because some Survivors theoretically were, I had been remiss in not thinking further about what Anthony was.

The look on my face must have conveyed too much of this doubt because she added, "I'm only telling you this because I'm assuming you've noticed."

"Of course I have," I lied.

Adelaide rose to her feet, dusting the snow off of her clothing. It seemed clear that talking about this had become too much. After all, how do you comfort someone when the thing eating away at her eats away at you too? "And Sadie? Just remember that Everett…he loves you despite …" She couldn't say the rest. *Despite how genuinely crazy you are.*

"And so I should love him despite," I nodded.

She leaned over and kissed my forehead. "I think you're going to save him, Sadie. And for that, I'm eternally grateful." Save him from what? I wondered.

She walked away without another word.

—◆—

LATER IN THE DAY, I SAT BY THE FIRE, PLAYING WITH MY PHONE. I PULLED UP Corrina's number and almost called her, but I stopped myself. Then I typed out a long text message, but I deleted it too. She didn't want to hear from me, and I knew it. I didn't need an unanswered phone call or text to confirm that.

If only I had other humans, I thought. If only I had someone else to talk to, someone who knew nothing of this situation in the slightest. Someone who would listen to anything I had to say.

I pulled up Cole's number on my phone and stared at it for twenty solid minutes before convincing myself that the best thing I could do for him was leave him alone.

—◆—

WHEN EVERETT GOT BACK LATE THAT NIGHT, I WAS ALREADY IN BED, TRYING TO sleep again. I heard a soft murmur of hushed voices in the living room, then they faded and Everett's footsteps came softly down the hall. He paused when he reached the door, hesitating.

He cracked the door open and slid inside. "Why aren't you asleep?" he asked.

I smiled a bit, sitting up. "How'd you know?"

"Breathing's different when you're sleeping," he said, reaching down to pull off his shoes and socks. He shrugged out of his coat and sweater. There were rips in his soft V-neck t-shirt, though I wasn't sure from what. The stone skin beneath them, though, was entirely intact. I cringed, wondering where they came from and trying to not wonder at the same time. "Will you try to sleep?" he asked.

I shrugged. "I'm okay without it," I said, though I was feeling more exhausted than I had been even in the six months I had stopped sleeping.

"But will you try? Can we just lie here together for a while? It's been a long day," he said. I slid back to the center of the bed and let my head fall back and my hair spread gently across the pillow, a clear indication of my assent. This was the problem with Everett. His presence was so convincing, so intoxicating, that all day I'd been thinking of his monstrous side, and now I felt safe lying next to him, unprotected.

I simultaneously loved and hated that he was capable of that.

Everett lay on his side, the line of his body mirroring mine. I looked into his eyes. I began to lightly trace the lines in his arms he had huddled in front of him in the distance between us.

"How was your day?" he asked softly.

"Uneventful," I said. "Are we going to stay here?"

"Have somewhere you need to be?" he asked.

"We need to be in Montana, obviously. Or out trying to find my family and stopping them before they do anything like I saw in the vision again," I said.

Everett tensed. I felt very strongly that he was holding something back, but before I could ask, he kept talking. "We can talk about it on Friday. Tomorrow is Mark's birthday, and even though we've had thousands between us, it's a big deal to my mom for the family to be together, so we have to stay for that," he explained.

"Should I go ahead and leave for Montana so that I'm not here when you're celebrating family things?" I asked, suddenly insecure, afraid of imposing.

"Are you kidding me?" he asked incredulously. "When we use the word 'family' now, you are included. I thought you realized that." I shrugged sheepishly. It frustrated him that there was any question. "You're a hard girl to love, Sadie. You don't take it well," he said. Something about that felt more insulting than he meant it.

"Sorry," I whispered. I was embarrassed.

"Nothing to apologize for," he said. "Hey, didn't we lie down so you would sleep?"

"Sleep doesn't come easy these days," I said. My fingertips continued their glide over his satiny skin, down his arms and back up, from his collar, up his neck, and across his cheeks. I laid my palm on his cheek and stroked it. He tilted his head and placed a slow kiss on the inside of my wrist. He wasn't breathing.

I let my hand drift down his neck again and then across the material of his soft undershirt until my fingers found his cool skin in one of the tears in the shirt. Everett shivered and inhaled sharply. I slid my fingers down the shirt until they found another tear, this one larger and more on his side. I let my fingertips rub back and forth across his granite skin, feeling the hard ridges and grooves of his muscles. Everett closed his eyes and swallowed hard.

"Are you okay?" I whispered, my own voice breathier than I expected.

He nodded. "What are you thinking?" he asked.

"How I'm touching a part of you I've never seen," I said.

"I noticed that," he said. *It feels amazing*, he said in his mind, entirely by accident. His guard was down. I was able to feel warmth wrap around my body, radiating off of him — a kind I didn't feel from him often, even in our more tender moments. A kind that found something deep in my core and embedded itself there, creating a hum of alertness, heat, and tension in the scariest way. The best way.

I moved my hand from the open tear and back to the t-shirt, trusting the security even the thin fabric gave me.

I don't know how in control he was, but I knew he didn't want me to stop. I laid my palm flat against the valley between his stomach muscles, and I took a few deep breaths to steady myself. I was having my own conflicting but powerful emotions, and I felt his too as he let his guard down. Though my battle for control was entirely different from Everett's, it was still a battle. How far was too far? How far wasn't far enough? Everett and I had once confined our physical relationship to what our 19th century selves would be more comfortable with, rather than our 21st century selves. Or, at least, we planned to.

And yet, here we were, lying in bed together, my skin undeniably magnetized to his.

I suddenly slid my hand under his shirt so it rested exactly where it had been only without the barrier between us. His breathing caught but then steadied again. I didn't know what I was doing.

He was so lean, his body so smooth and taut. "I think I would like to see this part of you," I said, pressing my palm lightly into that place where his sternum hollowed out. I watched the thought cross his mind a fraction of a second before he acted. I never even saw him move, but instantly he was in the exact position he had been, only now more of his pale skin was glowing in the dark room. He'd taken off his shirt faster than I could see it.

I let my eyes rake gently over his bare chest and arms. "Still okay?" I asked, my voice a whisper.

He nodded. "And you?" he asked sliding a cool hand against my cheek, cradling my face. I nodded, too. I wondered how close were we to the 21st century. And how far from the 19th? Very slowly, he leaned in to me and pressed our foreheads together. "I love you," he said.

"I love you," I said. And then he touched his cool, sterling lips to mine. We kissed for a few moments before he tentatively put a hand on my hip. I responded by putting my hand to his side. He parted his lips and let his tongue escape, past my lips and into my mouth, which he had never done before. We walked a thin line between an innocent kiss and a venomous bite, between my safety and my becoming like him. But soon I lost myself in the kiss, deciding to trust his control. I tightened my grip around his waist, and he pulled me closer in kind. He wrapped both arms around me, hugging me against him. I felt the muscles in his back ripple with even his tiniest movements.

I broke my lips away and kissed along his jawbone and then down his neck. Nuzzling my head into the crook of his neck, I let a few lazy kisses fall on his collarbone. But then I took a long, deep breath, and suddenly froze in place. What was I doing? He tensed beside me as I did this, likely afraid one or both of us had pushed past lines we had done a poor job defining in the first place.

Dangerous. It was dangerous. But it was enticing. It was addictive. It seemed…worth it.

Almost.

I let my head rest back on the pillow, thinking maybe I was too brash. But my hair fell away from neck, leaving it long, exposed. I was surprised, even rattled, when Everett bent to kiss my throat. He didn't let our bodies break apart, and so quickly he was on top of me, carefully hovering so almost none of his weight pressed into me. We looked at each other intently for one long moment.

And then, in a flash, he was lying beside me, his body only an inch away but not touching me at all. It had become too much, and he knew it. I should have been able to stop us, but I wouldn't have. I wanted him that close to me again. I felt guilty and scared for being so uncontrolled but at the same time more in love with Everett Winter than I even wanted to be.

He said, "I'm sorry."

"Nothing to apologize for," I said. "If anything, I'm sorry. I started it."

An excruciatingly long pause hung between us. Finally, he smiled, "I didn't mind it."

I worked my way back into the shape of his body — my forehead against his jaw, my chest and shoulders against his stomach. He took my cue and wrapped his arms around me again.

"How bad was that for you?" I asked. "You know…bloodlust-wise," I said, to be clear on what I was asking about.

He frowned. "Doable, apparently," he said, "But I wouldn't trust me." I said nothing. "How was that,…you know,…19th-century-wise?"

I laughed softly. "Intriguing. More powerful than I might have expected," I admitted, "But I'm fine."

"Sadie, you've got to tell me if this ever isn't what you want. You've always got to be honest with me on this stuff, okay?" he said.

I nodded. "And you have to tell me the same thing," I said. "I mean, not just when you can't get in control. You should tell me when you don't…want…" I wasn't sure what I was saying, but I was suddenly nervous. These were the kinds of moments where 145 years of living somehow added up to me feeling like a teenager — an inexperienced teenager at that. I was never confident. I never knew what I wanted. And I really never knew what I was doing.

Everett put a gentle finger to my lips. "Let's just put this out there. There will never be a 'don't want to' situation. The 'want to' is what makes the control part so hard," he said. His voice was soothing and affectionate. He was being gutsy admitting that. It sent electric charges up and down my spine to hear it.

As he regained composure, I could sense fewer and fewer of his feelings.

"Sadie, we need to talk about something."

I steeled myself and swallowed hard, suddenly scared for reasons I couldn't explain. "Okay," I said.

"Ginny and Mark have been looking for a trail to follow to find your missing family members," he said.

"Like tracking?" I asked.

"No, more like detective work. They found a news story about the girls from last night," he said, stroking my hair. I felt a pang in my stomach. This was why he was being loving and calm.

I had never doubted that the murders were happening while I watched them, so I wasn't sure why this hurt to hear. "Where were they?" I asked, my voice weak.

"San Francisco."

"That's awfully close to your California house," I said to him. Pacific Grove was less than an hour's run — for our kind — from San Francisco. "You think there's a connection?"

"We don't know," he said truthfully. "Princess, you should understand. They killed four last night, but they've killed more than that overall."

"How do you know?" I asked.

"We found instances of an alarming number of unsolved murders over the last few months," he said. "We can't necessarily tie them all to the rogue Survivors, but in the last three weeks there have been a string of them. They've been in towns in a straight line from Canada to San Francisco — several incidents in British Columbia, then Washington, a bunch in Oregon, then four in California."

"What do you mean by 'incidents'?" I asked. "As in someone died in each of those places?"

"As in," he said, softly, "a lot of people died in each of those places."

My throat closed. "So last night wasn't the worst?" I choked.

"It was the…least," Everett said apologetically.

Least? That horror, that obscenity? That was the *least* bad it got? I swallowed hard.

"Sadie, it's not your fault," he said, knowing where my mind was going. Had I not left my family in Montana, likely none of the others would have left either. And if none of them had left…

"How many?" I asked. He didn't answer. "How many?" I repeated. "I want to know," I said, *the damage I've done,* I thought.

"Eighteen incidents," he said. "Eighteen that we can be sure they had a part in."

"How many murders?" I demanded.

Everett's face was like stone. "A hundred thirty-eight," he said.

The magnitude of the number struck me like 138 swords. A small percentage of my family — maybe not even all 28 rogue relatives! — had killed at least as many humans as family members they left behind. It was exactly how the nosferatu lynxes in Romania had explained the violent *vieczy* to me. This is what they said to expect, and yet I couldn't.

I wanted to cry, to scream, to throw things, to take it all back. But it was too late. 138 times, it had been too late.

"We're going to stop them," he said. But if we were really going to, wouldn't we have done so by now?

I said nothing. I only closed my eyes and pretended to sleep until I felt early sunlight shine in through the broad windows, the metallic taste of blood and the ringing of those girls' screams never far from my mind.

CHAPTER FOUR

tikka masala

THE NEXT MORNING, THE WINTERS PRETENDED NOT TO KNOW THAT I now knew the of the 138 deaths. I wasn't sure if that was to spare my feelings or if it was simply because it was Mark's birthday and everyone was in a celebrating mood. There was so much birthday festivity packed into these few days. And yet, for all my years, I'd never celebrated a birthday. As Survivors, just like our parentage, our exact birthdays were also kept a secret from us.

Each of the Winters flitted around their home energetically, buzzing the same way humans do on such occasions. Watching the Winters celebrate like humans helped me keep the images of the murders and the images of a family I had grown to love in separate parts of my brain.

Adelaide was busy in the kitchen, cooking the least-green meal I'd ever seen them eat. This communicated to me that her birthday dinner was less about the strategic value of turning her family's eyes green and more about the love and celebration of family. All the younger Winters were gathered in the kitchen to help — or at least pretend to — except Madeline, who was wandering outside in the snow. It was a very joyous occasion, the kind I needed to take my mind off things. I hung close to the family even though that kind of socializing didn't come naturally to me. I'd been trying to do the things I ought to instead of the things I was inclined to. Thus far, it had meant fewer suicide missions and more camaraderie, so I suppose it wasn't a bad choice.

By the afternoon the house smelled like rich chocolate and spicy Tikka Masala. Apparently Mark had an affinity for Indian food and devil's food cake. As the cooking wound down, and the meal was almost ready, I sat by the fire. For a few solid seconds I felt content with my life.

Everett noticed this, I think, and sat next to me. "I want to give you something," he said. He produced a flat, square, turquoise box tied with a white ribbon — a Tiffany box — and handed it to me. Too big for a ring. Too small for…most else.

"When did you get this?" I asked.

"In Dallas, with a little help from Felix," he said.

"What's it for?" I asked.

"You don't celebrate a birthday, do you?" he said.

"Have I said that?" I asked.

"You didn't have to," he said. "I just got to thinking about it, what with Corrina and Mark and all. So I'm fixing that. Let's just call it a little bit of humanity for you."

"But if it's not my birthday, then I don't need a present. That's how it would be in the human world," I argued.

"Yes, because we two are fantastic at playing strictly by the rules of human society," he joked. "Just open it."

I untied the ribbon and opened the box, lifted the small suede pouch from inside, and untied it too. Attached to a very long chain — long enough to reach my stomach — was a very beautiful gold key. "Wait, let me guess," I said sarcastically, "the key to your heart." I laughed. "Do we even have hearts?" He was sentimental, sometimes corny even. I was not.

"Please, I remember a certain girl telling me I couldn't get away with using clichés, being immortal and all," he laughed.

"If not your heart, then what?" I asked.

"It's the key to our forever," he said, his burgundy eyes meeting mine.

There was that word again. It seemed less scary when he said it in moments like this, when I was perfectly content — with my life and my immortality. Still, I was flighty, I admit, and so it intimidated me.

"It's beautiful," I managed to say, sliding it around my neck.

"It's meaningful," he said. He reached for it where it dangled and lifted it, then dropped it inside the neck of my shirt. The gold was cool against my stomach. "It's better there, closer to you. I want it to remind you we're going to get through this. And when it's rough, I'll be there next to you. Beneath all the layers of couture, the defense mechanisms, beneath this ridiculous persona you're trying to project, this part of me will be there. We'll get to that vision on the beach, Sadie. We'll get everything we ever wanted. We'll get forever."

I kissed him. "Thank you, Everett. I really, really appreciate this," I said. I meant it. It was a lovely gesture.

"Okay, sappy kids, time for food!" Mark called from the dining room. Everett bounded over the couch and slammed into his brother. Mark went flying, but caught himself lithely.

"Boys!" Adelaide snapped.

"Sorry, Mom," they mumbled, righting themselves.

On the long table, there was a beautiful spread of food, mostly what I recognized as Indian foods, save, of course, for the three-layer devil's food cake in the middle. "Adelaide, I don't even like to eat, and this looks wonderful," I said.

"I'll take that as a compliment," Adelaide smiled. "Shall we?" she said, gesturing to the feast before us.

"Maybe a prayer before?" Patrick suggested. "Sadie might want to…"

"Oh," I said, nervous on the spot. "In my family, it's always the patriarchs who offer thanks." I nodded to Anthony.

"I'd be honored," Anthony said. He bowed his head. "We're thankful today for being together for Mark's birthday, especially in this trying time. We are thankful for triumph over conflict, for family new and old, near and far, Survivor and Winter. For our health. For my family's happiness. For strength to persevere."

He went on, but I didn't hear the rest. I was too distracted by how emotional I had become at his inclusion of my family. It meant a lot to me to envision a life in which Survivors and Winters would be together as one. The terrible night at the bonfire had become a distant memory.

Over dinner, we spoke of happy things, normal things. Our trip to Dallas before the blackout. Ginny and Mark's fighting over driving my car. My bickering with them when they said my car was lame compared to their cars in California. Patrick telling funny stories from a century ago. Madeline quiet next to him.

When everyone had enough, Mark, Everett, and Patrick cleared the table — good boys that they were — and then we sang Mark "Happy Birthday." He blew out number candles — a 10 plus a 1 — and then cut the cake.

Adelaide handed me a slice. I groaned at the sight of it. "I can't," I laughed. "I will actually burst." I noticed Madeline ate nothing.

"More for me," Mark said and grabbed the plate, toppling my slice on top of his own.

A nice quiet had fallen over the table, each of us content with the meal and the celebration.

Anthony interrupted it. "Sadie," he said, "when the vision found you the other night, are you sure you were not looking for the rogue Survivors?"

Forks clinked against plates, and everyone looked up at one another. "Dad," Everett said, tension in his voice.

"I'm sure," I said, ignoring Everett's hostility.

"And this was the first time that had ever happened?" Anthony asked.

"Of course," I said. "That's why it was so startling."

"Let's not do this now, Anthony," Adelaide asked, her tone somewhere between pleading and warning.

"I just want to clarify a few things," Anthony said. He turned back to me. "Has the vision recurred since then? Or was it just the one time?" he asked.

"I don't know how much of a vision it was, Anthony," I explained.

"I think it may have been," he admitted.

"The girls were killed two nights ago. I saw it happen. It was in the news," I argued. "I do not have the gift of premonition, Anthony. You know this," I said, uneasy now too. I could tell what he was getting at.

"Perhaps you have acquired it," he said casually, sipping coffee.

"Acquired? As in killed someone to get his or her power? You're joking," I said.

"No one would blame you if you had taken it upon yourself to acquire more powers. There is a war. All powers will be useful. I just ask that you tell us if you do so we know what we have in our arsenal," Anthony said. His nonchalant attitude toward murder was absolutely infuriating. It was also frustrating that he was asking me to tell him what powers I had when the full Winter arsenal, so to speak, was a mystery to me.

"Anthony, I have not killed anyone. I never have, and I never will. My life is not a constant search for power the way yours is."

This changed his mood. He was being cordial, albeit accusatory, before. But now I'd angered him. "Don't pretend you're better than we are, Sadie. At least our destructive quests end in something useful that protects our families. What do your quests end in? Scars and failed suicide attempts? Who is that going to help?" His voice was cold.

"That's enough." Everett slammed his fist on the table. A glass of water next to him cracked and toppled, and the water spilled on the table. "That's out of line, Pops, even for you."

"Just calling a spade a spade. If Sadie gets to call her death wish 'research' instead of what it is, then surely we can find an amicable way to describe our process of acquisition?" Anthony said. He reminded me of John, which made me hate him a little.

I was afraid I was going to scream. Say things I couldn't take back. Open wounds I could never close. But I couldn't insult Anthony without insulting them all. "Excuse me," I said, setting my napkin on the table and rising to my feet. "Thank you for a lovely meal, Adelaide."

"Don't walk away from me," Anthony hissed. "We are not done yet. How do I know you aren't lying?"

"Because I'm not you. Just because you're still hiding something, doesn't mean I am," I seethed. I turned to walk away.

Anthony rose to his feet angrily. "You will NOT walk away from me!" he bellowed, the sound reverberating through the house.

"Watch me," I snapped angrily, storming out of the room.

"Smooth, Dad," Mark said, rising to his feet.

"I can't believe you," Everett said, on his feet already.

Don't follow me, I said in my mind, knowing Ginny was listening.

"Give her a minute, guys," Ginny warned. They backed off.

By the time I got to Everett's room, I could hardly breathe. I couldn't pinpoint why Anthony's accusation upset me so badly. It was insignificant that he, a creature who didn't consider killing a big deal, had, essentially, called me a killer. But it confirmed to me that Anthony and I didn't value the same things. I valued *life* (fine, if even not my own). He valued *power*. Even worse, he believed it was okay if life became the cost of power. It was ironic that I felt this strongly about life, but I did value it. I had never tried to take anyone's but my own, and I was beginning to think my heart was never really in my attempts in the past. If it had been, maybe I would have succeeded.

I felt trapped. I had wanted so badly to get out of Montana, so we went to Dallas. Dallas was supposed to be the ultimate reprieve for me — an escape to my human life — but it had gone so terribly wrong. Corrina all but hated me. I had cut myself off entirely from the human world for which I lived. And then we came here to recover from my horrific vision. Now this. I couldn't stand to stay here any longer.

And yet, I had nowhere to run.

—◈—

EVERETT KNOCKED ON THE DOOR A FEW MINUTES LATER. "SADIE?" HE SAID. There was uncertainty in his voice. I sensed he didn't know what to do.

"Yeah?" I asked. I was pacing.

He looked uneasy. "Hey, princess," he cooed. He put his hands on my cheeks.

"I need to go back to Montana," I said. This was less than optimal, but where else would I go?

"Okay," he said. "When do you want to go?"

"I'll go now, I think. It isn't snowing too badly. I'll drive."

"Now?" he asked. "You couldn't wait to get away from there."

"Yes, but now I'd like to be away from *here*," I said.

Always running, he said in his mind, a thought I likely wasn't supposed to hear. I pulled away from him.

"You can stay here if you want. Or maybe you should go back to Pacific Grove. I know the weather is killing you," I said, flinching at my word choice.

"I'll be fine," he said, pulling on his coat and picking up a suitcase neither of us had unpacked. "I'm a big boy. I can handle myself here, in Montana, or wherever else you are," he said. It was a lie, of course.

I knew he was aching with need. But he wouldn't let me out of his sight. He knew it. I knew it.

We went downstairs, and I was surprised to find Ginny and Adelaide standing in the entryway with coats and boots on. "We'll come with you, if that's all right," Adelaide said. I nodded.

Mark came up beside me and swung an arm around my shoulders, pulling me into him. "I'll be along soon," he whispered into my ear. "After I have a good talking-to with the warriors in there."

"Set them straight," I whispered back.

"That's what I'm here for, little one," he said, giving me a tight squeeze before he bolted out of sight.

From the blowup at the dinner table until the time we got in the car, no more than fifteen minutes had passed. I handed Everett the keys and let him drive so I could check out completely.

<hr />

WHEN WE ARRIVED IN THE MIDDLE OF THE NIGHT, WE PARKED OUR CAR AT THE end of the last mountain road just up the mountain from Swan Lake where we always left it.

Lizzie was waiting for us at the gate. "Welcome home," she said.

"Thank you," I said. I managed a small smile, but it was half-hearted. Though it had been my home for the most of my life, the world inside these walls never felt like home to me.

"Might I take Sadie with me?" Lizzie asked the Winters.

"Sure," Everett said. "We'll be at the house." He and Ginny took off with our things toward their new home on the square. Lizzie and I walked on toward the church, away from the others without another word. Adelaide followed.

"Mind if I join you?" she asked sweetly and walked in step on my right side, Lizzie on my left.

"No," Lizzie and I said in unison, though I was certainly more uneasy about this than Lizzie was.

"Sadie has had a hell of a time these last few days, Lizzie," Adelaide said. "She had a strange experience, almost like an intrusive vision. We'll need to speak with Andrew and Hannah about it. Regrettably, we'll need to tell John and the other elders about it, too, but maybe we can hold off on that."

"Certainly. We can meet in the room off the church. Should I get them now?" Lizzie asked.

"It would be best," Adelaide said. Lizzie nodded and flitted off toward Andrew's home.

I was shocked that she planned to meet with the eldest Survivors without Anthony. "What are you doing?" I asked her.

"I'm doing you a favor," she said. "I'm letting you break the news to your family that you saw their children killing humans without Anthony around to make it any more stressful for you."

I was in awe. "But…"

"But nothing. He *was* out of line today. He knows better than to accuse you of hurting anyone, and as a *person*, he should know better than to bring up your more sensitive subjects. I'm mad at him, and he knows it. He'll be along in the morning, I'm sure, but until then, you can have this moment with your family." I was so grateful for her in moments like this. I felt that Adelaide understood me better than any of her family, better than any Survivor. For weren't we the same? We were both witches, in some ways, who loved creatures with an aggravating need for human blood. "I love you, Sadie," she went on. "I love you like you were my own. I have since before I even knew you, before I even knew you were destined to be with my Everett. I can't explain it. I was always missing a piece, even with all the joy my family brings me. You're that piece."

"Oh, Adelaide. What would I do without you?" I said tenderly, dropping my head to her shoulder.

"You'd survive," she said. "You'd survive."

THEY HAD NO WORDS WHEN I FIRST TOLD THEM. THERE WAS ONLY STUNNED silence and quiet fear before the denial set in.

"But you don't have premonitions," Hannah reasoned. "Perhaps it was a dream?" I could see it on their faces how hard they were working it out in their minds, trying to rationalize away what I'd seen.

"It wasn't a premonition, and it wasn't a dream. I was awake," I said.

"Then a hallucination," Andrew said firmly. "You are under a great deal of stress. Perhaps you hallucinated your greatest fear."

"The Winters confirmed that the incident took place. It was in the news in the outside world," I said stiffly.

It felt like slow motion when I watched it sink in. Lizzie's breath grew haggard, and she began to hiccup, soft tears streaming down her red cheeks. Hannah pulled her knees to her chest and did much the same as Lizzie. Andrew sat with his impeccable posture and stared straight out ahead of him for a few moments, and then he crumbled. He bent over the table, put his face in his hands and was quiet for a long time.

Since I'd told them of Anthony's prophecy, and since I'd explained the transformation our rogue family members would undergo in the outside world, we had known this day would come, the day when members of this family, when *Survivors*, had become destructive. Careless. Gluttonous. Murderers. But I hadn't imagine it would feel this awful. How could I have?

"Can we stop it?" Hannah asked.

"If they are anything like any other *vieczy*, no," Adelaide said. "Only by destroying them."

The hope I saw flicker in Andrew's eyes faded. "So it's a choice, then, between our family or innocent humans." I was grateful to be in the room that absolved us of our powers. I wouldn't want to feel what they were feeling or hear what they were thinking.

"I don't know how much choice we have," I said. "I've failed at finding them, and, even if we did, who is to say we could destroy them?"

"Certainly we could," Adelaide said. "My family knows how to destroy all matter of creatures. They're the same kind as my children. It's difficult, but it's not impossible."

"Now if we could find them," I said, "we have at least until April before they'll come here because there will be snow until at least then, and you recall that there was no snow on the ground in Anthony's vision. We've got to be ready, even if they don't show up until the last day before the snow begins next fall. We need to keep doing what we're doing. Patrick and Mark can keep working with the youth, teaching them combat, refining their powers. Ginny can keep working on her mirroring of each power. Lizzie and Sarah can work together to see if there is a way to split and merge powers, like we've discussed. I am still convinced if a power can be acquired, a power could also be merged, split, or even stripped. And I'll keep looking for our family and researching what we need to."

"Adelaide and I can teach you a few things I think may be helpful in your future," Lizzie offered. "If you're interested."

"Of course," I said, my curiosity piqued.

"Good. Come with me," Lizzie said. She rose, and Adelaide followed. They walked to the far end of the room, opposite the now-invisible entrance. Lizzie put her hands to the wall, and a glowing outline of a door appeared, just the way it did when someone opened the entrance from the church corridor — the only door I had known was in this room. She reached for what seemed to be an invisible doorknob and pushed the wall open. From where I was standing, I could see a long dark hallway and not much else. "Come along, Sadie."

I was mesmerized. Were there other doors in this room I hadn't seen? And where did they lead to?

Andrew took my hand as I passed him. "We trust you with everything we have, Sadie. I hate to burden you with another secret, but…"

"I won't say a word," I promised.

"Thank you," he said, and let me go.

CHAPTER FIVE

apothecary

I FOLLOWED LIZZIE DOWN THE STRANGE NARROW HALLWAY, CRAMPED against dusty walls. I could feel my powers come back to me the moment I crossed the threshold. Adelaide followed behind me, and the door closed and faded back into the wall. We were in total blackness. Lizzie whispered something under her breath and the hallway lit up from what seemed to be a torch, but when I looked at Lizzie's hands, I saw a ball of fire hovering inches above her open palm. I audibly gasped. Adelaide laughed.

"Lizzie, the church backs up to the mountainside. Where are we?" I asked, deciding not to ask about the fireball she was controlling.

"Inside the mountain," Lizzie said matter-of-factly.

"Has this always been here?" I asked.

"We built it before we built the church," she said.

"How come I never knew about it?" I asked.

Lizzie stopped abruptly and turned on her heels to face me so that the fiery light was between us. I felt its heat on my face. "Because you are not an elder, and so you are not privy to all our secrets. I know you have forgotten that you once had a place in this society that was not at the top of it, and I do not ever remind you of it, though I should. There are some things you do not know because you are not supposed to know them. Our unique circumstances have made it so that we have recently told you things we otherwise wouldn't, but please don't take that for granted."

She turned around and continued down the corridor.

"Adelaide knew," I muttered.

"Because Adelaide is a witch. She could teach me things," Lizzie said.

"But she isn't even a Survivor!" I argued.

"Now you are being childish," Lizzie said, and I shut up.

We continued walking deep into the earth. Eventually, I saw a faint glow coming from the end. When we reached it, Lizzie closed her hands around the fireball, extinguishing it.

We walked into a room that was nearly the size of the church. The walls were misshapen and angular, as if carved haphazardly, which they likely were. In the middle of the room, small lights barely brighter than oil lamps formed a large circle a few feet above our heads, as if they were a part of a giant chandelier. But they were attached to nothing. I checked.

A very large, circular table sat beneath them. Vessels of all kinds, many of which were filled with brightly colored liquids, packed the table's surface. There were a number of set-ups that looked like old-fashioned chemistry sets, along with kettles and cast-iron pots. Many hovered above small fires, attached to nothing. Small glass jars filled with herbs and powders, wooden spoons, mortars and pestles, and various other utensils littered the large surface of the table.

Lining the walls beyond the table, huge wooden cupboards seemed to have held up well considering they had likely been built when the Survivors arrived here over 300 years ago. Along the sidewall, from floor to high ceiling, there were tiny wooden drawers with markings on the front of them, looking much like old card catalogs in libraries.

Lizzie went to the far side of the table. As my eyes adjusted to the dull lamp light, I saw Rebecca, John's wife, and Sarah, Lizzie's closest friend, awaiting us.

"Hi, Sadie," Rebecca said warmly. "Adelaide," she nodded.

"Hi, Becca," Adelaide said. *Becca?* I thought incredulously. "What is all this?"

"The apothecary," Lizzie said. "It's where we make things."

"Like what?" I asked.

"Enchantments, elixirs, that sort of thing," she said.

"You mean spells? *Potions?* You *knew* you were witches!" I yelped.

All three of the elders laughed. Sarah said, "Oh, Sadie. You always did think you knew everything."

I wanted to but did not say that, for the most part, I did know everything. At least compared to the rest of the Survivors.

"We knew we were capable of these things, yes," Lizzie said. "Whether or not we are labeled as witches…well, we decided that was irrelevant."

This alienated me a bit. I had always had a fervent desire to know *what* I was, if I was something the world knew of. "You couldn't have told us that?" I asked, frustrated.

"Shall we have the talk again about how you weren't supposed to know everything?" Lizzie asked. "Only the elders may use the things in this room. Adelaide has been helping a number of us with several projects lately, and she has graciously taught us far more than we ever knew before. Because you seem to be in the middle of everything, I think it's time to see if you have the ability to do what we can do."

I was instantly uneasy. If I couldn't do what they did, then I was not a witch like they were. And if I were not a witch, then what was I? A nosferatu? A *vieczy*?

Or a freak. But I might be a freak even if I could do what they were capable of.

Lizzie seemed to understand my line of thinking, something she was inordinately good at. "You have made it clear to us that what is happening to our family members outside these walls has something to do with *what* they are," she said. "Unable to know exactly who is what, then — more specifically, what you are or are not — I have no way of knowing what you could or could not do. But I am hoping you can do at least some of this." She was flustered and suddenly trying very hard to keep her mind clear. I looked at her carefully. I wondered if she knew I could tell she was lying. I didn't know which part of that was a lie, of course, but some of it had to be. They were so full of secrets.

"So how do we find out?" I asked, ignoring whatever she was hiding, as it was ingrained in me to do so.

"We'll start small," she said.

"No fireballs," I laughed.

She smiled, relieved that I had chosen not to ask more questions. "No fireballs," she said. "What do you think we should start with, Adelaide?"

"Becca and I discussed trying a protection elixir of some kind," Adelaide answered.

"We've been thinking of the most basic one," Rebecca said.

"We have some flowers to start with," Sarah added.

"Excellent," Lizzie said. She turned to me. "We're going to make an elixir that's a very simple version of something we make often. There are only a few ingredients."

I nodded, following only slightly.

"Come here, Sadie. Let me show you around. We can start with the recipes," Rebecca said, bringing me close to her. She walked me to the furthest cupboard and opened the door. There were shelves lined with notebooks — at the bottom were very old notebooks, covered in skins with delicate, thin pages inside; others were marbled black-and-white composition books like I'd seen in drug stores; and on top there were a few plastic-fronted spiral notebooks. It was an interesting chronology of the progress made in this room. Also interesting to know that of the few things from the outside world the Survivors brought in here, they valued the practices of this room enough to warrant buying modern notebooks.

Rebecca pulled a skin-covered notebook from the bottom of the stack. I presumed it was one of the oldest. "This is where you can find recipes or guides for how to do things. I wish I could say there was a better way to find what you are looking for, but you really just have to know. They aren't organized at all. We wrote things down as we discovered them — successes, failures, they're all in here," she explained. I nodded.

"So you figured out how to make this elixir early on?" I asked, wondering how one just *figures out* something like that.

"Indeed, we did. When we first arrived here, not all of us had stopped aging, and so we needed a way to protect food for those who still needed it since we came across real *food* so rarely, and it would freeze or spoil. Eventually, we needed to protect our bodies. Lizzie and I began wondering if the old remedies our mothers had taught us could hold up against our special kind of bodies. We made salves and syrups to heal skin or preserve breads and meats, and we had many failures. Eventually, we found a weak mixture that protected some things," she explained.

"What did it work on first?" I asked.

"My skin," Sarah said. I watched the same old memory playing in the three elders' minds. "Rebecca and John's first child was a feisty baby, and I took care of it the most at the beginning. It'd scratch the living daylights out of me, and I hadn't stopped aging yet, so I could feel every single scratch! I was desperate. I told them to try their salve on me," she explained.

I couldn't help but notice that, even here, in a room that no other Survivor from later generations knew existed, Sarah was careful not to let on to who Rebecca and John's first child was, even saying "it" instead of him or her.

Amusement radiated off of Rebecca, Lizzie, and Sarah. Adelaide, who surely experienced the same thing if not worse with her children (who I could only assume were prone to biting at a young age), laughed with them. But these were exactly the kind of stories I'd heard about infants of apparently all species that made me unsure what was enticing or endearing about them.

Rebecca flipped through the pages of the antique notebook until she found the page she was looking for. "Here we go," she said walking back to the table. "First we need a cauldron," reaching for an empty cast-iron pot from the stack of them. "And heat," she said. Standing over one of the burned-out fires, surrounded by stones, she held her palm open parallel to the ashes, and slowly a trickle of smoke was emitted from the ashes. Then, as if someone was blowing on the cinders, they began to smolder, then glow, and then a soft flame appeared. Rebecca handed me the pot. "You can start a fire in all the ways humans do, I'm sure, but this I need to teach you. Hold it over this flame, just an inch or so above it," she instructed. I did as she said. "Now. Close your eyes and focus your mind on making this pot hover over the flame," she said. I looked at all the other cauldrons floating around the table with no one or nothing holding them place, and I felt deeply unsure that I had in me the ability to make that happen.

"That's it?" I asked doubtfully.

"If you focus, it should work," she said.

I closed my eyes and obliged. I focused all my energy on the vision of the pot hovering over the small flame. "Now what?" I asked.

"Now let go," she said.

Trying desperately to keep my focus, I did as she said. Before I opened my eyes, I heard a loud thud as the cast-iron pot hit the table and then a crash as it knocked over a stack of pots and a few glass jars in the process. I cringed with embarrassment, "I'm sorry. I can't do this."

"Nonsense," Lizzie said, walking close to me. "There is not a single thing we ever tried and got right the first time. Here," she said, handing the pot back to me.

"I'll get this," Adelaide said. She put her fingertips to her forehead, so they spanned out over her eyebrows. The pots on the table restacked and the scattered contents of the broken glass jars found their way back inside the vessels, the shards of which had pieced back together until it appeared as if nothing had ever happened. I was stunned.

"Again," Rebecca said. I obliged, and again the pot toppled onto the table, this time rolling onto the floor before it took out any other materials.

"Again."

Again, it dropped, but this time Adelaide caught it midair — without touching it — and sailed it back into my hands.

"Again."

It landed hard on the table and took out one of the chemistry sets. Again, Adelaide put it back together as if nothing had ever happened.

"Again."

Crash.

"Again."

Thud.

"Damn it," I murmured, but the words came out like a hiss in frustration. "This is pointless," I said, crossing my arms. "I can't do it. I obviously am not like all of you."

Lizzie sighed and looked at Sarah, who shrugged.

"We shouldn't give up yet," Lizzie urged. She came next to me and took the pot in her hands. "You just need to focus," she said as she closed her eyes and held it out over the flames.

I felt a surge of heat in my chest, a pull in my stomach as Lizzie did this.

"Like that," Lizzie said, letting go of the pot, which floated effortlessly.

"Wait, do it again," I said, testing a theory. Lizzie obliged and within seconds the pot hovered over the low flame. The heat wasn't powerful, and the pull in my stomach wasn't strong either, but I definitely felt it again.

"What is it, Sadie?" Lizzie asked.

"Will another of you try?" I asked.

Rebecca took the pot from Lizzie, focused and suspended it over the small fire. I felt exactly the same things in my body when Rebecca did it as when Lizzie did.

"Sarah, you try," I said. I closed my eyes and focused now on sensing Sarah. I watched her mind go clear, felt her emotion focus on the task, felt her gut as it powered the pot to hang in the air. Same heat. Same pull. If I could emulate these thoughts and actions, I felt certain I could duplicate the result.

"What are you doing?" Lizzie asked.

"I think I can sense what you're doing to make it happen," I said, smiling and sensing triumph.

"You can do that?" Rebecca asked.

"I can do that," I said happily. "Let me try again." Sarah handed me the pot, and I stood in front of the fire. I held the pot, now warm from the flame, and I focused all my energy on doing what I felt each of the three elders do. When I opened my eyes, the pot was suspended, an inch above the flames.

Lizzie exclaimed. "I knew it!"

"We should have known Sadie could do anything we could," Sarah said.

"That's incredible," Rebecca said. "Using your individual talents to capitalize on and learn talents from others. I can see why you are so powerful. What a model for a Survivor." I tried not to laugh. Above all things else that I *was*, a model Survivor was chief among the things I was *not*.

"Come now, let's make the elixir!" Lizzie squealed. She clapped her hands together in excitement. I felt a surge of pride for having made her so happy. I so badly wanted to please Lizzie; her approval meant the world to me.

Rebecca showed me where to find the ingredients for the elixir. Bottles of liquids — from olive oil to a formula I had learned on the outside was called sulfuric acid — were stored in the tall cupboards next to the recipe books. Each little drawer on the sidewall was home to a different sprout, flower, spice, grain, animal tooth, or piece of dirt. I couldn't imagine the elders having traveled far and wide enough to have gathered all these things, then I realized that was because they wouldn't have. They might have gathered some of it — the olive oil was in a grocery store bottle — but likely Joseph had created the rest. There was not a substance in the world he couldn't manufacture. His talent was particularly useful in this way.

After gathering everything together, I put them in one by one as the recipe described, just like I'd seen Corrina follow steps in a cookbook. At the end, there was a murky white elixir swirling around the bottom of the cast-iron pot. I took the delicate flower bloom Rebecca handed me and dipped it in the liquid.

Lizzie held out her hands and made another small ball of fire. "Put the flower in it," she said.

I held the bloom in the middle of the flame, so close my hands burned. But the tiny white flower was unscathed, pushing the fire away from itself like a miniature but effective forcefield.

Lizzie smiled up at me, beaming. "Success."

LIZZIE, REBECCA, SARAH, ADELAIDE, AND I CALLED IT QUITS FOR THE DAY, HOPing not to push our luck with my early success in the apothecary. As we left, Lizzie lifted her palm toward the lights in the ceiling, and as she closed her fist tightly, the oil-lamp chandelier went dark.

In 144 years, I'd had no inkling that the elders could do this or anything else beyond the talents or powers everyone knew they had. This made it so hard to trust them — even Lizzie, whom I adored. I know she had reminded me of my place, growing frustrated that I felt I had a right to know these things, but didn't I have a right? I was risking absolutely everything — most notably, my freedom — to be here, to help them and to protect them, but they were keeping secrets. As we wound down the earth-walled tunnel back to the church, I was upset — not because they were still keeping secrets (I had come to expect it), and not because I would never uncover those secrets (I was sure I could), but because there might never be a way for me to determine when I had figured it *all* out. After all, how could I know what I didn't know?

When we got to the end of the tunnel, Rebecca reached her palms out to the wall to open the missing door.

"Wait," I called. "Can we see if I can do that? What if I'm in here alone and can't get out?"

Rebecca quickly put her hands to the wall, as if I hadn't asked her anything. "What?" she asked, once the door was open. "Oh, sorry, Sadie. I didn't hear you in time," she said. A lie. I clearly heard her think, *Goodness. We might trust you, but there would be no occasion for you to be in our apothecary by yourself.*

Light poured into the hallway from the room inside the church. It was already morning. I was surprised to find several of the elders meeting around the giant marble table, including John. My stomach clenched. As soon as he saw me, he jumped to his feet. "What is *she* doing in there?" he said in a growl to the others, not even bothering to address me himself.

"We've had this discussion," Lizzie said, the only one among them comfortable with defying John.

"And I thought we agreed we'd stop telling the girl everything she wanted to know," he barked.

"This was my idea, John. We need to know what she's capable of. There will come a time when we need to know what all Survivors are capable of," Lizzie said.

John scoffed. "These are not your secrets to give away! And they aren't yours either," he shot at Adelaide. "What were you even working on in there?"

"Merely a discussion of protection elixirs," Lizzie said, but John cut her off.

"Protection? Good Lord, you told her she is incapable of being bound by your protection charms and elixirs? What did you hope she would do with this information? Suddenly be loyal and help us reinforce the barriers around the city with her own irreverent breed of magic?

"John — " Lizzie interjected.

"It is imperative that we stop telling her these things. It is bad enough that she already knew that we knew not to let anyone outside of this sacred city. What of our secrets haven't you given away?" he asked, heated.

Lizzie pursed her lips together. "We were merely talking about protection elixirs in the apothecary. Simple, primitive versions. We were going to educate her on the things we learned first. So, until you said that just now, Sadie didn't know about the barriers, so now it is you who is — what was the phrase you used the other night? — 'impulsively giving away our most trusted strategic information to Sadie and the Winters' I believe it was?" Lizzie smiled, but there was an edge to it.

"What barriers?" I asked. Just how much were they talking about me when I wasn't around? And what did they mean about knowing not to let anyone outside, I wondered. I didn't actually know that. I don't know why he thought I did.

All ten of the elders in the room exchanged glances.

"There are protections around the walls of the city," John said, defeated. He sank back into his chair. "No Survivor can cross them, except for those who created them."

"All of you, I presume," I said, and he nodded. And it clicked. They wanted me to learn to make protection elixirs, however basic, because, as Lizzie said, they used them often. Surely they used their more advanced protection elixirs for these barriers? And what else did they use them for? "Did the barriers not work...before?" I asked.

"They weren't strong enough, apparently," John said callously, looking at the women standing around me. He blamed them. How convenient for him.

"But they are now?" I asked.

"They are," Lizzie said before John had a chance to answer.

"Did you make an exception so that I could cross them?" I asked, thinking about how I freely went in and out of or over the gates and walls of the City.

"No," John said. His fury was evident on his face. He didn't give any further explanation, but he turned to Lizzie.

"Or...for the others?" I asked.

"No, not for your rogue brothers and sisters either," he conceded. "Happy now?" It didn't take my powers to feel the disdain he felt toward me, possibly even toward Lizzie. She stared him down, but the gaze he returned was just as icy. "Now, you can leave us," he said, turning his attention back to the elders at the table.

"Meeting you don't want us to sit in on?" Lizzie asked, provoking him. "I think I'll stay," she said. She was testing his patience, and I liked this about Lizzie. I'd heard her think often about how John, too, needed to remember his place. He may be some kind of patriarch to this family, but he was not one of the three original elders, and she was. Though the hierarchies other than the basic elder-children divide in our family were relatively subtle, this was one she wanted to make sure was clear, at least to John.

"Fine, just *her*, then," he said, not even looking at me.

"We'll go," Rebecca said feebly as she hurried toward the exit of the room. Sarah and Adelaide were fast on her heels, but I sauntered, in no hurry to please him.

When I walked by him, I heard him whisper, "What a disgrace."

—◆—

WE FOUND EVERETT AND GINNY IN THE SQUARE TALKING TO ANDREW AND BEN-jamin. Everyone seemed to be in a pleasant mood, which was a relief.

"Good morning, princess," Everett said as I approached them. I hadn't realized that we'd been in the apothecary all night.

Andrew smiled. "Did you enjoy your time with your elders here?" he asked, gesturing to Sarah and Rebecca beside me. "Not to discredit Adelaide's presence," he added.

"I did enjoy it. Successfully," I added.

His face lit up. "Good! Praise God," he said.

Everett stepped toward me and put his arms around me. "Where's Lizzie?" he asked.

"She chose to stay in the church. John was holding a meeting and she crashed it — just to irritate him, I'm pretty sure," I said.

Andrew chuckled softly and looked at his feet as he kicked at the snow. He loved Lizzie for all the reasons I did. He lifted his gaze to meet mine, but then met Rebecca's unforgiving glare and the smile evaporated quickly. Rebecca clearly did not condone Lizzie provoking her husband, much less Andrew's approval of this. "Sorry," he whispered.

After that, we all split up. Rebecca retreated into her house, and Adelaide retreated into ours. Andrew went to the church, and Ginny went with Sarah to practice what they had been practicing for weeks. Sarah had one of the most unique talents among the Survivors, one that had been almost irrelevant until now — power bestowal. She could give the powers of one Survivor to another temporarily and without diminishing the power of the Survivor she was taking it from. Ginny had the most difficulty mirroring this skill, and it was potentially one of the most important powers we would need in a war.

I had theorized that Sarah might be able to do more than just bestow power. I believed that she could strip a power from someone entirely and give it, intact, to another. Essentially, I believed she could do what Anthony, Patrick, and Mark did when they acquired powers, only she could do it without killing someone to make it happen. By all accounts, this had never been done. But if there were any hope of power evolving, she'd have to spend time around humans. That's when my powers evolved so rapidly. I knew she'd never do this, not even if it meant success in the war.

Combined with Lizzie's power to merge, I envisioned a battlefield where Sarah and Ginny could pull powers from the enemies and Lizzie could quickly combine them and give them to our warriors or allies who needed them. Ginny, Lizzie, and Sarah spent an enormous amount of time together trying to make this happen. So far, they had been unsuccessful.

This left Ben, Everett, and me. Ben quickly got nervous in this trio, so he trailed after Ginny and Sarah. In an attempt to be in the middle of as much as he could, he'd often offer to be their guinea pig. He'd described the feeling of having one's powers separated and sectioned off, however temporarily, as a soul-splitting sensation. I had no idea what he meant by this, but I wondered if it was anything like what I'd felt at the bonfire six months earlier, when half my soul went with Everett and the Winters and the other half was rooted in this ground in the Survivors' City.

I sighed. In that equation, where was the part of my soul that belonged to the human world? Or the part that belonged to me?

"What is it?" Everett asked as we watched Ben walk away.

"Nothing," I said.

"Something," he said, taking my hand as we walked toward our house.

"Missing my humans," I admitted. "Maybe just my human life."

"It's funny to me that you refer to it that way. It is not as if you ever were a human," he said.

I shrugged, saying nothing.

"You should try to sleep," he eased. "You haven't since Monday, and it's Friday now." I nodded, though I knew I wouldn't. I wondered if I would ever sleep again. "Did you have fun being witchy with Mom and Lizzie?" he asked, changing the subject.

"How'd you know about that?" I asked.

"Andrew told us. I knew Mom had to be up to something very… Adelaide," he said, which I had learned meant doing something only a witch could do or, more specifically, something he could not. "But Andrew told Ginny and me so you wouldn't have to keep it from us. He figured you have enough to worry about." That was sweet of him, I thought. Andrew seemed to be the elder most concerned about my stress level, which I attributed to our nearly father-daughter relationship. I was grateful for it.

"I see," I said.

"So was it fun?" he asked.

"I'm not certain that fun is the right word. It was successful, though," I said.

"So you can do what the witches can?" he asked.

I nodded. "Does that mean that's what I am? That all this ridiculousness about me being special is just that? Am I really just one of them?"

Everett bit his lower lip. "I don't think it means that," he said.

"John just told me something that didn't sit very well with me. A few things really." We'd reached the front door of our small home.

"What's that?" he asked.

Crossing the threshold into the much-warmer inside, I said, "He said they have protections around the city walls — barriers, you could say — designed so that no one can cross them. But I can."

"Just you?" he asked, kicking snow off his boots and wiggling out of his exterior layers in the entryway of the house.

"And presumably the rogue Survivors, as they had to get out somehow," I said. "You and your family obviously can, but that's because you aren't Survivors." As I said, I realized how unique this was. Most gates existed to keep threats out. The elders' barriers existed to keep us in.

I shrugged out of my coat and hung it on a hook by the door. "It's just weird. Yes, I'm like them. No, I'm not like them. Yes, I can do what they do. No, their protections don't apply to me. Nothing makes sense! No one can even tell me what I am," I said. The distress in my voice was more obvious than I'd like.

Everett put his hands on my face and looked at me. "I know what you are," he said very seriously. I stiffened and braced myself, wondering what he could possibly know but ready to hear anything. He had always kept secrets. This I knew. "You're a Sadie. And I love that about you."

CHAPTER SIX

remembering

LATER THAT NIGHT, I DUCKED ACROSS THE SQUARE, DOWN TO A house that backed up to the thickest parts of the forest. Its faded red paint was peeling heavily, exposing the thick horizontal wood planks beneath. I ran my hand over small cracks around the thin doorframe. This house, Lizzie's house, was the home in which I'd lived most my life.

It was sort of an amalgamation of the time the elder Survivors had spent here in our city. The roof was thatched with a thick wheat-like substance I'd never learned the name of, but I knew was common in homes that predated the ones in which they lived in Salem. The planks, too, were original to the building of the place in the late 17th century. But on the doorframe were tarnished brass hinges you could buy in any hardware store, attached to a solid carved wood door Lizzie had bought in Kalispell maybe 20 or 30 years ago. I'd helped her install it.

Until the Winters built their house here, I had never stayed another night in any house in the Survivors' City. The house unofficially became Lizzie's and mine together, functioning like what I knew in the human world of roommates. As the other three girls in my generation I grew up with — two of whom mated — moved out to their own houses, I stayed with Lizzie. It lessened the pressure of being alone. There were years over the past century and a half when Lizzie and I would live alone, as of yet not responsible for any of the youngest generation, but as the decades would pass, a new generation came around and we'd invite two or three more into her — our — home. Lizzie became my friend and closest confidante, but I kept so much from even her. There were so many things I'd want to say but feared saying because she was an elder and I knew her primary loyalty would always be to that role.

I knocked on the door, and Lizzie quickly opened it. "Sadie?" she asked. I could hear the surprise in her voice.

"Hi, Lizzie," I said. "May I come in?"

"It's your home, Daughter. Always has been," she said, stepping aside.

Lizzie's house was modest like all in our town were. It was a main room much the kind that I'm sure they had in Salem with dusty wood floors and low ceilings, a laddered loft overhead where a few of us slept, if we slept. In Salem, that space would have been used to hold supplies and the like, but what supplies did we really need?

Lizzie was sitting on the dusty floor of her home, poking at her fire pit. I suppose that was unlike the original Salem homes. The Survivors' homes had fire pits in the middle of them with an opening at the top to let out the smoke, much more like a tepee than a New England home. From what I knew of colonial homes in both their primitive and advanced stages, fireplaces were built into walls and were very deep. Great for space, awful for circulating heat. And in a winter that could reach 40 below, immortal or not, heat was the priority.

I looked around the small room and glanced up into the loft only inches from my head. "It seems empty," I said.

"That's because it's just me," she said.

"But you've never lived alone," I said. I couldn't believe I hadn't noticed this in the months I'd been living back in the City.

"Because I had you," she said. "You're too hard to replace." She smiled, but her thoughts told a darker story. I tuned out of them.

I noticed a cast-iron pot hovering over the flame and changed the subject. "Are you working on apothecary-like things?" I asked.

She smiled. "Surely it isn't a foreign sight to see a pot over this fire."

"Hanging over it? No. Hovering? Yes," I said.

"You know all those years I had to fight with that stupid iron pot hanger…I could do this. I just couldn't let you see it. Isn't that something?" she laughed.

It was something. I remembered that pot hanger. It was awful. It fell over, ruined meals, splashed boiling water all over the tiny house. "I can't believe you faked it for so long," I said.

"We do what we have to do, I guess," she said. *Do we?* I thought. Is that something that counts as *have to?* Lizzie seemed to walk this thin line between wanting to tell me everything and wanting to tell me nothing, just like the rest of them. She interrupted my thoughts when she said, "So what brings you here, my dear?"

"Just wanted to stop by. Apologize too, I guess. For how I acted in the apothecary. You're right. I'm not supposed to know everything," I said. I don't know if I believed this, but I understood the value of saying what needed to be said.

"Thank you for your apology," she said.

"I also wanted to say that I don't take for granted all that you've shared with me. In fact, I'm very grateful for the support the Winters and I have received from you, Sarah, Hannah, and Andrew. It means a good deal to us," I said genuinely.

"You've been here for months, but now you came here just to say that?" she asked. Her eyes had a soft but knowing look.

"I don't know why I come anywhere anymore," I said. The words came out before I thought them, but it was oddly true.

"Well whatever the reason, I'm glad you're here. I worry about you, you know," she said.

"I assumed."

She kept her head to her work, nodding to herself as she said, "Good. I like to think you haven't forgotten how much I think of you, how much I care for you."

"Lizzie, that may be the only thing that brought me back here," I said.

This made her pause, but she never met my eye. She just nodded and returned to fiddling with the pot and whatever she was making.

"Why did you come back?" she asked softly. "Really?"

We'd never spoken of it. "I thought I had to protect you."

"Just me?" she asked.

I thought about it. "All of you," I said.

"Then I wasn't the only thing that brought you back here. It was loyalty and love for all your Survivor brethren. Do not discredit that."

I involuntarily scrunched up my face in a bit of aversion. I didn't think it was that.

Lizzie didn't like my reaction. "Sadie, you have a particularly interesting memory. For someone who has the supernatural ability to remember everything, you sometimes forget what matters most," she said. She gestured for me to sit down, and I joined her on the ground.

"What do you mean?" I asked.

"Do you know that you had a good life here?" she asked plainly. I thought the question was rhetorical, so I waited for her to continue, but she didn't. She meant it as a question. Did I know? she wondered. Like it was fact.

"Lizzie..." I began. She continued to wait for me to say more, the silence enveloping me. "It's a bit more subjective than that."

"No, it isn't. We gave you a good life, and somehow you've forgotten it. Maybe many are forgetting it now. But your life was made up of days where you children would roam the hills around our city or in the woods, just doing as you pleased. Do you not remember the times that you and Noah and Ben would spend in the woods, simply spending time together with no one bothering you? Inside these walls, you wanted for nothing. You were allowed freedoms we would have never been afforded in Salem. We changed our belief system to give our children a better life than we had. It has hurt me in a particularly strong way that you think this is not the case. That you've forgotten you had a good life."

141 years I'd lived in this house, and she'd never spoken to me about this. The pain in her voice was real. I had truly hurt her, and I hadn't come close to knowing it. "Maybe it wasn't about my life in here."

"Then what?"

I chose my words carefully as I looked out her window and could see young Survivors milling around the square, chasing each other. Playful sounds filtered in through the cracks and crevices of the house. "Maybe it was about knowing that there was a life for me, out there," I said, my eyes fixed on the moon.

"You have always felt drawn to a world we've kept from you. But was it really about that world? Not just a desire to leave? To rebel?" she asked candidly.

"I think it really was. I felt…pulled to go out there, to live out there. To tell the truth, I never thought another soul would leave these walls. I, more than anyone, was shocked when my 28 brothers and sisters left here," I explained, and that was the truth. I hadn't even believed Anthony when on that cold night in Romania he'd told me that some Survivors would abandon our family. It seemed an actual impossibility.

"We were all shocked," she said, a grave regret on her face. "With you, I at least saw it coming a bit. But they weren't like you all along. Their lives were not hardened until they left here. Yours…it hardened so long ago. "

I wondered how many of my secrets Lizzie knew. If she knew why I left the city — the *real* reason and not just that I wanted to go — if she knew about or sensed my troubles once I was in the outside world, the death quest, the isolation. I wanted suddenly to tell her everything. As a warm tension formed in my chest and throat, I felt truths and admissions bubbling inside me, pressing against my carefully crafted dam.

But Lizzie spoke before I had a chance to. "You know, parenting isn't what it used to be," she said, a kind of ironic lightness to her voice. "Once it was so simple. We had discussions amongst ourselves, considered our values, our priorities, what we wanted for our children and our community. Fourteen of us have raised, with the most recent births, 153 children. And, for the most part, the process has been the same. There weren't many of you who made us question our principles, who made us wonder if we were doing it right. But there was always you, here inside these walls, and I always knew we weren't doing what was best for you. I don't know what else I could have done, given the circumstances, because I maintain that we gave you a good, solid life. It should have worried me more that you couldn't see that. I'm to blame for so much of this," she said.

"Lizzie! No. That's not it at all. You were wonderful," I encouraged. I didn't blame Lizzie for anything. She had been my only saving grace.

"I should have talked to you. Been more honest with you," she said.

I made a noise as if to speak, but no words came out. Inside these walls, many things were sacred. Honesty had never been one of them.

"But it was too dangerous! Don't you see? I have a loyalty to my position as elder. I have a loyalty to the decisions we make as a group," she said.

But I thought about it. When she let me out to read the books, to escape briefly to the world outside, that went against what many of the elders believed was right for me or for anyone. She'd been bending the rules for me for over 25 years, probably longer if I thought about it.

Her train of thought was on the same line mine was. "And I know there have been times where I've betrayed that loyalty, but it was always to do what I thought would save you," she said, only tears were welling up in her eyes. I wished I could read her mind more clearly, but she'd become so expert at blocking me. Here she was opening up, only to shut me out. What was Lizzie afraid of telling me?

"Lizzie…" I trailed, surprised by her emotion. I felt she wasn't just talking about the bookstore visits. "Let's talk now. I might not be an elder, but I'm also not a regular Survivor. If anything, I understand the nuances and gray areas of what you all consider right and wrong and what might actually be right and wrong. I understand how pressure has forced you to make difficult decisions. You can talk to me."

"It's not so simple," she said. "But you're right about the pressure. It's become so much harder to parent these children now. So much harder to lead this society. We were a peaceful people with simple values and a quiet life before you abandoned us. And once you left…it was just chaos. Children of all generations scared that something had happened to you, crying in the streets, convinced after weeks that you had died. In your leaving, you made every Survivor ask a question of themselves they'd never asked before. 'Should I go?' They all asked it. Every one of them, I guarantee it. And the ones who'd believed you dead, they had to ask another much harder question. 'Can I die?' And do you know how much harder it is to parent a child who asks those questions? I do because I raised you. But the rest of them? They had no idea."

This hit me like a wrecking ball to the chest. They cried over me? They had to ask themselves hard questions, questions they'd been protected from asking because of me? I had never even considered that I had become a source of anguish for the other Survivors. I just knew enough of them hated me that I didn't care about them. But this was misguided, selfish. I understood that now. "I'm sorry," is all I managed.

"I just wish I could have made it right for you while you were here. I tried to compromise. I tried to help you. I indulged you. I let you go to Bigfork, read the books."

"It wasn't enough," I said, but the words came out harsher than I meant for them to.

"And yet I don't know what I could have done differently. I gave you an outlet to your pain by letting you read the books. I kept your secrets, let you live here with me under a kind of protection from those like John," she said. She paused and looked up at me, her eyes appraising my reaction to the elder's name. I replayed the last moment in my head. I had visibly flinched when she said it. Carefully, she said, "I believe…that you…that you know what he wanted to do with you before you left. You wouldn't hate him so much if you didn't."

"You know what he wanted to do to me?" I asked. My voice was thick with emotion. I didn't like thinking about this, about the time that John openly told other elders that I hadn't done my job as a Survivor because I hadn't procreated. I listened as he had vowed that he would see to it that I would get pregnant, no matter to him that I didn't want to. Hearing the man who was supposed to be our leader hatch a plan that involved deception, rape, and forced impregnation wasn't my favorite moment to relive. It was, after all, the final straw in my imprisonment. It had been that very night that I'd abandoned the Survivors nearly four years before.

"Of course I knew. Why do you think I kept you so close? Fought so hard for you with him, even now? Do you know that every night you slept in this house, I stayed here, watching over you even though I can't sleep myself? Do you know how many nights that John arrived at that front door with a boy in tow, one he'd enlisted in his sickening plan? I kept you close to keep you safe," she said. Her voice was thick now too, and her eyes reddening.

Her words sank around me like stone. He brought others into his plan? A plan that began long before I heard of it that day? I felt nauseous. If he was willing to do that, what else had he done in the last 320 years?

"I ran to keep myself safe," I said quietly.

"Because you think no one loves you enough to protect you. That's where I failed you," she said. She wasn't the first person to point this out to me.

"No! That's not it," I said.

"Isn't it? Is this the first time you feel safe here, now that you have a pack of angry-eyed Winter children to protect you from the world? From threats inside these walls?" she asked. She was getting angry now, but I couldn't tell the direction of it. At John? At the Winters? At me? She was feeling so many things that I couldn't filter through them fast enough. How much she hated John. How betrayed she felt by this entire situation, by forces larger than me, by probably even God.

I wanted to say "I've never felt safe anywhere" but it seemed that would only make it worse. Worse for her or for me, I wasn't sure. I had, after all, spent the last few months beginning to think that I had found a safe place with the Winters. What did it mean that I was about to admit that wasn't true?

I was uncomfortable then. I felt vulnerable, too vulnerable even with Lizzie who was my lifelong safe haven. So I rose to my feet, needing to get out of there. "Lizzie, you did a wonderful job raising me. Of raising all those who came through your household, who've ever been born inside these walls…all of us. And I'll never be able to repay you for how much you've done for me, or how you apparently protected me in ways I could have never dreamed. Just know that I love you more than I've ever loved another creature. And I'm sorry if it was hard on you to watch me hate myself," I said in earnest.

"It's still hard," she said coolly. I nodded understanding. "I love you, Sadie. Just as you are. I just hate that you've never felt whole."

What a way to put it. "There's just something about me…" I agreed. "I'm different. Crazy, maybe. Broken. But different. It's in my bones."

Lizzie just stared in the flames as I opened the door to her tiny home. In her mind, where I wasn't supposed to hear it, she said, *If only you knew how true that was.*

unlikely enemy, unexpected friend

IT WAS A LATE EVENING IN MARCH WHEN I WAS REMINDED OF THE horror. When my body recoiled and my mind revolted. When I tasted the blood again.

As others spent their time preparing for battle, I'd spent countless hours inside the apothecary, able to do what the elders told me it had taken them a century to learn to do, always on the first try, once I had learned to emulate their exact actions. It sent my mind swirling. The more I learned they *could* do, the more I knew they were hiding.

I'd reread *Theogony* for the 2,018th time in my life, literally, and I'd spent hours staring at the **1696** printed on the inside cover. Until recently, it was the one thing I was *certain* the elders had lied about: They had given me a book printed after their exile from Salem, which meant they had gone outside the city walls long before they had claimed to. Going into the apothecary changed the stakes of the game we were playing. They hadn't only lied about what they had done, where they had been, and what they had seen. They had lied about what they could do. They had lied about who they were. Who *we* were.

And then, late on an unseasonably cold Friday night, something clicked in my head, and I snapped the book shut, got up from my sunken chair and went to find Everett. I had something to tell him. Something important.

I threw on a coat and walked out into the yard to the as-yet moon-less night. The whole family was there, talking with my four favorite elders — Andrew, Lizzie, Hannah, and Sarah — in the pale light of old streetlamps that dotted the lane. I whispered to Everett that I needed to talk to him. In my mind, I told Ginny to get Mark and to come too. I made it two steps before I collapsed.

Wherever they were, it was warmer. Noah was running, surrounded by a large group of the rogue Survivors. There was sand under his bare feet, and a warm sea breeze on his cold skin. They ran along a deserted beach until they reached a lighthouse, and then turned toward the road.

I knew the road they were on. I knew they would turn left where they did, and I wasn't surprised when the long, glass-fronted house came into view at the end of the road. It was the Winters' home in Pacific Grove.

The pack broke in front of Noah, and burst through the front door, splintering it. A security alarm sounded, feebly at first, but then it got louder. The house was dark, but I could see perfectly. They tore the house apart, knocking over furniture and smashing breakables as they fumbled through every room, looking for something or someone.

I felt the tension rise in Noah when he realized that what he was looking for wasn't there.

I wasn't there.

"She isn't here," he said. The security alarm had picked up steam after the first minute, and it was blaring a loud siren now.

Derek, ever the ringleader, knocked a painting off with a flick of his wrist, and then he laughed.

"Stop it," Noah cried. "Let's go!" he screamed over the deafening alarm. Then he froze. They all froze.

"Smell that?" Derek asked, grinning maniacally.

Noah inhaled, and I could smell a warm, piquant scent hanging in the sea air. My mouth began to fill with liquid like it had before. "No," Noah whispered, but he did smell it. The scent got stronger as I heard muffled voices outside the house. I had no idea what it was — though Noah clearly did — but whatever it was, it was the most enticing thing I'd ever smelled. My body tightened and my stomach prickled.

"Humans!" Derek yelled.

They ran outside. People had spilled out of their houses at the sound of the alarm on the quiet street in the sleepy town.

Derek lunged first, but the rest followed quickly. Only Noah held back. Only Noah seemed to hate what he'd become. "No, no," he said — I said — again. I didn't know if it was he or I screaming.

Fifteen Survivors leaped into the crowd of pajama-clad neighbors. One after another, they tore at the necks of the humans, their blood pouring onto the pavement. It was hardest to watch those who made it outside in time to see their loved ones being torn apart, realizing their own fates were sealed as well. The looks on their faces were burned into my mind.

As the blood began to spill, the scent became unbearable. I felt dizzy. "No, no!" Noah cried. I felt intoxicated. And I couldn't resist.

I reached for a young teenage girl — thirteen or fourteen years old — and I held her close to me. "I'm sorry," I heard Noah's voice whisper. He kissed her neck before he bit her, his apology before his razor-sharp teeth sank into her flesh, opening her carotid artery.

Her screams faded quickly, and her blood began to cool the fire inside of Noah. Once her body went limp, he laid her gently on the ground and closed her eyes.

And then blackness.

EVERETT'S HANDS WERE ON MY FACE. THE BACK OF MY SKULL WAS POUNDING again, and there was pandemonium around me. I winced as I opened my eyes, too weak to move.

"She's coming around," Everett said.

"Answer the phone," I said feebly as I swallowed, trying to erase the taste.

"What phone?" Ginny asked, exasperated.

Then Adelaide's phone rang, and everyone froze. "Hello?" she asked.

I opened my eyes and closed them again. I saw spots. My body felt hot even in the snow, but nothing like the fire at the base of my skull.

"Who is it?" Anthony asked her. She held up a finger and listened.

"The security company. The alarm is going off at the house in California," she told him.

"But how did Sadie…" Anthony trailed.

"It's happening now," I managed. "They're there." I reached for Everett to pull myself into a sitting position. "They just killed eighteen of your neighbors."

They all stared at me in horror.

Anthony rubbed his face with one hand, then ran it through his hair. His tell of stress. "Patrick, Madeline, you go. Find out what happened. *Now*," he snapped. The pair took off running immediately. "Sadie, I'm sorry…"

I said, "Now you know I was telling the truth."

"Anthony, go with them. You should be there. The police could…" Adelaide said.

"Oh damn, police," Mark said. "That will not make this any easier."

"Go with them," Adelaide insisted. Anthony hesitated, looked at me, and I nodded. He sighed and quickly caught up with Patrick and Madeline.

"What happened?" Everett asked.

I closed my eyes and collapsed back in the snow, the burning pain in my head still raging. "Ginny can tell you," I said.

"No, I can't," she said. "When you blacked out, your mind went blank."

I screamed. "Damn it! I hate this!"

Lizzie broke through the Winters and came to my side. "Are you all right, child?" she said, both hands on my face.

"No," I admitted.

"Maybe she should rest," Lizzie suggested to the hovering crowd.

"We have to know what's happening," Everett said. His voice forceful and as icy as the snow I lay my head in.

"We can give her some time," Andrew said, coming to Lizzie's side.

"No," Everett barked. "We need to know now."

I looked at him, incredibly surprised. Ginny stared at him in disbelief, and spoke softly, "Everett…"

"Am I the only one who takes this seriously?" he snapped. In the dim light of the old street lanterns lining the lane, I had to squint to see that his eyes were a glowing crimson red.

"Everett!" Adelaide snapped.

"No, it's fine," I said. It wasn't fine, really, but I had no idea what was going on.

"Let's go to the church room," Andrew said. "There's better protection against sound."

I was unsteady on my feet. "May I?" Mark asked, reaching to scoop me up. I nodded. Everett had already begun to walk toward the church, and he didn't turn around or offer to help. Mark tucked me against his chest, but I tensed. Seeming to understand that I hated this display of weakness, he threw me over his shoulder in a flash, like he was giving me a piggyback ride. I appreciated him for that.

Inside the church room, I recounted it all in gory detail, nauseous as I talked about the smell and taste of blood, about the horrified looks on the families' faces. But I didn't tell them Noah kissed that girl's neck before he killed her. That detail was just too eerie.

Andrew spoke. "We must find them, if only to stop them. Even if it means our family will fall apart. Even if it means we'll lose ourselves in the process. Even if we have to kill them all."

Hannah looked uneasy. "Do you mean that?" she asked Andrew.

"They've brutally murdered 156 people that we know of," Andrew said. "We will have to risk everything."

"He's right," Lizzie added.

I put my head on the table, just wanting to be anywhere but here, living anyone's life but mine.

I'd be lying if I said the first image that came to mind was anything other than Cole Hardwick's sun-kissed face.

"We need to let Sadie rest," Andrew said, rising to his feet. "Come on. Out with you all." He opened the door and we filed out of it. Everett went on ahead without me.

"Everett," I called him, but he didn't turn around.

Not good, Ginny said in her mind.

"Everett!" I called again.

He snapped around. "What?" he screamed.

"Shhh! Everyone will hear us!" Ginny snapped.

"What do you want?" Everett repeated, this time quieter but not by much.

"What the hell is wrong with you?" I asked, only slightly stronger now. I rubbed the spot on the back of my head where the fire had finally started to subside.

"With me? What's wrong with you? You think it was easy to sit there and listen to you talk about how disgusted you are by my kind? How sick we make you? It's good to know what you really think of me."

"You've got to be kidding me," I said, unable to process what was happening. He had never been like this before.

"Ev, man. Shut up," Mark said. His voice was even, cooling.

"Am I talking to you?" Everett shot at Mark.

"Everett, I was just telling them what I saw. Something I didn't want to do, might I add, but *you* forced me," I countered, now close to him.

"Like that's an excuse for the shit you just said about me?" he argued.

"About *you*?" I asked incredulously.

"Okay, we need some space apparently," Mark said, realizing no one was listening to him. "Let's walk," he said, and he grabbed Ginny's arms and mine. But Everett followed. He was picking a fight.

"You are being ridiculous," I said. My eyes began to sting, and my throat tightened as if I were crying.

"What do you want, an apology?" he spat. He was on my heels.

"It would be a nice start," I said quickly. We cleared the city gates and stopped a few feet outside of them. I stopped to look at him then. The fury in his face terrified me. Paired with the hurtful words, it was as if he were an entirely separate person from the one I'd come to love.

"Why should I apologize? This shit is all your fault to begin with," Everett said coldly. "We wouldn't be here if it weren't for you, right?" He paced back and forth a few feet from us, one hand scrubbing his face and running through his hair. Just like his father.

It was suddenly hard to breathe. "You don't mean that."

"You're the one who's always saying none of this would have happened if you hadn't left this place. Maybe you're right," he said callously.

What he was saying, the way he was acting — these were possibly my worst fears coming to fruition: The last loyal ones turning on me; the tragedies happening around us blamed on me.

"You need blood," Ginny said. She grabbed her brother's arm. "Sadie, I'm sorry. We'll be back, and he'll be more polite, I promise."

Everett shrugged her off. "I don't need a babysitter, thanks," he spat, turning toward the woods.

"No way you're going alone like this," Ginny said, chasing after him. She grabbed his arm again, but he took her wrist and pushed her, hard.

Mark was between them faster than I could see him move, his hand on Everett's throat. "You do *not* touch our sister that way. And you don't talk to Sadie that way either. Say you're sorry, and then we're going to go get your head straight. You understand?" Mark demanded.

Everett fought Mark for a minute, but then he relented. "Sorry," he choked.

"Good," Mark said. "You okay?" he asked Ginny. She nodded, frustrated. "We'll be back by morning, Sadie. Sorry one of us can't stay, but we need to be there to watch out for him."

"Just go," I said. And they did.

Alone, I sank in the snow, pulled my knees to my chest, and put my head down. Things were going very poorly for me.

I took a pen out of my pocket, rolled up my sleeve, and began to make marks down my arm. From the crease of my elbow, down toward my wrist, over smooth skin and faded scars, I wrote a thin line of fifty tally marks. Below it, another line of the same. And another. I started a fourth line and wrote only six marks on that row. 156 marks in all. One for each of the dead I felt responsible for.

I hated that I knew what Everett and his siblings were doing.

Just then, I heard Ben call my name. He was standing inside the city gates, looking out on me.

I got up and went to him. "What are you doing here?"

"I want to talk to you," he said.

"Of course," I said. I opened the gate to let him out. He walked through effortlessly. I assumed that since I had been the one to open the gate, he could get through it.

I hadn't spoken to him much since we'd returned, but he spent a lot of time with the Winters.

"Walk with me?" he asked. I nodded and we began to saunter into the forest. "How are you managing, Sadie?"

"Being back, you mean?" I asked.

"Being hated," he said.

Oh, *that*. I chose my words carefully. "I'm handling it, I suppose. I'm not sure what I'd do without the Winters here and those few of you who are good to me." The last hour made me question just how helpful the Winters — or one in particular — were. "And I miss my life out there a lot," I said. "But I'm okay. How are you dealing with all of this?"

He shrugged. Of all of the people in my generation, Ben was the most dedicated to my family's way of life. He'd had his youthful indiscretions — like the time he made his own wine and sneaked Noah and I out to drink it with him — but most of that was a century behind him. Now he was loyal Survivor. His presence — even his mind — reminded me very much of Andrew's. He had a gentle but powerful nature. He was a traditionalist, though, the way that Andrew was, so I feared he would hate me over this mess more than he actually did. "I pray about it a lot. The trouble is, I don't seem to know what's right. Do I like to see our family split apart, as they are now? Of course not. But do I want the rogue ones to come back and start a war? Obviously not. It seems there is no easy answer."

"One thing I learned out there is that there usually isn't," I said.

"But that's the thing, Sadie. It used to be simple here. That was what made it such a paradise. We've had no conflicts. No tragedy. No trouble at all. Then you came back here with that family of Others and told us that our brothers and sisters are killing humans? And that they'll come back here to start a war, presumably to kill us? How did we get here?" he asked.

I couldn't tell if his question was rhetorical, so I answered it. "It's my fault, of course. I'm sorry, Ben. I'm sorry this has happened. If I had stayed, it wouldn't have been this way," I said. Ben did not respond,

but in his mind, he was trying to decide whether to comfort me. He
didn't want me to blame myself, but he saw it the way I saw it. He was
feeling guilty, too, though, which was out of place among his thoughts.

"They sent Noah and me after you when you left," he said quietly.

"They did?" I was stunned.

"As soon as they'd realized you'd gone. Lizzie went to Bigfork, and
when you weren't at your bookstore, she came back here and told them
she thought you had gone," he said.

"But you couldn't find me?" I asked.

"Of course we could have. Your trail was easy to pick up," he said,
offended I had suggested such a thing.

"Then what happened?" I pressed.

"We couldn't do it, Sadie. Noah knew what you wanted, that you
had wanted to go for so long. And it killed him to see you go, but he
couldn't make you come back here. So we cleared the city gates and
got far enough away to talk, and we decided we couldn't steal your freedom from you. If they wanted to bring you back, they couldn't use us
to do it," he said. His face was in his hands as he said this. I could see
now that he blamed himself for having let me go. The same guilt I was
carrying, he had been carrying, too.

"Did you tell the elders that you wouldn't track me?" I asked.

"Of course not! We couldn't disrespect them like that. If we had,
they would have found another way. Your freedom would still have
been in jeopardy. We pretended we tried and failed. This was the best
we could do to protect you," he explained.

"Where did you go?" I asked, enthralled in his story and still in
disbelief.

"We headed east where we weren't in the path of any humans. We
were afraid of them, I suppose. We found some beautiful waterfalls and
landscapes we had never seen. We rested there for a while, enjoying
being outside the city walls. We came back about three weeks later.

They never sent anyone else. They figured if their only trackers couldn't find you, no one would," he explained.

"You let me…escape," I said. Hearing it aloud didn't make it seem any less unbelievable. "How did you and Noah know what I wanted?" I asked.

Ben sighed again. "I suppose it doesn't matter if I keep his secrets now seeing as he's abandoned us, too," he said. He angrily snapped off a large branch from a tree we passed, snow falling off it onto the ground around us. This was a rare display of emotion for Ben. "He can see inside your mind," he told me.

"What?" I stopped walking.

"Not always. But for a long time he's known what you're feeling, and sometimes what you're thinking," he said.

"Can he do this to everyone?" I asked.

"Only with you. Only sometimes," Ben said. "But after 140 years of living with you and trying to protect you, he understood the basics. You wanted to get out. You want to be a human. You want to die." I looked at Ben, surprised and scared that he knew about my shameful search for mortality. "Don't be alarmed. We've known this for a while. We've never told anyone. We're good at keeping secrets." A faint, sad smile crept into the corners of his mouth as he said this. "There's no reason to expose you now. They all hate you enough," he said.

"Thank you," I managed.

"For what?" he asked.

"For keeping my secrets," I said. "And protecting my freedom," I added. I was so surprised to learn that there were people in my family willing to sacrifice what they believed in for my happiness. For 141 years, I never knew anyone gave a damn. All this time I had felt so alone. It was a shock to learn how wrong I'd been.

Ben smiled at me. "If I could have one thing in this life, do you know what it would be, Sadie?"

I shook my head.

"I want my family to be happy. That's all I've ever wanted."

I felt a pang deep in my stomach. Had I ever done something only because it would make my family happy? "You're a better person than I am," I said.

"Nonsense," he said. "I will admit I am a better Survivor. You, of us all, know the distinction."

I felt guilty again. That's all I was supposed to be, wasn't it? A Survivor? All I had to do was *survive*. And what did I want to do? Become a human. And die.

"What are you thinking?" he asked.

"This shouldn't be so hard for me — to stay here and be with my family," I said.

He didn't say anything. What could he say? He agreed with me.

I continued. "But there's more to this world, Ben. More that I wish all of you could see. Things I miss since I've had them and now I don't."

"I've read our three books, Sadie. I know there is more from *Beowulf*, *Macbeth*, and *Theogony*. It just doesn't interest me," he said.

"They don't do it justice. You can't understand it because you've never seen it. All you know of the outside world, you learned from looking down on a town many miles from here. A town that is smaller than any other town I've been to, so I can't explain how little that tells you."

I tried to explain. "To you, the world is something you see from afar, like a line on the horizon. But what if the horizon isn't a line? What if it's a flat shape, like a circle or a square? You can see that from where you stand. You'd only see the edge of the shape and think it was a line. What you see of the world outside, it's the smallest edge of the smallest shape. There is so much more."

"I imagine you are like a sphere, then," he said.

"Why do you think that?" I asked.

"There's no edge to a sphere — it's three dimensional and continuous. We could always see the sphere and know it was different. That was you in here," he said, rubbing his hand along the city wall we were walking around. "And out there, I'm sure you are different. That's what upsets you the most. So they, the narrow-minded ones out there, can see you too. If you were a sphere, we'd all be able to see you, and we'd all be forced to realize our perceptions were wrong. A three-dimensional, continuous entity could never hide in a world of two-dimensional shapes. So you'll always stick out. It would be the same with the Winters. You'll never be able to hide," he said.

"Comforting," I muttered.

"But there is an advantage. With any of you who have learned to live in this world and that one, you'll always have a vantage point that others won't. But you'll never be able to hide. The question, of course, is how you became a sphere because a sphere would be the most enlightened of us all, able to see everything — all the shapes, as you say — on the ground below. You know about our world and the one beyond our walls. You know everything, by comparison."

This caught me off-guard. Ben was describing a philosophy I'd read about in the human world — Abbot's notions from *Flatland* — only he had come up with it on his own. My family, despite having such little world experience, had powerful things to say. I do not know why I believed that they were incapable of seeing the world as I did. That wasn't it. Although some would never want to know a world unlike their own, some of them could if given the chance. But I was not so special among them. They were as intelligent and gifted as any human I'd met. It was out of immaturity or ego, perhaps, that I had assumed this wasn't the case.

"So you think that what I learned out there isn't all bad?" I asked.

"I think anything a person can learn can't be bad, as long as you don't let it change you. Sadie, sister, I realize that you are not like us in every way, but you are like us in the ways that count. We all came from the same place. You're still a Survivor, and we still love you. Even the ones who don't show it," he said.

"I appreciate that," I said.

"It's what one expects of one's family. And if it is any different out there, I hope you haven't let that color your perception of your own family. We will always love you, even when we cannot understand you. I realize that lack of understanding might be the challenging part for you — it is for us all — but I cannot imagine that the Winters understand you any better than we do. They seem even less human than we are, despite having lived in a human world," he said. He was right, of course, but I hated to admit it or to give any Survivor another reason not to like the Winters. "Might I suggest that you find a human to talk to, Sister? Surely in your travels, you've met one you can trust with your truth?"

"Maybe," I said. I was grateful for Ben's suggestion, and that he understood he could not provide what I needed. But had I met a human I could that much of? It didn't feel like it. Except Corrina. But now I had alienated her terribly. I was sure she hadn't forgiven me. I wasn't even sure she'd let me in if I arrived at her door.

But there was one human who would always answer the door for me, I was sure.

Cole Hardwick.

I stopped where I was and pulled my cell phone from my pocket, as Ben wandered on. I pulled up Cole's number, stared at it, and the I put the phone away. I couldn't do this in a phone call. He deserved better than that if I were going to ask him to let me back in his life. It wasn't fair to ask this of him, but he had once promised me — before I walked out on him in London — that he would listen to anything I wanted to tell him.

This time, I acted quickly, so as not to allow myself the twenty-minute deliberation that would end in me leaving Cole alone.

"Ben, Everett and the rest of them will probably be back tomorrow. Can you tell them I'll be back in a day or so?" I said.

"You mean can I lie for you and not tell them you are going to see some human they don't want you to see?" he asked.

I bit my lip and nodded.

"What is it that Ginny always says? Done and done."

CHAPTER EIGHT

human contact

I'D LIKE TO SAY THE DECISION TO SEE COLE HARDWICK WAS ONE I could write off as impulsive. It was not.

I went back to the house to get my things. Thankful that Adelaide was not in it, I grabbed my traveling tote bag, threw in a bunch of books into it along with the usual contents I always traveled with — my Moleskine journal, *Theogony*, my passport, and the like — changed into nicer clothes, and grabbed my Fendi Spy bag. I left without a word to anyone. I called the airline on my car's speakerphone on the way out of Bigfork and booked a flight to New York.

Just the fact that I flew to New York instead of running there was a clear sign of premeditation. This journey was not one that could be written off as a crime of passion.

But I felt like I had no choice. The cold air had begun to penetrate my skin, my *soul*, in ways I had never previously imagined. The cold used to be a refuge for me, and it used to be one of the solitary fond reminders of the place I came from. But now the cold was menacing, contorting and controlling the man — er, person,…no, thing? — I loved in ways I couldn't understand and couldn't forgive. All I wanted was to be standing in the Mississippi heat I'd felt before all of this began. And then Everett could stand by me without his attitude, his standoffish moments. "But who was I to judge?" he might say if he were here, since I would be standoffish in the Sahara desert, the Swiss alps, and everywhere in between.

It was mid afternoon when we landed. I took a cab to Union Square. I didn't know where Cole lived, but I could sense his mind so easily, I knew he wouldn't be hard to find. I traversed the sidewalks of Manhattan in four-inch platform-heeled suede and snakeskin Prada ankle boots, following my supernatural senses. It did not escape me how strange this was.

I was glad that it was a Saturday. I might find him home alone, wherever home may be. After being pulled south and west for a number of blocks, I found myself on Spring Street in front of a large building made entirely of glass and steel; it looked very much like a giant glass house.

I could read Cole's mind clearly from the sidewalk. He was reading *Harry Potter*, which I found incredibly endearing for reasons I could not entirely explain. He was just starting the seventh book, and he was excited about it. He was sitting on a couch, wearing pajama pants even at this time of afternoon, feet propped up on a coffee table in front of him. Music was playing in the background and light cascaded in through the floor-to-ceiling windows of the loft-like home. He was such a normal human. I understood why I'd come.

I walked into his building and was greeted by his doorman. "Who are you here to see?" he asked.

"Cole Hardwick," I said. It was the first time I'd said his name aloud in months. It felt strange and velvety on my tongue.

"Is he expecting you, madam?"

I hesitated. "Er... no," I said. I hated that I had to let his doorman call Cole to announce my arrival because it would give me away. But I supposed that, on the chance he wouldn't want to see me, it would be easier for me to overhear that from a phone call with the doorman than from his beautiful face.

"Ah. Your name then?" the doorman asked.

"Sadie Matthau," I said. I was exponentially more nervous than I expected to be.

"Very good," the doorman said. He picked up the phone dialing Cole's number.

It only took a moment for him to respond. "Hello?" he asked, his mind curious. He hadn't been expecting anyone.

"Good afternoon, Mr. Hardwick. There is a Ms. Matthau in the lobby to see you. May I send her up?"

Less than one second later: "Sadie Matthau?" I could hear him ask in disbelief. There was a strange smile in his voice — I could hear it at the same moment I felt it. "Yes! Send her right up," he beamed. All the tension in my body released.

The doorman took me up to Cole's floor and directed me to his door. I moved quickly, trying to keep to a human pace.

He was been standing behind his door in what I could sense was fervent anticipation. I knocked and, too quickly, he opened.

"I can't believe it!" he exclaimed as he walked toward me. He threw his arms around my waist and lifted me off the ground.

When he put me down, I had a chance to look at him. His features were so friendly, his eyes as clear blue as an ocean, just as I had remembered them. Though, as before, I had forgotten how beautiful he was. His sandy blonde-brown hair was sweetly disheveled and his eyes were still as blue as sapphires. He was wearing a vintage Mighty Mouse t-shirt over knit pajama pants. This deconstructed version of him was candid and warm.

"I'm so glad you let me in," I confessed as we stepped into his loft apartment.

"Why would I not?" he asked. He ran a hand through his hair and shook it out of his eyes nervously as we stood there. I'd missed the mannerism.

"Because," I said vaguely, not wanting to relive the details — or the emotions — of the night I'd walked out on him in London.

"History's dead, kid. You're here now. That's what matters," he smiled. "Oh my gosh, where are my manners? Sit down! Can I get you anything to drink? I'm having coffee, but I can make almost anything. I'm handy," he laughed, his smile like a sweet reprieve.

"No, I'm good. Thank you, though," I said politely and followed him into the main room. It was very masculine, with thick charcoals and rich espresso wood blanched over the concrete floors and steel fixtures, but it had all the touches of thoughtful design, right down to the spray of three vases of varying heights set off-center on his coffee table in front of which I sat. I quickly deduced he either hired a designer or had help from his mother, whom he had always talked about with great admiration.

"I have to apologize for my appearance," he said as we sat on his couch. "I would have looked more presentable if I knew you were coming. How long have you been in New York?"

"About an hour," I said.

"You came to me first?" he asked, his voice cracking. His mind instantly swam back to familiar images of the Sadie-and-Cole Happily-Ever-After sort they'd been in Tupelo and again in London. Clearly, it was a mistake to have admitted this. Here I was giving him the wrong idea less than two minutes after arriving.

"Oh, um, yeah," I stuttered. That was the best I had?

"What are you doing in town?" he asked.

"Visiting you?" I said. It was a question, sort of.

"That's…unexpected," he said. *Don't get too excited,* he said to himself.

"I was on my way to Europe, so I thought I'd make a stopover here," I lied. I panicked, realizing only then just how weird it was that I had flown across the continent to see him like this, unannounced.

"That's very thoughtful of you," he said calmly. *Stay cool. Stay cool. Stay cool!* he commanded himself mentally.

"Is it?" I asked. "I don't know. I've not been very thoughtful of you so far," I said. "I need to apologize."

He waited for me to go on.

"I was out of line in London. I was even out of line in Tupelo when I acted the way I did. It's not fair to you when I'm so unpredictable and...flighty," I said. I didn't like to think of myself that way, but it was pretty accurate.

"The apology for London, I'll take. I won't lie, I was pretty bummed. But you have nothing to apologize for in Tupelo. It was a fantastic weekend, and I wouldn't trade it for the world," he assured me. He looked me in the eye for a moment as we sat, facing each other. Oddly, my mind played a memory of Everett looking into my eyes the night we'd first kissed in Twin Falls, when I had counted to see how long we held each other's gaze. We'd made it to sixteen.

"I'm really glad you're here," Cole said. I started counting, but I made it to only four before I deflected. "I've been worried about you," he admitted.

"Why?" I asked, now nervous. It didn't end well for me when others started worrying.

He was saying just what he was thinking, as he was thinking it, so I was getting very little lead on our conversation. This was a tactic he used to keep himself from backing down from what he wanted to say before he could lose his nerve. It made my life, in that moment, exponentially more difficult.

"It didn't seem like you, what happened in London. You weren't the same as you were when we met. It seems that something tough is going on in your life. And if that's the case, I'm concerned," he said sincerely.

I didn't say anything. This happened with him: He could see through me when I wanted to hide.

He went on, "Corrina thinks the same thing, but you won't talk to her about whatever it is. We all know something is wrong, we just don't know what."

"When's the last time you talked to Corrina or Felix?" I asked. I needed to know if he knew about Everett. If he did, he hadn't let on.

"Weeks? Months? I don't know. I've been pretty busy at work. I got pretty busy with a project at work, so it's been a while, I hate to admit," Cole said. I relaxed. He had no idea Everett Winter existed, much less that I had run out on Corrina and Felix the way I had.

"I'm surprised you think about me that much," I said honestly.

You're kidding, right? "I haven't stopped thinking about you since the moment I met you," he said. *Before that, even.*

"I think about you," I said. That was true but probably not the right thing to say. I didn't think of him the way he thought of me, that was clear. Or if I did, I wasn't supposed to.

The memory of Everett and me in Twin Falls persisted as Cole and I chatted. I suppose some part of my mind was trying to make me feel guilty, or was simply trying to remind me of the butterflies I could feel with Everett — like those I was reticent to admit I was having just then with Cole. But that's not how the rest of me took it. Before Everett and I had truly kissed that night, I'd asked him to kiss my forehead like Cole had done at the wedding. I suppose this had been to even the score in my mind. Compare the two side-by-side.

It would be only fair, then, if I didn't write off my feelings for Cole until I'd had a chance to be with him like I'd been with Everett. Deconstructed. Intimate. Attached.

I put my hand to my forehead, as if to erase these thoughts. Even I could tell that was a dangerous line of thinking.

"Everything all right?" Cole asked, laughing nervously at my expression.

"Fine, fine," I said quickly.

An odd silence hung in the air between us. Then Cole said, "Sadie, do you think you'll ever settle down?"

"No," I said. *Not until I'm a human,* I said to myself, which was something I didn't count on anymore.

He reacted instinctually, flinching visibly. That was not the answer he anticipated. "Nothing would motivate you to?"

That was some sort of proposition. It was subtle, but I caught it. Barely.

So I chose my words carefully. "I would love to, Cole, but I have a hard time fitting in. I'm comfortable by myself," I said.

"You feel comfortable with me," he said plainly.

"I do," I said. An image of me in a wedding dress flashed in Cole's head. I bit my lower lip.

"So the trouble is..." he led.

"Complicated," I said.

He sighed. "You could give me a chance to give you what you want. Come spend some time in New York. No commitments. No strings attached," he said. He had this interesting way of offering things. It was unobtrusive yet sincere. I wondered if it meant I might be so at ease that I'd agree to something and not know it until later.

"I understand you better than you think, Sadie. I'm not saying you have to give up the parts of your life you like, maybe just the ones you don't. And I know there are parts you don't like. If you came here and sat still for a little while, maybe, just maybe, you'd be a little more normal," he laughed. He didn't mean that with any kind of malice. Instead, it was like he saw right through me. He knew that I wanted to be normal more than I wanted anything else, and he was offering it.

"Maybe," I said quietly. Normality offered from Cole's smooth lips and rosy baby face sounded more enticing than anything I could dream of. I don't know what it was about looking at him that made me quietly forget everything else.

I absent-mindedly fingered the gold key hanging from my neck.

"So what's going on in your world that brought you to me today?" he asked.

I selected a tiny sliver of my mental armor and pulled it down. "Family drama," I said.

Cole's eyes widened. "You never mentioned you had any family," he said.

"Do you assume everyone is without family if they go unmentioned?" I asked.

Of course not, but Corrina... "No, of course not," he said. "You just... well Corrina mentioned that..."

"...that I had no family?" I guessed. I'd never told her that, but I had been telling her lies of omission on three years.

"Something to that effect," he said, stumbling over his responses.

"Well, I do. I just never mentioned them."

"Want to talk about it?" he asked. I shrugged. *Nothing? You came all this way to give me just that much, and then you won't tell me anything else?* he said in his mind. He was frustrated.

I leaned back and pressed my palm to my forehead. "Everything is just so ridiculously stressful," I said.

"And you need an outside opinion?" he asked.

"Perhaps..." I paused, unsure of what it was I needed, other than just someone *outside,* someone human.

"A shoulder to cry on?" Cole offered.

I stiffened. I would never let myself cry my tearless, hollow sobs in front of Cole. I hated showing vulnerability to anyone because it always felt like someone was invading me. Even to him. Especially to him.

"Sorry. I didn't mean to shoot you down," I said. I always fumbled around him. My words were always wrong.

Cole crossed his arms across his toned torso and leaned back on his couch, definitely more relaxed than I had ever seen him. I think he felt more confident since I was on his turf. Either that, or he was falling out of love with me, and that made everything less problematic.

He could tell I had just closed off again, so he was direct. "Sadie, what can I do for you?" he asked.

"Do you remember London *before* dinner went awry?" I asked.

"Of course," he said smoothly. *I'd never forget it. It felt so real,* he added in his mind.

"Maybe, if you're not too busy, today could be like that. I need to get my mind off things," I said, hoping desperately he'd want to spend the whole day with me.

"Say no more," he said. "Give me a few minutes to make myself presentable, and then we'll get a cab to midtown. I imagine Fifth Avenue might be a good place to drown your sorrows?"

I smiled. "Sure," I said. Truth be told, it wouldn't take Fifth Avenue. So far, it had only taken twenty minutes of feeling like a human for my so-called sorrows to slip away. Anywhere with him would ease my mind.

"Great," Cole said, hopping to his feet. "I'll be right back. Make yourself at home." That phrase was more alienating than anything any human ever said to me. I had never felt at home in any place at any time — except in Everett's arms when he was being less…wintery. But even that wasn't home. It was just closer to a mirage-like feeling I'd been chasing all my life: peace.

—◆—

COLE AND I SPENT THE DAY ROAMING MANHATTAN. IT FELT LIKE A VACATION. Cole radiated simplicity, normality, happiness.

The weather was mild for this time of year, and it was bright and sunny. It took me a little while to get used to the cacophony of voices and visions coming from eight million other people, but before dinner in some white-tablecloth restaurant on the Upper East Side, I had gotten it under control.

I had never turned my phone back on after the plane ride because I didn't want to deal with the angry voicemails and frantic lists of missed calls from the Winters. They would be back in the Survivors' City by now, aware that I had gone off on my own while a pack of rogue Survivors was roaming the earth and looking for me. They would call their disdain for my independence a faction of "looking out for my safety" when they lecture me upon my return. They would say traveling together was for my protection. And I would think but not say that it did not feel like a precaution; it felt like chains.

Cole asked far fewer questions than he did in our previous encounters, which was good because then I had to lie or deflect his questions less often. His feelings were not much different than they had been in London, but now he was more wary. Still, his visions of us together were vivid in his mind. I didn't mind them. They were peaceful, respectful, and normal.

I felt like hitting myself for thinking this way. I had Everett. I loved Everett. His whole family were putting their lives on the line to fight for my family. I finally started to feel guilty for what I was doing. I had come here in need of a friend, and Cole had been that friend. But Everett would not see it that way, though, and who could blame him?

In the cab back to Cole's, I turned on my phone. A mistake. Forty-seven message in my iPhone's voicemail list: six from Family 4 (Lizzie), three from Family 1 (Andrew), seventeen from Ginny, four from Adelaide, four from Anthony, twelve from Mark.

There was only one from Everett. I'd listened to only the first two or three seconds of each, but his I listened to in its entirety. "Good thing my heart is already stone because otherwise you running off to Cole would hurt like hell," his voice said. There was a clear razor edge in his otherwise calm cadence. By far, it stung the most.

But this at least confirmed he knew where I was. I should have guessed Mark would track me. I just thought it might take a little longer.

"Everything okay?" Cole asked, as I flipped through some of the voicemails.

"Sort of," I said.

He raised his eyebrows, asking without actually asking what was going on. I just shook my head.

"How long will you be in New York?" Cole asked, switching subjects and swallowing the frustration of me evading another question.

"Not long," I said. If the Winters knew where I was, it was only a matter of time before they appeared out of nowhere.

"When is your flight?" he asked.

"Hmm?" I asked, looking at my phone.

"To Europe," he said.

"Oh," I said, remembering the lie I'd told, "tomorrow morning."

He had an interesting calm about him when he said, "So you can stay with me tonight."

I looked at him in surprise. "I have a guest bedroom," he added quickly, then worried he'd overstepped.

"That would be nice," I said. As soon as I agreed, I regretted it. I still hadn't slept since Dallas. The odds were strong that I wouldn't be able to tonight either. I was exhausted, sure, but I had just agreed to a night of lying in his guest bedroom, wide awake and alone with my thoughts.

"Great," he smiled, quiet again for the rest of the ride.

I couldn't help but wonder whether a human life would be this way — lazy weekends with Cole? Holidays with his family in Tennessee? Vacations with Corrina and Felix?

I wanted that so badly. So badly, it hurt. By the time we reached Cole's door, I couldn't tell whether guilt or longing was stabbing at my stomach.

I was so confused. In the middle of this mess, when my *love life* was more trivial than it ever would have been, my head was clouded by this confusion. By these *feelings*. I hated it. And any path I chose would hurt someone. Every path I chose would hurt me. Or maybe it just felt that way.

"Do you want to watch a movie?" Cole asked as he locked his door behind us.

"That sounds nice," I said. I dropped down ungracefully on his couch and stared at the TV as he put in a movie.

Out of the blue, that spot at the base of my skull began to feel hot. It didn't hurt; it didn't even actually burn. It just felt warm. Like a human.

What was I doing here? I needed to call Everett. Urgently, I felt the need to make things right.

"Hey, I'll be right back," I said. "I need to make a quick call." I went into the guest room and dug my phone out of my bag.

When I looked up, I had to put my hand over my mouth to keep from screaming.

duel

A MENACING MARK WINTER STOOD IN FRONT OF ME. "WELL, ISN'T this nice?" he hissed. I wasn't used to animosity from him. I had grown accustomed to him siding with me.

"What are you doing here?" I whispered and hit his arm. I was still in shock from having watched him materialize. And I was hostile because I was busted.

"Trying to make sure young *vieczy* haven't ripped you apart. Now that I know you're fine, I might ask you the same question. What exactly were you trying to pull, running off like that?" he asked. He leaned in toward me as he said this, so close his signature motorcycle jacket hung off him and brushed against my skin. It was threatening.

"I needed a little human contact. Is that such a bad thing?" I asked.

"When there are twenty-eight out of control *vieczy* out there who are *looking* for you? I should say so," Mark said, pacing.

"What did you expect me to do after how I left things with Everett? Sit and wait for an apology? I had to get away," I argued. It was one of my more unflattering character traits that I got defensive and argumentative in moments like this.

"So you ran off to the only human man on the planet in love with you? Because you thought that would *help*?" he sneered.

"I never said he was in love with me."

"Please," he scoffed. "You didn't have to."

My patience wore thin. "Get out of here. I'll come back tomorrow, and in the meantime, I'll be plenty safe," I insisted.

Just then, Cole knocked on the door. "Everything okay?"

"Fine," I lied, narrowing my eyes at Mark. "Leave."

"No can do," Mark said.

"I don't want trouble," I said.

"You've been off the grid for nearly twenty-four hours. Trouble is about to arrive at the front door," Mark said.

"They're coming?" I said in dismay.

"Your phone has been off! You could have been dead!"

"Never so lucky," I muttered.

There was a knock at Cole's door.

"That'll be Everett," he sighed.

"Damn it!" Mark disappeared, I'm sure only to reappear outside Cole's door with Everett and, I'd guess, Ginny.

I hurried out of the bedroom. "Cole," I said, clear warning in my voice that he didn't read.

"Hold on, Sadie, someone's at my door. Must be a neighbor since the doorman didn't send anybody up."

I held my breath as Cole opened the door.

Everett's immortal face had never looked angrier. Ginny and Mark flanked him.

"Can I help you?" Cole asked with great surprise. But as Everett emitted a sound that sounded like a faint growl, bold waves of defense rolled off of Cole; he was only concerned with protecting me from the menacing strangers. "Who are you?" he cried.

"Why don't you let Sadie introduce me," Everett said, striding boldly into Cole's home.

Cole looked at me, concern and confusion in his eyes. "Sadie?" he asked.

"Cole, this is Everett Winter," I said helplessly.

"Who?" Cole asked, leaning back to put space between his body and Everett's since Everett wouldn't let up.

"Her boyfriend," Everett said roughly. I didn't like the sound of it that way. It was like he was proclaiming ownership.

Cole looked at me in disbelief. "*Boyfriend*?" he asked, the disbelief clear in his voice. I could read that he was angry with me for lying and at Everett for hearing the same cold possessiveness in his words that I did. He was jealous that I had someone who was not him, and he quickly felt inadequate looking at Everett's strangely beautiful face. He felt betrayed. And buried beneath all that, he was absolutely terrified of the three angry immortals who had stormed into his home.

"Boyfriend," Everett confirmed. "And you must be the fair-haired Cole Hardwick. I've heard so much about you," he said, smiling menacingly. He had yet to acknowledge me.

"Funny, she hasn't told me a thing about you," Cole said, the hostility in his voice evenly split between Everett and me.

"You think this is funny?" Everett's words came out like a snake's hiss, and Cole's eyes widened.

"Leave him alone!" I yelled. I stood between them and pushed Everett back.

"Why? You couldn't," he said.

Mark reached for Everett's arm and pulled him away. "Not the plan, brother. Let's try this again," Mark said. "Cole, I'm so sorry for my brother's actions. My name is Mark Winter. This is my sister, Ginny, and that's our hot-headed brother, Everett, who, yes, is with Sadie now. Sadie hopped a flight to come see you without telling anyone where she was going, and we've been very concerned ever since. Ginny suggested she may have come to see you, so we called her friends Corrina and Felix and found out where you lived."

You really called Corrina? I asked Ginny quickly.

Tried. She didn't answer. He wasn't exactly hard to find, though, she said.

Cole was obviously unsure what to believe or how to respond. "Is that true?" he asked me. I nodded. Cole looked back at Mark. "I do understand," he said. They were all ganging up on me. Had I been *that* reckless?

"Thank you for understanding," Mark said politely.

"I do not understand that little standoff, though," Cole said, nodding toward Everett. "She isn't property."

Everett swallowed hard, ridding his mouth of venom, no doubt. "I'm sorry, Cole. You're right. I highly doubt *you* did anything you shouldn't have," he said calmly. He was careful, I noticed, not to absolve me of *my* sins.

"We should go," Everett said coolly.

Cole looked at me, wondering if it was safe to let me go with them, searching for guidance. "You could all stay. You've come a long way, and it's late now. We could find a place for everyone to sleep," Cole offered. He was stalling — half afraid to let me go with Everett, half afraid to let me go at all.

"That's very generous," Everett said, "but we'll be on our way. Thank you for taking good care of her."

"Are you sure?" he asked, looking at me.

No, I thought. "I'll be fine," I said. "Let me get my things." I walked back into the bedroom, Cole on my heels.

"Are you sure you want to go with them?" he whispered, blissfully unaware that the Winters would hear every word.

I sighed. I didn't want to lie, so I said the other thing I had to say. "Cole, I'm so sorry I didn't tell you about him. Things are just so complicated with us. With everything."

"That's your favorite word," Cole said. He was trying to be brave, but his eyes looked watery and red. His pain stabbed at me — my throat felt right, and I felt a sharp pain on the left side of my chest where a heartbeat should have been.

How hard it was to explain to anyone the consequence of my talent in moments like these, for no one could understand what feeling each terrible thing you made a person feel, as they felt it, could really do to your soul. "I really am sorry," I repeated.

"I don't understand it," he said, "but I don't want to talk about it anymore." He was building up his own walls, cutting me off. I didn't like it.

Everett appeared in the doorway. "Ready, princess?" he asked, smiling.

The Winters stepped into the hallway and went toward the elevator, leaving Cole and me in the doorway.

"You call me if you need me," Cole said softly, and I nodded. He put one warm hand on my cheek and hesitated before he leaned in and kissed me on the other.

Enough, Everett said icily in his mind. I pulled away from Cole and skulked down the hallway.

I felt Cole's parting thought as I got on the elevator: *It never gets any easier to watch you walk away.*

—◆—

"WHAT DO YOU THINK YOU WERE YOU DOING BACK THERE?" I SCREAMED, thrusting my hands at Everett's chest as we spilled out onto the streets of Manhattan. It was nearly eleven o'clock, but there were people everywhere, and they were staring. "You had no right to bust in on him like that."

"I wasn't busting in on him, Sadie; I was busting in on you!" Everett said plainly. Just like his father, his even tone in response to my fury fueled my fire.

I yelled. "You could have killed him!"

He reached for my elbow and pulled me toward him, whispering into my ear, "You think you could try calming down? You're scaring the humans, sweetheart."

In a huff, I walked in front of them, immensely frustrated by the waves of people and stoplights that halted my forward movement. The three of them stalked half a block behind me for three short blocks before I stopped. The cold night air swirled around me. We had passed hundreds of people in just the few blocks we'd walked. It was unfair to make them follow me through the crowded streets this way.

In Ginny's mind, I could not only hear her thoughts but feel her thirst, and worse, the tension and battle for control inside of her every time an unsuspecting New Yorker stepped in front of her or slammed into her on the packed city sidewalks.

I turned around to face them, waiting for them to catch up. Everett's eyes were closed tight, and he was wincing as if in pain. Ginny had stopped breathing, and she had her left arm wrapped around her waist, her right hand to her mouth, literally chewing on her index finger. Mark was staring at the ground. Their desire was simply too much to control. If I had eight million minds invading mine, they had eight million heartbeats taunting them.

"Let's get a cab," I said.

Thank you, Ginny said, clearly embarrassed.

I hailed a cab, and the three of them piled into the backseat. I rode in the front, trusting only myself to be this close to the driver, though it was only denial that made me believe that the thin, plastic divider between the front and back seats would protect him from the Winters. "Fifty-ninth and Fifth," I said.

Where are we going? Ginny asked.

Central Park, I answered.

Isn't that supposed to be dangerous at night? she asked.

You're worried? I asked. She laughed. It was the first remotely happy sound I'd heard out of any of them since before I blacked out the night before.

As we drove with a heavy silence between us, the low foreign chatter on the driver's radio lining my ears, I was surprised when I heard Everett's mind. *I don't want trouble,* he said.

I turned around to look at him. "Then you shouldn't start it," I said.

Am I entirely to blame for this? he asked. I didn't respond. *It is impossible for you to see any situation from any perspective other than your own. Why is that?* he asked, his mental voice more hostile now. I didn't say anything back.

The cab let us out where I'd asked, a block from Central Park. I knew it was entirely unsafe for humans to be in there at night, but I was hoping we'd run into so few that it may be the only place on Manhattan where the Winters could think clearly. We walked deep into the park, away from the roads and open areas until we were in the more forested parts.

"Are we going anywhere in particular?" Mark finally asked.

"Feel like you're going to kill someone in the next ten seconds?"

"No." he said.

"Then we're done wandering," I said, stopping.

"Thank you so much for getting us off the street, Sadie. It was too much to handle," Ginny said. She hugged me tight. "I'm sorry this happened this way. We were just so scared."

"I'm sorry I didn't tell you where I was going," I said, shrugging out of her arms. "But you never would have let me go if I had told you."

"Of course we wouldn't have!" Everett barked. "Why don't you get this? You are going to get yourself killed!"

"Why do you all of a sudden think you can make my decisions for me?" I asked. I didn't want to fight with him, but he was being ridiculous. "It's not your job."

"Bullshit it's not. Remember I told you I'd fight for your life because I knew you never would?" he said, genuinely hurt. Of course, I remembered when he said that. It was that night we returned to the Survivors after Moscow. He had promised exactly that. "I was serious then. I'm serious now. I will protect you whether you like it or not."

"You want to control me."

"I want to love you. There's a difference," he said. He dropped his voice and stepped toward me. "I'm sorry for the way I acted last night, but that Montana winter is getting to me. I'll keep it in check, and I'll never yell at you again," he said.

"Yes you will," I said. His face creased, disheartened as I said this, so I clarified, because I apparently only ever said the wrong thing. I reached for the gold key around my neck and held it up. "If forever means forever, then of course you'll yell at me again. I'll yell at you. We'll be normal-ish."

Suddenly, his eyes filled with emotion. He nodded that I was acknowledging the future he believed we were going to have. The stress of our situations made this tough for both of us, I knew. We didn't want to be mad, but were these the kind of things to just let go of?

Mark cleared his throat. "We love you, too, for the record," he said softly.

"And so you're stuck with us looking out for you, too," Ginny added.

"Yeah, little one, because like Everett said, you'd never do it for yourself," Mark said. "'Cause you're a little, you know," he said, making the sounded of a cuckoo clock and spinning a finger next to his ear.

I smiled in spite of myself and smacked Mark's arm. Ginny and Everett laughed. I was uneasy, then, not sure if it was right to have shifted moods with my anger still so heavy in my throat.

"I don't know that we're done talking about all this," I said.

"Oh, we're not," Everett said, "but I don't really want to get into it anymore tonight. It's been a hell of a day." I nodded even though, until this, my day had been lovely.

"We should book a flight, I guess," I said, settling my feet back in reality.

"Actually, we don't need one..." Mark wore his most smug grin.

"Or we have one," Ginny added, "however you'd like to think of it."

"I'm missing something," I said.

"Just here to treat you like a princess, is all," Everett smiled. He slid his phone out of his pocket and made a call. "Hey, yeah. We're coming now. Can you pick us up? Yeah. There's fine. Thanks," he said.

"Want to fill me in?" I asked.

"Come along for the ride," Everett said. He took off running through the park.

———◆———

I KNEW THIS DAY WOULD COME. A TOWN CAR MET US AT THE EDGE OF THE PARK. He drove us out of the city and into New Jersey, to Teterboro, an airport I'd never been to, and right onto the runway where a Citation X jet was waiting.

I didn't ask any questions.

The ride was smoother and significantly faster than a commercial jet. Ginny and Mark bantered back and forth, and Everett and I talked quietly. We weren't affectionate yet. I was still upset that he had behaved as he had the night before, and he was more hurt than he admitted to that I had not only run from him but also to Cole. But the animosity between us had drained.

As we flew, I let my mind wander, which was dangerous. Except for panicked moments — like the one I'd had when I went off the grid and got on a plane to New York — I had gotten very good at not looking at the big picture in my life. I just handled each day, one by one, and, until recently, slept each night next to Everett, like wiping my slate clean. And every morning, I determined what I needed to work on, how much time I could spend pretending I was someone or somewhere else, and what it would take to get my family — the Survivors, the Winters — through another day. It was when I thought of the big picture that it became too overwhelming.

The visions had been the thing to tip the scale over to overwhelming. They drained me. I'd had only those two, but they were powerful enough to keep me awake, to jar my insides, to break my heart. And here and there, I'd been able to spend time with the Winters as a family, or with Ginny pretending to be a normal girl, with Mark pretending to be a normal little sister, or with Lizzie pretending to be a student or even a daughter. But with Everett, I was just myself. I could be afraid, or I could be strong. I could cry, or I could be stoic. I could act like a normal young human, spend my energy testing the limits of our relationship. Or, I could be a war strategist who needed an adviser, a friend who needed another friend, or a girlfriend who needed her boyfriend. He could be what I needed, and, in turn, I could be what he needed in these scary times, too. So when I sat across the plane from him, our interactions still strained, I put my feet in his lap and laid back my head, I whispered that I loved him — because I did love him — and knew that, without a doubt, my life was better since the moment I met Everett Winter.

"You love me how much?" he asked. A slight smile broke across his face. "More than life?" he asked.

"More than death," I whispered, knowing that's the answer he was looking for.

He removed my shoes and rubbed my feet. "And how long will you love me this way?" he asked, his old charm back.

I held up the key from around my neck. "You know how long," I smiled.
"Say it."
"Everett…"
"Come on, say it!" he said.

I rolled my eyes. It wasn't the Maserati or the Ray-Bans or the ocean-front house or the hand-through-his-hair I fell in love with the absolute moment I met him. It was that smile — and that Victorian gentleman underneath. He really was a hopeless romantic. He tried to hide it under all that West-Coast edge and pretty-boy charm, but I could see through it.

Because I loved that gentleman and some tiny part of my cynical soul believed in our beach vision, I said, "Forever."

The co-pilot got up to stretch his legs, and Everett asked him how much farther we had. "Not far. We should be on the ground in half an hour," he said. He'd just walked back into the cockpit and closed the door when I began to feel woozy.

It happened just the way it had before. For a moment, I heard Ginny and Mark teasing each other, mixed with sounds foreign to the plane. Then my vision went. Noah's thoughts were again inside my head.

They were running through a dense, snowy forest. Noah was leading the way, so I couldn't see who was there. "Close?" someone called from yards behind him.

Noah turned around, and stopped. The rest of them stopped, too. The faces of twenty-seven of my family members looked back at him. "Just ahead," he said. "We're going to be careful, right? Not hurt anybody?"

Derek stepped forward. "Of course not," he said. He put his hand on Noah's shoulder. "We're not trying to hurt anybody ever, but some-times we can't help it, right? That's just what we are now. But these people aren't humans, so why would we hurt them?" Noah believed him, but I did not.

Satisfied, Noah ran again. I felt as he was driven toward a place, a thing. He was tracking, but differently from the way I tracked. He used his senses in ways I had never learned to, felt magnetized to the thing he was looking for, like it was finding him and not the other way around.

Abruptly, the trees broke apart and they found themselves in a clearing. Sheets of white and silver metal and glass appeared to rise out of the snow in a jumble of fallen trees. It took me a moment to realize where I was: the Winters' house in Canada. There was one light on.

Then I was back. I felt the plane's descent. Everett, Mark, and Ginny's faces alarmed me, and I snapped back to reality.

"Who is at the Canada house?" I asked.

"Mom," Everett said.

Then panic hit. She was the only one of them unable to defend herself, unable to fight the way her *vieczy* and *nosferatu* family fought.

"Adelaide!" I shouted. "They're there! They're going to get Adelaide!"

The Winters jumped to their feet. They understood. "Sadie, focus. We should be near Calgary right now. Are we closer to the house or to the airport? Can you figure that out?" Mark asked, his hands on my shoulders.

I reacted instinctually, my mind searching the ground below us for clues. But before I could figure it out, I could sense Adelaide, and Noah, and an ear-busting humming pitch that came from a place I was absolutely certain had to be their house. "We're nearly over the house right now," I exclaimed, unable to understand how I knew.

"Are you sure?" Everett asked, frantic.

"I don't know!" I shouted. I wasn't sure. I couldn't even tell what I was sensing, what I was going off of. What if I were wrong? What if we were too late — because of me?

"Sadie, come on!" Mark shouted.

My throat closed up and my head swam. The humming and buzzing of unfamiliar minds and visions and verbal thoughts of familiar ones clouded my mind. "I can't read her mind. It's too jumbled!" Ginny screamed.

I felt myself being pulled this way and that, and I was just so scared. The sounds came to a crescendo in my head that I tried to block out to focus. I shut my eyes tightly, pressed my fingers to the top of my skull and pressed hard, hoping this would relieve it, hoping this would block out all the sound.

"Oh my god," I heard Ginny say.

"What is that?" Mark and Everett asked in unison.

I opened my eyes. From my fingertips on one hand, grey-violet wisps that swirled like smoke but were opaque like metal trickled from each of my fingertips. My fingertips burned, and the pads of my fingers were a dark red where the strange substance attached to them, each finger on my left hand trailing the things for several inches.

"What is this?" I screamed.

"I don't know," Mark said.

"What is this?" I repeated, more urgently.

"I don't know!" Ginny screamed, her eyes glistening nervously.

"Mark, do something!" Everett barked. So he did. Mark grabbed my wrist and pulled my hand to his own head, jamming my fingertips against his scalp. He inhaled sharply. The burning stopped. My fingertips returned to their normal color, and when I pulled my hand away, the wisps were gone.

"What on earth?" Everett whispered.

Mark exclaimed. "She just gave me what she was thinking. There. I recognized it. We're almost over the house NOW."

"We need to get out of the plane," Everett said.

"Out?" I asked.

"Done and done!" Ginny screamed. She strapped my precious travel bag to her body, and then she kicked the door open. Air came whipping into the small cabin. Alarms went off and the pilots were screaming at us, no idea what had happened. Ginny was sucked from the plane. Just as quickly, Mark was too.

Everett grabbed me around the waist. "Don't let go!" he warned, then he leapt out the door. The air sliced at us as we fell, down and down toward the ground. I held to him tightly.

With a loud clatter, the earth beneath us fractured as the three *vieczy* landed on the ground. They took off in a sprint, Mark leading the way. Everett put me down so I could run with them. I'd never run so fast in my life. In moments, we were there, busting through the blood-red doors and into the metal house. I heard a scream. I shuddered.

Beside me, Everett's voice cracked in pain. "Mom!"

CHAPTER TEN

encounter

"GET AWAY FROM HER!" EVERETT ROARED. A LOUD GROWL BUBBLED out from deep in his chest, and he snarled, exposing his shiny white teeth. He crouched close to the ground, a predator waiting to pounce. "I said put her down!"

Derek had Adelaide by the neck of her nightgown. She was shaking and gasping for air, her eyes wide in terror.

"Derek, put her down!" I screamed. He laughed maniacally. I hadn't spoken to him in years, but now I vividly remembered images of him sucking blood from a dying girl's body in my visions — twice. He looked just as threatening now, his mouth inches from Adelaide's throat. "Let her go! You aren't here for her!"

"No, but she could be an added bonus," he said, running his nose along Adelaide's neck. Everett lunged.

"Everett!" I cried, but they already had him. Four of my brothers had met him mid-jump, their agility and speed matching his own. He couldn't escape. He may have been the strongest *vieczy* in his family, but that was no match for the four bloodthirsty ones holding him. I knew I was helpless against my siblings if they turned on me, but I wasn't afraid for myself.

"Now, now, Sadie," Derek said. "We won't hurt your little boyfriend...yet." He motioned for two of the others. He released Adelaide to them and walked toward me. Even with these six preoccupied with Adelaide and Everett, there were still twenty-one other ruthless creatures crowding the living room.

"What do you want?" I hissed.

"Sadie, we're family. I don't even get a hello?" Derek said, pacing now. *We haven't even hurt your stupid friends yet, so why are you so angry now?* he thought. I suddenly remembered that none of them knew I could read minds.

"Hello," I said petulantly. I flipped through his thoughts for plans or information that could help me. I was hit with a strange electric current the second I tuned into Noah's mind, now purposefully. Noah seemed not to notice, but since Ben had told me Noah could connect to my mind in some way, so I had to be careful.

Ginny, I think Noah can hear us, I said quickly. I looked at him, but he wouldn't meet my gaze.

"That's a little better," Derek said. He was circling me. "We don't want to bother you, but it's been brought to our attention that you've done one hell of a job adjusting to the world outside the walls of the old homestead, and we were thinking maybe you could help us out."

I was about to throw some retort Derek's way when Everett's thoughts stopped me. *Don't let them know what you know.*

I swallowed. "How can I help you? Everything I know about the human world is stuff you don't care about, like cars and nice clothes."

Good, Everett said, encouraging me.

"We were thinking more along the lines of how you operate so quietly. We seem to be attracting the attention of humans wherever we go. They tell each other when they find dead bodies," Derek said. It was interesting to watch members of my family, other Survivors, interacting with the world when they understood so little of how it worked.

They think you're one of them! Everett screamed in his head. I nodded slightly, never looking in his direction, but I was confused. Hadn't

Everett told me I smelled more like a human than a witch or anything else? Couldn't they tell?

"Humans care a lot about death," I said. "They take it very seriously. You can't just go around killing whoever you want without repercussions. There are whole teams of people — police, they're called — who will catch you and imprison you for killing."

They laughed. "They could not catch us! And, even if they could, we could fight them off," Peter, one of Derek's sidekicks, scoffed.

"But if you fight them, and then they know you aren't human, you have a real problem. You need to keep quiet, blend in with the world around you. Otherwise, it could mean very bad things for our family," I explained.

"The Bible-beaters on the mountain no longer interest us," he said.

"They're good allies to have," I said.

Derek's eyes narrowed. "Are you working with them?"

Lie, Everett said.

"Obviously not," I said. "I live here with these friends of mine. You think the elders would allow that?" I asked. I was surprised at how easy it was to lie.

Derek and the others seemed to consider this. "That's a good point," Peter offered.

"We thought you might want to come with us," Noah admitted. He'd been silent the whole time.

"I've got a good setup here," I said coolly. "But thanks for the offer."

"I think you should come with us, Sadie," Derek said, his voice more hostile now.

"I like it here," I insisted.

"Because of your little friends, right?" Peter asked.

"Well, we can take care of that," Derek laughed as he lifted Adelaide off the ground by her neck. She let out another cry of pain.

That was it. Mark and Ginny lunged at him, and Adelaide dropped to the ground. I dove into the scuffle and dragged Adelaide out of the pile just as the rest of the Survivors jumped on top of Everett, Mark, and Ginny. I held her close to my chest into the night and bolted as fast as I could.

"Sadie, wait! Here!" Adelaide yelled. I skidded to a stop in the snow. She staggered back a few feet, and put her hands to a giant tree whose trunk was as thick around as the two of us. One side of the tree slid open, like a mechanical door. "I'm safe here. Now go!"

I didn't stop to ask questions. As I burst back into the house, I launched myself into the fray, which seemed to confuse everybody. The Survivors weren't trying to fight me and the Winters wanted to protect me. Suddenly, the earth beneath our feet shook as Patrick, Madeline, and Anthony burst in, taking out a floor-to-ceiling window with their arrival. I had no idea where they'd come from or how they knew to come, but I was grateful they were there.

"Where's Adelaide?" Anthony asked as he grabbed a rogue Survivor by the neck.

"Safe!" I screamed back.

I'd directed my attention to trying to free Everett. He had gotten himself at the bottom of a scuffle beneath five of my siblings. Anthony and Mark helped me free him as Ginny and Patrick grabbed lunging Survivors midair, binding them from afar. But the rogues resisted the bindings and could break free if they lost focus at all. With Everett free, all of the brothers, Ginny, Anthony, and I stood in the middle of the giant room, backs and shoulders touching so that no angry Survivor was hidden from view. The Winters seemed to be able to fight one or two of them at a time in hand-to-hand combat while simultaneously using their powers to fight Survivors clear across the room. I tried to follow, but I was oddly out of place, regretting having not spent more time with them when they worked with the young Survivors in Montana to prepare for combat.

The Winters and the rogues ran into each other with loud cracks that sounded like explosions. Their shark-like teeth bit furiously at each other.

I was of no use. I'd reach for my siblings and try to pull them off the Winters, and they'd shake me off. I didn't want to hurt them unless they hurt the Winters, which didn't appear to be happening. Nor did the Winters' sharp teeth penetrate the marble skin of the *vieczy* Survivors.

Mark grabbed at heads and snapped them in different directions, several at a time with his ability to manipulate bodies, but to no avail. Everett and Patrick together managed to rip an arm from one of my family members, but as if drawn by an intense magnet, the arm — laying on the ground — instantly shot back up to the body it belonged to, reattaching as if nothing ever happened.

"Mark! Fire!" Anthony yelled. Mark made a giant swooping motion toward three of the rogues and a gust of flames erupted in midair. He wrapped the fire around them, but they didn't burn.

While we were watching, Noah backed away and launched at me. He grabbed me and bounded out of the house. No one saw it happen.

Just outside, he stopped. "We didn't come here to hurt you," he said, setting me on the ground. "You stay out here," he said. Then he bounded back into the house.

I could hear faint sounds of battle through broken windows and open doors, but the thunderous crashing and clanking did not carry into the night air in the sleepy Canada forest.

Then I heard voices. "Ginny, help me. Come on, focus! You've got to focus or they'll be able to break the bindings," Mark said.

"Where's Sadie?" Everett asked, frantic.

"Out here," I said, making my way back inside.

In the living room, twenty-eight red-eyed Survivors were tightly packed against each other on the floor. Mark, Ginny, and Patrick were standing over them, their hands outstretched, all their energy focused on holding their opponents in place. This had been the first power I saw Mark Winter exhibit the night I met him. The Winters saw that they could not defeat the *vieczy* Survivors, so they had changed their strategy to capture.

They all looked exhausted, their clothes ripped and hanging haggardly from their bodies.

"What do we do now?" I asked.

"We take them back to your family, as Andrew asked," Anthony said.

"You think you're so smart," Derek cackled. He was bound so tightly that only his head could move, but he still managed to look around him to the other rogue Survivors and ask, "Peter, you're on. Ready, guys?"

"Wait!" Noah exclaimed, panicked. "Can't we take Sadie with us?"

"She'll come when she's ready," Peter answered. "When it's time." He squirmed against the Winters' weakening bindings and loosened one hand from the mix. He shot a bare left arm into the air and, on it, I saw three strange blue and green symbols. "Now for our magic trick," he smirked. He opened his palm then snapped his fingers, and all twenty-eight of them disappeared.

"What the hell?" Mark asked.

"Check outside! Quickly!" Anthony barked. We did as he said, spread out around the house and combed the woods, but there was no sign of them.

"Damn it!" Anthony yelled. We gathered back inside the house. "Mark, go get your mother," Anthony directed. He ducked out the back and into the woods without a word. They both returned moments later.

"What a mess," she said, not letting the tension of the scene affect her calm front. She put her fingertips above her eyebrows and closed her eyes. There were loud cracking and splintering sounds as the front door pulled itself back together, sealing closed. Broken glass drifted into place in window frames. Wrecked furniture mended itself. Punctures in the sheetrock walls smoothed over. Pictures and mirrors repaired and rehung themselves on the walls. The back door found its hinges and closed. Items fallen off shelves found their place back on them. In less than thirty seconds, the room looked the way it had when I left it on Mark's birthday.

"Is the sound barrier intact?" Anthony asked Adelaide.

"I wouldn't forget it, old man," she laughed. Like Mark, she'd push herself into joking around in these tense moments. Then again, it was easier for her. She was the only one who hadn't seen what we had: an enemy we couldn't defeat, an enemy who disappeared.

But Anthony wasn't amused. "We need to talk to the Survivors," he said. Abruptly, he took off running.

CHAPTER ELEVEN

point of origin

I WAS BEGINNING TO DETEST THE SMALL CONFERENCE ROOM OFF the church corridor. It seemed like each time was in it, I was telling my family of more horrors perpetrated by my siblings.

We were all crammed into the tiny room again. We told them of my vision, of the mad dash to save Adelaide, of the losing fight with the rogue Survivors, and of their disappearance. We spared the details of jumping out of the plane (okay, of the existence of planes), and, at my request, of the strange solid-smoke pieces that extended from my fingertips that, as best I could tell, were physical manifestations of my thoughts.

"I thought you said you knew how to kill them!" Andrew exclaimed.

"We had no way of knowing they'd be impervious to the usual methods," Anthony responded, trying to stay calm. "We thought you were all witches, and that *they* were *vieczy*. But there's something different. Something we've never seen."

"Their defenses were incredibly strong, which is uncharacteristic for their kind. We are not used to such opponents," Patrick added.

"But there were twenty-eight of them and so few of you, and you came out unscathed," Andrew reasoned.

"That's because of our powers. Mark and Patrick able to fight several at a time without touching them, while simultaneously fighting hand-to-hand with another. Ginny can do the same by mirroring their powers. I have some talents that aided us, too," Anthony explained. I noticed how he could not say the same for Everett.

"But still," Andrew said.

"We think they don't know how to destroy their own kind. Much like you don't know how to destroy Survivors, they are unaware of how to harm themselves and so they can't harm us," he explained. It was always interesting when Anthony characterized himself with his children as if he were a *vieczy* himself. He wasn't. So how did he fit into this?

"That means we have a chance against them!" Andrew cried.

"A chance for a peaceful ending!" Lizzie beamed.

"No," Patrick said. "It's means we've got a good chance we'll be massacred as soon as they figure it out and get their focus under control."

Their faces — and hopes — dropped instantly.

"Killing them was our last resort, and now we can't even do that!" Andrew screamed. He banged his fist against the marble so hard a piece of the ancient rock severed under the blow. This was the first time he'd lost his temper.

"We have to find them again," I said. I could feel heat rising in my face, an uncomfortable mix of excitement and fear of Everett's reaction of what I was about to say. "We need to put all our resources into finding a way to kill a Survivor."

They all went silent.

Everett scoffed. "You mean, now we have a reason to let you put all our resources into finding a way to kill y-..." he paused and looked up at everyone, "kill Survivors." He wouldn't look at me though. This had landed in the exact place he hoped it wouldn't.

He'd understood what I had: that by determining how to kill the rogue Survivors, we'd have to find a way to kill me.

I ignored him. "We have no choice. Even if we don't look for them now, even if we choose not to kill them *now*, we have to be prepared for the war. What happens when they come bounding over those city walls like in Anthony's vision, and they kill all of us?"

"How do we even know they can kill us?" Sarah asked.

"Or that they even would if they could?" Lizzie asked. I looked at her pale blue eyes, the fair snow-kissed hair in waves framing her face. She looked so young to be so old. She couldn't bear the thought that the day would come when any Survivor would hurt another.

I thought back to our conversation about John. Hadn't that day come and gone?

"It is unwise to assume that they won't find a way. We also can't assume that they wouldn't," Anthony said, his voice as forgiving as he could make it. I was grateful to him for this. "Even though that is what we all hope for," he added, uncharacteristically.

"Best defense is a good offense," Patrick smiled, trying to help. The reference was lost on the elders.

"So we have to know," I said.

"What do you suggest? Trying different ways?" Andrew asked incredulously. I cupped the ends of my sleeves in my hands.

"Not exactly," I half-lied.

"Then what?" John spat.

"I'm not sure," I said softly. "If only there were other Survivors. Then we could ask them. Then we could know…"

All fourteen of them stiffened. "There are no other Survivors," John said quickly.

"Were there never, though? Didn't you come from somewhere? Isn't there a chance that there were Survivors before, who made you?" I asked, knowing I was on thin ice threatening their beliefs in this way. Believing that there were other Survivors meant believing that they were not a God-chosen people, selected to Survive. It could mean that they were, in fact, witches. That they were as guilty as common criminals — or demons, more likely, as that's what they'd been accused of in Salem — and that was simply too much for this group of Puritans to believe. The first rule to Surviving was the undying, undoubting belief in God, and, really, in the belief that we were a chosen people. The second was to believe we were the only ones like ourselves. (The third was to never stray from the sacred city walls.)

Catherine, John's most vocal ally, leaned into the table and spoke. "God made us the way we are." She hadn't spoken to me since I returned, but her patience had worn thin. "You haven't lost your faith in this, have you, Sadie?"

"Of course I haven't. And I don't doubt that God made us how we are. I just wonder if others were made this way as well. You all had parents, and I'm sure there was someone in Salem who was like you — at least someone you suspected?" I said.

They resisted. "None of us knew anything about this when we were in Salem. As far as we knew, we were unjustly accused of witchcraft. All those other accused — the ones they hanged, had to be innocent because they died. Though we didn't, you know we aren't terrible creatures like they thought of us in Salem."

"Of course I know," I said as tenderly as I could manage. "None of you were related to the accused, were you?" I asked.

"No," John said. This made it unlikely that any of those accused were actually witches, then. What were the odds of a town the size of 17th-century Salem having more witch-blooded families than the thirteen that produced the fourteen Survivors sitting in front of me?

"But none of you ever suspected any members of your families? Never thought someone was a little…off? Parents or aunts or uncles? Older siblings, maybe?" I asked.

"No," John said flatly. All the elders were deep in thought. I wondered if they had decided long ago not to entertain the idea that their families might have been like them. After all, if their families were Survivors or witches or whatever, they would still be alive out there. That would produce a reason to leave these hallowed walls, and they didn't want that.

Lizzie said finally, "There's no sense digging into the past."

"But there is," I insisted. "It's going to be the only way to figure out how a Survivor can be killed, *if* a Survivor can be killed. You all had to come from somewhere, and so somewhere on this earth, either there is a Survivor older than all of you, who will help us understand more about Surviving, or there is someone who killed a Survivor, and so he can tell us how," I explained. I saw many furrowed brows. "Look, research is my thing. I can track history, read anything, find people, ask the right questions. I need to know where we come from. When I find that out, I'll either learn how to kill a Survivor or prove that it can't be done."

"What do you need from us to do this?" Andrew asked.

"Honesty," I said. As soon as I'd said it, I knew it was too blunt. I needed to learn to finesse.

"You think we lie, child?" John hissed.

"No, I mean you'd have to be forthcoming with details. Answer my questions. Someone in this room knew they were special, knew *what* they were before they left Salem. Did that person have parents like themselves? Did something happen to all of you when you were young? Was there someone you all had in common? Things like that," I said. Lizzie looked uncomfortable as I said this, which didn't surprise me. If talking about their life in Salem was something she was comfortable doing, maybe I would have heard about it in the 141 years I lived under her roof. I never had.

The elders exchanged uneasy glances. "We'll need to discuss this," Andrew said.

"I respect that, Andrew, but we're losing time. If you don't help me, I don't know what we'll do," I said as sincerely as I could. I hated that

I had to come here and make a case to them, and they had to deliberate because they didn't trust me.

"Give us time, Sadie," he said, a warning in his voice.

I rose. The Winters followed. "I need to go into town. I'll be back in an hour or two."

Andrew dismissed us with a wave of his hand, his eyes fixed on the table, lost in thought.

CHAPTER TWELVE

fortuitous error

WE TOOK OFF IMMEDIATELY FOR BIGFORK. I DIDN'T WANT TO BE TWID-
dling my thumbs while I waited for the elders' response. I
knew it was going to be no. My protective detail — Everett,
Mark, and Ginny — followed me. Electric Avenue, the main
drag, and the street beside it sat flush against the mountainside, so we could run from my family's city, past Swan Lake,
over another mountain range, and up to the edge of Bigfork.
There was a break between stores and houses just off Electric
Avenue where we could walk onto the street as if we'd just
gotten out of our car or emerged from a vacation rental
condo. It was a convenient little spot.

"They're not going to help us," I said, as we passed the tea
cottage and rounded the corner of a street I knew like the
back of my hand.

"What makes you say that?" Ginny asked me.

"If they were going to, they would have agreed to it by now,"
I said as we passed a souvenir shop and crossed the street.

"That's jumping to conclusions. Let's wait to hear a no
before we act like we already have," Everett warned.

"They never talk about Salem. And there's something
Lizzie doesn't want said," I reasoned.

"But Lizzie is our greatest ally among the crazy fourteen," Mark said lightly. "She shouldn't be any trouble at all."

"You underestimate her. She's also the most guarded," I said.

"She was like your mother," Everett said.

"And best friend!" Ginny added.

"So? It's not like you can't love someone who is strong-willed. I never once talked about Salem, Massachusetts, with her. Not once. I lived in a four-hundred-square-foot house with her for nearly a century and a half, and it never came up once. She doesn't talk about history, she doesn't talk about herself. And she never does anything she doesn't want to do. If she had our backs in there, she would have said something," I argued.

"So you think we're on our own," Everett said.

"I do," I said. We reached the fourth store on the right of the small street we were walking down, a brick-and-glass storefront with an updated and yet still fading green-and-white sign bedecking the top of the door that read *Books and Ladders*. I stopped in front of it, the dim cling of wind chimes in my ears from the few hanging down from the overhang above the windows. They had icicles hanging off them. It was the first time I'd been here since I left four years ago.

"This is the famed bookstore?" Everett asked.

"It is," I said, as I pushed through the door. I ducked under the beads hanging from the inside doorframe and made my way into the tiny shop, the Winters behind me. They looked around, perplexed and a little disappointed. The store was narrow — no more than fifteen feet across — but it was deceptively deep, with several small rooms like this one behind it. Books lined the walls from floor to high ceiling, and there were old-fashioned library ladders in each row. There was some order to the sections, but still the place felt in disarray. A few homey, mismatched armchairs had been stuck haphazardly in corners where they could fit without obstructing the walking paths. In places, stacks of books littered the floors. Faded and worn oriental rugs covered the old wood floors, overlapping so that you couldn't tell the floor was wood at all. Eclectic mixes of lamps had gathered over the years, giving light to each cozy nook. The air smelled like old books. If there were ever a place that felt like home to me, this was it.

Behind the counter, a woman with greying waves falling into her eyes and most of the way down her back was half-leaning on a tall stool, reading a thick book with a door of some kind on the cover, emblazoned with the words *Dark Places*. She wore black cat-eye glasses and thick knit sweaters in layers. Dozens of charms hung from her neck, and she had elaborate rings on every finger. Her skin was chapped and beginning to wrinkle, though prematurely, for she was still too young yet to look *old*. I knew her face almost like I knew the faces of my family. She'd been here the first day I walked into *Books and Ladders*, and every time I'd been here since.

It took her a moment to pull herself away from her book. Still finishing the page she was reading, she said, "Good morning to you. Anything I can do for…" but her voice trailed off as she looked up at us, crowding the tiny front room of the shop. Her face went pale. "Sadie," she breathed.

"Hi, Beverly," I smiled. I anticipated this. I had come to this shop every day it was open for twenty-three years, and then one day, I just stopped. Finally, here I stood again.

"You…you…" she stuttered, her eyes wide.

"I'm sorry I haven't been in — "

"Years! Nearly four years!" she said, a look of shock still on her face. But then a smile broke across it. "You're okay!" Snapping out of it, she ran toward me and threw her arms around me. "You're here!" she repeated. "And you brought friends! You've never brought any friends!" In her mind, I heard her think, *There are more of you! I knew it!* This concerned me.

Sadie, Ginny hissed in her head. *A word.*

Give me a second. "It's good to see you, too, Beverly. I'm not back for good, but I'm in and out of here a lot now. I thought I'd stop by."

"I'm so glad you did. Days have been dull around here since you left and...wait..." she paused, closed her eyes as if she'd remembered something terrible, "How's Lizzie?" she asked, nervously. Waves of tension rolled off her, and I tasted anxiety on my tongue.

Sadie! Ginny snapped.

"Lizzie's come here?" I asked.

"Not often, but yes. But how is she?" Beverly pressed, clutching my hand between hers.

"She's fine," I said.

"Oh, thank the stars," she said. "What can I help you with?" she asked, her mind lighter suddenly.

Now! Ginny yelled.

Okay, okay. "I think we're just going to look. Maybe I'll show my friend here the comic books?" I said, thinking quickly of what was in the back room, far from the front of the shop and from Beverly's ears.

"Comic books?" Mark said, perking up. I looked at him quizzically. "Lead the way!" he enthused. A reminder that he was sometimes just a nineteen-year-old boy.

I led the Winters into the farthest of the four back rooms of the bookshop, where one wall was lined in comic books. Mark was giddy, and even Everett was distracted by them. There was so much I didn't know about them — even just the little things. Golf, a house in Bahamas, a house in south of France, a secret passageway inside a tree, and comic books. I was keeping a list.

"What was that about?" I asked Ginny.

"How long have you known that woman?" Ginny asked.

"Since I started coming here," I said. "She's lovely."

"Didn't you start coming here twenty years ago?" Ginny whispered.

"Closer to twenty-five. It was 1985," I said.

Mark and Everett turned their heads, now listening to our banter. "Sadie! This is so careless!" Ginny said urgently.

"What are you talking about?"

"She's a human!" Ginny exclaimed. I looked at her blankly. She rolled her eyes. "You've looked the *same* for twenty-five years! You can't just pretend you're human and be so careless as to come to the same places for that long. People will see that you're different. She *knows* you're different!"

I was dumb-founded. This problem had never once occurred to me. I thought hard about so many things about being a human, so many details about what I would do and how to control myself, how to act, how not to. But never that they would notice I hadn't aged! What did the Winters do? Leave cities entirely after a few years before people got suspicious? Fake their own deaths?

"That's exactly what we do," Ginny said, following my train of thought. "We should go."

"No! Guys, if she's figured it out —" I began.

"She has," Ginny interrupted.

"Well, she hasn't said anything to anyone in twenty-five years. Why would she now?" I asked. They considered this. "I mean, the damage is already done."

They talked among themselves, reasoning that there wasn't anything we could do to reverse the damage. "You kids keep plotting back here. I'll be looking for what I came for," I said. I didn't take their worries too seriously.

Beverly helped me comb the shelves for more world mythology books. I had many of them already, but, as I was sure the elders were going to shoot me down, I needed all the help I could get. Then we compiled some travel books. I bought any she had on places I had never been. We may be traveling quickly to new places, and I wouldn't have time to research the areas in advance.

I knew I was just spinning my wheels, but it was better than staring at the church, waiting for them to come outside and tell me no.

Everett emerged from the back rooms. "Adelaide called. The elders are out. Andrew wants to talk to you," he said.

"Let me just pay for these," I said.

As Beverly was ringing up the books we'd picked out, the little bell on the front door sounded. I turned around.

She looked out of place here, and here in the human world, it became clear to me how young she'd been when she stopped aging. Her clothes were outdated, and she was wearing shoes and a coat she'd likely not worn in over three hundred years. She never left the city, and both were superfluous accessories to most of our kind.

"Hannah?" I said, the surprise in my voice obvious.

"I need to talk to you," she said. She looked around the shop, clearly overwhelmed, confused. "But not here," she added.

"Of course," I said.

"I'll get this," Everett said. "We'll catch up."

"I'll see you, Beverly. Thanks for your help," I said.

"Come back," Beverly said.

"I will," I said and followed Hannah out of the shop. We retraced the same path we'd taken into town. Hannah's heart was racing and her nerves were on edge. She held her jaw taut and looked at the ground as she walked. Whatever she had to tell me, she wasn't supposed to, and doing it in an unfamiliar place outside the city walls was adding to her tension. I felt bad. I wished I could relieve her stress.

When we reached the end of the street, she paused, as if deciding if we should walk back home or stay in town to talk. "Is there somewhere we could talk among the humans and not look out of place?" she asked.

Her question reminded me again of her innocence. Little Hannah, 331 years old if I had counted correctly, not only looked but also acted like a twelve-year-old. "Of course," I said. I looked around quickly to see what was open. This time of year, half the stores were closed. I saw lights on in a café across the street. "This way."

I led her across the street to a shop called Bearfood, set back in a courtyard. I'd never been in before. It had brown concrete floors and three little black wrought-iron tables like I usually saw on patios. Pictures of buffalo dotted the walls. It had an eclectic amalgamation of things and food. There was the obligatory mixture of local fare — a wall of Flathead Cherry jams and candies, huckleberry taffy and syrup, alongside a few odds-and-ends racks of organic clothing and touristy t-shirts, boxer shorts, and infant onesies adorned with moose, black bears, or fish, and an array of local coffees and sodas, including Mark's favorite, Flathead Monster. All of this just like every other store on Electric Avenue and unlike any other store anywhere else on the planet.

Hannah carefully and cautiously appraised her surroundings, wondering in her mind if this was what all shops looked like on the inside.

"Would you like something to eat or drink?" I asked Hannah. She thought about it for a minute, asking herself when she would have a chance to eat food on the outside ever again. It baffled me that she thought this way. She could leave whenever she wanted to. She read the menu on the wall carefully: espresso, smoothies, ice cream, cokes, quiche, pies, and cupcakes. She had no idea what the words meant. "What do you feel like?" I asked, trying to help her.

"Something sweet, if they have it," she said, smiling sheepishly. "And cold. It is hot in here!" she exclaimed, fanning herself. Of course, I thought. She'd never felt central heating.

Obliging, I ordered ice cream for her, ignoring the odd looks from the woman behind the counter for ordering ice cream in Montana when there were three feet of snow on the ground. I got her two scoops, not knowing what she'd like: one Mint Chocolate Chip and one called Moose Tracks. That was Corrina's standard order so I figured it was worth a shot. The woman handed me the cone, and Hannah stared at it, unsure of how to eat it. I quickly grabbed a cup and a spoon, flipped the cone upside down and handed it to her that way. She smiled as we made our way to a small table against the window.

The Winters were still in the front room of Beverly's shop watching me.

Hannah picked up her spoon and took a giant bite of the green minty ice cream. "What did you need to talk to me about?" I asked Hannah. She'd gotten giddy upon her first taste of the dessert.

"Andrew would be upset if he knew I was talking to you before he could, but they're not going to answer your questions about Salem," she said.

"Of course they aren't," I sighed.

"Do not be discouraged, daughter Sadie," she said, nervous still, but happy she was about to relieve my anxiety. "I don't think they could help you anyway."

"Why?"

"Because," she said, a thick spoonful of ice cream in her mouth, "they didn't know about themselves in Salem. Well, one exception, but I can't speak on his or her behalf." I dropped, disheartened, until she said, "But I knew."

My body seemed to come alive. "Did you already have your powers?"

"Yes," she said.

"The same as they are now?" I asked. I had always known that Hannah could see the future, but I didn't know the details of it. Unsurprisingly, details were never discussed.

"No, they've advanced quite a bit. But the visions are about the same things now that they were then."

"Specific things?" I asked.

"Yes," she said.

I hoped my face didn't convey my thrill that she was telling me about this. "Go on," I urged.

"I only see things about Survivors," she said, "and about a group of people I've never met, whose skin is darker than ours. They live in a place where the terrain is similar to that on the mountain."

It had never occurred to me to wonder whose future a person with the power of premonition might be able to see. Did Anthony only have visions about the Winters? Or did he also have them about strangers? "But who did you see when you were in Salem? You didn't know who the Survivors were then."

"I saw them about Lizzie, Andrew, Sarah, Thomas, Jane, Mary and Catherine, Rebecca, John, Ann, William, Joseph, and James," she said. I wondered if she never called them "the elders," or if she were trying to make a point by listing their names this way. "And my father," she added quietly.

I wanted to let out a cry. Her father? "Do you think it means he was like us?" She nodded. She was telling me there was a Survivor before the fourteen of them, that she *knew*, all this time, that the hand of God didn't come down and wrap them in some holy protective swaddling clothes the winter they trekked across the continent after they were expelled from Salem. She knew they were born this way — or at least she was.

"Does this mean the story the elders tell us about the winter you became what you are… Does this mean they know it isn't true?" I asked gingerly, afraid to overstep my bounds.

"They believe it to be true. They think it is irrelevant that I could see my father in the visions, and they don't believe he was like us," she explained, a little hostility in her voice. They didn't take her seriously, which offended her.

"But you do," I deduced.

"I do," she said coolly.

"He told you?" I asked.

"He never said anything about it," she said. She looked at the ceiling for a moment, then added, "To me."

"To someone else?" I asked.

I knew she was trying to cloud her mind with fuzzy memories and unrelated thoughts to block me from it, the way Andrew and Lizzie — the others who knew I could read minds — had no doubt told her to. "I can't break a confidence," she said. "Don't ask me to."

"I won't," I said. But her mind had already betrayed her. I watched a sleepy, young Hannah stumble awake and into a room in a Puritan-era Salem house where seven men I'd never seen sat around a table with Lizzie. And though I couldn't explain how, I knew it was connected. I knew Lizzie had to be the other one who knew *what* she was before they left Salem, that Lizzie was the one Hannah's father had talked to. That's why she was going out of her way to not talk to me about this.

I wouldn't press the issue. "What about the others, the ones you've never met? Do you think they are like us?" I asked.

Hannah shook her head. "That part is a mystery I'll never fully understand," she said, "I don't think the Bloods are like us though, at least not really," she explained. I wasn't sure what she was fabricating in that statement, but I knew she was lying or omitting something important.

"Why do you call them the Bloods?"

"That's what they call themselves," she said, matter-of-factly. This was a piece of information I had no idea what to do with, so I filed it away and would try to make sense of it later.

Hannah scraped the bottom of the dish with her spoon. It was endearing somehow.

"So you've always known it was possible that there were more of us out there?" I asked her.

"I did," she said. "I didn't believe there were, though. I don't now," she clarified. I raised my eyebrow, and she went on. "I thought about what you said about our parents, about them dying," Hannah said. "I suppose my father must have died at some point. If not, he would have come looking for us, wouldn't he? I was his only daughter, and I was accused as a witch, and he knew he *was* a witch. He couldn't have just left me here. He would have come for me," she said confidently. "Sadie, that means we Survivors do have some weakness. If my father died, then we can too, and we can defeat the rogue children. That's good news, isn't it?"

"I suppose it is," I said. "But now I have to find out how he died. That's the only way it will help us."

"How can you find that?" she asked.

"I don't know. Let's say he is dead. That would mean someone killed him and, presumably, someone who could kill a Survivor must be immortal too. If that's the case, then whoever or whatever killed him is still out there. There must be a trail — some human out there who's noticed they aren't normal. I will have to find them," I explained. "Either way, there should be an immortal creature out there who has so far been impervious to my tracking methods."

"But what kind of humans would this creature have interacted with so much that they would know what he was?" she asked.

I shrugged, considering this. Then, a light bulb. "Beverly," I whispered to myself. I caught Ginny's attention in my mind and asked them to meet us outside.

I turned back to Hannah. "Come on. If he's alive, I know how to find him. If he's dead, then I know how to find the story."

I got to my feet and scrambled out the door of the café quickly, Hannah on my heels. As the Winters crossed the street toward us, I nodded in the direction of the forest. "I need to get back," Hannah said at the end of the road. "Don't mention this." I nodded in agreement before she took off running toward the Survivors' City.

I led the Winters to the clearing where we entered the town. "What's up?" Mark asked.

I filled them in on what Hannah had told me about her father. "I have a plan," I said. "Beverly has got us figured out."

"Thanks to your carelessness," Ginny said.

"The point is she's probably not the only human to have noticed people like us," I said. "If Hannah's father is alive and we can't find him, or more supernaturals like Survivors, then we can track the humans who swear they knew someone like him. And if he's not, we can track whatever killed him in the same way. I'm sure that...*thing*...is still alive, if her father isn't." They all nodded at this.

"The plan?" Everett asked.

"Everett, you can pack us all — assuming you three are going with me? Ginny, you can be on standby to book plane tickets once I figure out where we're going. Maybe you and Everett can figure out who needs to go with us, but I would consider it a personal favor if you could keep Anthony from joining us."

"What about me?" Mark asked.

"I need your brain," I said.

The siblings laughed. "That's a first," Ginny scoffed.

"For what?"

"You're going to help me scan the thoughts of six billion people and see if I can find something. A lead. A conversation about supernaturals. Anything."

"And where are you going?" Everett asked.

"To follow the human trail," I said.

"We'll go with you," Everett said.

"There's no need to. You guys get started. We need to leave as soon as possible."

"I thought we agreed you weren't going anywhere alone," Everett said.

"Well, *you* did, but we know now that the rogue Survivors aren't going to hurt me. And Bigfork is about ten minutes from where you're going, not 2,000 miles, so I think I'll be okay," I reasoned. I would stand firm on this. I needed to have the kind of freedom my research necessitated.

Everett reluctantly agreed, and they took off toward the Survivors. I went back to the bookstore. Beverly was alone. I flipped the Open sign to Closed as I walked in the door.

Beverly looked up. "I need to talk to you," I said. Her face reflected my serious tone. She grew nervous, even slightly fearful.

"About what?" she said, her heart rate elevating as I walked toward her. I didn't mean to look menacing, but she backed away from me. On the counter, I saw the sixth or seventh book in a popular vampire series open facedown. I sighed, reading her thoughts.

"Well, first, I'm not going to hurt you, so you can calm down," I assured her. "I just need to know what you think about me." In her mind, she wondered if she could get away with giving me her opinion about my character. "What you know about me, I should say."

They always say they're not going to hurt you before they really do! she thought.

"Go on," I urged her.

She swallowed. "You're immortal, for one," she said, her eyes closed as a lot of unnecessary dramatic tension emanated from her. "Or maybe you just age really, really slowly. I saw that on a TV show once."

"How long have you known?" I asked.

"I started thinking it about ten years in. You were just *so* weird when you first came in. And back then, we were about the same age, but look at us now. My hair's going grey, and you're just as beautiful — and young — as ever."

"And?" I said.

"There's something up with you and Lizzie," she said.

"Like what?" I asked.

She peeled herself off the wall she'd backed into, intrigued that I didn't know what she was talking about. "Like she didn't know where you went when you left, but she knew you'd come back."

I considered this. I had gotten too much new information in the last hour to really process it, so I filed it in my memory for later.

"Anything else?" I asked.

"I don't think you're vampires. You and Lizzie that is. But those three that came in with you today..." she trailed off.

"What makes you say that?" I said, somewhere between impressed and alarmed.

"They're paler than you. And all of them were so beautiful! *Inhumanly* beautiful. The one who paid for your books was so cold. I touched him," she smiled, an adrenaline thrill emanating from her as she said this. I raised my eyebrow at this. Damn pop culture vampire obsession. It had made every small town conspiracy theorist out of touch with reality jump to this conclusion all the time. To be fair, it was true about the Winters, but you know they had to think this about other people who were not immortal vampires — just poor, pretty humans with a penchant for sunscreen who lived with cold hands from poor circulation. But people always believe the weirdest solution. And the worst.

"But you don't think I am?" I asked.

"Nope. Lizzie either. If you live around here and nobody ever dies in any kind of questionable way here...well, you do the math. Who would you be eating? It's not like there are people up on the mountain nobody's ever noticed!" she laughed, thoroughly amused with herself. Well, at least no one knew our city was tucked away on the mountain range. "Are they vampires?" she asked.

I sighed, massaging my temple. "*Vieczy*," I said.

"What?" she asked.

"Google it," I muttered.

Oh I will, she thought.

"Did you ever tell anyone about me?" I asked.

"Never!" she said, extremely offended I'd suggest such a thing. "I know I'm the only one you come to in this town. It's like you trust me. I could never betray that trust!"

I smiled graciously. If I were going to screw up and let a human figure out I wasn't human, I supposed Beverly was a good one to have screwed up with. "Thanks, Beverly."

"Anytime," she said, picking her book back up. "I'll see you soon?"

"We'll see."

CHAPTER THIRTEEN

the human trail

THERE WAS NO TIME TO WASTE. WE SPENT THE REST OF SUNDAY preparing. I gave everyone assignments. Ginny handled all logistics for the trip. Everett and Mark discussed with Anthony who should come with us. I had a serious conversation with Patrick and Madeline about how Peter had disappeared with a snap of his fingers and taken twenty-seven Survivors along for the ride with him. If we had that power, we'd be free of the constraints of human travel, and able to do exponentially more research in a fraction of the time it would normally take. Their goal on this trip was to find us this power.

This was the first time I had condoned acquisition. I should have felt guiltier about abandoning my principles, but that's the funny thing about abandoning principles, isn't it? It doesn't feel bad when you do it, and by the time you feel the sting of it, the crime has already been committed.

Lizzie was glad to have avoided my prying, and so she was content to help. She and Adelaide collected Sarah and Rebecca and spent the rest of the day and night in the apothecary, creating a notebook with the most pertinent recipes and incantations for me to take abroad. They packed a bag of all the essential ingredients they could find, and gave it to Everett.

And I sat upright and still on my bed, fingertips to the top of my head, noise-canceling headphones in my ears. In my months of advanced mind reading and tracking, I had been able to deduce this: Most people were thinking about ten or twelve things at once, even if they didn't realize it. They were often feeling about fifteen things connected to those thoughts on varying levels. At that moment there were a little over six billion, seven hundred million people on the earth and about two hundred thousand supernatural creatures I could sense so far, whose thoughts were quieter but whose instincts were louder. In any given moment, I was scanning through roughly eighty billion thoughts and one hundred billion emotions, searching for elusive clues.

Three things happened: One, I came up empty. Two, the spot at the base of my skull that burned when I connected to Noah's mind would ache, as if it were tired of looking into other people's minds. Three, more often than not, when I would pull my fingertips away from my scalp, purpley-metallic, solid-smoke pieces were attached to my fingertips. They wouldn't evaporate, no matter what I touched them to, until I finally would put them back against my own head, and for a fraction of a second, I'd have all the thoughts I'd just had all over again, as if they were entirely new. Talk about déjà vu.

When I would get distracted, I'd retrace over the 156 tally marks on my arm, this time in thin Sharpie. To make them more real.

By nightfall, I had a few shaky leads.

Mark sat next to me. I pulled giant pieces of thoughts from my head and implanted them in his. I was still afraid to put my thoughts in anyone else's mind, but for some reason, I trusted Mark. I also trusted I wasn't going to hurt him, since I'd inadvertently "given" him one of my thoughts before without incident.

He was overwhelmed by the volume of thoughts and minds I was scanning through, but he picked out a few salient things here and there.

Quietly, when we were both ready to give up, we played with the fin-
gertip-thought manipulation, and then, out of the blue, one time I
pulled my hand away from his head, after having inserted a thought
into it, and more shimmery, golden, glittering solid-smoke pieces dangled from my fingertips. They didn't burn the way my own thoughts
did, but instead they tingled. The color was, undeniably, the exact
shade of the Winters' venom.

"Whoa," Mark said, watching them dangle and swirl.

"What do I do?" I asked, fascinated.

"Put it in your head!" Mark boomed, his voice enthusiastic. I did as
he said, and suddenly an image of Mark driving his R8 down 17-mile-
drive in Pebble Beach popped into my head — a girl I'd never seen
sitting in the passenger seat in a too-short red dress.

"That's what you were thinking about?" I asked incredulously.

"That's *always* what I'm thinking about," he laughed.

Everett appeared in the doorway. "Everything okay?" he asked.

"Yeah, Sadie's just showing off," Mark said, shoving me. I shoved
him back. He fell off the bed.

Everett raised an eyebrow. "Come here, Ev," I smiled, reaching my
hands out to him. He obliged. "Think of something really random that
you've never told me about."

"That you wouldn't mind her knowing," Mark added, joking.

"What?" Everett asked, confused.

"Just do it!" I laughed, pleasantly surprised to find myself so amused
by this evolution of my powers.

Everett nodded and did as I said. I put my fingertips to his forehead
and quickly pulled gold wisps — identical to Mark's — from his mind.
His eyes widened, watching this. I put them against my scalp, and
quickly I saw a flash of images from a time maybe fifty or sixty years
earlier. They were in a diner. Everett was dressed in a white crew neck
t-shirt and stiff, dark jeans, cuffed over penny-loafers and white socks.

His hair was slicked back at the roots. Mark, dressed just the same, was dancing with a young girl maybe ten feet in front of where Everett sat, cramped in front of a jukebox and unapologetically crowding the small aisle. Ginny was sitting across from him on a brown vinyl booth, her hair in pin curls and a pink cardigan sweater buttoned around her shoulders. She said something to Everett — he couldn't remember — and then she walked off toward an old jukebox to join Mark, a poodle skirt swishing as she walked.

"Peggy Sue's Diner? Yermo, California? 1956?" I asked, after the thought had evaporated.

A look of awe dawned on Everett's face. "Impossible," he said, barely more than a whisper.

"She's good, isn't she?" Mark asked, still amused. Power always amused him.

"She's good," Everett agreed, and pulled me into him, kissing my lips for the first time since before our fight on Friday night.

MONDAY MORNING, EVERETT, MARK, GINNY, PATRICK, MADELINE, AND I LOADED up one of the Winters' snow-chained, jacked-up Land Cruisers at the end of the road near Swan Lake. A number of the elders came to see us off, but Lizzie's absence dimmed the light of the others' presence. She contributed to this trip in the form of recipes and supplies from the apothecary, but the message was clear. I seemed to have gravely offended her by asking her to talk about Salem.

Andrew emerged from the woods as we were getting in the car. He had Ben in tow. This was quite a distance for the two of them to have come to see us off. "A word?" Andrew asked.

"Sure," I said.

"I have another favor to ask, and I will understand if you turn it down since we turned you down," Andrew said. He felt guilty, which confirmed to me that it was not he but Lizzie who had urged the elders not to talk to me about their time in Salem.

"Name it," I said.

"Take Ben with you," he said.

"But Andrew, you're trying to keep everyone…in, away from the world out here," I said.

"We need to know if it will happen to all our children. If going out there…" his voice trailed off. Images of the rogue Survivors sitting in church pews flashed through his mind, blood on their mouths. People's minds were particularly complicated. "I want one of us out there with you. You needn't be the only Survivor going, since we are the reason for this quest."

I didn't know what I could say.

"I told him about the heartbeats," Ben interjected. "That you and Noah determined that you and the other twenty-eight are the only ones who don't have them. Well, I've got one. We think I'll be safe."

"I was unaware that you knew about the heartbeats," I said coolly, wondering how many of my secrets Noah gave away to Ben over the years and, in turn, Ben had given away to Andrew. "Do you want to go?"

"Not forever," Ben said carefully.

"Which is why I trust him to go," Andrew said. "Don't you?"

"More than anyone else in those walls," I conceded.

"Andrew, even if I wanted to, we can't get him on a plane. He doesn't have any kind of identification that humans need to fly," I said.

"Will this work?" Out of his pocket, Andrew produced a newly minted passport with Ben's name and photo on it. He'd used Matthau as the last name. "I hope you don't mind. I borrowed one of yours and showed it to Joseph. He was able to reproduce it exactly." I looked it over, comparing it to my own. I knew it would be sufficient. Joseph had reproduced the matter of my passport, not just the look if it.

"We need to get going if we're going to make our flight," Ginny said.

Your call, Everett said in his mind.

I relented. "Fine. Let's go," I said.

Ben got in the car with us. As we drove through Swan Lake and back toward Kalispell, he pressed his face to the window, looking at the town. He was awestruck at this world he'd never seen, but he steeled himself and tried to remain unimpressed fearing that any sign of excitement would betray his loyalty to his walled-in world.

I had decided we would go to France. I had an image of cave art in my mind and couldn't shake it. I picked France because the oldest known cave art in the world was in Lascaux, in France.

We planned to fly commercial, as I hadn't — and wouldn't — ask about what happened with the Citation X jet we ruined when we jumped out of it. Ginny had managed to get a ticket for Ben before we arrived at the Kalispell airport. At the airport, the Winters casually encircled Ben, no doubt worried that upon his first contact with humans, he'd turn *vieczy*. But it was anti-climactic. Ben had no reaction to the humans, other than being appalled by the affection they publicly displayed and the amount of the skin they showed — in winter in Kalispell, Montana, no less. This only got worse once we caught our connection at Sea-Tac.

More than anything, his senses were bombarded by a million sights and sounds he never knew existed, and it overwhelmed him. I couldn't imagine leaving the Survivors — before I had read any of the books — and entering the world like this, with people in cars, in airports, on planes. In over 150 years, Ben had never gone farther than wherever he and Noah camped out while they pretended to track me three years before. Now, in the morning, he'd wake up in Europe. And trying to explain to him that we were going to *fly*? Well, he just read a book

Ginny gave him and never believed that's what we were doing until he was in the air. Even then, he doubted it was happening.

Ginny sat next to him, her protective instinct over him stronger than I expected. Ginny's thoughts usually revolved around Ginny.

Everett and I surfed the Internet — how useful Wi-Fi on planes was turning out to be! — looking for stories, however extreme or loosely supported, of lost cultures around the world. I just kept thinking that, if I could get on the ground, I'd be able find what I was looking for. In research, I always did my best thinking on my feet, guided by the indescribable sensations I felt in my core.

Once we arrived, Patrick and Madeline immediately took off to find the disappearing power I asked them to acquire. The rest of us went right to Lascaux. I didn't know if the prehistoric paintings themselves would be of any use to us, but I wanted to learn anything I could about of cave art. I couldn't say why.

⸺◆⸺

WE SPENT A SOLID MONTH ROAMING EUROPE WITH VERY LITTLE TO SHOW FOR it. We sank into a routine of clambering footsteps and sighs. Heavy waves of tension, frustration, and doubt covered me at every moment. The group let me lead without question, and they rarely voiced aloud their concern at our lack of a plan. But I could feel their patience waning by the hour. And Everett was the worst. He seemed to be living with a perpetually short fuse, angry at someone at all times, difficult even when he was calmer. I couldn't help but notice this only intensified as we'd wander into unseasonably cold temperatures or spend nights in frigid, open landscapes or hideaway mountains in rural Europe and Russia. The calendar might say it, but spring had not come for Everett, and so it had not come for me.

The rest weren't much better. Ginny seemed to get impatient with us even faster than usual, and she was a whirlwind of emotions. Ben was scared everywhere we went, and even though Mark was nothing but a help, calming his siblings, taking care of Ben, and convincing the group to keep quiet and follow me, it still wasn't enough.

Precisely why I wanted to travel alone.

In our month abroad, we mainly visited ruins and archaeological finds: the site of a ten-thousand-year-old city in Danube, Pompeii, the Parthenon, and other ruins in Greece. I don't know what I was looking for, but I knew this was what we had to do.

Every few days or so, the Winters took off in shifts. Ginny and Mark would go first, and then they'd come back for Everett while Ben and I slept, as if that would somehow make it better. He was doing the same thing whether I watched him leave or he disappeared in the night. I didn't know why the charade was necessary. On more than one occasion, once they'd all return, I'd catch the news in a town we stayed in, reporting an unsolved murder or two several towns away. I convinced myself there was no connection, denial turning out to be a far more useful tool than I could have imagined.

A few days before the end of April, as the reaching edges of a European winter were starting to give way to an actual spring, we went to the ruins of Ephesus in Turkey. Ben and I knew Ephesus from the Bible. It was a city in early Christian times where several important Biblical figures worked and lived and prophesized at one time or another. The city is comprised mostly of intricately carved ruins — facades of buildings, crumbling amphitheatre columns, as well as a large library, revolutionary for its time. We went to the gladiator graveyard, which had been discovered only a few years before. I felt an unexplainable electricity surge through my body.

We had gotten in the habit of frequenting these places at night so that we could explore in any way we saw fit. I stood under a pale moon, desperately seeking a lead.

"Something feels...off," I said to the others. "Like I've tracked something here," I said. But that wasn't quite it either. "Like I've tracked... myself here."

Ben came and stood next to me. He closed his eyes and focused his energy. He said, "There," and pointed toward the amphitheatre. He was tracking in the same way I'd felt Noah do in one of the visions — in a way that was completely foreign to me, albeit wildly successful.

"Where?" Everett asked.

"The hill the amphitheatre is carved out of. Something is there," I said, understanding with certainty what Ben was drawn to. I just didn't know why I didn't feel it until he pointed it out.

Ben and I led the way, walking up toward the hills and eventually entering the amphitheatre, trying to locate the source of the thing pulling us. But I wasn't sure what I was looking for. Would it even be a thing we could see? Or was this a more intangible feeling? We carefully climbed the steps of crumbling stone until we were at the top and could go no further. Ben and I both felt whatever we were looking for directly below us. "We have to go inside," he said.

"We can't harm anything," I warned, knowing that Ben didn't understand the value of world monuments like the one we were standing on.

"Down here!" Mark called. We bounded over the top edge of the amphitheatre, landing on the hillside that made up the back of it. At the bottom, Mark had begun burrowing a small tunnel. "It's hollow inside," he said as Ginny and Everett dropped to their knees to help him.

"How do you know?" I asked.

"I projected in there and landed in a room and not in the middle of a mountain," he said.

I couldn't argue with that. They dug a tunnel large enough for us to crawl through into the room Mark saw. We all just fit inside it, but we were in total darkness. My body felt hot, and my extremities tingled. Ben felt the same way. For just a moment, I felt what I could best describe as a pulse in my left wrist. It left as quickly as it had come.

"Mark, a light, please," I said.

Two torches set about five feet off the ground and six feet apart burst into flame with the flick of Mark's wrist. They were attached to stone fixtures that looked as old as the ruins outside, though they had pieces of red paint flaking off of them. The whole thing was incredibly eerie.

In the sudden light, we saw a pyramid of symbols on the wall. At the top, a fading red cross. Below that, several hundred symbols that got progressively smaller the closer they came to the bottom. Some of them were simple Xs or circles with dots around them. Others had many lines, forming complicated shapes with lines that crisscrossed and curved. Most had a number of dots or small lines off to the side accompanying them. No two were identical.

"Behold," Everett said. "Sadie's cave art."

"Is this what you've been looking for?" Ginny asked me.

I was unable to talk. I felt a tangible pull toward these symbols. Like they were a part of me. Like they were people I had known and lost.

"What do you think they mean?" I finally asked them.

"Probably just a hieroglyphic-like language," Everett answered.

"Who would put them here?" I asked.

"Sadie, you told us this city is important in Christian history. There's a cross at the top. Put two and two together," Everett said.

"I don't think they're Christian symbols," I said.

"I don't either," Ben said, backing me up quickly. "I can't explain it, but they're not."

Everett sighed audibly. "Are we just going to keep doing this? Saying we can't explain why we feel something, but somehow we *know* it's important?" he asked, his frustration apparent. I had so hoped the mild air would make the Everett Winter I fell in love with come back to me. As he made these comments, this seemed less probable.

"She's right. They predate Christianity," Ginny said, coming to my defense. "Look at the cross. That's not the way a cross is portrayed in Christianity. The horizontal line is closer to the center of the vertical line than it should be. This city existed before Christianity, so the symbols probably did too."

I nodded in agreement, my hand hovering inches from the symbols.

"Do you think they have anything to do with Survivors?" Ginny asked.

"I don't know," I said.

"They do," Ben said. "I know it." He felt what I was feeling, something I had no way of explaining to the Winters. This electricity radiating off the symbols. This feeling of familiarity.

Mark sensed this. "What are you thinking?" he asked, studying my face intently.

"I've seen them before," I said, more to myself than to him. "Not these exact symbols, but this style."

"Do you know how many symbols on this earth, in all the places you've been and in all the books you've read probably look something like this?" Everett asked. "They're lines, circles, dots, Xs, Os. They're bound to look familiar."

"Do you always have to doubt her?" Ben asked. Everett shot him a venomous glare.

"Where do you think you've seen them, Sadie?" Ginny asked.

"I have no idea." I had a supernaturally eidetic memory, but this I could not remember. I wanted to smack my head against the wall.

We heard a voice. "Trespassers!" The voice was distant, and the word was in Turkish.

"We've been found out," I announced, translating the word they'd all heard. "What do we do?"

"Go out the way we came?" Mark laughed. "Is there an alternative?" Mark said. His calm reminded me that he likely spent time in places he shouldn't fairly often.

He led the way out of the tunnel, and I followed him. Scrambling to my feet outside, I saw a flashlight searching the area. Someone had heard us but hadn't yet determined where we were. "Show yourself!" the man's voice said. He was muttering expletives to himself, frustrated by what he assumed were kids or vandals.

But as he rounded the corner and saw Ginny climbing out of the tunnel, he dropped his flashlight and let out a cry. In the dark we saw him cross himself, and whisper, "*Kurtulan.*"

"What did he say?" Mark urged.

Uneasy, I whispered, "Survivor."

THE MAN TOOK OFF RUNNING. THIS WAS A RESPONSE I DIDN'T EXPECT. MARK and Everett were amused by this, so they let him run in terror for a few seconds before they outpaced him in one bound. The man let out a startled cry as they grabbed hold of him.

"Be nice!" I shouted.

The boys held him as the rest of us caught up. The moon had gone behind the clouds, and I could hardly see a thing. "We need light," I said.

"I got it," Ben said, and he closed his palm and opened it to a ball of fire.

I looked at him, dumbfounded. "That's not water," I said. His individual power was to manipulate water in all forms, but, if nothing else, fire was the opposite of water. He could do that? But he just shrugged.

"What's your name?" I asked the man in Turkish.

With eyes wide, he stuttered, "Berkant."

I gestured for Ben to hold the light toward Berkant's face so I could see him better. He was a small, frail man with a wiry beard. But the defining feature of his face was a grisly scar that cut diagonally from the top of the left side of his head between his eyes, across his nose, to his right ear.

"Please!" he begged, shaken to his core.

"We won't hurt you," I responded. "I promise. We just need to talk to you. They'll let go now, if you won't run."

"Just talk?" he asked, hesitant. He wasn't looking at me.

I nodded, and he relaxed. They let him go. "I have some questions. Is there somewhere we could go? Perhaps somewhere warmer?" He had to be cold.

He nodded and pointed up a long hill that led up and away from the ruins. There was nothing else on it, save for scattered trees. We followed him for about a mile until we came to what can best be described a shack. We all went inside, where his wife and a young son were. He said nothing to them, and they said nothing to us. The woman and small boy didn't even look us in the eye as they clung to the corner of the room.

Berkant would address only Ben, Mark, and Everett, until it was clear I was doing the talking for us. I wasn't unfamiliar with the fact that there were cultures on this earth that still didn't equally respect or even acknowledge the existence of women. I learned early on this was the case. But if I could grow up among dozens of Puritans who evolved in such a way that they never treated a woman as less than a man, then I could assert myself in front of any man in the world. Berkant would have to deal with me. I wasn't going to coddle his prejudices.

Then I told the others to go outside, knowing our collective presence was overwhelming him.

"Why did you call us Survivors?" I asked.

"You were in the Survivors' Cave," he said. "My family has watched this monument for seven generations, ever since an old Survivor instructed us to do so. Since then, only a handful of times has someone come there. They called themselves Survivors, and so I knew you must be Survivors too."

"Did you know them?" I asked, my mind hot at the thought.

His wife, who sat quietly in the corner, crossed herself and said a prayer under her breath.

"I met an old one...once." A penetrating image flashed across Berkant's mind of an angular-faced man with dark hair and dark eyes, dressed in black. He reached out and put his hand on Berkant's face until he felt a white-hot pain across his whole face. It was a cross between the burn of branding and the raw pain of a sliced-open wound. The memory faded out as blood ran into Berkant's vision and his stomach lurched from the pain. I understood that this was how he'd gotten the scar on his face. The pain of the memory churned my stomach.

"He's the one who hurt you," I said, understanding. Berkant nodded. I pulled out my Moleskine notebook and made a note:

"Survivor" who mangled Berkant, maybe the one who killed Hannah's father, if he were killed?

"And the generations before you?" I asked.

"He marked each of my forefathers in some way. Some had scars like mine. Others, he'd take an eye or a limb. But all of us were marked — his guarantee that we'd stay here and be loyal to him." Berkant said, his voice sad. "That is how it has always been. The old Survivor told each generation to work and keep his children here, that we have to watch that cave. He made us take a *berkant*, a solid oath. Each of us has been named that ever since," he explained. This rubbed me the wrong way, that the old Survivor had named him. It was a form of proclaiming ownership. "Each father teaches his son that this is our purpose. And who can defy his father? We are loyal people," Berkant said, his young son on his lap now. He hugged the boy close to him. I understood Berkant's loyalty to his father, better yet his unwillingness to defy his family. Half of me did, anyway.

"You all have lived here for seven generations?"

"My son will be the eighth," he said, grief now emanating from his small body. He hated to think what the Survivor might do to his son.

"How did you meet your wife if you never left?" I asked.

"He brought her to me."

"So you would have a child," I said, understanding.

He stroked his son's face. "I can only hope he will spare my boy. He will stay here and guard Ephesus and the Survivors' cave without such pain," he said.

My throat was tight with the guilt and fear in Berkant's voice. "He's the only one you've ever met?" I confirmed.

"There was someone with him. A loyal friend," Berkant said.

"Do you remember anything about this friend?" I asked.

"He called his friend Sam."

I nodded, scribbling furiously. "What do you think a Survivor *is*?" I asked.

He considered this. "Something not of God," he said.

A fair — albeit offensive — description, I thought. "What if I told you we were Christians?" I asked.

"Your old Survivor, he thinks he is a kind of messiah," Berkant spat. "He can be no Christian."

"Do you think the old one put the symbols in the cave?" I asked.

"I assume so," Berkant said.

"I thank you for your help, Berkant," I said, rising to my feet. It was time to leave the man. He and his family had been scared enough for one night. I picked through Berkant's thoughts quickly, determining all I could about what he knew.

"One last question," I said as he walked me outside his small home.

"Yes?" he asked, the color coming back to his face now that we were leaving.

"What did they call him?" I asked.

"*Kuzgun,*" he said.

"*Kuzgun,*" I repeated. "Raven."

THAT NIGHT WE WENT INTO SELCUK AND GOT ROOMS AT THE HOTEL BELLA. Mark stayed with Ben, to show him the ropes of everyday things like running water and to make sure he didn't lose his mind flipping TV channels. Ginny had her own room, and Everett and I had one.

I took a long shower, washing off weeks of traveling dirt. Ginny had taken our clothes to wash, so I wrapped myself up in towels and sat on our bed, hoping it was not too inappropriate. Everett's eyes lingered on me when I came out of the bathroom this way, but he said nothing. My eyes widened a bit, too, to see him clad only in boxer shorts. This was the most I'd ever seen of him, but I said nothing either. We were even. Evenly uncomfortable. Evenly interested.

Everett fiddled with the contents of his traveling bag. His temperament had been fairly smooth for the last few days as the weather got milder here, staying between forty and fifty-five degrees. As the feel of winter faded, his anger and needs subsided. This was a welcome reprieve after months of recurring tension between us.

His alabaster skin was glowing in the lamplight of the room, except for the shadows under each deep cut of musculature in his frame. It was hard to focus.

"Your trip seems to be coming together, princess," he said.

"In some ways," I said, burying myself under the covers. I had an awful lot of fabric on my body to still feel so naked. "We aren't any closer to finding out how to destroy Survivors just yet."

"But you're many steps closer to your point of origin," he countered, coming to sit next to me on the bed. He was trying with all his might to not think about the fully-covered-but-still-naked situation that was thoroughly occupying his mind. I knew this because he was so distracted by me that he was letting his mental armor slip.

"If the one Berkant called Raven is the point of origin then, yes, we are closer. I know he exists now and is possibly still alive," I said.

"Do you think he's the one who killed Hannah's father?" he asked, as he laid down. "Or that he could be Hannah's father?"

"Surely they wouldn't be the same person. Berkant's Raven is a monster, and Hannah's father was a quiet Puritan. It leads me to believe that maybe the monster killed him, as you suggest. Or maybe it doesn't. Maybe this Raven and Hannah's father have nothing in common. We don't know enough yet."

"Maybe Madeline and Patrick could go to Pickering and dig around. See if they can find part of the human trail there," he suggested. Pickering, in Yorkshire, England, was the town where Adelaide's family lived in Britain in the sixteenth century. This was a good idea, I realized, as it was one of the few sure instances of witch-families in a certain place at a certain time.

"Hand me my phone?" I asked, afraid to move and disrupt the mound of fabric I'd covered myself in. He obliged. I dialed Mark.

"Oh my god, it's a full time job taking care of this kid," Mark said.

"Is he okay?" I asked. Mark was not known for his patience...or purity.

"He's asleep, finally," Mark said. "But now I'm stuck here and going stir crazy. Tell me you have something you need us to do."

"Can you fill Patrick and Madeline in? If they're still in Northern Europe, have them go to Pickering and see what they can find," I said.

"Symbols or sources?" he asked.

"Either," I said. "Thank you."

"No, thank *you*," he said. "It's the least I can do if you can make the Angry Winter over there be a little more…"

"California?" I asked.

"Precisely," he said. "The air is heating up. Heat him up the rest of the way, and maybe he'll be the Ev I know and love three quarters of the year."

"Mark…" My throat closed up from embarrassment, and I couldn't find my words. If I were capable of blushing, I would have been.

"Shush. I've got this, little one. Now get him." Then he hung up the phone.

Everett laughed, watching me shrink beneath the covers. "How badly do you wish I couldn't hear him just now?"

"Pretty badly," I admitted. "Is Ginny coming back with our clothes any time soon?"

"I doubt it," he said, an amused smile on his face. "Is this too much?" he asked, gesturing to his bare skin. He was only half-serious.

"No," I half-lied. I reached up to push my hair out of my face.

"What are those?" he asked, running his hand across the tally marks on my arm. I had retraced them so many times that the shower had only faded them, not cleaned them off. There were more of them now. In the last few weeks, I had two more visions that I'd concealed from my traveling companions. Nothing relevant happened in them anyway except that in one, I wasn't in Noah's head, I was in someone else's, though I couldn't figure out whose. And the rest of the rogues were there, so why did the difference matter? There were only ever more deaths. Twenty-one more, to be exact.

"The body count," I said. 177 marks in all.

"It's up to 177?" he asked.

"How did you count them that fast?" I asked, laughing.

"I don't count," he said. "I just…see. It's called subitizing, I think."

"What is that?" I asked.

"I can see quantities of numbers without counting them. All people do it, theoretically. But humans can only do about four things at once and I can do…well, apparently, at least 177," he said.

I creased my brow. "Right…"

"Never mind," he said.

He sighed, lifting my arm to his mouth to kiss it. "177 new scars, I suppose," he said.

"They aren't scars," I said, offended. I had not tried *anything* to end myself. I had kept up my end of the bargain.

"Aren't they?" he asked, his eyes knowing. Of course they were scars. On my record. On my soul.

He continued to kiss my arm, then my shoulders and across my collarbone, up my neck and lips.

I lost my mind in moments like this. The humming and buzzing in my head quieted. The voices faded away. My skin felt electrified, and my head literally felt hot. And all I wanted to do was be closer to him.

We stayed like this for hours, kissing and dancing on boundaries, relishing the freedom of lying next to each other, enjoying the tiny bits of skin that we otherwise never exposed to one another as layers of fabric began to fall away. We said more than once that this is what it must feel like to be like human — the twenty-one-year-old quiet girl from the Northwest who fell in love with city life, the twenty-four-year-old California boy with the fast car and the good looks. And for a few seconds at a time, I believed we were those kids, just vacationing for the holidays in an exotic locale and enjoying our lives.

But then I'd see those tally marks.

CHAPTER FOURTEEN

soulless

PARADISE WAS SHORT-LIVED.

Before dawn, Ginny came knocking with the clothes, and as soon as he heard us talking to her, Mark came in. I was still wrapped in only towels and blankets, and so I hid behind Everett as we talked.

"Where's Ben?" I asked.

"Trying to breathe," Mark said. "He had a panic attack, not that he knew that's what it was."

"Is he okay?" I asked, alarmed.

"He's fine," he said, scrubbing his hand across his face and then through his hair. "Sadie, he needs to go home," he sighed.

"What do you suggest I do? Put him on a plane?" I asked, feeling stressed and guilty.

"Of course not. If you're okay with it, I'm going to get Adelaide to meet us. She'll take him back," Mark said.

"But he was helpful, and Andrew asked me…" I said.

"He needs to go home," Mark repeated. He had obviously had a conversation with Ben that I had not, so I had to trust him.

"Okay," I said.

"Great. The quickest way for Adelaide to get here from the Survivors is to drive to Seattle, so she is already en route. I got her on a flight into Bucharest via London. It was the best

I could do. It's about 1,000 miles from here. She'll be here in twenty-four hours, so we have some time to kill," Mark said.

"Look at Polly, learning to handle logistics," Everett smiled.

"'Bout time," Ginny jeered.

"What about Patrick and Madeline?" I asked.

"They were in Norway. They're following a lead, but then they'll head to Pickering. No magical transportation power yet," he added.

"So what's the plan, boss?" Everett asked.

"I want to go to Ephesus again so I can see it in the daylight.," I said.

"You won't be able to look at the symbols again," Ginny reminded me. "It's a little harder to covertly destroy part of a monument in the daylight with tourists watching."

"I know. I just…" I trailed off hating to again say that it was for reasons I couldn't explain.

Everett seemed to understand. "All right," he said, "everybody out. We need to get dressed."

I KNELT OVER THE GLADIATOR GRAVEYARD. I HAD READ ABOUT GLADIATORS in a history of the Roman Empire, and I was shocked to learn of what I could best describe as murder for sport. Now that the ethics of murder and the value of life, human and otherwise, was a constant question in my life, I couldn't think of anything more despicable than the gladiator tradition.

So why did I feel this electricity in this place?

"Do you feel it, too?" I asked Ben, who was hovering near me.

"Like lightning in my bones," Ben said. "And…"

"Sadness," I said, feeling what he was feeling.

"Right," he said. I also felt guilt, but Ben did not.

We made it to Bucharest a few hours before Adelaide's flight arrived. We found a café with Wi-Fi and waited there. I pulled out my laptop and searched for anything in Romania that might help us while we were there. The last time I'd been in Romania we'd encountered the nosferatu lynxes in the mountains to the northwest. I wondered if Narcisa, Valentin, and their dwindling coven were still there.

Everett, Mark, and Ginny were starting to lose patience with each other. Their dispositions had changed. The air in Romania was much colder, and it had been days since their last excursion. They needed to feed.

We greeted Adelaide at the airport close to midnight. Their flight back to London left at six in the morning. Adelaide was with her children for two minutes before she lectured them on the dangers of going too long without blood.

"We can't leave Sadie," Everett said.

"But you can't go without your brother and sister. It's for your own protection," Adelaide reminded him, stroking his hair out of his eyes. It was very maternal. I wondered why.

"I'll be fine," I said.

Everett started to protest, but Adelaide stopped him. "She will be fine. You have to go before you get dangerous, and that's that. Now, you three go," she said. None protested. They simply hugged and kissed and went on their way. "Sadie, I'm going to take Ben somewhere he can rest before our plane ride. You can come with us, or…"

"I have some things I'd like to do," I said.

"Then you do them. And take care," she said, kissing my forehead.

Ben was looking at the ground as it came time for our goodbye. "I'm sorry I couldn't be of more help," he said.

"You were great. You were brave," I said.

He nodded, and then backed away. We had never shown each other affection. Now didn't feel like the time to start.

"I'll keep him safe," Adelaide said, hugging me tight.

—◆—

THE SEASONS WERE MELTING, ONE INTO THE OTHER. MOST THINGS I CARED about had fallen by the wayside. Any version of who I used to be had faded. Thinking about it, I supposed I could include my faith in that list. Perhaps that's what motivated me to go to Densus.

I ran straight there to see the famous Densus Church. Like Ephesus, it had a pagan history that predated its Christian history. The church wasn't quite that old, dating back only to the seventh century, though it had been sacred ground for centuries before that.

I roamed the hills surrounding it for several hours, waiting for that pull. But I felt nothing.

An hour before dawn, I worked my way inside the locked church. I knelt at the altar and prayed for guidance. For protection. I gave thanks that, so far, we had all made it through this debacle in one piece. And I asked for forgiveness for the million bad choices that had landed me here, and for wishing I hadn't been roped into this. I regretted hurting my family, but I also regretted helping my family, and that made me a terrible person.

Before I knew it, I was crying. I was on my knees, alone with my God, and vulnerable on a cold dawn in a foreign land. I knew these mistakes I'd made and the hand I'd been dealt were irreversible, that there would be no lazy Saturday afternoons with Cole or couples' getaways with Corrina. There would be no human life for me. Just more of this. More of the same.

This is why I wanted out so badly.

I realized how lost I had become. My faith had always been my true north, the direction all other paths I took were based on. But now I wasn't so sure. I had lost sight of so many things I once thought, once believed, and that was dangerous. Everyone has that internal compass, and everyone's true north is a part of who they are. By abandoning my internal compass, I was guilty of abandoning who I was at my most basic. I was falling apart. I understood then that it didn't matter what was at someone's core — love, faith, a god, art, philosophy — if it was neglected, it would give way. Abandoning my core had put distance between the deepest parts of myself.

I pressed my forehead to the ground and prayed, curled up in front of the altar, in front of the crucifix. I repeated prayers this way for twenty minutes. It felt like the only safe place to lose it. In front of God. In front of myself.

Then I heard them coming: Three minds in the distance, running toward me at a faster than human pace. I assumed it was the Winters, tracking me far more quickly than I expected them to. But as they got close, I heard three distinct mental voices, uninhibited by mental shields. If it were the Winters, I wouldn't be able to that with anyone but Ginny. I stood up, on my guard, and made my way out of the church.

"What do you know?" she called, still a distance away, her long hair whipping wildly in the wind. I recognized the shock of white-blonde hair on the muscular man beside her before I could make out her features. They had a girl with them I didn't know.

"Narcisa!" I called and ran toward her.

"Don't forget me," Valentin said in his native Romanian.

"I'm so glad you're alive!" Narcisa cried as she threw her arms around my neck.

"Wouldn't I be?" I asked, laughing.

"You had low odds if you'd been traveling with that crazy lot of *vieczy*," she said.

"I still am traveling with them," I said, then I added, "I'm meeting up with them soon."

Up close, I could see the girl with them was beautiful, her frame was more petite than her companion's. She had long, straight black hair and creamy mocha skin and light eyes that gave her an exotic look with her rich coloring. Her features and skin were ethnically neutral; she could have been from anywhere. Out of place with her disheveled traveling clothes, she wore a pendant around her neck that hung as low as they key I wore around mine. On it, there was a monarch butterfly. "I'm sorry, I'm being rude. I'm Sadie Matthau," I said, as I stuck out my hand to shake hers.

She took it. She had pulled her shirt-sleeves out from under her jacket and cupped them in her palm. I picked up on this whenever I saw anyone doing it since I did it myself, and, as if guilty by association, I wondered what she was hiding. "We've met," she said, in Romanian, her voice sounding different than Valentin and Narcisa's.

"Have we?" I asked, puzzled. I had never seen her face before.

"This is Samantha Parker," Narcisa said.

"Call me Parker, please. Everyone does," she said.

"You met her in her lynx form," Narcisa told me.

"The smallest and darkest, fuzzy one," Parker smiled. Of course. I had her teeth marks scarred into my side. Everett had to heal them because whatever Parker had done to me kept them from healing on their own. They were slightly shimmery and cool now.

"What are you doing here?" I asked.

"You're in trouble, aren't you?" Narcisa asked, a cheeky grin on her face.

"Not exactly…" I said.

"Nonsense. We've heard something about a war between witches. Is this true?" she asked.

"Between members of my family, yes," I said, wondering who she heard that from.

"Then you need allies. We'd like to help," she said.

"But I'm working with the Winters. I know you hate them," I said.

"That's the wrong word," Valentin said. "We just wanted to protect you. Now it looks like that means working with them."

"You seem to know an awful lot about this," I said, regretfully wary of Valentin's altruism, despite how genuine it seemed. How much did I know about these nosferatu anyway? And how did they find me here? And what would motivate them to lay down their lives to fight in a war that didn't involve them, let alone fight alongside a family they attacked only months before?

But what position was I in to reject help?

"News travels fast," Parker interjected.

"We'd like to hear it all from you. Have time?" Narcisa asked.

"Plenty," I said.

We caught each other up quickly. In the months since I'd last seen them, the remaining members of their coven had split apart. These were the only three of them traveling together now, and they had become nomadic. Parker got wind of the war first, and after hearing more about it, Narcisa and Valentin assumed I was involved. Valentin picked up my trail outside of Bucharest by happenstance only hours before.

I told them what had been happening — about the rogue Survivors and our quest for the Survivors' point of origin. I told them about the visions, about how they had been right to warn me about what a *vieczy* was capable of.

"Well, pretty girl," Valentin said, "we're in to help you. Anything you need."

"We're just traveling now. Researching," I said.

Suicide attempts? Narcisa asked in her mind. I shook my head. "Then we'll travel with you," Narcisa declared, "if it won't inhibit you?"

"I'm sure it won't," I said, not certain that was true, "If we find what we're searching for, we'll head back to the states soon, and then there will be a war."

"Which we will fight in," Valentin said. I knew the lynxes had always felt some protectiveness over me that I never understood, but offering their lives was extreme, even for them. As if to ease any doubt

I felt, he added, "This is what we do. It's why we took you when we did. We've seen what supernatural creatures are capable of. We try to limit the bloodshed."

"Awfully noble of you," I said.

"What else could we do?" Parker asked. "We can't live among humans. Few *nosferatu* have that kind of control over their shifts."

"And we've lived among the animals for too long," Narcisa said. "We're unfit for the human world."

"But yours we can handle," Valentin smiled. Of course. There was so little humanity left in my world.

My phone rang. Everett's voice came on the other end. "Meet us in Pickering, princess. Pat and Madeline have something you'll want to see."

"On my way," I said. "But I'm bringing allies. We'll call you when we get there."

Quickly, Narcisa, Valentin, and Parker morphed into their lynx form, and we took off into the night.

fateor

WE RAN BACK TO PARIS WHERE WE COULD CATCH A TRAIN THAT RAN under the English Channel. It had taken only six hours to run the 1,200 miles between Bucharest and Paris, sticking to rural, roundabout routes so we wouldn't be seen, but we were slowed down when we had to resort to human methods of travel in the more populated areas. Once in London, we took a train to the far suburbs above the city. Then, once in the countryside, the nosferatu could take their lynx form again and we could run.

The sun dipped near the horizon by the time we met up with the Winters. I was reminded of the eerie hours of darkness that clung to Moscow. I had lost all track of time by then.

We came upon them in a grassy plain just north of Pickering where Valentin, Narcisa, and Parker morphed back into their human forms. Ginny had heard us first, her senses awakened by my proximity. I could sense she was wary of my companions.

"How unexpected," Patrick called as he spotted us in the distance. As if to declare his party's sentiments, he walked straight up to Valentin and shook his hand. The gesture seemed out of place here among this group who'd recently tried to kill each other.

"Patrick," Valentin nodded. "Good to see you, I think."

"Sadie?" Everett asked, looking for an explanation.

"They found me in Romania. They've gotten word of the war, and they've come to help," I explained, refusing to ask anyone's permission for Narcisa, Valentin, and Parker to join us.

"Do we need help?" he said under his breath. I ignored him. When was spring? Or, more accurately, weather warm enough to make him stop acting like *this*?

"I'm sorry. I'm being rude," I said, reaching for Parker and pulling her toward me. "Parker, I'm sure you remember the Winters, but since you've never officially met, allow me to introduce you. This is Patrick, the eldest, and his wife, Madeline. Everett is with me, his sister, Ginny, and the youngest, craziest of the lot, Mark," I said as I went around the group.

She nodded to each, acknowledging. She was fidgety and fingered the monarch pendant.

"What have you got for us?" I asked, eager to get down to business.

Patrick said. "We thought you may be best at figuring it out. We were following a *draugr* from Norway—"

I cut him off. "A what?"

"A *draugr*," he said. "The *draugar* are Scandinavian vampires that hunt other dead — okay, well, not living — things."

"Like *vieczy*," I said, understanding. "Wait, is it *draugr* or *draugar*?"

"Both. *Draugr* singular. *Draugar* plural," Patrick clarified. "Well, we got into it," he said, sheepishness in his voice. Of course, if Patrick had an excuse, he'd get into a fight with anything. "They are known for their strength, so Madeline and I had a hard time fighting him off. They can also sink through earth, so you can't corner them. If you back them against a stone wall, they'd just sink through it and come back at you from the other side. He took off. We found him about fifty miles north of here, and followed him."

I looked at the flat plain around me, the low sun casting long shadows. "Followed him where, exactly?"

Patrick and Madeline exchanged wary glances. "Right here," Madeline said.

"And then?" I asked.

"Then he disappeared," Patrick said.

"So why are we here? Can't he probably just disappear?" I asked.

"We're here because of this," Patrick said, turning his back to me and taking a few steps into the field. He held his hands up in front of his body, palms forward, until they were bent backwards, as if he'd run into a wall. "Something's here. We called you because all matter of vampires, shape-shifters, and the like can't produce charms or spells like your kind can, so this must be your kind of magic."

They all moved forward and felt the invisible wall. "Is it possible this is where Adelaide's family lived? Perhaps they hid their village or something?"

"I already called her," Patrick said. "She doesn't know anything about it."

I reached out my hands to the invisible wall, and I felt stone under my fingertips. More strangely though, I felt a quick shock, then a red glow illuminated above my hands, as if someone were casting a red light onto the stone wall. I jerked my hands back.

They all saw it. "Do it again," Mark urged. I must have looked uneasy. "Come on, it won't hurt you. Trust me, kiddo," he said with his trademark instigative smile. Always the adventurous one.

"Be careful," Everett warned. Always the cautious one. Mark rolled his eyes.

I tentatively put my hands out toward the empty space again until I felt cool stone beneath them. The shock was more elongated this time, like a dull electric current passing through my body. The red glow emerged and grew brighter until it formed a triangle about the width of my shoulders. At the top of it, the red glow gave way to the same off-proportioned cross we'd seen in the cave at Ephesus. A blank spot formed in the middle of the triangle below the cross.

"What do I do?" I asked.

"I think it wants you to put something in the circle," Ginny offered.

"But what?" Patrick asked.

"Well that was the weird cross we saw in the cave at Ephesus. Maybe you need to put one of the other symbols in there," Everett offered.

"What symbols?" Narcisa asked.

I kept pacing. They kept talking. Their voices spinning around my head in a frenzy.

"The symbols we saw at Ephesus. There was a cave there," Ginny explained.

"There is no cave at Ephesus!" Valentin cried.

"There is when Mark digs one," Ginny scoffed.

"Always the troublemaker, are you?" Valentin kidded, punching Mark in the arm.

On and on and on they went. So many voices.

My head began to throb. Then I heard it, a voice, smoky-thin and far away. *Use the spells.*

"SHUT UP!" I screamed. They froze. "Who said something about spells?"

They all exchanged glances. None of them knew what I was talking about.

"Quiet," I snapped. I closed my eyes and tried to filter through the multitude of sounds in my head, listening for the distant voice again.

Suddenly, the other sounds in my head faded.

Use the spells, I heard again. It was Noah.

A pointed burn at the base of my skull flared. And then he said, *Revelations.*

Everyone instinctually sensed my panic. Unsure of what was happening, they had surrounded me. The nerves in the air made my own stress elevate exponentially, which in turn made them panic more. The effect was sickeningly and instantaneously cyclical.

"Everett, Ginny, give me your bags," I said hurriedly, dropping my own pack to the ground. I poured out the contents and began rummaging through plastic pillboxes in which Lizzie had packed the herbs and ingredients. I held the notebook she'd given me, running my fingers across Lizzie's thin, formal script in the inside cover:

Elixirs and Incantations

"Noah told me to use the spells," I said. "I have to find one that can get us in there."

Everett looked up at his family with doubt in his eyes, and then he looked all around us. "Is Noah here?" he asked.

"Don't be stupid. Of course not," I snapped.

"Then, Sadie…"

"Impossible, I know," I said, flipping through the thin pages.

Then I stopped. Across the top of a page:

Fateor

The Latin word for "reveal." That must have been what Noah meant when he said *Revelations*.

Below it, Lizzie had carefully written a description: "The Fateor Elixir shows the secrets of a thing, however hidden or protected." She included a list of ingredients.

"Ginny, help me. I'll read the ingredients out to you." As I read out the list — dried white chrysanthemum, olive oil, balsam, ginger root, cumin seeds, sepia, wolfpaw clubmoss, and red clay — Ginny pulled the needed herbs and roots out of the pile and mixed them in Everett's hands. He ground them together, his stone-hard knuckle and palm acting as mortar and pestle. "What's next?" she asked. "Earth of the hiding place," I said, reading the last ingredient on the page. Mark grabbed a handful of soft dirt from the ground directly in front of the invisible barrier and added it to Everett's hands.

I turned the page, and my eyes widened. It contained only two lines.

Fateor, continued...
Add blood of the discoverer.
1:3

"Damn it," I said under my breath.

"What's it say?" Everett asked.

"It just has numbers," I said, "and something about blood."

"Whose blood?" Everett asked, his brow creased.

I didn't answer him. "What could it mean when numbers are written with a colon between them? Like one-colon-three?"

"Could be a ratio," Mark offered. That wasn't a bad guess considering we were working, essentially, with a recipe. But which ingredients in ratio to what? Did it mean the blood? One part of my blood, for three parts the other ingredients? Vice versa?

"What else?" I prompted. Everyone furrowed their brows, thinking and frustrated by having no quick solution. I scanned quickly through my mind to determine what the 1:3 could be referring to. I ran down the list of ingredients, thought of the blood, about the word Fateor, Noah's voice saying Revelations.

And then, the obvious. "The Bible," I said, mostly to myself.

"Leave it to the Puritans…" Ginny said, rolling her eyes.

"Here, someone pull up the Bible app on my iPhone," I said, holding it out for someone to grab with one hand while I began digging for something else I carried deep in the pockets of my bag. None of the Winters reached for my phone. "Hello?" But they were frozen. "Help me!" I said again.

"We can't," Ginny said, her voice emotional, which seemed an odd response to my asking for them to help me with my phone. Stuttering, she explained, "i-i-iPhones work with electric charges emitted from the skin. We don't have those b-b-b-because we're…"

"Dead," I said. "Or not alive. Same difference."

I flipped through the visual images of all the interactions I had with the Winters and realized, only then, that neither Patrick, Ginny, Mark, Madeline, nor Everett ever once touched mine or their parents' iPhones. I sighed. A million tiny things I didn't know about them. Or hadn't thought of yet.

I threw the phone to Parker. "Can you work one of those?" I asked. She nodded. "Good. Find the app."

"What are you digging for?" Everett asked, still on the ground next to me.

"Something else I need," I said, deflecting him again. He could sense it and emitted a faint growl.

"Got it," Parker said. "What am I looking for?"

"The book of Revelations, chapter one, verse three," I said.

Parker read: "Blessed is he who reads aloud the words of the prophecy, and blessed are those who hear, and who keep what is written therein; for the time is near."

"Does this mean anything to you?" Patrick asked.

I knew the passage. I just needed to hear it again, as if remembering it wouldn't do the trick. "It's about the second coming of the Messiah.

That seemed an awfully weighty thing to throw in here," I said. "That can't be why Lizzie put it there. But what did she mean?"

"Hey…Mom told us to remember something about a prophecy," Ginny said.

I had just located a tiny makeup case I carried in my bag for over two years. I idly fingered the vial and arrowhead inside it.

"What?" I asked, trying to leach onto her train of thought.

"I remember it too," Mark said. "Covets and resents…" he trailed off.

"Yes!" Ginny cried.

Mark closed his eyes tightly, and thought. Melodically, he said, "And because of good things that the Heavenly Powers have given in the past, we must be careful not to ignore the shape of things to come."

"What kind of prophecy is that?" Everett asked.

"What does it mean?" Valentin asked. Our nosferatu companions were trying very hard to stay out of this mess as much as they could.

"I have no idea," I admitted. I played the verse from Revelations over again in my head. *Blessed is he who reads aloud the words of the prophecy, and blessed are those who hear, and who keep what is written therein; for the time is near.* "But it doesn't even matter. The verse in Revelations just suggested reading it aloud. I think that will make the elixir work. If you hear it, maybe you'll see what I see when whatever is hiding in plain sight reveals itself."

"Now what?" Everett asked.

"One final step," I said, opening the makeup case in my palm. "Question, though. How far away does your spidey sense work?" I asked, trying too hard to be light-hearted when I was about to do something troublesome.

Mark laughed. Less amused, Everett asked, "Which spidey sense?"

"You know, the one where you can smell blood," I said. I ignored the worried glances.

It was, of course, Mark who answered me. "Like *really* smell it? Eyes go bright red, contort-and-go-crazy smell it? Half a mile, give or take. To know it's near? Miles."

"Great. Ginny? Madeline? Pat? You kids are going to want to take Everett and hang back for a bit. I'd say, go half a mile or so."

"What?" they asked in unison, everyone suddenly alarmed.

I pulled out the vial of ricin, a natural poison that was easy to preserve, and I coated a sharpened arrowhead in it. A cursed arrowhead dipped in poison was the first way I'd learned to break my skin, and it'd been my stand-by ever since. "Seriously, you need to get out of here, quickly."

"Not me?" Mark asked.

"Think you can keep it together without killing me?" I asked as I rolled up my sleeve.

Everett yelled. "You promised you wouldn't do this!"

"Calm down. The last step calls for my blood. Cliché, I know, but I didn't make it up. Now give Valentin here the stuff we've already mixed, and get away," I explained. None of them moved. "Now!"

"Everett, *go.*" He felt trapped. I had trapped him. He could leave and know I was about to do something to myself, or stay and potentially quite literally eat me alive.

Relenting, he poured the half-made elixir into Valentin's hands and sprinted off over a shallow hill and out of sight with the rest of his siblings, save Mark.

I uttered an Etruscan incantation, a curse in a language from a culture dead for centuries. The poison-tipped arrowhead glowed a faint pearly blue at the end, and without hesitation, I stabbed at the crease in my right elbow near where blood was usually drawn. I dragged the sharp edge downward so that the wound was a few inches long. Valentin and Narcisa flinched as the arrowhead pierced my skin. Mark looked away. Strangely, though, Parker stared in fascination.

"Now the fun part," I said, gritting my teeth, I squeezed my arm as tightly as I could, forcing blood out of it. When enough wouldn't come, I opened the wound wider and coated my thick blood on my hands.

In the distance, I heard a sound. The sound of one stone body fighting against the others. I wanted to believe it was the uncontrollable Madeline who the other Winters were having to hold back, but it was probably Everett.

I scraped the blood off of my hands and into Valentin's, and made a paste with the ingredients he was holding. He was understandably revolted. Then Valentin poured the gritty-red substance into my hands. It began to change. It became smooth, ran off my fingers and into my cupped palm. It had become a mysterious silver-clear liquid with the texture and look of mercury, though it felt weightless. It stuck to my skin, but it would easily roll off if pressed.

"I think that means it's working," I said to them. They nodded in agreement.

"Congratulations, kiddo. You're a witch," Mark winked.

"Now what?" Valentin urged.

"First aid first," I said. "Mark? Fix me." I cupped the Fateor elixir and my left hand and jutted my wounded right arm out to him. He inhaled sharply, closing his eyes and twisting his head away at first. After a moment, he regained control, and he put a knuckle behind his front teeth and pressed. Soon, a molten golden liquid trickled down his fingertips. I realized he could milk himself for venom the same way you could milk a snake. He gingerly spread the liquid over the wound. It tingled and felt cool.

But it wasn't enough. The wound was too deep, and the thin layer of venom wasn't covering it. "Damn it, Sadie," Mark growled in frustration. Then he repeated the milking process without even bothering to wipe my blood from his fingers. His eyes burned fiery red, but he remained calm (though not without effort, I am sure). He laid on another layer then lit the venom over the wound on fire. A white-blue flame went out as soon as it had ignited. The pain was as gut-wrenching as you'd expect it to be, but I steeled myself.

Mark inhaled deeply. "Sorry, but they won't be able to smell it this way."

"What about the blood in the elixir?" I asked, swishing the substance around my palm.

"Must be quite the magic potion. Can't smell it at all," he said. He called the others back.

"What the hell is that?" Everett asked, gesturing to the blackened, cauterized wound on my arm.

I didn't answer.

With an edge to his voice, Patrick looked at me and said, "You're walking a thin line here, Sadie."

Through clenched teeth, Everett breathed, "Tap-dancing on it."

"We're ready to reveal." I placed my hands on the invisible barrier, which again lit up with a red glow. With my hands covered in the elixir. I spoke aloud Mark and Ginny's prophecy. I felt exactly the same current as before. "And because of good things that the Heavenly Powers have given in the past, we must be careful not to ignore the shape of things to come."

Immediately, the blank space in the triangle lit up with an indigo-violet symbol, eerily similar to the ones we'd seen in Ephesus:

In moments, the triangle and its symbols disappeared and the faint red glow spread outward until a decaying stone structure about six feet tall and two feet wide appeared.

"That's it?" Everett asked.

There had to be more to it than this. "That can't be it," I whispered. I reached down and wiped the rest of the elixir off my hands on the grass in front of the statue.

"Sadie, look!" Ginny cried, pointing to the pasture beyond us. As if someone had ripped a giant cloak off them, several rows of structures appeared. There were just foundations at first, and then murky outlines, but quickly shacks, houses, adobe squares, tents, even tepees came into view. They were of every size and every shape a house could be, and came from all over the world and from all different time periods. They sat close together, facing a central lane.

We stepped into the clearing, crossing whatever barrier had kept us out before. It was unnaturally silent, and the air was impossibly still. I felt as if we had just walked into another time. Or into a mausoleum.

"Does anyone sense that?" I asked, shaken by the feel of it.

"Sense what?" Everett asked, calmer now. He had stepped up next to me and was holding my hand.

I breathed, "Death."

CHAPTER SIXTEEN

ava bientrut

THE STRUCTURES RANGED IN SIZE FROM A SHODDY LEAN-TO THAT only two people could sleep under to a two-story sage-green-sided modern block townhouse that looked like it had been plucked from in between two other condos, with no one the wiser.

"Do you think we can go in them?" I asked, unsure of the protocol.

"I don't think we should be here at all!" Parker blurted out. We all turned to look at her — I, for one, was surprised she even had an opinion. "I just think…they're not… Why here? What will this tell us?"

"We just spent a lot of time and energy to reveal a hidden city — "

Mark cut me off. "I'd say more a mixed-era neighborhood."

"Fine, hidden neighborhood — and you don't understand why we want to see what's here?" I asked.

"Maybe we shouldn't disturb anything," she added. She was speaking English now, I realized, so everyone could understand her. The cadence of her voice was unnatural and sounded forced. Was it simply that her English was not as good as her Romanian? Though I remembered making a mental note that her Romanian had had a strange accent to it, too.

"I don't think anyone's coming back to them," Everett said, rattled like I was by Parker's strange sentiment. "Let's look."

I stepped forward to the first doorway, a rotted, wood-plank door barely serving as an entrance to an adobe shack.

We'd found the death. Beyond a little table and shoddy chairs and a firepit that acted as a stove, was a fabric and straw palette on the ground. Two dead bodies laid on the aging bed, obviously ancient yet preserved. One appeared to be male, the other female. Their skin looked dried but remained intact. Their eyes were open, milky-grey irises perpetually staring at the rough ceiling above. Thick white cobwebs clung to their bodies as if chaining them to the bed.

We all edged inside the small room. The Winters seemed unfazed by death, but the nosferatu — Narcisa, Valentin, and Sam — were shaken and uncomfortable. Odd because they had once seemed so calm about mortality.

"I smell old blood," Mark said. "Good news for us."

"How's that?" Narcisa said, her nerves wearing thin.

"If there's old blood, that means they were both human and have decomposed, even if they don't appear to have decayed all that much. One of us," he said, gesturing to himself and to his siblings, "could lay still and cover ourselves in cobwebs, and we'd look and feel dead too," he explained. The thought sent shivers down my spine. If these creatures hadn't been entirely *alive* in the first place, like the Winters weren't, how could I know they wouldn't wake? That they weren't a threat?

"I wonder why they haven't decomposed," I said.

"Who knows? Why were they left here inside a shack, hidden by magic — a couple hundred years and a couple thousand miles from wherever it was they began?" Mark asked.

"She's not convinced they're dead," Ginny said, rolling her eyes. She was right. I wasn't.

"They might be listening to every word we say, waiting to attack," I reasoned.

"Let's settle this." Narcisa closed her eyes. "Valentin," she called, tilting her head toward the bodies.

Valentin took a deep breath to overcome his fear, knelt by the bodies, and laid his palm on the man's forehead.

"What's he doing?" Mark asked.

"Reading them," Narcisa said.

"He's a *reader*?" Patrick asked in disbelief. "You couldn't have mentioned that?" he asked, looking at me.

"Is that rare?" I asked.

"About as rare as Ginny's mirroring powers," he said.

"Human. Both of them," Valentin said.

"How certain are you?" Patrick asked.

"Are you asking if I'm a real reader, or just someone like Sadie who can sense supernatural presence?" Valentin asked.

"That's exactly what I'm asking you," Patrick said, his face cold.

"I know the heritage of every individual in this room, if that's what you are wondering. I am sure I'm among the most precise readers you've ever met," Valentin said, his voice and presence strong in the line of Patrick's accusation.

I knew Valentin had a power to this effect. I could tell I had been *read*, per se, when he first shook my hand in Romania. But the kind of reading Patrick and Valentin seemed to be tossing around now? That was a far more significant trait than I'd realized.

Every individual, he'd said. And so what did he think I was? I'd have to ask him at a more appropriate time.

"Sadie, look at this," Everett said. He stepped forward and held out two aging documents he picked up from the small table.

They were in a language I couldn't read. I showed them to the others. "Does anyone recognize this language?" I asked, passing the parchment-like papers around the group. Everyone shrugged.

"What do you think they are?" Everett asked.

"They're important, if they're here," I said. "Take them with us. Let's go to another house."

We went back into the lane. "Which next?" Valentin asked.

"That one," I said, picking the largest and most modern of the homes. On the way, we passed a lean-to and a tepee with the front drawn open. I could see no bodies inside, but there were papers lying on the floor in each. I took them, too.

We walked up the whitewood stairs to the front of the big, new home. I opened the friendly wood-and-glass front door and walked inside. My throat caught when I crossed the threshold. It couldn't be a particularly good omen.

The home was immaculate. There were wood-plank floors covered in thick oriental rugs, a velvet, nail-head couch, and a print wingback leather chair. Art hung from the walls, a flat-screen TV hung above the fireplace, a DVR and video game system attached to it. Then I understood. Kids. They had kids.

I walked backward into the kitchen and found more documents laid out on the kitchen table. These were in French but had a Canadian seal, so I assumed they were from Quebec. The first one I read was a birth certificate from June 7, 1972 for a Jean Paul Gaulet. Beneath it was a Canadian passport, life insurance, a car title, and the loan paperwork from a house. At the bottom there appeared to be a page from public record listing the birth date, sex, city of birth, and parentage of 80 children with sequential birth certificate numbers, the name Jean Paul Gaulet, birthdate 6/7/72 as the 29th on the list. Paper-clipped to it was a copy-machine copy of an identical page containing only 79 names, Jean Paul Gaulet missing from the list.

It was the same for a Merit Winot, married name Merit Gaulet, born November of the same year in Quebec City, Quebec. Similar documents for a Jean Paul born in 1996, a Linore born in 1998, Marion born in 2001, and Christian born only in 2004. They were records of their existence, and doctored records that made it so they never existed at all.

"What are they?" Mark asked, now looking through the same stacks.

Everett, who'd read over my shoulder, said. "It's the record of a family."

"A record that's been erased," I confirmed. I stacked the documents together and handed them to Ginny. We had to explore the rest of the home to see if there were any markers of the fate of this family.

The home looked untouched. Two pots sat on the cold stove, a wooden spoon rotting on a spoon rest next to one of them. A stack of mail sat untouched on a side table by the stairs. Two textbooks with notebooks and open backpacks were strewn across the living room as if two of the children had been doing homework when we walked in the door.

"Keep looking down here," I said to my group. "I'm going upstairs."

I mounted the steps. Everett, Mark, and Valentin came with me, but the rest stayed downstairs. A narrow hallway at the top of the stairs had three doors along one side and one at the end. The first and third doors had brightly colored signs hanging from them. The first was in pink and silver, and read Marion and Linore in curlicue handwriting. My chest ached with fear about what was behind those doors.

"We can look for you," Mark offered, sensing my hesitation.

I shook my head and composed myself. "It will be good for me, hardening to do this," I said. A painful truth considering the circumstances to come.

Two twin beds flanked opposite walls, decorated in matching bedspreads that matched the pink and silver of the sign on the door.

They looked as if they were sleeping. The younger of the two — Linore, I remembered from the birthdates — was so small that her tiny frame was only half the length of the twin bed. She could not have been more than five or six. She was wearing shoes and tiny jeans, which told me that they hadn't been here when it happened but were put here to rest afterward. A tiny worn white stuffed bear was tucked against her body. Someone had put that there, I knew. I shut my eyes trying to forget it, but I knew I would not. It would haunt me.

Marion was older than her sister, but she was still young and still small. A brown stuffed rabbit was tucked under her arm. They both had long straight chocolate-brown hair that was spread out across the pillows. Valentin read them as he had before. I caught Mark caressing their cheeks and closing his eyes as if in prayer.

"Were they human?" I asked. Valentin nodded.

Just as it had been with the two in the adobe flat, there were no obvious wounds or outward cause of death.

I headed out of the room and opened the third door, a black-and-white checkered flag with a Ferrari logo in the corner of it hanging on the door and, as I had expected, a ten- or eleven-year-old boy laid on a red, plastic race car bed. A miniature Ferrari Testarossa perched on his still chest left as the form of comfort.

Both parents were in the last room. The father was still and on his back, but the mother's arms curved as if holding an infant, but her arms were empty. French doors opened into a small nursery to the side where a small toddler was tucked in a crib. I knew he had been pulled from his mother's arms in her final moments. Such tender care was taken with the children, such violent irreverence for the mother. The juxtaposition was unnerving, and it was extremely purposeful. Extremely personal.

Mark, Everett, Valentin, and I said not another word to each other as we descended the stairs.

"What did you find?" Patrick asked.

"The family," I said, and explained no further. "Anything else down here?" I asked.

"Nothing," he said.

"Let's go. More to see," I said stoically.

We found similar scenes over and over again: Papers accompanied by corresponding bodies, or sometimes empty houses with papers. All the bodies had been human, and none of them were very decayed, a sign of supernatural forces at work.

I stood in the lane and spread out all the papers as others brought them to me, trying to understand what had happened. Judging by the variety in shelters, we could assume the victims spanned nearly a thousand years of history, and given that the strange cross from the cave in Ephesus was here, I knew we were in a place relevant to our search.

But I could not make these puzzle pieces fit. Were these humans just unlucky bystanders? Or people who made up the human trail — like Beverly — and knew too much?

I had begun to create a vision of Berkant's monster Survivor in my mind, and I had imagined the blood of all of these people on his hands. Who else would have spanned time in such a way? But I didn't know enough for this to be a logical argument. I was making him up because I wanted someone to blame for this, but the facts had not led me here.

Suddenly there was movement between two old wooden shacks at the end of the row. We all flinched, having sensed it, and before I could even register who or what it was, Patrick and Madeline had launched themselves at the source of the disturbance. There was a crash of stone against stone and then a blood-curdling scream. Patrick fell backward into sight, a mangled mass in his hands.

It was a head.

Bolting down the lane toward him, we saw Madeline straddling a decapitated body.

"Oh my god!" I cried.

"Relax," Patrick said. "It was the *draugr*. He was hiding in here, and I was tired of chasing him," Patrick said. "Polly, can you take care of this?" he asked Mark. Grotesquely, he tossed the head toward Mark the same way you'd toss a set of keys, but before it reached him, Mark flicked his wrist and set the head on fire. Flaming, it landed on the ground and was quickly reduced to a pile of ashes. "Did he have any powers, love?" Patrick asked, hopping to his feet.

"None!" Madeline growled, clearly aggravated that their chase had resulted in nothing.

I must have looked horrified. The Winters, on the other hand, were true to their warrior nature and were entirely untroubled by the scene. I didn't want to think about that.

"Sorry for the distraction," Patrick said, smoothing his clothes and then sliding his hair back out of his face. But he quickly froze. Only his eyes moved, surveying what was around him. "Do you hear that?"

"Are there more *draugar* you need to behead?" I asked, likely rude from my wracked nerves.

"Not *draugar*. Breathing. It's in there," he nodded, indicating the house we stood in front of.

Tired of surprises, I flung open the front door with such force that it ripped off its aged hinges. Then I let out a startled cry. She screamed back.

My confederates stormed the room in moments and surrounded the figure hunched in the middle.

But she just laughed.

"Go ahead and try," she croaked, the wry words razor-edged in regret. She had ashen-brown skin that looked like the bark of an oak tree, and her hair was a coarse, ratty mixture of black and grey pinned back behind her ears. Her voice was smoky — dusty, even. "You'd only do old Ava a favor," she smiled, a sullen smile revealing rotted black teeth. As she cleared what sounded like centuries of grit from her vocal chords and wheezed out her words, I heard that her speech was colored with an accent I couldn't place. Perhaps Creole, or a Caribbean of some kind, though she spoke English clearly. She was also impervious to my mind-reading abilities. I hadn't heard her outside the house, and I couldn't sense her now.

"Back off," I said, calling off the guard. The woman was covered in shawls and sitting in a rocking chair. Aside from speaking, she had been completely still. "You're alive," I breathed.

"Perpetually," she sighed.

"But all the others..."

"Dead," she said knowingly. "Of course they are. He killed them all. He kills everyone he meets. Terrible trait in a person."

"Who?" I asked.

"Now, now," she said. "We're getting ahead of ourselves. First, you tell me who you be."

"I'm Sadie," I said.

"And are you all Survivors?" she asked, her eyebrows high.

"How did you...?"

"Only Survivors can enter our little city," she explained.

"I'm the only one among us," I said.

Ava coughed and sputtered a wheezy laugh and made a cooing sound. "Oh they just keep getting more inventive, your lot! And the rest of you?"

"Patrick and Madeline, there. Ginny, Mark, Everett...Parker, Narcisa, and Valentin. They travel with me," I said, indicating each one. "Now, who are *you*?" I asked.

"I's called Ava Bientrut," she said. She said it *Byee-en-chrut*, which reminded me of the way they spoke in Louisiana. I remembered someone telling me about a Bienville Parish there that they'd pronounced *Byee-en-vull*, and so I would spell it Bientrut when I wrote this down in my notes.

"And why are you here?" I asked.

"Because I cannot go," she whispered. With what looked like great effort, she wiggled her fingers, which I took to mean she could move no more than this.

"Chained," I muttered, thinking of the image I kept in my mind of the chains of immortality. Only her situation was clearly more literal.

"Come now, pull up a chair. I never see people, so I would love to sit like regular folk. Let me pretend I am living a life, not a life sentence," she said.

We did as she said and pulled chairs into a sort of circle around her. Three chairs short, she called, "You…Madeline, was it? And, Samantha — there should be three more upstairs."

The two girls hesitated at the tiny, frail staircase that led to another level of the old home, but ascended as instructed and returned moments later with three more shoddy wooden chairs.

"So where to start?" Ava smiled.

"You said only Survivors could come here. What about the *draugr*?" I asked.

"I suppose there is that exception. If you've been before, you can come again," she said.

"So he had to come with a Survivor?" I asked. "Are there so many of us that people come here often?"

"You, like all the others, think you are unique. He has made it so," she said.

"He?"

"Your creator," she said.

I wasn't sure if she was speaking of an actual person or an ethereal being. "We don't know him," I said.

She cocked her head to the side and eyed me warily at this. "You know not who made you?" she asked.

"As in, a person?" I asked.

Her eyes narrowed further. How I wished to be able to read her mind! "Then maybe you are not who I think you are."

"Who do you think I am?" I asked, but she said nothing.

"We should go," Parker blurted out.

I looked at her and then at Narcisa. *What is her deal?* I asked, indicating Parker.

Narcisa shrugged. *A million little secrets, that one.*

"Ava, tell me about your creator," I urged.

"He's tall," she cackled. I rolled my eyes. "Oh come now, I have to have some fun. I can tell you he's no saint. I've known him for nearly 400 years, and I've only ever known his wrath."

"You know him personally?" I asked.

"It is a fairly personal thing, selling your soul," she voiced wryly.

"Is that what you did? You weren't born a Survivor?" I asked.

"I am *not* a Survivor. I've been kept alive against my will, and against God's. That isn't *surviving.* And, no, I wasn't born this way. If that were so, I could blame the heavens for this. Instead, the fault is only mine, child," Ava lamented.

"How long have you been this way?" I asked.

"318, 319, maybe 320 years?" she guessed. 320 years ago, there had been a witch-hunt in Salem. It could not be a coincidence.

"I want to know where Survivors come from," I told her. "Can you help me?"

"I cannot," she said plainly.

Frustrated and sure she was lying, I asked another question. "I want to know how to kill a Survivor as well. Do you know anything about that?" I asked.

"I do not," she said. I knew she knew more, and I hated to think we had come this far with someone who knew the creature we were searching for without getting any answers. So, rising to my feet, I hovered over her and placed my fingertips on the top of her head. She gritted her teeth and moaned for a moment and then let out a startled cry. I retracted my hand, hating to hurt her, but there was nothing attached to it. I couldn't pull a thought from her mind.

"Stop that," she hissed. "You think he let me keep my *memories*? You think he let me keep my *thoughts*? My punishment is isolation. When he took my freedom, he took everything I could have enjoyed and anything I could have used against him. I'm sorry, Sadie-child."

"But you know that there are more of us?" I asked.

"Nay, child. There's just one," Ava Bientrut breathed, her voice labored now.

"There are a lot of us where I am from," I said.

"Apart from your lot, then," she reasoned. Quietly, she added, mostly to herself, "Just one last, lone Survivor." She stared out in front of her.

"Ava?" I called. "Ava?" I said again, waving my hand in front of her face.

She didn't respond. We sat there for a few moments, unsure of what to do. I finally said, "We should go." I let everyone go before me, and before I left, I followed the line of Ava's stone gaze. Branded into the wall of the aged house, were 24 tally marks in a single row.

"Just one...last...Survivor..." she whispered, her eyes still fixed on the tally marks, her smoky voice fading into nothingness.

CHAPTER SEVENTEEN

cold heart/
warm heart

AFTER OUR STRANGE CONVERSATION WITH AVA BIENTRUT, WE COL-
lected all the documents, counted all the bodies, and left. We
recovered documents for 114 people, and found 96 bodies.
There were 47 houses in the field near Pickering. I didn't
even look through each structure myself. On the train to
London, I took out a red Sharpie from my bag and marked
my right arm below my healing wound — a different color
and a different arm for a different set of crimes. I had made
only six tally marks before Everett took the marker from my
hand and pleadingly said, "Stop."

We decided to go to Heathrow and devise a plan. I, of
course, had already devised a plan for myself. I just hadn't
shared it with them.

When we walked into the airport, I said, "I need to go to
Salem, and I need to do it alone." Everett, Patrick, and Ginny
all opened their mouths to speak, but I held up a hand. "I
know you aren't okay with that, and so I ask that Mark come
with me. It's kind of difficult to travel inconspicuously with
all of us, and Mark can project back to you if he needs to.
This is a fair compromise."

All three frowned, frustrated by my solid logic, I suppose.

"What about us?" Everett asked.

"I think you should go to California for a few days. You could use the warmth," I argued.

"What, like go home to Pacific Grove? Are you kidding? Go back to police tape and an entire city trying to recover from a massacre of 18 people killed on a sleepy street? Yeah…no thanks," he said.

"Fine, then go wherever you want. We can all meet back in the Survivors' City in maybe five days or a week, but, in the meantime, you could use the warm weather," I said.

"That's a long time to be on your own," Everett protested.

I didn't entertain his objection.

"What about us?" Valentin asked.

"We could use you," Patrick interjected. "If you are going to fight with us, there are some things you should know. Perhaps we could use this time to catch you up."

"Certainly," Valentin said. Narcisa agreed.

Parker narrowed her eyes. "I want to go with Sadie."

Again, another remark from her that came out of left field. Pushing a thought outside the bulwark in his mind, Mark hissed, *I don't trust her.*

I didn't either. "Why?" I asked her, my voice clearly displaying my suspicion.

"If the Winters get one of their clan on your protection detail, I want one of ours. I can project, too, like Mark. Two is better than one, right?" she argued.

That sold Everett. "Two *is* better than one," he agreed.

I glared at him. Mark did too, but he didn't back down.

"Fine," I said. I didn't trust her, but if nothing else, maybe this would be the time to figure her out. "It's settled then. Mark, Parker, and I will fly to Boston. Ginny, Everett, Madeline, you'd like what?"

"San Francisco is fine," Ginny nodded.

"Patrick, where am I sending you and our guests?" I asked.

"Calgary," he said. I got in line the first class line at the ticket counter. Thirty minutes and over £5000 a ticket — about $78,000 — later, we had procured nine first-class tickets back across the Atlantic for flights that left within the next three hours.

—◆—

"YOU ARE SUCH A LIAR," MARK WHISPERED IN MY EAR.

"I don't know what you're talking about," I said calmly as we waited at security.

He held up his plane ticket. It read:

DEPARTURE:
28 Apr 13:40 LHR (London)

ARRIVAL:
28 Apr 16:25 JFK (New York)

"Do those letters spell Boston?"

"Of course they do," I said coolly. "I can explain to you how that spells Boston in a about two hours, when everyone else is on a flight back and we still have an hour to kill before our flight — *to Boston.* Okay?"

"You should tell him," he mouthed.

"I realize."

"You're trouble," he breathed in my ear. And he said not another word.

—◆—

WITH SOME TIME TO SPARE, EVERETT AND I SEPARATED FROM THE GROUP AND walked hand in hand down a corridor in our terminal, away from the British Airways lounge where we'd left the others. Our traveling tribe had attracted negative attention in the airport. We didn't exactly look like your typical international traveler. To begin with, we were dirtier.

"So what do you need to do in Salem?" he asked softly. We shuffled into a coffee shop and ordered coffee we wouldn't drink, just to sit and look and feel normal.

"Research, of course," I said. "I need to learn what really happened here. There's more to Ava Bientrut's story. I have to figure out what it is, how it connects."

"If I trust you with anyone, it's my baby brother," he said.

"I figured," I said.

Everett's face was serene. He had a way of just looking at me — silently, contentedly — that communicated his admiration for me. In this instance, when things had been so complicated, I was happy to silently gaze back, submerging myself in the peace that was buried somewhere in our relationship.

So I noticed when he blinked. I could see it when he twitched his head. Closed his eyes. Stopped breathing. Bit his lip.

It didn't take the crimson flecks in his eyes when he reopened them or the gold shimmer on his lips to know that something had just gone wrong.

"Ev?" I asked, watching him try to fight whatever was happening.

He gritted his teeth and exhaled sharply.

"Everett?" I repeated.

He couldn't even answer. He clenched his fists, and pressed them on the table until the wood splintered and then broke under his grip.

"Everett!"

Suddenly, an airport cart with a siren blared outside the café. It was red with white crosses, clearly the airport ambulance.

I needed him to tell me what to do. I needed to know how badly this was about to go. Frantic and unsure what else I could do, I reached forward and placed my fingers against his head and pulled thoughts from his mind. I closed them in my palm then discreetly put them in my own head underneath my hair. I was instantly overwhelmed by the same burning thirst I'd felt in Noah's mind before. Only this made me feel out of control. I could tell from the times I'd actually smelled blood that someone, somewhere was bleeding. Profusely.

I had to act.

"Come on," I said, quickly rising to my feet. I grabbed his wrist. "Now," I said.

He followed. I tried to think quickly on my feet, darting right when the airport ambulance had gone left. I saw a family restroom two gates down, and I walked toward it as fast as I inconspicuously could, never loosening my iron grip on Everett's wrist.

Inside, I locked the door and pushed him against the wall. His breathing had shortened, and every muscle in his body was taut.

"Listen to me," I said sternly.

"I'm sorry, Sadie," he breathed. His face was pained.

"Don't be stupid. Open your eyes, Everett. Look at me," I urged, my hands on his shoulders, my body inadvertently pressed against his, keeping him still.

He bit his lower lip again, the venom thicker now.

"Look at me," I repeated, now planting my hands on either side of his eyes. He finally did as I said.

"Sorry," he whispered again.

"I want you to think about the beach vision. What do you love about it?" I asked.

"Forever with you," he said, his body relaxing a bit. "And warmth. I think lots of warmth."

"Yes. The water's warm. The air is mild. What else?"

"You'd be mine," he exhaled, his face still creased but his breathing slowing.

"What else?"

"We're married in it, right?" he asked, a tiny bit of a smile edging into one corner of his mouth.

"Presumably you're the one who gives me that diamond," I joked, stroking his hair.

"Then I guess by then you'd be *all* mine," he smirked, letting his hand slide down from my neck, down my chest, on my side to my back. I knew what he meant.

"How 21st-century of you," I smiled, staying light if it could keep him light.

"Please," he smirked. "Marriage consummation is not a 21st-century phenomenon."

"Touché," I said. I got him to focus on me for a moment, his eyes fixed again on mine. With my thumbs, I wiped the venom from his lips, and he swallowed hard, probably to get rid of the excess. Very gently, and very carefully, I kissed his lips.

I don't know if it was that we were far enough away from the bleeding, if it had stopped, or if I had actually calmed him down, but I was grateful for the relaxation.

"Thank you, princess," he cooed, his voice velvety and sincere. "Thank you for understanding and taking me, cold heart and all."

"Please, all you put up with from me…well, it's the least I could do," I said. He smiled genuinely, the relief clear on his face. His body relaxed into mine.

—◆—

MARK AND I WERE SEATED NEXT TO EACH OTHER ON THE PLANE. HE WAS FIDGeting with his TV screen, flipping channels absent-mindedly. He groaned audibly when the captain announced we were lucky to be missing the fluke mid-spring blizzard about to hit New England by fly-

ing just south of there into New York. I was disappointed too. Just when
he was breaking free of himself, I was there to drag him back.

En route, I tried to explain to him that going to New York was not
about Cole. Specifically, it was not about going to see Cole without
telling Everett.

The truth was, I needed money. I wasn't going to be out of money
in the next twenty-four hours or anything, but I'd need it soon. It was
expensive enough traveling the way I did, but buying *nine* plane tickets
at over £5000 a piece that day made me realize how my life had gotten,
at the least, nine times more expensive lately. When we got to New
York, it'd be more hotel rooms or a bigger suite that I'd have to get to
fit the three of us. We had gone to Europe with only traveling packs,
so we needed clothing and supplies. This pattern of spending would
just continue, so it was time to arrange the sale of the other red diamond I'd been carrying around with me for three years. I could sign it
over to Christie's, and they could do what they were good at doing.
And then, hopefully before I needed it, I'd have more money.

Mark didn't buy this for several reasons. One, he thought it logisti-
cally impossible for someone like me who owned no home, no
diamonds of her own, had only one car, and flew commercial airlines
everywhere could go through the kind of money I had in just three
years. I asked him if he'd ever met his sister. He was not amused. Then
I reminded him of the not one, but two Land Cruisers he'd purchased
for me, his prized possessions that *I* had invested nearly six figures a
piece in. Then he shut up.

Mainly, though, he believed I felt a need to fix things with Cole, a
point I wanted to argue, but it was true.

I thought there would be a way to fix things without further thick-
ening the mess I was already in with Cole and jeopardizing Everett's
trust in me. But that is why I needed to go to Manhattan now. If not

now, then when? If I couldn't fix things with him now, then when would another opportunity arise?

Mark vehemently disagreed, but he didn't try to stop me. He knew better. I had to love him for that. A good brother — a good ally — he was turning out to be.

When we arrived in Manhattan, I asked Mark to help Parker understand why we needed to not tell the others where we were. I wasn't sure if she would play along. After all, what loyalty did she have to us?

I'd found a suite big enough for the three of us at the Soho Grand on short notice with the help of a Centurion American Express concierge who had worked wonders for me on more than one occasion when I found myself stranded somewhere on the globe. The next morning, I took all three of us to Bergdorf to buy new clothes since I'd made a particularly useful relationship with a stylist there. For nearly three years, she'd helped me procure things I was looking for that usually never even made it to the racks, so clothing the three of us in a few new outfits seemed like an easy task by comparison. After picking out a particularly tailored Proenza Schouler black and mustard gold blazer and skirt ensemble to wear out of the store, I stuffed the tattered and filthy clothes we'd been wearing for over a month in a laundry cart in our hotel and playfully imagined the maid who would end up finding a several-thousand-dollar outfit simply in need of a good washing in the trash.

Midday, I put in a call to my contact at Christie's, and by late afternoon, I sat at the bar in the hotel with Parker and Mark, working up the nerve to call Cole. Biding time, I watched in amazement as Parker downed four martinis and Mark grew evermore charming. I hadn't thought about the nosferatu being susceptible to alcohol, but of course, they would be. After all, all you needed to get drunk was a metabolism.

I imagined this is how it went for Mark before he met me and when he could get time away from Anthony's acquisition trips. Find some girl — presumably not a human, but apparently not just a *vieczy* — wine and dine her. Flirt. Flash that Winter smile. Be brazen. Be…hot.

And maybe this is how it went for most girls. Sit at a barstool with a Mark-Winter-type leaning in toward you, flip your hair and laugh, put your hand on the chest of his motorcycle jacket, get drunk, and get easier and easier to woo. He was all over her, and she was.eating it up.

But I'd never been like most girls — and not just because I was physically incapable of drunkenness.

Unable to watch this courting ritual any longer, I ducked out and went back up to the room, braced myself, and called Cole.

It rang four times, each ring reverberating in my skull and putting further pressure on my head and chest.

He didn't answer.

This was unsurprising, sure. I left him — three for three of the times I'd ever seen him — but this time with a more open wound, my then jerk-off of a boyfriend pulling me away from him, proclaiming that I was *his*. God, just remembering that made me so mad at Everett. Those moments — his worst — were a source of doubt that would cloud our relationship forever.

So of course Cole wouldn't answer the phone. He had a quiet life, and what did I do but disrupt that quiet and mess with his head? *Just get your head around it, Sadie. You're never going to hear from Cole Hardwick again.*

Then the phone rang. It was Cole. Wow, I was fantastic at letting my thinking spiral out of control incredibly quickly.

"Does your boyfriend know you're calling me?" he asked, without even a hello. Not even his abruptness could pluck the casual Southern charm from his voice.

"It's nice to talk to you, too," I said.

"Ah, Sadie. How I've missed you. Or is it that I've missed how you manage to evade every question I ask?" he asked. But his tone was surprisingly light. I sensed this might be as mad as you could make Cole. Mad enough that you knew it, but not so much that it made him any less…Cole.

"I've missed you," I said. "I owe you an apology. And an explanation."

"Do you ever get tired of apologizing?" he asked.

"Depends," I said. "Do you ever get tired of needing an apology?"

"All the time," he cooed.

There came a natural silence. I wondered if all this awkwardness was just a sign that I should stop trying.

"I'm in New York," I said.

"Who didn't see *that* coming?" was his retort.

"I understand if you don't want to see me," I added. In my mind, the offer sounded compassionate. Out loud…not so much.

"But you know I will. It's who I am," he sighed. *Why am I not ready to give up on you yet?* he asked himself. *Ah, yes. Because it was love at first sight.* Mind-reading through the phone was always interesting. It was very difficult to tell when someone said something and when he thought it. I judged that last part he'd only thought and not said.

"You really don't have to. I don't want to put you through anything…" I trailed. Painful? Awkward? Invasive? I wondered which was the right word to use. "…unnecessary," I decided on saying.

"How long are you in town for?" he asked.

"Until the fifth," I blurted out without even thinking. What day was it now? We should actually be in New York for at most another day before heading to Salem. I'm not sure what I was thinking by saying this. Did I just lie because I could now?

"And are you alone?" he asked, assuming I was not.

"I'm with Mark. You remember Mark?" I asked.

"How could I forget Everett's brother?" he asked in reply. Got it. Point taken.

"Well I'm here with him and our friend Parker," I added.

"Parker? How many poor fools like me are you toting around this planet?" he asked, mistakenly assuming that Parker was a guy. This was the first thing I'd said that had actually angered him. Probably because I was only a mile away from him, I could see in his head that he wondered how many other men I dropped in on in cities all over the world, toying with their hearts, until Everett pulled me back. It was, hands-down, the least flattering version of me that anyone had ever falsely assumed. I hated it.

"Parker is Samantha Parker. She's a family friend," I explained. Awkwardly, I'm sure, I said, "I am only dating one person. And the only city I come to repeatedly to see someone in is New York."

Judging by how long it took Cole to stumble over halves of words before he responded with the kind of thing that you only had to say because someone else said something that didn't make sense first, I knew I had said something terribly off. Awkward. I was so, so awkward.

"If you do want to see me, when are you free?" I finally asked.

He laughed a little. "What are you doing right this second?"

———◆———

HE MET US IN THE HOTEL BAR. HE ORDERED A BOURBON FOR HIMSELF AND SPUN it around the glass for a few minutes before he said much.

Parker, now drunk, provoked him. "You're awfully quiet, Blue Eyes."

"You're awfully sloshed," he sighed. "And my name, though you may not remember from five minutes ago, is Cole."

Parker giggled. "I remember. But they're *so* blue."

Now I laughed and elbowed Mark. "Some effect you have on women."

"She's easily distracted," he glared.

"So what are you kids doing here without the rest of your family?" Cole asked Mark and me. "I thought your boy didn't like you being out of his sight."

"Her boy," Mark said stiffly, "sent me as her chaperone. We'll be back with the rest of them soon enough."

Cole took a long sip of his drink and considered how much more this angered him.

In the stiff silence, Mark tried for another conversation topic. "So, Cole. How's good ol' Tennessee?" Mark asked him.

"Wouldn't know. I can't think of the last time I've been," he said.

"Christmas?" I asked.

"I didn't go home for Christmas," he admitted. This surprised me. Avoiding his family at a holiday seemed like a fraying edge in a tapestry I'd woven in my mind of Cole's perfect Southern gentleman, perfect *human* image.

"Everything…okay?" I asked.

"Oh yeah. Just too much work to do. Family offered to come here, but they're afraid of the city, and they wouldn't let me pay for their plane tickets if they came and…" he trailed. "It's complicated." This fit better. I understood that in his line of work, extreme hours and limited time off came with the territory. I also understood his family in small-town Henderson, Tennessee, probably didn't have the money to fly them-selves up here or to do a lot of the things Cole did. He, of course, tried to take care of them. Tried to pay for things. Tried to help them. But for reasons too personal for me to understand, they refused this aid.

"So what have you been up to?" I asked.

"Not much, to tell the truth," he said, gazing into the bottom of his glass. I thought of every song lyric I'd ever heard about seeking answers in the bottom of a glass or a bottle, and watching him I understood what that meant. "What about y'all?"

Where to start? Chasing a ghost, cave arts and ruins, interrogating terrified humans, having a complete breakdown on the floor of a church 5,000 miles from where I sat now, discovering dead bodies in hidden cities, training for a war... That's what I'd been doing. "We were traveling," I said.

"Per the usual. Go any place interesting?"

"I went to Ephesus in Turkey and Densus Church in Romania," I said.

He perked up at this. "Weirdly, I've always wanted to go there," Cole said. I smiled, sipping a hot tea I'd ordered. "Very interesting. And where's the rest of the clan now?" he asked.

Mark answered. "My brothers, sister, sister-in-law, and parents flew back to California. We'll meet up with them soon. Sadie had a few things to do in New York and Boston, and we thought we'd keep her company," he said, wrapping his arm around Parker's shoulder and bringing her in close to him. That was close enough to the truth, I thought.

"I see," Cole said, his eyes suspicious. So unaccustomed to receiving answers from me, Cole wondered if we were lying.

"And Boston is next?" he asked me. I nodded. "What's there?"

"Genealogical research," I smiled. Also close enough to the truth, I thought. I liked this. I liked that we were telling him things that weren't incriminating. It was warming him up by the second.

"Weird, but okay," he shrugged.

This whole time, Parker had been staring at Cole in a really odd way, something all three of us noticed and were trying to ignore for very different reasons. But suddenly, her eyes refocused, she shook her head and quickly — too quickly — she stood up.

We stared at her in confusion.

"I have to go," she said abruptly, and before we could ask any questions, she was headed for the lobby.

"You think she's okay?" Cole asked.

"Going to find out," Mark said, on his feet and behind her now. The way we were sitting, Cole was facing me and the rest of the bar, while I was facing the open doorway of the bar and into the lobby. I watched Parker get into an elevator and Mark catch it just in time to get in as well. A second later, Parker got out of it and headed for the streets of Manhattan, Mark on her heels. I caught Mark's eye. *You stay,* he said — pushing words outside his mental barrier the same way Everett did — and so I did.

"It's pretty unfortunate that you didn't get to go home," I said.

"I told you the day I met you that the city is wearing on me," he said. "I love the life I've made for myself. I'm proud of my accomplishments. But what am I doing here? So far from anyone I love."

"You want to go back?" I asked.

"It's not that. I just hate that I have to compromise. Success or my family. Freedom or my job," I explained.

Freedom. My word. "Do you ever feel trapped?" I asked.

"Every day," he said coolly. I related.

I pulled a move from his book. I leaned in very close to his face, and without even blinking, I whispered, "Tell me, Cole, what do you want most out of life?"

You, he thought. But he gazed back, those sapphire-shine eyes penetrating me and breathed, "Mortality."

"Touché," I laughed. "Seems like I don't have the monopoly on evasion."

He shrugged, happily. "You think this Everett guy is the one for you?"

"Only time will tell," I said. I realized, three tenths of a second too late that, I should have said 'Yes' in this instance, even if it were completely false. (It wasn't *completely* false.)

Cole smiled mischievously at this, cocked his pretty-boy head to the side, and eased, "Then it's a good thing I have all the time in the world."

My phone lit up. EVERETT WINTER in big writing popped up on the screen. Fourth time that night — but first time it had been in Cole's line of sight. "Man, he's got good timing."

I ignored the call and texted him back: *With Mark & Parker. Place is loud. Call later?*

"I realize what I should have asked," Cole said, his mood having dipped a bit. "I should have asked if he thinks he's the one for you."

"Unequivocally," I said, finishing the text.

It lit up again. From Everett: *I just talked to Mark.* Damn. Caught. I texted back, stalling: *What did he say?*

"So where's the discrepancy? Why does he think one thing and you think another?" Cole asked.

"He believes in destiny. Takes things as a given. Takes me as a given," I said, surprised to hear myself say the words out loud when I'd known all along that that's what I thought.

"And that bothers you," he said.

"Wouldn't it bother you?" I asked.

"Of course it would. I mean, it does bother me. That's the problem I have with him, Sadie. It's not a territory issue or even straight-up jealousy. I hate that he stormed into my place the way he did. I hate that he feels like he owns you. Maybe I just hate him," he said. Those were strong words for Cole.

"He's not all bad," I said, suddenly defensive.

"He was just so angry. It was terrifying," Cole argued.

"He's not always angry," I said, not answering an unasked question.

"Ah," he said, nodding. "Bark is worse than his bite, eh?"

I smiled in spite of myself. "I wouldn't exactly put it that way," I said. Cole raised an eyebrow at me, and I shook my head. "He's just careful with me. He worries about me," I said.

"Yeah, I can see it all over his face that he feels it's his job to protect you," Cole said with a snarl, his hostility evident.

"And it is, in a way," I argued. I didn't want to say all bad things about Everett. I loved him. I *hoped* it would work out the way it was supposed to. He was still mine, cold heart and all. Sitting twelve inches from Cole's warm heart didn't change that. "Look, I'm reckless. You get that, right? You can see it? It's what's driving you insane about me.

I travel all the time, and I take off doing weird things, and I often don't tell people where I'm going. It's a personality trait. It's possibly even a flaw. If your life was less boxed in, if you weren't tied down by a job or a regular life, and I was your girl? Well, wouldn't you go chasing after me? Especially if you heard I was doing dangerous things? Especially if I had a track record of getting hurt in the past?" I asked.

"Do you have that track record?" he asked.

"Like you wouldn't believe," I said. Phone buzzed. *Says he's looking for Parker.* I texted back: *He can't find her? They just walked out of this bar together. Mark told me to stay right here and he'd be back. I figured they were just making out somewhere.*

He narrowed his eyes as at me as I texted, pausing before he admitted, "I can't say what I'd do. But I can't think that I'd do anything you didn't want me to."

"Don't say that," I said.

"Don't say what?"

"Don't make promises you can't keep. You have no way of knowing how you'd act if we were together," I said.

"I know I'd treat you with respect," he said firmly.

"Everett treats me with respect," I said. "But he has to deal with a lot, and so do I. A lot of wild cards you know nothing about. So don't sit here and say what you want is to be with me and promise me that you would do better. You don't know that. You don't even know that you would do it differently," I said.

"I didn't say I wanted to be with you," he wagered.

"You didn't have to," I countered.

"Then tell me about the wild cards. Answer the questions I've been asking you since the day I met you," he pleaded.

Phone buzzed again. *I'm sure he's got it under control. And making out? I'll have to hear that story later. Are you alone?* Everett asked. I texted back: *I'm talking to Cole,* I admitted. *He met up with me and Mark. We weren't alone on purpose.*

In Cole's mind, he said, *Can you not just put the phone down long enough to talk to me?*

I set down the phone, knowing that that admission to Everett might blow up in my face. "I can't tell you, Cole. Telling you is dragging you in, asking you to hurt more," I said.

"You don't know how I'd react," he said, throwing my own argument back at me.

For possibly the first time, he was frustrating me. I'd been able to fantasize about a human relationship with him all this time, but I kept my mind from going too far and my mouth from saying too much. Cole had not been returning the favor, and I'd coped with that. Cole's patience with me was running out. Like so many do, he thought he could wait for what he wanted; he'd said so only moments before. But waiting is a funny game, one where your world is taken over by the absence of a thing. In waiting for something, you are consumed by a perpetual nothing.

Phone buzzed. Everett's text: *It's okay, princess. I trust you.*

I exhaled deeply. Cole was right. Everett had excellent timing.

"Why did you even come here?" Cole asked, his voice bitter.

I didn't like where this was headed. "I wanted to be your friend. To make things right between us. Apologize for the last time." He didn't respond, so I continued. "I hoped we could find a way to be in each other's lives," I explained.

"Be my friend like you've been Corrina's? I hear I don't have the monopoly on being walked out on, either," he said, that edge still in his tone.

"That's a low blow," I said, building a wall between us, sealing myself off from being affected. Corrina was my most tender of Achilles heels, which he undoubtedly knew. If he was going to play dirty, I was going to play icy. "But it's only one of a million things you don't know the whole story on, so you don't have a right to judge."

"Fine. Here's what I do have a right to judge. I don't think he's right for you," he said.

I rolled my eyes. "In what world do you have a right to judge that?"

"I'm serious, Sadie. I know what you want. I knew it from Corrina and Felix. I saw it at the wedding. I feel it when you come here to me. You come here because you want something different. You want what I can give you," he said.

"And what is that exactly, Cole?"

"You want to sit still," he said.

"You know nothing."

"Come on, you've got to be tired of this running. You have got to want a life. Everyone, no matter how adventurous, wants it at some point or another. This could be your point," he argued. He was alienating me further.

"Don't do this," I pleaded.

"Pick me, Sadie," he said, his eyes deep, sincere.

"Cole..."

"I'm serious. I'll give you what you want. Anything you want. But you have to pick me to get it."

"You can't say that! Don't make promises you can't keep!" I said.

"I know plenty. Pick me."

Now I was getting callous. I may say something stupid in 3...2...1... "Are you giving me an ultimatum?"

He raised his eyebrows. *Good idea*, he thought. "Yes," he said plainly. "Me or him. Now or never. Be with me, or don't. Let me love you, or stop doing this. Stop coming into my life in shambles without letting me pick up the pieces."

"I don't need anyone to pick up my pieces," I said.

"That's a lie."

It was silent. Another text from Everett: *Sadie?*

"Come lay your head on my chest. I'll show you what normal is like," he said.

Tempting.

"You know, you setting terms like that isn't any better than Everett doing…whatever he does," I argued.

"I'm not him," Cole shrugged. "I'm better than he is."

"I can't believe you," I said. I texted Everett back: *I love you. I'll call soon.* My heart was closed off and about as cold as that boy of mine's back in California.

"Could you put down the damn phone and look at me? He gets you every other night of the year. Can I have your attention tonight?" he said.

Cole was a mixed up mess. He doubted himself. He felt angry toward me. He loved me so much it suffocated him. He was proud of himself for putting his foot down, and frustrated with himself for having lost patience and done this. He feared it was too soon.

He took the last sip in his glass. "Let's just stop this. Let me love you, or leave."

Now who was being callous?

Frustrated, and a lot less in love with the idea of Cole Hardwick, I said, "You've made that an easy choice." I rose to my feet, grabbed my bag, kissed him on the cheek, and left without a word.

CHAPTER EIGHTEEN

the salem
witch trials

IT TOOK TWO DAYS TO TRACK DOWN MY CONTACT AT CHRISTIE'S TO arrange the sale of the diamond, and in that time, I started reading into the sordid history of Salem, Massachusetts.

It was more than a little odd, I realized, that I had never done this before. I knew little about Salem and the witch-hunt that sent my ancestors into exile. Perhaps I couldn't bring myself to hear the real story. Maybe I was afraid. Maybe I hadn't cared until now.

I was so shocked to learn the real story of witch hunts throughout history that I barely got past that before we arrived in Salem. I found that witch-hunts in Europe pre-dated those in Salem by nearly 1,500 years. In 367 AD, the Roman Emperor, Valerian, declared witch hunts fair game. Later, in the 12th century, accusations, convictions, and executions happened frequently — and off the record — across Europe. But in 1231, Pope Gregory IX had ordered an inquisition into the practices of witchcraft, and by 1484, Pope Innocent VIII declared that the practice of witchcraft was punishable by death, taking many of those off-the-record pursuits into the public — and legal — arenas. From that point on, it seemed like any kind of witch hunt was acceptable. A book called the *Malleus Malificarum*, known as the Hammer of Witches, was published in 1486, and it gave detailed instructions on how to locate, identify, and persecute witches. I read in more than one place that it has been estimated that millions of people were executed across Europe in witch hysteria.

But in Massachusetts, it all happened in 1692, and 19 people were convicted and hanged — not burned at the stake like so many believed — though countless more were accused and others died in other ways. Some documentaries I watched said 200, some 500, other sources claimed 150 were accused in all. Whatever number they cited, I didn't believe it anyway. There was, after all, no record of the twenty-six souls who I knew to be accused, imprisoned, and then exiled. There was no record of the fourteen who survived. And in the public record, there was no record of the deaths of the nineteen who were hanged. For all the records there seemed to be, there were numerous holes. Sources of doubt. Places where whole parts of the story — like the twenty-six accused children who were exiled and never tried, much less convicted — were missing.

The one question history had never had been able to answer was, Why Salem? Why 1692? I knew that the hysteria over witchcraft happened in Salem in 1692 because there had been some matter of witches in the village — the people I knew as our Survivor elders. I felt guilty that so many innocent people died when so many of my own guilty ancestors survived.

Mark, Parker, and I boarded a train to Boston a few mornings later. My two traveling companions had been growing increasingly affectionate, but Mark was still on edge after he lost Parker in the city. I had returned to our hotel suite after leaving Cole, and Mark came back without her an hour later. We spent the rest of the night tracking her, at first remotely from the hotel, and later that night, traversing the city on foot looking for her. At dawn, we found her standing outside the

Ferragamo store at 52nd and 5th Avenue, staring at the window displays. She greeted us cheerfully but never offered a word about where she'd been. Two trackers on a twelve-mile island, and we couldn't locate one warm-blooded, unprotected girl. It was odd.

From Boston, we went immediately to Salem. I headed straight for the Visitor Center in the middle of town.

"All the hype about you being this experienced global researcher, and your strategy includes starting at a visitor center?" Mark quipped.

"Never underestimate looking for answers in the most obvious places," I said.

Towns in New England looked so drastically different from other places I'd spent time in within the states. The streets and buildings were so much older, for one. And everything was so close together, tightly and conveniently packed within even a regular person's definition of walking distance. But they had a quality I couldn't quite place that set them apart from the towns and cities in the South, on the West Coast, and especially those in the Northwest.

"What are we looking for, exactly?" Parker asked.

"We're not exactly sure," I said. "That's kind of how it works with me. I'll know it when I see it."

Parker rolled her eyes and scoffed audibly, actions indicative of her personality as a whole. She seemed quite like an annoyed Mean-Girl type all the time. Except of course when Mark ran that hand through his hair and called her Sugar — then the ice queen melted. But right now, as she trudged in her boots I'd bought along the freezing pavement of Salem, she was frustrated that following me meant doing everything on my terms. This, of course, made me wonder why she'd come in the first place.

We passed a number of little shops or storefronts that advertised palm reading or divination, witch supplies, and haunted tours. Many of them felt touristy, but others felt like they believed in their craft. An odd amalgamation of the history, persecution, study, and practice of witchcraft dotted the lanes of Salem, Massachusetts.

Inside the Visitor Center, there was a large model of a ship, and mostly pictures and displays relating to maritime history. "Ships not witches?" I asked, mostly to myself.

"Um, Sadie?" Mark said, a few yards from where I stood. He pointed to a sign on a display that read, in bold letters:

TRIALS 1692

I walked toward him.

There was a sign below it that read:

HOW MANY WITCHES WERE EXECUTED IN SALEM DURING THE TRIALS IN 1692?

This angered me. It was widely and rightfully believed that those who died in the witch trials, as well as those who were accused, were innocent humans. But here, in a building owned by the state of Massachusetts, they referred to them as *witches*. I walked away without even opening the flap to see the answer.

In the center of the display was a large map of the region in 1692, with different townships highlighted in different colors. On either side of the large map were corresponding lists of the names of accused witches who had been executed from each town.

I couldn't stand to see it written this way. Those nineteen hanged, one pressed, and four dead in prison — those *lives* — commemorated for all eternity, grimly immortalized, on goddamn color-coded note cards.

I can't say why it bothered me the way it did. Is this what we would mean to the world, if discovered? Is this how my elders would have been immortalized if they'd stayed? It might be distant history to the other people milling in and out of the Visitor Center a decade into a different millennium, but to me, it was significant. These could have been my family members.

"Are you okay?" Mark asked, finally removing his Ray-Bans. His eyes were very red, and he looked exhausted. I owed him one for dragging him here through this cold.

"Fine," I murmured. "Let's get a map and get going."

"I'll do you one better," he said. He handed me a dozen pamphlets and brochures for all the museums and historical sites in town relating to the witch trials. One read "Witch House," and another read "Witch Dungeon Museum." Yet another was emblazoned with a quote from one of the executed, Rebecca Nurse: "Oh God help me, I am an innocent person." There were more for the Salem Witch Museum and the Witch History Museum and the like. "Where to?"

"This one," I said, pulling the Witch House brochure to the top. The picture on the front looked eerily familiar. I had to see it in person.

Mark put his sunglasses back on, took the stack of brochures from my hand, and gestured, "Lead the way."

—◈—

PARKER HAD DISAPPEARED AGAIN BY THE TIME MARK AND I HEADED TOWARD the Witch House. I decided this must just be a part of her M.O. Once is a fluke. Twice is a pattern.

The Witch House was a two-story home built in the mid 17th century. It belonged to Jonathan Corwin, a magistrate who had presided over many of the interviews in the witch trials. In the world of black-and-white lines, of good guys and bad guys, that made Corwin a bad guy.

His home was perfectly preserved. We entered through a small doorway in the back of the house where we both had to duck to keep from hitting the doorframe. We paid our admission, then ambled through the wood-paneled, low-roofed rooms of the home.

The front door was blocked off and not used as a working doorway, but I went to it to see the vantage point of one entering the home so long ago. There was a rickety, uneven staircase in the center of the foyer. To the left, a room with a long dining table in it. To the right, there was a larger room with a variety of furniture in it. I stepped to the doorway of this room and looked at the chairs and another table, a loom and other small tables, a large fireplace, and the other household items that cluttered the space, and I knew I'd seen it before.

The house where we found Ava Bientrut.

From the moment she told me how long she'd been imprisoned, I knew that she had some tie to Salem. Standing in the room of Corwin's house, I also knew that the home we'd met her in was one exactly like this, unequivocally from the same era and region.

"Doesn't this look like…" Mark trailed.

"Yes," I said, knowing he saw what I saw.

"Like, strangely so," he reiterated.

I took in the details of the space around me, the finish on the walls, the worn patterns on the stones inside the large fireplace, even the beams on the ceilings. And there, on the aging wood plank ceiling, carved into a beam, were tally marks just like the ones Ava Bientrut stared at.

Mark watched me as I closely examined them from below. "Got something?" he asked.

"Nothing," I said, shaking my head.

In the gift shop, they had tons of reproductions of primary source documents for sale, a real rarity in the kind of research I did. I bought every one they had. Timelines. Arrest warrants from 1692 carrying Corwin's and John Hathorne's signature. The piecemeal transcripts from trials or interrogations that had been recovered. Narratives and first-hand accounts of the events from that time that you could find published nowhere else. A copy of the infamous *Malleus Malificarum* and the 17th century's *Enquiry into the Nature of Modern Witchcraft*, another piece I'd seen referenced in documentaries and the like. Much like the *Malleus Malificarum*, there were countless pages of how to identify, accuse, torture, convict, and kill alleged witches.

We next visited the Witch Dungeon Museum, whose ominous name filled me with dread. Instead of it looking like a regular museum, we first stood in a small room with a cash register, a girl about my human age behind it, and behind her, a wall plastered with headshots of actors. The images didn't fit.

"Welcome to the Witch Dungeon Museum. Two adults?" the bubbly blonde asked. She was dressed in period clothing, presumably remakes of what a girl her age might wear in the Puritan era.

"Uh…yeah," I said, sizing her — and the wall of headshots — up as I put my credit card on the counter.

"Great. Next show starts in fifteen minutes," she smiled, her voice so awkwardly syrupy for being someone behind the counter at a place called the Witch Dungeon Museum. Mark and I exchanged glances. *Show?* I mouthed. Mark shrugged. "You can look around our gift shop while you wait," she said and pointed us to the only other doorway out of the room.

We were the only two visitors here. Inside the small gift shop, I began to look for the same things I'd found at the Witch House. Here, though, there were far more touristy items, including a black silhouette of a witch (I use the term loosely) wearing a pointy hat and riding a broomstick, emblazoned on a bright orange flag. Upon closer surveillance, I found an entire Halloween section.

I felt bad that we'd have to wait fifteen minutes. I could tell Mark was already bored with following me.

I pulled a few books from the shelves: *A Guide to the Salem Witchcraft Hysteria of 1692*, adorned with a strange headstone from 1696 on the cover, and *The Devil in Massachusetts*. I was most interested to find a Witch's Almanac, filled with spells, incantations, rituals, and stories of good and evil. I pulled Lizzie's old notebook from my bag, and flipped through the two, side by side. They were filled with much the same things.

Above the bookshelves, there were decorative pieces of art. I saw a recurring theme in some of the sculptures, mirrors, and hanging ornaments in which a crescent moon lay on top of a bright sun. Unsure of what they were or signified, I grabbed a small, wood-carved version and added it to my stack.

As other people filed into the waiting area, Mark came over to check on me. "Finding anything useful?" he asked, flipping the pages of the books I'd stacked together and fingering the wood grain of the small ornament.

"Lots to look up," I said. I turned around and saw him pulling a plastic tube from a basket labeled "Magic Wands." The tube was filled with glitter and sequins shaped like stars, suspended in water. "What are you?"

"*Avada Kedavra,*" he hissed, pointing it at a statue of a black bird, a fierce stare on his stone face. Nothing happened. Pouting, he whined, "Hey, it doesn't work!"

"Was that the killing curse from *Harry Potter*? Really, Mark? Man, what if it *had* worked?" I joked.

"That raven looked like it needed killing," he joked.

A raven. *Raven.* Weird. I made a mental note and moved on.

"We're opening the doors!" our period-era actress cried, popping her head in from what looked like a theatre. "Did you want to buy those?"

I nodded, and put what had become a large stack down on the counter, Mark slid the purple and gold-glitter plastic magic wand on the top. I looked up at him incredulously. He smiled sheepishly.

⊷◆⊶

THE REENACTMENT DIDN'T TEACH ME ANYTHING I HADN'T ALREADY KNOWN, other than helping me understand what they meant by "spectral evidence." As our cashier — now turned re-enactor — was crying and screaming as if possessed by the astral projection of a supposed witch torturing her, I began to understand the hysteria effect. Mark had to put both hands over his mouth to stifle his laughter. I suppose he couldn't take any of it seriously, able to do all the things they had accused people of doing back then — astrally projecting, torturing people without touching them — himself.

But the dungeon was another story. After the show, they walked us downstairs into a claustrophobic stone space. It wasn't the original dungeon — that had been destroyed half a century before — but the recreated one gave a good feel of it. It was pitch-black inside, the stone walls cold. Mannequins were in chains inside prison cells so small that people wouldn't have been able to sit down. We listened as the tour guide explained how, at the height of the witch trials, there would have been up to 150 people stored in this hallway not twenty feet long and narrower than ten feet across. There was no light, no air circulation, no plumbing. People were chained inside cells and, in the open space, chained to the walls, with raw sewage and rats rising to their knees as the freezing Salem river overflowed into the underground space in times of heavy rain.

I couldn't imagine it. There were about fifteen other people on our tour inside the hallway, and it was closer than I liked to be to people, and claustrophobic enough that Mark had begun clenching and unclenching his fists because the scent had gotten too concentrated. I imagined the fourteen original Survivors here, chained, imprisoned in these conditions when they were just kids, and I could barely stand to think of them this way. Some of the prisoners had stayed here for months on end — years even, if they couldn't pay their court costs. My elders spent only a week in these conditions, but I was nauseated after five minutes, even with light, without the stench, and only a fraction of the people.

"Let's go," I said to Mark. It had become too much to bear.

He stepped in front of me, and pushed back against the small group, cutting a clear path for me to get around them and back to the entrance. As we got there, we heard the tour guide explain that the only artifact that was original to the actual dungeons was a the large ceiling beam overhead. "Supposedly, if you touch it, you'll get good luck," she explained. Mark touched it as we passed beneath it. I reached for it as he had, and crimson red sparks flew between the old wood beam and me. Mark saw it. I saw it. With bulging eyes, our bubbly blonde tour guide saw it.

"Our exit cue," Mark breathed, grabbing my arm, and taking the stairs back up two at a time.

———◄◆►———

I OFFERED TO TAKE A BREAK. ENTHUSIASTICALLY, MARK CHOSE A PAN-ASIAN restaurant off the square to sit in. I ordered tea. He ordered six vegetarian dishes, each entirely green.

"Tired of the sunglasses, eh?" I asked, neck-deep in my stack of books.

"I can't get away with it here like I can in California," he sighed. "There they think you're a hotshot. Here, they think you're…"

"Weird?" I offered.

He scrunched up his face. I forgot — Mark hated being anything but utterly, painfully *cool*.

"Feel like you're learning anything?" he asked as his food arrived about fifteen minutes later.

"Oh, I'm learning," I nodded, pushing through my fourth book since we sat down. I had to slow down to read the *Malleus Malificarum*, which I had purchased in its original Latin. A poor choice.

"Anything fun?" he asked, inhaling his seaweed salad in two bites. It was interesting watching him navigate chopsticks. He had to be so careful not to break them into splinters.

"Oh yeah," I joked. "My favorite so far in this one? 'If she be a witch, she will not be able to weep,' they suggest."

"So? You can't cry," Mark shrugged. I thought it interesting that he had noticed this.

"Yeah, but the other Survivors can. Well, the rogue bunch excluded," I said. "Not to mention, so can your mom, so…wrong on that account. Says a witch can't say the Lord's Prayer, either."

"Wrong on that account as well," he nodded. "Any mention of your ancestors in there?" he asked.

"Doesn't seem to be," I said, which was true. "But there are a few weird things. Like here's this letter from Governor Phips, the governor at the time, to the king of England. He's begging King Philip to offer him a solution, tell him what to do with the accused witches. He doesn't think they should kill them because the evidence is too circumspect, but he doesn't think they should ignore the accusations either. He's asking for a compromise."

"Like exiling twenty-six kids instead of killing them," he suggested.

"Yeah, exactly. Not to mention, the Survivors didn't get tried. They were accused and exiled. That was it. And that was supposedly December 1692, which makes sense now because the court that did the most of the trying in that year — the Court of Oyer and Terminer — was absolved by Phips in October," I said, showing him to a large timeline I'd bought at the Witch House. "The next entry on the timeline is December 29th when Phips instituted a day of fasting and prayer, as if asking forgiveness for what they'd done."

"Like, say, exiling and leaving twenty-six kids who were accused as witches to die, after executing 19 or 20 and imprisoning hundreds of people that year?" Mark suggested.

"Exactly," I nodded.

"What else?" he asked.

"Not much else that could help me piece in the Survivors' story, but there's a lot of talk of the devil or the Man in Black or what have you. The devil's book. The devil's mark. Oh, and predestination."

"Predestination, as in your soul is destined for heaven or hell before you're even born? Well, that's not *as* weird," he argued, diving into his plate of garlicky broccoli.

"You *would* say that," I said, rolling my eyes as I muddled through the Latin. "You believe in Anthony, so you believe in fate."

He cleared this throat, a gesture meant to be dramatic. "I was going to say I thought it wasn't as weird because people still believe it today," he said. "Doesn't mean I agree with it."

"Mark, if you don't believe in fate and predestination, then you don't believe in your father's power," I argued.

"I don't think they're the same, Sadie," he said. "I don't think you were destined to leave your family and start up this whole mess before you were born."

I looked at him quizzically. "Then you don't believe the vision," I said.

"Sure I believe it. It's going to happen," he argued, shucking through edamame.

"But he had the vision of the war when you were born. Your whole life, that's been your destiny," I said.

"You think Dad didn't make sure I turned out this way, just in case? I mean, he believed without a doubt I'd be his great warrior because of the vision, but then he spent the last hundred years training me to be exactly that. He named me after warriors. Taught me everything he knows about killing, about strategizing. Helped me acquire limitless power. Sounds like a self-fulfilling prophecy to me," he said.

I had never heard any of the Winters doubt Anthony in this way. It turned out that Mark was more reasonable than the rest of them, I supposed. But I had known that for a while now.

I wanted to know more about this philosophy of his, but just then Parker sauntered in the door of the restaurant and plopped down at an empty chair at our table.

"Man, I'm starving," she said, picking up a menu. "What looks good?"

Mark and I looked at each other in incredulity.

"Okay, dude, one thing that you disappear. Entirely another that you pretend you don't," Mark said to her. He had switched from "sugar" to "dude." That couldn't mean good things for their...er...relationship.

"What do you mean?" she said, her shoulders rising in sync with her intonation. It made her look animated.

"Um, like how the other night you were gone all night, and when we found you at dawn, you acted like nothing had ever happened?" he suggested. I was grateful he was fighting this fight instead of me.

Parker snickered. "You didn't seem to mind." Muddled flashes of her hot and his cold, of skin, of lust, and then of the two of them naked in the bed of our hotel in New York hit my head. I shuddered — even gagged a bit — at this very sensory image. Mark winced, realizing what I'd just seen.

"Let's focus," I said, gritting my teeth. "Where did you go?" I asked her.

"If I said Mexico, would you believe me?" she laughed, pulling that damn butterfly pendant this way and that, making a grating sound on the chain.

I was fed up with her games and regretted having brought her along. I pushed my books and documents back in the bag and stood up. "I'll be outside, whenever you two are...finished," I said and went to wait in the square, a weird place dotted with park benches and a giant statue of Samantha from *Bewitched* on a broomstick.

Impatiently, I stood up and wandered toward the old cemetery I'd marked on my map. I walked up and down the rows, the path obscured by melting snow. The headstones were buried nearly to their tops, and only the carvings above the names showed. I knew from the plaque outside, though, that the earliest bodies had been buried here fifty years before the witch trials. Unable to see names or dates, there wasn't much to look at except for the strange graphic skull and angel wings carved on most of the stones. This seemed out of place for the time. I took a picture of several of the skulls, and ambled back toward the restaurant.

They emerged not long after, and I said not a word to them as we walked to the Salem Witch Museum, our last stop. Its major exposition was a show there, and we arrived just as one was starting. There were just as few people here as there had been at the Witch Dungeon Museum. We sat in the middle of a tall theater, where life-size dioramas lined the walls — scenes of Puritan homes, shouting men and women in courtrooms, dingy dungeon jail cells, and bodies hanging on Gallows Hill. At the beginning of the presentation, a large red circle on the floor began to glow. On it were twenty names that I recognized as those who were executed during the Salem Witch Trials.

The lights were dimmed, and then, one by one, the wax scenes were illuminated as a voiceover narrated the scenes, telling the complete tale of the witch-hunt.

The story began in the Reverend Samuel Parris's house. His slave, Tituba, was the first accused. We'd heard her name at each stop, but I hadn't read much about her. It was the Reverend's daughter, Betty, and his niece, Abigail Williams, who had accused Tituba of witchcraft. It was her stories of black magic and voodoo from her indigenous Caribbean roots that sparked the allegations of witchcraft in Salem. After half a dozen screaming girls accused her of witchcraft, she was shackled and imprisoned, like some two hundred would be. She eventually confessed — most scholars believing she did so only under extreme duress, like all confessions gathered then — and then gave testimony of a man in black who had come to her and bade her sign the book of the devil I'd read about before. She referred to him as a tall man from Boston. But despite Tituba's confession, she was not executed. She was used to help find other "witches," pitted against the townspeople as if being an "actual" witch led her to know of the others. And after that, she was simply sold back into slavery, with no further record of her existence beyond that.

This rubbed me the wrong way. I knew what the holes in the history could mean. Holes in the historical record led to those 165 supernatural creatures living in isolation on a mountainside. Holes in records could mean those 96 bodies in Pickering. Holes in history could mean Tituba was still alive.

There was so much more talk of the devil. Of evil. Of the fabled man in black who solicited Tituba's involvement. Of the horrendous spirit that supposedly drove these accused witches to commit crimes they likely never committed, that drove young girls to make up accusations that would lead to the death or imprisonment 150 people in a single year. The presentation closed with three question that rang in my ears: "Who is the devil? What side was he fighting on? What side does he fight on even now?"

I was exactly what they condemned in those times, wasn't I? Me, my family, my love, my friends? Weren't we all some version of the beings the Puritans feared? Did we have the devil in us? And what side were we fighting on?

I tried not to think about it.

In the second exhibit, there was an enormous timeline of witchcraft and witch-hunts in the western world. Drawing comparisons between the witch-hunt in Salem and McCarthyism, racism, and discrimination based on sexual orientation, the timeline featured an interesting formula:

Fear + Trigger = Scapegoat

I wrote this in my notebook, and then I ran my hands over the words. Was that what I was in my family, the reason they hated me so much? A trigger of their fear of the outside? Was I just a scapegoat, and not actually to blame?

Over the door, I saw a quote from *Macbeth*, Act 1, Scene 1: "When shall we three meet again? In thunder, lightning, or in rain?" My stomach caught at this. It made me miss Noah. *Macbeth* was his book. When would we meet again?

I tried not to spend as much time in this gift shop, already tired of lugging around what I'd bought. I let Mark and Parker look around while I made notes.

Mark brought me a necklace with symbols on it we couldn't read that looked similar to the ones in the cave at Ephesus, and a small stack of a postcards, trinkets, and magnets with images of black birds on them, all labeled "Raven."

"Could be a coincidence..." he trailed.

"I don't believe in those," I said.

"I know," he said. "Can we go? She's getting antsy," he nodded toward Parker.

"Sure thing," I said.

"I'll go get these for you," he offered, taking all the trinkets from me.

"Hey, how do you think you spell 'Tituba,'?" I asked him.

"What, didn't teach you phonics on the mountainside?" he laughed. I glared at him. In fact, they didn't. "We'll look on one of the displays in the lobby. I bet it's there," he offered.

We found a plaque discussing the death of Sarah Osborne. I remember having read her name as one of the three who were the first accused, along with Tituba. But her name was not among those on the red circle on the floor of the museum.

The plaque listed the names of four persons who died while imprisoned. These names weren't included in the twenty on the memorial circle at the museum. Twenty executed and four who died in prison. I thought for a moment about the tally marks at the Witch House and those on Ava Bientrut's wall. I looked at my own arm: 178 tally marks, one for each of the dead.

Of course. Twenty-four tally marks. Twenty-four dead in Salem.

Pieces were falling into place.

Mark and Parker ambled out into the lobby. "Ready?" he asked.

"One sec," I said, trying to make it all fit.

I scanned the rest of the plaque, found Tituba's name and wrote it down. Then Mark laid the Raven postcards in my open notebook. I saw *Tituba* in my own handwriting and RAVEN in print on the postcard.

"Rearrange the letters…" I said to Mark, pointing at the two words.

Parker heard me, and her face grew angry.

"Rearrange the letters," I said again, with more force. I scribbled furiously, writing it to make sure, checking off one letter at a time. "Rearrange the letters of her name. Tituba   Raven has the same letters as Ava Bientrut. He named her after himself. Marked her, just like Berkant. In Pickering that was…"

"Tituba?" Mark asked, his face alarmed. "That's why the house looked like the Witch House here. It was from the same time and place," he said. "But, Sadie…you really think she was still alive?"

"You heard them. She was sold back into slavery, never to be heard from again, the only one that even history can admit they lost track of," I reasoned. I began pacing. "That has to mean the Raven that disfigures Berkant's family in Ephesus — who's still alive — and the Raven who imprisoned Ava Bientrut all those years ago… they're the same person! He was here. He was in Salem. He must have known the Survivors!"

I burst out the front doors of the museum, needing air and a space where I could talk louder. I pressed my fingertips to my forehead, and tried to breathe.

Mark edged up behind me, protectively. But Parker followed cautiously, a loud and nerve-wracked inner monologue plaguing her mind. *Go or don't go? GO OR DON'T GO? Does she have it all figured out? SHUT UP!* she screamed to herself. *SHE CAN HEAR YOU.*

I still held the postcards Mark had given me. The second one had the red memorial circle with the names of the executed on it. On the outer ring, the names of two of the accused sat next to one another: Sam Wardwell and Mary Parker.

Samantha Parker. Sam Parker.

"You!" I cried, pointing at Parker. "Of course. You're in this. Ava Bientrut called you Samantha!" I played the moment again in my head. I hadn't understood it till now. She'd asked Madeline and *Samantha* to go get the chairs from upstairs in the ghostly house. Samantha. *Sam.* "She knew you! I introduced you as Parker, but she knew your name was Sam!"

"What?" Mark asked, his face alarmed.

"And Berkant called Raven's friend Sam! How stupid of me. I assumed it was a guy! But Sam can be anyone, girl or guy. And it's you. You're Sam!" I cried. "I'd bet everything I have that he named you too."

I had said too much.

She lunged at my throat and pushed me against the building we stood in front of, right there in broad daylight in the middle of the street. In a fraction of a second, Mark grabbed us and flung us into an alleyway.

"What are you going to do about it, goody two-shoes?" Parker cackled.

"It's true? What are you, some kind of spy?" Mark asked, his face distraught. I suddenly realized he was feeling betrayed on many more levels than I was.

"Boys are so easy," she grinned.

On some strange instinct, I hit her across the face so hard I knocked her to the ground. My strength far outweighed hers, especially in her human form. "You used him in all this," I said angrily, now my chance to be protective of my inherited big brother.

Despite the seriousness of the situation, Mark burst out laughing.

"You prude," she hissed, spitting blood. "If you had any sense, you'd use those looks of yours too." As she got to her feet, she lunged again, but this time Mark caught her and pinned her to the wall by her left forearm. As she struggled against him, her sleeve slid down her arm enough that I could see three small green and blue symbols on her wrist that looked just like the symbols in Ephesus, only in different colors. That's what she had been hiding under those long sleeves.

Then the final piece.

Suddenly I knew where I had seen the symbols in the cave in Ephesus before. "Mark, the symbols..."

"Ephesus, I know," he said. He stepped back and let go of her, binding her now with his power. She thrashed against his invisible bindings.

"They were on Peter's arm in Canada," I explained.

"Which one's Peter?" Mark asked, his own head reeling, trying to keep up.

"The one who could disappear," I said, and turning to Parker, I realized out loud, "And you keep..."

"Disappearing?" she smirked, her eyes dark with a malevolence. She opened her palm and closed it tightly.

She was gone.

CHAPTER NINETEEN

unraveled

WE CAUGHT THE LATEST FLIGHT OUT OF BOSTON BACK TO SEATTLE, where Mark and I said very little. Each of us was so frustrated. He was, I'm sure, frustrated with himself for quite literally sleeping with the enemy.

"Mark… I'm sorry she…" I tried.

He put a hand up, signaling me to stop. "She wasn't the first. She won't be the last." And that's all he said about her.

My frustration ran deeper. I began making a list in my notebook of all the things Parker had done to lead us up to this conclusion that, unfortunately, blindsided us. How could I have not seen this? She was weird from the moment I met her. In her lynx form, she'd maimed me, sinking her teeth deep into my flesh with some kind of concoction that kept the wound from healing itself. In her human form, she was awkward, fidgety, and unpredictable. She had been the one who didn't want us to go into the hidden houses outside Pickering. She had been the one who weirdly volunteered to go with Mark and me to Salem. She disappeared all the time, and not just out of sight, but out of trackable range — which, for me and Mark, was the same as disappearing entirely. She was a shape-shifter, and I had mistakenly assumed that she could shift only into animal forms. But the symbols on her wrist and her ability to disappear led me to believe that she had been impersonating Peter at least since the battle at the Canada house. But for how long? And where was the real Peter?

But what unsettled me the most was why Sam had come with us. As Raven's sidekick, was she sent to find me? Was Raven looking for us? Or had he found us? Did it mean that, all the time I was looking for Raven, Raven had been looking for me?

I sat on the plane and gathered as much evidence as I could from the literature I got in Salem, about who Raven might have been, about what role he could have played in Salem, what role he might be playing now. Once I read everything carefully, the evidence screamed at me from the pages.

In 1692, many of the accusations had dealt with accounts of signing the book of the devil or meeting a Man in Black. The stories of the Man in Black were very consistent. They all stated that he'd asked "victims" to sign away their souls or invited them into witchcraft. In return, he promised a kind of salvation. And they always knew, just by looking at him, that he was magical, which, to them, meant something terrible.

You could look at any of us — me, the Winters, the rogue Survivors — and see that we were magic too. People doubted it because they doubted the existence of the supernatural at all. But something was off about each of us who was less alive than we were dead.

Witches — ancient ones, those thought to exist in Salem, even Wiccans and various others today — often referred to a Man in Black as their leader, specifically over multiple covens.

In a collection of non-fiction narratives from Salem Village in 1692, Deodat Lawson gave first-hand accounts of happenings during the Witch Trials. Often these accounts included readings of or references to bible verses from the book of Revelations, which Lizzie had used in many of her spells. Most notably, Lawson told of an account in which an afflicted person was read Revelations 5:9, which read, "And they sang a new song: 'You are worthy to take the scroll and to open its seals, because you were slain, and with your blood you purchased men for God from every tribe and language and people and nation.'" I couldn't help but think of our mysterious Raven in this case who, I could already tell, had had his hand in evil doings from many tribes and languages and peoples and nations. I wanted very badly to know, then, what they — an unknown they — had done in his eyes to purchase men for him. He surely saw himself as a kind of god. Even Berkant had said he thought of himself as a messiah.

I had to find him. He had to be our point of origin, and, as I suspected when I began this hunt, he'd have the answers.

But first I had to speak with Lizzie. She had to talk. I'd been thinking back to the conversation I'd had with Hannah in Bigfork. She said she only had visions about the Survivors, and so in Salem she had them about the fourteen would-be Survivors and about her father (and about the Bloods, but I wasn't sure how this fit in). But she had them about her father, and no other adults from Salem. Wouldn't that mean that Raven wasn't in Salem, as I'd deduced? Or if he had been, that Hannah would have seen him in her visions?

Or it meant that Raven was Hannah's father, which was a haunting conclusion I didn't want to draw.

When we got to Seattle, we called the various parts of our scattered troop and asked them to assemble in the Survivors' City. We met at the gates at dawn, a week into May. As patches of snow at the middle elevations began to give way to the ground underneath, I realized we were nearing, maybe even within, our original window for when the war would take place. How close were we?

"Where's Parker?" Valentin asked when Mark and I arrived by ourselves. I looked at Mark, whose original disappointment and betrayal had boiled into anger and resentment on the flight, and asked him to tell the story. He obliged.

Hannah and Sarah were waiting for us, but Lizzie was nowhere in sight. "Did you find my father?" the youngest elder asked me.

"No," I said.

"Did you find what killed him, then?" she asked, running to keep pace with me as I walked to the square.

I sighed. "Not yet, but I'm close."

"We should leave her be, I think," Sarah said to Hannah, her hands on Hannah's shoulders.

I turned to look at her, and Hannah's dejected expression made me feel bad. She had been such an ally. I owed her more than this. "Wait," I said to them as they walked the other way. "Hannah, you can help."

"I'll do anything," she said.

"What was your family name in Salem?"

"Raven," she answered.

I dropped my head. "Thank you," I said, and turned on my heels. There was only one thing to do. I went straight to Andrew's house and knocked on the door.

"Daughter Sadie?" he greeted me with a question mark.

"I need to talk to her. You know that what she has to say is valuable. I need her help, Andrew. Now. She'll know where to find me," I said.

He kissed my forehead and closed the door.

I walked into the forest and sat against the tree I'd first started hiding behind when I was sixteen years old, 129 years before. I thought of the things I'd carved into it, the questions I'd asked, hoping someone would answer if I made them visible. I thought of the way Noah would follow and sear off the bark, erasing my heretical questions, absolving me of my sins. As early morning brightened into day that faded into night, I thought about how I missed him. Lizzie kept me waiting, so had plenty of time to do so.

She knew this was my refuge. She respected my privacy in this place and never came looking for me here. But on this day, finally she did.

Seeing her there, after we'd been so jarringly distant from one another, I felt like we were separated by a two-foot-thick wall of glass: doomed only to look at one another but never to connect again.

I could tell her mind and heart were torn over her failure to help me. She tasted regret on her tongue. But why? She could change it, if only she would.

"Did you find what you were looking for?" she asked. I saw in her mind a flash of her conversation with Andrew. *We are in dangerous times, Lizzie. Now is not the time to hold grudges. Now is the time to seek solace in the ones you love. Go to her. She needs you,* he'd said. It was only on his urging that she had come at all. Had he not intervened, how long would she have continued in this charade?

"I found some of the pieces of an unfinished puzzle," I said stiffly. "But did I find a way to destroy our kind? A way to defend ourselves? Or even the person or thing who has this information, which is so crucial to the protection of this family? No. I didn't find that." Guilt emanated from her. I didn't care. I laid it on thick because I was sure she had the answers. She had kept me out of her mind, out of her past for a reason.

And, even now, she said nothing.

"Lizzie, I need to tell you what we did find, though, and I need you to hear me. There were at least two people in two different countries who called me a Survivor. There were symbols I can't explain or translate. There were dead people, stashed away in a hidden town that *our* magic unlocked. And people who spoke of an old Survivor, a kind of monster who had maimed or killed or imprisoned them or those they loved," I explained.

She was rocking back and forth uneasily.

"They called him Raven," I said, quietly.

She froze.

"You know him?" I asked.

"I know no monsters," she said coldly.

"You aren't going to tell me anything?" I asked. She didn't respond. "Fine. Then I'll tell you what I think. I think Raven is Hannah's father. I think he made us what we are, or made the elders that way, and then you all created the rest of us. I think you knew he was evil, you knew you shouldn't trust him, but you were so scared of becoming a witch that you'd listen to anyone who didn't want to hang you for your crimes. I'm even going to guess you did something terrible, likely for him, and the guilt weighing on you is why you won't tell me what you know. I understand that you're afraid, Lizzie. Whatever he bid you to do is not your fault. But we are in trouble now, and I need your help to get to him."

Infuriatingly, she remained still.

"I went to Salem," I said. She looked up, her eyes wide, shocked to learn it was still there. "It's not the same as it was then, but parts survived. I went to the dungeons. I saw where they kept you. I heard how terrible it was." I watched her fingernails dig into her skin. "I can't imagine what it was like, but I can imagine that you must have some resentment toward Hannah's father. From what I've read, he might have been the cause of the whole witch hunt. The reason for the witch trials. The instigator of what history has decided was the hysteria of misguided teenage girls. He let all of you take the fall. He wasn't there with you in the dungeon, was he? He didn't care what happened to you," I said. I felt guilty for coming on so strong, but I would do anything to get her to talk.

It worked.

"You have it all wrong!" she cried. "Alexander Raven was a good man!" Tears formed in her eyes and fell down her cold, pink cheeks. She may have seemed vulnerable, but waves of anger and resentment rolled off her.

"So it's true," I breathed. "Hannah's father…Raven…"

"Alexander," she said, an edge entering her voice, "He told me what I was, mentored me in a time I thought my body, my *soul* was betraying me. He held my hand and guided me through what I was becoming. Whatever this stupid witch-thing is." She cried, and as she did, she conjured a ball of fire in her hands and threw it to the ground where it sizzled in the remaining fragments of snow. "He protected me. He warned me of the witch-hunt that was to come. He told me we would be exiled."

"How did he know?"

"He could see the future, a trait Hannah got from him," she explained. She sounded defeated, as if her secrets had been the source of all of her strength.

"So you knew what you were. And you knew he was too. But how did you all get accused? No accusation like that is on record. The odds of accusing all fourteen of you were astronomical. Someone else had to know what you were," I reasoned. "Or there were more of you."

"No one else knew," she insisted quietly. "And we were the only ones."

"Then how..."

"Her father is the one who accused us," she said stiffly.

"What?" I said.

"You heard me."

This shocked me. "Why did they even believe him? He was just one man, and he accused 26 of you all at once? Wouldn't it be more likely that he was guilty of something that all 26 of you could attest to?" I asked.

"He was an important man. Considered a confidante of the Governor's, even well-respected by Reverend Parris. They considered him a hero. Who else but a hero, a man loyal to their horrendous cause would incriminate his own daughter? Condemn her to a fate worse than death?"

"Still..."

She shook her head. "It was a time of great fear, Sadie. Of great hatred and suspicion. In those days, in that world, it was entirely believable that one would choose his allegiance to God over his own family," she said regretfully. And yet, this family had been set up in a way that didn't align with this belief. "Besides, there was the spectral evidence."

"Evidence against you?"

"Yes. Abigail Williams, that girl who lived with the Parris family, the one they called his niece, was supposedly afflicted by all 26 of us. We haunted her, tortured her, and so on. Or so she said," Lizzie explained stoically. I wanted to ask how that had happened, how she had known to accuse them to fit in with Raven's original plan. And yet in Lizzie's mind, there was a painful misunderstanding. She never understood that part, never understood how and why the poor tortured girl would say she and the other accused were torturing her when they did not. And so I didn't make her admit this aloud.

"I cannot believe you ever forgave him for that," I said.

I had offended her. She cried, "He accused us to protect us!"

"You're defending him? You would not be on a mountainside in Montana three centuries later if it were not for him!"

"Exactly. We would be dead or worse. You misunderstand. He said he would come for us. He said it wouldn't be this way. But the winters got too harsh where his team of horsemen left us to die. We came farther west to this place, and he must not have been able to find us. Don't you see, Sadie? We've waited for him, all this time. And it's my fault he hasn't come! He only warned me, only told *me* to keep this group together where they left us, but I let us move here. I should have understood the consequences. I let him lose us. It's *my* fault!"

Solid drapes of guilt swept off of her and onto my shoulders. This was her secret, a secret she'd kept from everyone since 1692. "You never searched for him?" I asked.

"I prayed. I hoped so badly that he would find us, but we couldn't search. He warned me of the dangers of letting our kind go free in the world. He told me we had to remain isolated. And it turns out he was right, doesn't it? Look what happened to those who left."

"It didn't happen to me," I said quietly.

"Yes, of course not. Because somehow you're impervious to everything," she laughed in that crazed, sad way as she swallowed tears.

"He isn't what you think he is," I said carefully. "He *is* a monster. Evil."

Her temper flared sharply at my accusation. "Preposterous! I know no evil," she said, "none but those you brought behind our walls."

"The Winters?" I asked, hurt.

"The blood drinkers, yes," she said.

"How did you…?"

"I'm not stupid, daughter. You have always thought you were the one who knew everything! But some of us know more than you, child. And it didn't take being out *there* to learn it!" she fumed.

"When I returned here last summer, you and the other elders are the ones who sent me to Mark Winter! You told me to bring him back!" I argued.

"Because I thought he might be Alexander Raven!" she cried, having reached her breaking point. "I thought he had come to save us! He promised he'd come for us! Three hundred nineteen winters have passed, Sadie, and he never came! Don't you see? I thought the powerful sorcerer you spoke of was my Alexander Raven," she mourned. "Not some stupid blood-sucking kid."

"So you never wanted to meet others of our kind…" I whispered. Of course! How could I have been so stupid? They hadn't changed. They hadn't *evolved*. They were still the same, infuriating elders I'd known my whole life.

"Of course not! Inside these walls, we are safe from the world out there. But now you brought that world here. You ruined everything!" she hissed. Her words cut at me.

"You were the one who introduced me to the outside. You gave us books," I argued.

"I tried to convey some of the more important messages, yes," she spat. What an odd way to phrase it. Were *Theogony, Beowulf,* and *Macbeth* among the more important messages in the world in Lizzie's eyes? "But it appears that was a mistake."

"It appears trusting you at all has been a waste," I seethed. I had never fought with her like this, and I so feared regretting my words. But she was so infuriating!

"It matters not to me if you trust me because you have not been the one running this family. You have not been the one to bear the burden of guilt or of responsibility. I have done everything I could to protect this family. I made the error of allowing our group to travel to these mountains three centuries ago, and that might mean I have doomed us forever, and for that, I am sorry. But everything else, I've done right."

"I freely gave up my life out *there* to help this family. Because all I knew was this place. All I knew was how to be loyal to you, and so I came back!"

"And you brought a war with you!" she fought.

"A war that isn't my fault," I pleaded softly, a vain attempt to convince her, to convince myself. I was growing tired of this. "It doesn't matter to me what you think anymore, Lizzie. I'm going to find your Alexander Raven. He's the Point of Origin."

"Of course you will. You think he's a monster, and so you go chasing after him. If he were the good man I make him out to be you'd probably have no interest. Do you hope he'll try to kill you? Do you fantasize about dealing with evil, Sadie? Are you excited that he may help you find more ways to slit yourself open, to destroy the temple God gave you?" she asked, grabbing my arm and ripping back the sleeve violently. "You are such a heretic. And such a *child.*"

I yanked my arm away forcefully. "I'm the heretic?" I cried, my voice cracking from suppressing tearless sobs. I didn't know she knew about the scars. "Who's the one who wrote a *spell* to make a *potion* that not only used the Bible's words in a heretical way but called for my blood? How do you even know how to procure your own blood, Lizzie? Surely, the process required trial and error," I argued.

"I don't have to answer to you. I won't. I am so tired of this. I am so tired of worrying what regrettable decision you'll make next." Lizzie just laughed angrily. "You sat in our sacred church and convinced your elders to *help* you find a way to kill yourself. You coerced us — and the Winters — into legitimizing your death wish! You are the very definition of failure to me. You have the devil in you that only the world outside could have put in you, and I hope, I *hope* you find the end you're looking for. I hope you get there only for God to send you where you belong. You think *this* is eternal suffering? You know nothing."

My throat tight with emotion, and my heart heavy with betrayal, I managed to whisper, "We have to know how to kill Survivors so we can kill the rogues before they kill us."

"Or so you'd like us to believe," she said callously, her back turned to me. "I hope you do find Alexander Raven. I hope you do bring him back. And then I hope he saves us all. Except you. You have never been satisfied within these walls, never grateful for what we've given you. I hope you get left behind," she said.

"Lizzie, Alexander Raven is not some kind of savior," I said carefully.

"He is good," she hissed, turning her back on me.

"He's *evil,*" I insisted.

"You've met him? Looked into his eyes? Held his hand? You know this to be true?" she argued.

"No, but…"

"But nothing."

"Lizzie, listen to me. In England we found houses hidden that I could only see using your Fateor Elixir. There were bodies in them. Humans that *Raven* had killed and erased from history, probably the way he erased all of you. We found one living person there. Her name was Tituba Raven."

"That's impossible. Tituba wasn't one of us. She cannot be alive." What did she know of Tituba? I wondered.

"He made her into one of us at some point, kept her alive, and imprisoned her. She has been sitting in the same room, unable to move for 319 years, kept alive just to be tortured. He did that to her, Lizzie. He even named her after himself to leave his mark on her." Lizzie didn't respond. "Do you understand? Alexander Raven is a terrible creature. He would not be coming here to save you."

"He was like a father to me," she said.

"He used you!" I cried.

"For what?" she countered angrily.

"I don't know that part yet," I admitted.

Lizzie scoffed. "There you go with your half-cocked theories and plans. You are so selfish, so terrible sometimes!" she screamed.

I knew it only a matter of time before everyone in my life felt this way about me.

"Don't you understand? You think he wishes ill on this family but he warned us, Sadie. He warned us that out there we would become demons. He tried to keep us from becoming evil. That's more than I can say for you," she spat. I didn't have an argument against this. If he *were* evil, as I had come to believe, why would he warn Lizzie to keep us together and isolated, away from humans, apart from the catalyst that turned Survivors into bloodthirsty *vieczy*? Had I miscalculated?

We were quiet then.

"I tried so hard to save you," she finally said, mostly to herself. "I cannot spend my life doing this anymore, Sadie." Tears rushed down her cheeks a wary juxtaposition to her stoic expression and her stony voice. "I hope you're happy with the decisions you make. And I hope you can live with the consequences," she said flatly. Then she turned on her heels and without another word, walked back toward the town.

CHAPTER TWENTY

the lay of the last survivor

I TRIED TO CONVEY SOME OF THE MORE IMPORTANT MESSAGES, YES. Lizzie had said.

I'd replayed our vitriolic conversation over and over again in my head, repeated it, even, word for word to the entire Winter clan when I returned to our house on the square. And that's the line that stuck out to me because the rest of the conversation was about hate and denial and how I was wrong and how I was selfish and how I was awful and how Lizzie believed Raven was good and the world out there, bad. So there was just that one piece that didn't fit.

I tried to convey some of the more important messages, yes.

But *Beowulf? Theogony? Macbeth?* Were these the more important messages, a story of a hero and monsters, of the gods and their evolution, and of a kind of evil, both human and inhuman? Mainly, were they among the more important messages to Lizzie?

I allowed myself sleep that night. The last few weeks of research and revelations had given us such momentum that I had been running at full speed, but my conversation with Lizzie had sent me headlong into a stone wall at 200 miles an hour. Crushed my bones. Killed my spirit. Left me maimed in the snow. I needed the rest.

But the next morning, I took the three books and all my notebooks back into the forest where I could think. For safekeeping, I brought the other messages Lizzie had conveyed to me: her book of incantations and elixirs, and the Bible. I knew that somewhere inside the things I knew and the secrets I'd uncovered was a way to find Alexander Raven. Now I wondered if they were in Lizzie's books.

Everett and Mark sat with me now, their eyes intently watching me.

I opened up my Moleskine journal first, and I read everything I'd ever written in it. Keeping it open to the list of qualities about Sam, I bent down to lay it on the ground.

"I got it," Mark said. "Let go."

I did as he said, and the book floated off the ground, waist-high, open to the page. He smiled faintly. I nodded in thanks. Everett thanked him too.

I did this with each of the books. I leafed through the elixirs and incantations book. I left the Bible open to the book of Revelations. I reread *Theogony* and *Macbeth*.

Finally, the new copy of *Beowulf.* It was a new translation that I hadn't read yet, and so I began reading the epic tale again. It wasn't too different from other versions I'd read in the human world, but it was practically a different language than Ben's 17th-century edition.

And then, on the 121st page, at the 1,749th line, I involuntarily spoke, "Oh my God."

Everett and Mark both jumped. "What is it?" Everett asked hurriedly.

I read aloud, "'He covets and resents; dishonors custom and bestows no gold; and because of good things that the Heavenly Powers gave him in the past he ignores the shape of things to come.'"

Mark jumped to his feet. "Mom's prophecy."

"It's here. It's, word-for-word, in this version of *Beowulf*," I cried. "Mark, what did Adelaide tell you when she told you the prophecy?"

"She said there was a prophecy we needed to remember, that it would be a key, and Lizzie knew it was."

"Lizzie knew?" I asked. How many leads would dead end at Lizzie's silence?

"According to Mom," he said.

"Why didn't I know about this?" Everett asked him, heat in his voice.

"Because we weren't supposed to tell Sadie unless it became relevant, and you would have told her anyway, Mom knew," Mark spat. Everett was displeased, but he couldn't argue with that.

"Go get Adelaide!" I snapped. They did as I asked.

When she appeared, I held up the copy of *Beowulf*. "What aren't you telling me?" I asked Adelaide.

She sighed. She'd had her own loyalty battle here. Hadn't she formed some kind of alliance with the elders? But she helped me anyway. "When Lizzie wrote the Fateor elixir in your book, she didn't copy it exactly. Her old spell book said 'Read prophecy from Bewoulf 1749-1752,' but I saw her write Revelations 1:3. I looked up Revelations 1:3 and saw Lizzie had only given you half of it by putting that — instructions to read a prophecy but no prophecy to read. So, I asked Mark for your copy of *Beowulf* before we left for Europe, and I made he and Ginny remember the lines. I didn't want to betray Lizzie..." she trailed.

"But you hated to sabotage our search like Lizzie had," I said, understanding.

She nodded. "What do you think it means?" she asked.

"I don't know," I said, rubbing my temples, my eyes closed tight. "Clearly, she didn't want me to successfully make the Fateor elixir, but why?" I asked, pacing.

"Sadie, what if she's never made the Fateor elixir?" Everett asked. "It would stand to reason that she wouldn't want you making it since she hasn't, which is probably why she sabotaged it in the first place."

"Why do you say that?" I asked.

"How would they have even gotten the blood?" Everett asked. A fair point. I'd thought of that when I spoke with Lizzie upon our return, but I hadn't thought she'd keep me from making the Fateor elixir just because she hadn't.

"Thank you, Adelaide," I said, and she left us.

"Why would the prophecy have worked when it wasn't identical to whatever one Lizzie's referred to. She would never have read this version. I'd bet she has only ever read the version she gave Ben over a hundred years ago," I said.

"So we need that version," Everett deduced.

"On it," Mark nodded, bounding out of sight. He came back with Ben in tow — not what I needed.

"Don't blame me," Mark said. "He won't let go of it."

Ben was clutching the book to his chest. "Why must you take *everything*?" he asked.

"I just need to borrow it," I explained. "Please, Ben. Trust me. It's very important."

Uneasy, Ben handed me the book. I opened it to line 1749. The page was simple, unmarked, and no different than every other page in the book. What was I missing?

"I need more Fateor."

Mark rolled his eyes in a grand gesture. "Of course you do," he sighed.

"No, no way," Everett said sharply.

"The books are hiding something. I need to find out what," I said, not entertaining the protests.

"You are incorrigible," Everett said, gritting his teeth.

"We've come too far to not do all we can," I said strongly.

"I'm with you," Mark said.

"What?" Everett screamed in outrage.

I waited briefly to see if they lunged at each other, but once they didn't, I quickly began pouring together the ingredients like I'd done in England. "Hands," I said, and Mark obliged, holding out his hands to act as mortar and pestle as Everett's had. Once everything was together, I dug for my arrowhead and poison.

"No, no, no," Mark said, shaking his head vehemently. "Enough with gaping, jagged wounds." Mark looked at Everett who seemed to know what he was about to say. "Let me do it. I won't hurt you. I promise."

Everett let out an enraged growl. "I hate you sometimes," he hissed at Mark, which Mark pointedly ignored.

"Come here," he said to Ben. He poured the mixture in Ben's hands. "Hold this." Turning to me, he said, "You need to know I'm doing this only so you'll stop maiming yourself and because I can get the amount you need in a much cleaner, much faster way. Plus I'll be able to heal it."

"Got it," I said.

"Amount of what? What's happening?" Ben asked, his heart rate audibly escalating.

Stepping toward me, Mark said, "Staying still will keep this from being difficult."

"It's not difficult. It's impossible," Everett muttered under his breath.

We ignored him. "Got it. Stand still. Calm. Act like it's painless," I nodded.

Entirely on accident, Mark said in his mind, *Oh, sugar. It will be anything but painless.*

"What exactly are you going to do to her?" Ben asked

"Something you'll not want to watch," Mark warned. Steeling himself, he looked back at me hesitantly, and his eyes started glowing a low crimson. Venom pooled in his mouth and so he spit it out, leaving a thick gold-metal trail that sank into the earth.

I stuck out my bare arm toward him.

"Please," Everett said, begging us to stop.

"Ben? Hold him back," Mark said. Ben's eyes widened.

"Forgive me," he whispered quietly. Then he quickly pulled me toward him, one hand on my waist, one tucking my outstretched arm back against my side, and put his mouth to my neck. I heard Everett gasp and saw Ben quickly grab the stony *vieczy* body with all his might.

It wasn't a bite, exactly. Mark ran his top teeth in a straight line from my collarbone to my ear, slicing like a razor. I felt the burn of the venom greater than the sting of the wound itself as he closed his mouth around the wound. Since my blood didn't pump or flow freely, he quite literally sucked my blood.

My stomach lurched.

It was over in seconds. Mark stood over a horrified Ben, spitting my blood into his palms.

Everett was standing surprisingly still. Hauntingly still. His eyes bore into me with an intensity I couldn't name.

It was then that I realized the wound was burning. Burning badly. The kind of burn you get from salt and ice, or from subzero temperatures. The kind of burn that's so cold, it's hot. That's so hot, it's painful. That's so painful, you wish, you *pray*, you could pass out to escape it.

"Ev, she's okay," Mark said, his hand against Everett's chest. His breathing was ragged.

But Everett kept looking at me with the same intensity.

Mark kept talking. "Sadie, I cannot believe you actually stayed that still. You're insane," he laughed.

"Sadie?" Mark asked. His demeanor changed. "Are you okay?"

"She's burning," Everett whispered. "You idiot, there's too much venom. What did you do to her?" Everett screamed.

I realized I was on the ground. How did I end up on the ground?

"Damn it," Mark hissed, and took a deep breath. "I've got to fix it. Hold on," he said, kneeling over me.

"No!" Everett swooped in and knocked Mark backward. Mark slammed into a tree behind us so hard that it cracked and swayed.

"What the fuck?" Mark howled.

"Don't you dare touch her!" Everett cried, kneeling close to my body.

"Everett, let me fix it!" Mark pleaded.

"You stay away from her," Everett hissed. He looked to me. "Princess," he said gingerly, trying desperately to mask the desperation — the *fear* — in his voice. "Princess, I'm going to stop the venom and heal you," he said.

The burning escalated, and I could feel tightening in the rest of my body. This was such a different Everett than I'd seen, here in the cold spring mountain air with me, my neck an open wound. His eyes were on fire, his brow tense. His jaw was clenched so I could see every muscle and tendon ripple when he breathed. But something about him was different. He hadn't broken eye contact with me since I fell to the ground.

I was petrified. But Everett tucked his head into my neck and sucked, and the burning slowly dissipating, removing the venom I assumed. I was uneasy when I heard a gulp. Drinking. Now he was drinking my blood.

In a flash, I felt the warmth of seawater surround me, the grain of sand beneath me, and a taut Everett on top of me, his lips against mine. I felt heat. I felt life. Passion. Lust. Love. Safety. Security.

Happiness. A heartbeat.

Was I dying? Was he drinking too much? Unable to stop?

But he pulled away quickly, his level of control a marvel — I closed my eyes and reopened them three times to see that it was in fact Everett, not Mark, at my neck. When I found his gaze again, his eyes were wide with an emotion I couldn't read. It could have been fear, terror, or disbelief. And for one, fleeting second, I saw that golden-green sheen in his eyes I'd first fallen in love with in the California summer. Then he kissed me, without caution, without restraint, which was risky, I was sure. And though I knew it was odd, I was energized and pulled him close to me and kissed him in just the same way.

He swallowed hard, his efforts to catch his breath laborious. "Princess, are you okay?" he asked. I nodded, still unable to speak. He looked back at Ben and Mark, and then to me and whispered in my ear, "Did you feel it, too?"

I had felt it. I was — currently — feeling it. I nodded and managed a half-smile, though my expression must have been mostly dazed. I felt like part of me had been taken, inserted into him. A part of me inside of him. Him, a part of me. In an instant, Everett Winter had become a corner of my soul.

He lay back, trying to catch his breath, and I did the same, but as he moved even inches from me I felt a tug from deep in my chest and pressure in my throat. I reached out for him, and once I touched him, the pressure was alleviated. I had no idea what had happened.

Then, Ben's voice. "Sadie?" he asked, shaking.

"I'm okay," I said feebly. His body was pouring out waves of terror and protectiveness and mistrust. I got to my feet, trying to show Ben they hadn't actually hurt me, and I reached for my neck. My fingers sank into the deep wound though, and Ben winced. Everett reacted quickly, milking himself for venom now as I'd seen Mark do before, and put a thin line of it over the wound. I only felt a tingle then, exactly as I had all the times they'd healed me before. Then it was over, like it'd never happened at all.

But Ben wasn't relieved.

"I'm sorry, Ben," I said. I couldn't undo what he'd seen.

He shook his head signaling he didn't want to talk about it. "What do I do with this?" he asked, the ingredients of the incomplete Fateor elixir cupped in his palms.

I said the prophecy, and the mixture turned silver-clear in his hands as it did the first time. I picked up his ancient copy of *Beowulf* and said, "Here, drop a little bit onto this."

Uneasily, Ben did as I said.

The book flew open and the pages flipped themselves, stopping at the prophecy. Lines before and after the prophecy were outlined in a glowing green.

But the pages began to flip again. The book splayed open so wide, the primeval spine groaned and cracked. Three consecutive pages stood erect and glowed crimson, the color we'd seen everywhere along Raven's sordid trail. Some text on the red pages stood out in a luminous bright white.

I scanned these pages, trying to understand, but I had trouble with this version of the book. I opened my modern copy of *Beowulf* and read aloud line 2230:

> *"Because long ago, with deliberate care,*
> *somebody now forgotten*
> *had buried the riches of a high-born race*
> *in this ancient cache. Death had come*
> *and taken them all in times gone by*
> *and the only one left to tell their tale,*
> *the last of their line, could look forward to nothing*
> *but the same fate for himself."*

In the margin, there was an author's note, a brief description of the lines I'd read: *Long ago, a hoard was hidden in the earth-house by the last survivor of a forgotten race.*

"Because that's not cryptic," Mark said.

I scanned down the rest of the page. The passage spoke of life and death, of a forgotten race of people who had all been killed off, of hon-

oring those who'd lived in celebration with a funeral and worldly offer-
ings. I read it all aloud, trying to explain it. They all knew the story, of
course, Ben having no doubt read *Beowulf* as many times as I'd read
Theogony, but he had never heard it in this language. The next glowing
section in Lizzie's book read,

> *"My own people*
> *have been ruined in war; one by one*
> *they went down to death, looked at their last*
> *on sweet life in the hall. I am left with nobody"*

The last of them proclaimed,

> *"'Pillage and slaughter*
> *have emptied the earth of entire peoples.'*
> *And so he mourned as he moved about the world,*
> *deserted and alone, lamenting his unhappiness*
> *day and night, until death's flood*
> *brimmed up his heart."*

"What does it mean?" Ben asked.

"I don't know."

"So who marked the passages?" Mark asked.

"Lizzie, of course," I said. "It couldn't be anyone else."

I pulled out my iPad and Ben's eyes widened, trying not to lose focus
as images popped up on the screen. He had never seen a computer that
looked anything like this. "What are you doing?" he asked.

"Researching," I said, my eyes transfixed. I don't know why, but I
actually laughed when I looked up a description of *Beowulf* online. "And
there it is. That whole section of *Beowulf* is known as 'The Lay of the
Last Survivor.' She's talking about Raven, as if there was any doubt."

"You remember what Ava — er, Tituba — said, don't you?" Mark
asked me.

"One, last lone Survivor," Everett answered, repeating her words. That was her tip.

"This Alexander Raven sounds like a poor soul. Lonely. Forgotten," Ben said.

"That's what Lizzie wants us to think of him. She wants us to feel bad for him, feel bad that he has had no one all this time. But we know better," I said.

"Do you know better?" Mark asked. Everett shot him a venomous look, as if offended that Mark would question a conclusion I'd reached. How the tables had turned.

I looked at him, clearly perplexed. "What are you talking about?" I asked.

"So far, people have told you isolated stories about someone you've never met. Lizzie knew this man. She lived with him, was mentored by him. How do you know her version of Raven isn't the right one?" he asked.

I stared at him, blankly, as if I had never thought of this. I had, of course, though I hadn't seriously considered it. I was so used to lying that I never thought it possible that Lizzie's version was closer to the truth. But Mark had a point. And I was still haunted by Lizzie's final argument: Why would he warn us against evil if he were evil himself?

We were silent for a long time. I paced, fingers to my forehead.

Ben asked. "Do you think your book has secrets too?"

Everett got my old copy of *Theogony*. "One way to find out. Ben, if you would…"

Ben poured the elixir on it, and the process repeated itself. There was only one glowing passage — outlined in green like the first passage in Ben's book — and Everett read aloud the same lines from the modern translation:

"Now of the many children that were born to Sky and Earth,
These were the fiercest ones, and from the very outset they
Were hated by their father and he hid them all away,
As soon as they were born, deep in the earth; he took delight
In doing this wicked deed and did not let them reach the light.
But Gaia, thronging inwardly, prodigious, gave a groan,
And she devised a crafty piece of cunning of her own.
She made a kind of metal that was gray and very hard,
Fashioned a scythe and showed her children what she had prepared;
And though she grieved in her own heart, to make them bold she said:
'O children, born to me and of a father who is bad,
We'll take an evil vengeance on him, if you should agree:
If anyone was first to do things shameful, it was he.'"

"This is the story where the Sky — Ouranos — and Earth — Gaia — have three children who are terrible," I explained. "Ouranos doesn't want them, so he tries to kill them, but Gaia doesn't want them to die, and so she comes up with a way to fight him." The boys stared at me blankly. "Let's pretend Lizzie is Gaia," I said, "our proverbial mother, and that Raven is Ouranos. He's trying to kill his children, and she is trying to protect us."

"What, you think she wants you to kill Raven?" Mark asked incredulously. "That doesn't fit with a single thing she's said so far."

"What else could that mean?" I asked. "He's the father-figure, right? And he hid them all away, left us to die here. That's what that says, right?"

"But what about all of her crap about him being the good guy? Isn't that why she's not speaking to you?" he asked.

"So? let's just pretend everything Lizzie's ever said was a lie!" I cried, so angry I couldn't see straight. "I don't know what else it could mean!" I cried, my mind frantic from all of this. Realistically, I just wanted one of these cryptic immortal messages to support all that we'd found in

Europe and Salem. At least then we'd be looking for Raven with a 50/50 shot of knowing whether he was evil — as Tituba, Berkant, and, in a way, Sam, had suggested — or good — as Lizzie believed.

"Lizzie wants you to kill someone?" Ben asked, his voice cracking with nerve.

"No,…Ben…it's complicated," I said. What else could I say?

"What if someone else marked these passages?" Everett suggested.

"No, it had to be Lizzie. She's the only one who was so close to him in Salem," I reasoned. They didn't point out the glaring holes in my logic. "I don't know what else it could be."

"Or how this even helps us," Everett says.

"Why don't you ask your machine?" Ben offered. "Do whatever you just did to that," he said, pointing to the iPad, "and ask it a question. That's what it does, right?"

"You have to know what question to ask it," I said.

"Ask it about all the loose ends," he said, "the parts that don't add up."

I thought this over. "The Lay of the Last Survivor was about life and death, a funeral…" I said. I typed these words into a Google search bar and got 16.9 million results. "I need to be more specific."

"What about giving earthly things to the dead?" Ben suggested.

I typed *life, death, honor dead with gifts*. Results ran the gambit: organ donation, the Day of the Dead, grief counseling. "More specific," I said.

"They talked about laying these items together," Everett said.

"Like you would on an altar," Ben said, excited. I typed *life, death, altar*. 814,000 results, like The Altar of the Dead, a few books on Amazon about unrelated things. "More," I said.

They began to pace now, at the end of what we had from the passages — or from Beowulf, anyway. The pieces in *Theogony* seemed to offer nothing.

Finally, Mark said, "We need to think bigger. What doesn't add up in this whole search, not just in the books?" he asked.

I shook my head. What didn't add up? Everything and nothing.

"What about that list you're keeping about Sam?" Everett suggested. "Is there anything so weird it stands out?" Everett asked.

"The monarch butterfly pendant," I said. It had confused me since the first time I'd seen it. When we met, she looked raggedy from morphing in and out of her animal form, wearing a mix of clothes they'd likely stolen and animal furs slung over her like you'd see in old movies like Tarzan. But she always had that pendant on. "What could that mean?"

"Try it," Everett said.

I typed *life, death, altar, monarch butterfly.* 7,100 results. At least the first fifty were direct hits for "The Day of the Dead" and "Oaxaca."

"Where's Oaxaca?" I asked.

"Mexico," Mark said. "Famous for their Day of the Dead stuff," he explained as I read the screen.

"And how does all this fit?" I asked, aggravated.

Mark's eyes lit up. "In Salem, when you asked Sam where she'd been, she said *If I said Mexico, would you believe me?*"

"You're right! I can't believe she'd be cocky enough to actually tell us where she had been," I smiled.

"I can," Mark laughed.

"What do you know about the Day of the Dead?" I asked Mark.

Mark shrugged. "El Día de los Muertos? Sort of a half-Catholic, half-Pagan celebration in Mexico that coincides with Halloween and All Saints' Day, though the celebration is totally different. Locals believe the spirits of their ancestors come back once a year around the first of November, though the specific beliefs vary by village. They build leveled altars and leave the spirit's favorite things on them, food or drinks, cigarettes, that sort of thing. And they spend a lot of time at their dead loved ones' graves having a vigil that's also a celebration?"

"Oaxaca is the center of it," Everett added. "There are huge grave-yards there, giant celebrations, altars on street corners, in hotel lobbies, and for sure, in every home. It's insane." I looked at some pictures on Google of cemeteries crowded with people hovering over graves, all adorned beautifully with flowers, candles, and even little decorated miniature skulls. "That's how the monarchs fit too, actually. Monarchs migrate to Oaxaca every year around the time of the *El Día de los Muertos* celebrations. They believe the migration is the return of their loved ones' spirits."

"And the skulls?" I asked, showing him the ones I saw on the screen.

"Those are *calaveras de azúcar*. They're sugar skulls," Mark said. "Skeletons in general go with the whole thing. Figurines left on altars, artwork, the whole bit."

We were quiet then.

"You think that's where he is?" Everett asked.

"It's our best shot," I said. "And if Sam really was going to Mexico, then it's likely he's there now."

Looking longer at the skulls, I realized the only place I'd ever seen them drawn quite that way: on the headstones in the 17th-century graveyard in Salem.

"Come on."

CHAPTER TWENTY-ONE

the day
of the dead

I NEED A JET!" I SCREAMED AS WE BURST THROUGH THE DOOR OF THE Winters' house in Survivors' City. Adelaide and Anthony had been sitting quietly, enjoying a meal. They leapt to their feet, scrambling for cell phones and computers and whatever else it would take to complete my request.

"When?" Adelaide asked.

"As soon as inhumanly possible," I laughed, overjoyed that we were going to find him, and then I'd finally know a way to end this. My first thought, my primary thought, was realizing that I'd have an escape, if I wanted it. And though it should have hit me first, my second thought was that we'd have a way to defeat the rogues.

Mark gathered our things, and Everett collected everyone. I stood in the kitchen, thinking. If Raven had the right information, this could all be over. The war avoided. The misery ended. My life again my own. The beach vision a reality.

I went back to my computer, searching frantically to decide where in Oaxaca to go. It was an entire state in Mexico, and even the city of Oaxaca, the capital, had tentacles of villages reaching far into the mountains. I couldn't rely on sensing him on the ground because I had never sensed him before, so we had to know where to look. I found a photo of the inscription over the entrance to the Oaxaca city cemetery: *"Aquí la eternidad empieza y es polvo aquí la mundanal grandeza."* It meant, loosely, "Here eternity begins and the worldly grandeur is dust." The most spectacular photos I found were of a cemetery in the hills outside the city, in a place called Xoxocotlán. Partly because of the skulls on the headstones of the graveyard in Salem, partly because of the graves in the celebrations of El Día de los Muertos, and partly because I just felt it in my bones, I believed we'd find him in a graveyard. I made a list of all the major ones.

"There will be a jet at the Kalispell Airport in under an hour," Adelaide announced, quite proud of her accomplishment. The airport was only twenty minutes from the Survivors' City, running at top speed.

"You're amazing," I said, truly excited.

"Where are you going?" she asked.

"Oaxaca," I said.

"Mexico?" Anthony asked. "Do you need us to come with you?"

"Even odds that it will be peaceful or violent," Everett told him.

Anthony weighed the options. "I'll go. Adelaide stays."

I scoffed audibly. "Why don't we ask Adelaide what she thinks?" I said, my voice thick with teenage-style disdain. Anthony and Adelaide both raised their eyebrows. Even Everett looked at me in disbelief. *What?* I mouthed. Was *this* where the Winter boys learned to try to control their women?

Adelaide narrowed her eyes at me, but spoke to Anthony. "You'll be an invaluable resource to them if there's a fight, but we do have to put my safety into consideration since I'm not built the way all of you are. I should stay. And since you won't know what you're up against, so should Madeline." He nodded. I looked back at the table, embarrassed that she so vehemently disagreed with my disrespect of Anthony.

I sheepishly apologized to Anthony.

Patrick, Valentin, and Narcisa walked into the house soon after. "Narcisa stays," Valentin said, pushing his shaggy white-blonde hair out of his face.

"You have no more experience with them than I do," she argued.

"Fine, then I'll stay," he offered.

This satisfied her a little. In Romanian, she said, "No, you have to go. This crazy lot needs all the help they can get." She laughed. Back in English, Narcisa turned to me, "All right, pretty girl. I'm out." I nodded, understanding.

I idly wondered if I could talk Everett into staying, he the one of them who seemed the most unfocused — possibly even least skilled — in battle and the one I wanted least to get hurt. I dismissed the thought as soon as it had come to me. Wasn't I just as distracted by him as he was by me?

"Count this one in, too," Mark said, walking into the house with Ben in tow.

"No way," I said, shaking my head.

"He already made his case to me, and I buy it. I'll take responsibility for him," Mark said nodding at Ben, who nodded back. I didn't question it.

When Ginny and Madeline arrived, we said our goodbyes. Adelaide and Narcisa kissed their partners tearfully. Madeline tucked her head against Patrick's chest, and he kissed her forehead, their routine. Only once I boarded the plane did I realize that somehow we'd left behind the entire female half of our team — Ginny and I were outnumbered three to one. I sighed in frustration at these men, each of whom could not bear to endanger their partner. Only in so many ways, I empathized.

On the flight, we brought everyone up to date and explained why we thought we'd find Alexander Raven in Oaxaca. Then we had a long time to wait. Everett worked his way inside my sleeves and stroked my scars with his cool thumbs, his mind preoccupied once he realized all that we might encounter in Oaxaca. There was a lot we needed to talk about, but this wasn't the time or the place. I watched his eyes linger on the new slice down my neck. He had handled that both better and worse than I had expected him to. Better because I wasn't a *vieczy*. Worse because he hadn't even looked at Mark since he'd put his lips — and teeth — to my neck.

Then everyone got quiet thinking about the Pandora's box that awaited us. I was quiet too, realizing they had followed me blindly onto this plane and into a fight we knew nothing about. Putting them all in danger weighed on me heavily. It was only then that I realized that I had amassed a loyal following, a concept that could — and probably should — make me feel proud and loved. Instead, I felt burdened by the responsibility of it.

We touched down on a rural landing strip in the mountains west of the city, something I'm sure Adelaide and Anthony had finagled. Walking down the small steps of the plane, I heard the obvious quiet of a place with so few people. We ran east toward the city.

As it came into view, I felt a shock that brought me to a halt so quickly that I tumbled to the ground, skidding across snow and dirt and rocks. Ben stumbled too.

"In my bones," he said, catching my eye, answering my unasked question. The others circled back to us.

"What is it?" Everett asked.

"I can feel them," I said.

"Who?" Everett asked.

"Ours," Ben answered.

Of all the things we expected to find at the end of the sordid journey toward Alexander Raven, none of us expected to find the rogue Survivors.

"That way," Ben said, pointing east. I envisioned the map I'd studied of Oaxaca. In *that* direction were a number of towns and villages including Xoxocotlán. We headed there first. We walked so we wouldn't draw attention to ourselves, but we did not encounter other souls on the cobblestone streets. I heard no waking voices — aloud, mental, or otherwise — coming from any of the homes we passed. I did notice a similarity between the smaller adobe homes and the first home we'd entered in Pickering.

Then among the rows of colorful houses, the cemetery gates appeared. It looked very different from the pictures. The streets were empty and in darkness, and there was no sand art or sculpture or flowers like I'd seen in the pictures. There were no food vendors or people or anything else. I shouldn't have expected it to look like the festival though. These were just the bones of Oaxaca I was seeing. The festival decorations were the skin.

But a vibration in my core told me we were in the right place.

On the cobblestone in front of the closed gates, a bright red slanted scripted read *Aquí la eternidad empieza y es polvo aquí la mundanal grandeza*. It was written in blood. Suddenly, I felt certain no happy homecoming would come from this. I swallowed uncomfortably. These might be the gates of Hell.

"Parker is in there," Valentin said. "I know a member of my pack when I encounter one."

"Just as we expected," I said.

I grabbed Valentin. "Look, we have no idea what we're walking into. This may or may not be Alexander Raven, and he may or may not be evil. But, whatever he is, whoever is in there, I need you to read him. We need to know what we're up against, what he is. You're our most valuable asset," I whispered into his ear.

He nodded, understanding. "I can do it. I'll just need to find a way to touch him."

I took a deep breath, steadying myself. Anthony leaned in and said, "Now or never, Sadie."

We heard maniacal laughter coming from inside the gates. A number of voices broke out in a mocking chorus of "Now or never, Sadie. Now or never, Sadie." Indeed, they were waiting for us.

Everett hovered at my side as I stepped over the bloody message and entered the cemetery. The gravestones were bare, the pathways dusty. It was just another cemetery. Just another place.

We could see four women with deep olive skin and thick black braids hanging down their backs wearing beautiful long skirts in printed, hand-dyed wool and cotton. They were all lean and curvy, and though it was dark, I could see that they were strikingly beautiful. Their feet were bare, and they wore no coats: the dead giveaway they weren't human.

"*Miren a la guapa,*" one said to the others.

"*Dios mio, la bella ha llegado,*" another said.

"*Por fin!*" they all laughed.

"What are they saying?" Everett asked.

"They're glad I'm finally here," I said, "you might say."

"Glad indeed, pretty girl," one called.

"*A ellas hablan inglés,*" I said. "I mean, you speak English."

"You speak Spanish," the tallest one said.

"Who are you?" I called back.

"Witches," a smaller, round one laughed. "Don't you know?"

They smell human, even if they're not, Ginny told me in her head. I looked to her at my left, her eyes aflame.

"Do you know Alexander Raven?" I asked.

"*El Padre, por supuesto,*" the tall one said, as each of them crossed themselves — head, chest, shoulder, shoulder — as if he were their god. This disgusted me.

"They called him *the father,*" I said to the others. "Is he your father?" I asked as we got closer to them, only two graves now between us. I could see that they were standing in front of what appeared to be a mirror, though I couldn't imagine one was there. But I could see their backs, and I could see all of our reflections, but I couldn't see behind it.

"*Imbéscil! Idiota!*" they cried.

"Chicas, be nice," a voice said. It was low and velvety. "Our Sadie has done the best she can with what little education she received," it cooed.

Black smoke appeared in the mirror, and a man sauntered out of it. The Man in Black.

He put his arm around one witch's waist, and ran a pale hand down the curve of her side. He leaned into another's hair, inhaling seductively. "Thank you, girls. You've been successfully distracting," he said, slipping his hand under one of their shirts to reveal gaping wounds at their hips. He'd meant to throw off the Winters. He'd known — thanks to Sam — how susceptible they'd be to this bloody distraction.

He reached out to the two others, and they all disappeared.

My chest felt tight at the site of him. A long fur coat hung off his shoulders, dusting against the snow. His shoes were pointed, lace-up dress shoes in a shiny animal skin. He wore a crisp, Bordeaux-colored Ferragamo suit with an impeccably neat tie and tiebar, the top button of the jacket buttoned, a silk pocket square in the breast pocket. He looked immaculate, and not a thing like I expected. His jaw and cheekbones were sharply angled, and his skin was the color of espresso foam marked with heavy cream. It glowed. His eyes were as inky as the night sky in darkness, and his stiff, not-quite-black hair hung thick against his jawline.

He looked just like me.

He could have been my father, young-looking enough even to be my sibling.

"Daughter Sadie," he said, a refulgent smile on his thin lips. He stepped toward me. A funny thing happens when you find what you are chasing: You have no idea what to do to. I froze.

"I won't bite," he laughed, his arms outstretched. "Not like those blood-letters you travel with anyway."

Everett growled, and I squeezed his hand. "Don't," I whispered.

"Yes, Everett. Don't," Alexander Raven said, his steely gaze not leaving mine. He curved his hands and motioned them toward himself, asking for a hug.

"Princess," Everett hissed through gritted teeth. Patrick and Mark held him back.

Unwilling to have come so far to lose what I wanted by offending him, I stepped forward and let Alexander Raven's arms encircle me.

He made no sound. When he moved, he was silent. His mind was silent. There was no humming or buzzing, no heartbeat. He radiated nothing. All I felt was a pulse sensation in my own left wrist.

"Why do you say nothing, Daughter Sadie?" he asked. "You've searched for me. You've seen my enemies and my allies, met my conquests and uncovered some of my secrets. Surely, there is a lot you'd like to know about your Point of Origin?"

He knew our name for him. Sam hadn't spared a single detail. Just then, she walked out of the mirror. I hardly recognized her. Her ebony hair was shiny and clean and smoothed straight as if she'd just come from a salon. Thick eyeliner and glossy red lips glowed against her creamy mocha skin. She wore a slick leather jacket over a cashmere sweater that cut dangerously low, with a pair of Joe Jeans clinging to her muscular thighs, and high-heeled boots that went over her knee. The monarch pendant dangled below her cleavage.

"Parker," Valentin breathed. "How could you?"

"That's my favorite thing about you, Valentin," Sam laughed cruelly. "Like Sadie here, you believe the best of everyone. That everyone tells you the truth. That every cause is worth fighting for. It makes you so painfully easy to take advantage of."

"Enough," Alexander said coldly, silencing them. "Your quarrels do not interest me. Where were we? Oh, yes. Your brilliant nickname. I want everyone to start calling me the Point of Origin. It better signifies my position over you all."

"What exactly is that?" I asked.

"All in good time, my girl. You'll get your answers. But first, I want to show you something, a friendly reminder that I am capable of things you are not," he said.

He waved his hand casually, and the mystic mirror disappeared, exposing the rest of the cemetery and causing thousands of candles to illuminate. The last two rows of graves were decorated like they would be for the El Día de los Muertos celebrations. Rich goldenrod *cempacúchiles* and purple-red flowers lined the flat stones that extended out the length of each grave, in addition to traditional headstones. The *calaveras de azúcar* dotted the flower trim. Long lilies and gladiolas formed arches above the headstones.

Then I saw it, the dark centers of each of these shrines were not the empty stones, but were bodies.

"There are twenty-eight of them," Everett whispered, his ability to see numbers — subitize — useful in this moment.

I ran to them, fearing the worst. Their bodies were enshrined, perfectly still, hands across their chests, the strong scent of *copal* rising from burning branches in their hands. They were the 28 rogue Survivors. There was even Peter — he looked the worst of them. The most dead of them.

At my feet, I saw Noah's sweet, reddened, fair-headed face in perfect peace. I swallowed hard. "Noah!" Ben screamed and lunged forward. His face conveyed total distress and terror. He never showed this kind of emotion, but in that moment it looked like someone had ripped his heart out.

Raven laughed and froze Ben in midair. "Loyalty," he cackled, "is always entertaining." He flung Ben back to the Winters.

"Are they dead?" I asked. I heard a buzzing in my head, so I wasn't sure.

"Do not fret, my girl," Alexander said, wandering around their graves. "You can still sense them, can you not?" I nodded. "Then you know they are with us still. Day of the Dead beliefs are very interesting, half-Christian and half-Pagan. I think you can relate to that, Puritan witch?" I nodded again. "I love the idea that the soul can return for a visit, so I've used that as my inspiration. I've sent the souls of your siblings to a sort of limbo for now. Their bodies are here, but they will not wake until I choose for their souls to return. Which I will, should you all cooperate," he smiled darkly.

I turned to my companions. They were still yards away and straining against an invisible barrier. "Bound for our own good," Alexander said, looking back at the Winters. "Terrible lushes, these *vieczy*."

"They aren't all *vieczy*," I argued.

"Sweet girl, don't you know I know everything?" he asked, a chilly hand gliding along my face.

Everett cried out when Raven touched me, which amused him immensely. Then, unlike the others who struggled against the bindings, I saw a still Valentin fix his eyes on Sam. Soon he formed some connection with her that jarred her body, and he was able to break free.

Valentin reached out for Raven — to read him, as he'd promised — and Alexander Raven turned on him, grabbed his hand, and with no other effort, Valentin fell to the ground.

He was dead.

CHAPTER TWENTY-TWO

alpha and omega

"WHAT DID YOU DO TO HIM?" I CRIED, DROPPING DOWN BESIDE Valentin.

"I have no pity for the death of mere mortals. Their time will come eventually. It is no great disservice to bring it sooner," Raven said callously.

A pale green smoke rose from Valentin's lips. "Inhale!" Anthony cried, and, somehow in my daze, I understood him and followed his command. But Raven did also, and the smoke divided between us and came into both of our lips. I felt hot and then cold, and then an uncomfortable vibration down my spine, into my gut. My vision shifted slightly, as if every living thing had some faint other layer of color to it I hadn't seen before. A foreign feeling of what I believed to be nausea rose in my throat. I realized this was the process of acquisition. I had acquired Valentin's power — half of it, anyway.

Raven's face lit up as he felt the same odd things I did. "A reader! How glorious! It's so rare the nosferatu have any special powers to offer, but this is a real treat," he smiled. So now, Raven was a reader, too. Did that mean I was as well? I looked at Raven, back to the Winters and Ben, even down at myself, but I couldn't tell anything about us. I didn't know anything I hadn't known before.

I closed my eyes, trying to make sense of things. When I opened them again, everything was the same. All I saw was Valentin's body and Raven.

"And you a reader too, daughter Sadie? Now how could I go anywhere without you?" He reached toward me to pull me up, but I jerked away.

"You bastard!" Everett screamed. "Touch her again and I'll kill you."

Raven said. "You'll want to control him. It would be unwise to assume I need to touch him in order to destroy him," he hissed.

"Everett, *please*," I begged. "Be quiet." His red eyes were glowing like neon light in the night air. Mark had to cover his mouth. Where was that cool California boy now?

Ben cowered away from the mass of them, his terror real.

Alexander reached out for me again, likely to torture Everett. But when his hand touched my cheek, his eyes opened wide and he inhaled sharply. Something had shocked him. I realized quickly that it was by something he had *read*. "It can't be…" he whispered.

Then everything went black.

QUICKLY THE WORLD REAPPEARED. WE WERE IN THE SAME PLACE, BUT IT WAS lighter out, and we were alone. Raven was wearing different clothes. His hair messed up and out of his face. He wore blue jeans, a Henley shirt and an undershirt underneath it. His face was textured with a hint of scruff. He looked much more human.

But he had reimagined me completely. My hair was swept back out of my face and hung low at my neck. He had dressed me in a draped blood red jersey Elie Saab gown I'd seen on a runway. It was belted tight against my waist, cut high across my neck with sleeves that touched my palms. And it was slit all the way up my thigh. My feet were bare.

"Why do we look different?" I asked. "Where are we?"

"We're in a place inside my mind," he said, his voice nostalgic and distant as he wandered among the graves. So this gown, this bareness… it's how he had reimagined me. I instantly felt exposed and uncomfortable in a way words could never describe. "This is what I don't like about you, Sadie. You think there's an answer to every question, a reason for every sin. It is naïve. There are some of us in this world who are capable of things you'll never be able to explain. We possess power you can't trace, do things you can't comprehend. I'm one of those. I am above your laws and logic. I am above your human-like emotion and your stupid faiths."

Evil. I understood he was evil. Worse, since he was our Point of Origin, I knew that all Survivors came from the same evil place.

"I believe answers can be found," I said, surprisingly defiant for how terrified I felt. "Where are the others?" I asked.

"Where we left them," he said simply. "I must say, for such a conflicted, unfocused individual, you lead quite a coven."

"They are not my coven, and I don't lead them," I said. "They're my friends, my family."

"Who follow you to the ends of the earth unfalteringly. Think of it how you will, but you're the first Survivor ever to arrive at my feet with her own vampires and shape-shifters in tow. Much less the *vieczy* under your spell. They are the most notorious creatures on this planet. Aside from me, of course," he said.

I thought through what he said. "Do you mean that other Survivors have been here?" I asked.

Raven smirked, but he did not answer.

"What did you see when you touched me?" I asked.

"Only what Valentin must have seen any time he'd ever touched you," he said.

"What was that?" I asked.

"You don't know?"

"No," I told him.

A grin spread across Raven's face. He loved being in a position of power, and so he was going to make me wait for an answer. "Reading is a fine art, Sadie, one that takes time and practice to fully understand and utilize, which means if you got any of the dead nosferatu's power you'll not know what to do with it in time for it to matter."

"Why could you read me so easily?" I asked.

"Because I've been a reader before. Reading, really, is not unlike your tracking skill, I believe. Yours is a unique sense, a fully developed awareness and attraction to a thing. It must make you awfully bull-headed though," he said.

"Why do you say that?"

"You're drawn to things by nature. They call to you. Find you. Invade your mind and your soul. This carries over into your life and your attitude. You must be the type to get an idea and not let go of it. To believe there is an answer if you want one? To feel something for someone so strongly that it clouds your mind and your judgment? You must feel magnetized to that mate of yours. It's probably somewhat excruciating," he guessed.

"It is," I admitted. My love for Everett had come automatically, but it grated on me as time went on. It had grown in a paradoxical fashion: The more I loved him, the more the ache grew. This held true with whatever had happened with the wound on my neck the day before. I felt addicted to him now: a powerful high, an impossible withdrawal. And a total fear that someone would cut off my supply.

The line between pursuit and obsession had become blurred in the time I lived among humans. The line between cost and benefit was murky too. The line between seeking danger and self-preservation had disappeared entirely.

"How do you know this?" I asked.

"I've had a million powers. I've had one like your unique tracking ability, though not as acute."

"Did you love, then?" I asked. "Was it painful?"

"All love is pain," he said solemnly. "It's a fact of life. It has been since I was created. It will continue to be as the world goes on."

"But for you, was it more painful than it was for others?" I asked, oddly seeking solace in the monster before me. This was a good example of how my love for something could cloud my judgment. Overcome by the emotional battle I'd been facing all winter in loving Everett, and the newfound connection I felt with him, I couldn't even prioritize in this moment and focus on the task at hand.

He stopped his pacing again. "Again with your questions," he said. "That's a persistent goal, then, the seeking of truth?" he asked.

I nodded. That was an understatement.

He held one elbow in his palm, and tapped fingers against his chin, thinking. "All right, then. I'm willing to level with you. You are a special child, Sadie. One I've never seen. One I've only hoped existed. I will make you a deal," he said.

"What kind of deal?" I asked warily. Would any deal I made with him be a deal with the Devil?

"I'll answer your questions if you'll answer mine," he said plainly.

Deal with the Devil or not, that was an offer I couldn't refuse. "Done and done."

The corners of his mouth turned up and his eyes glowed like a child's. This made him happy. *Too* happy. "I did love," he said. "It was a love that history would not soon forget."

"One I've heard of?" I asked.

"I'm sure of it. Do you know the story of Achilles and Penthesilea?" he asked.

"Sure. The greatest warrior in Greek history and the Queen of the Amazons. The only time Achilles ever fell in love was when he killed

Penthesilea and their eyes met as she was dying. But it was too late to save her," I said.

"It's his tragedy that he killed the only thing he'd ever loved before even having a chance to love it."

"You're telling me that that was you?" I asked incredulously.

"In a way," he said. "You could say that Achilles gave me that curse."

I rolled my eyes. Achilles? Really? "What other rare abilities have you had?" I asked.

"I once had a reading ability that I cultured carefully over time," he explained.

"And?"

"Someone acquired it from me in a moment of weakness," he said stiffly. It was clear that Alexander Raven didn't like weakness. "It feels right to have it again. I ought to know what everyone is when I have been so influential in the supernatural world."

"How so?" I asked.

"You all come from me." He pulled back his sleeve to reveal a crimson symbol on his left wrist:

"You heretic," I said. "What do you see yourself as — some kind of messiah?"

"I walked this earth for two thousand years before your King of Kings was born. I had that symbol long before the Christians assigned it as a symbol of martyrdom. I'm no messiah, Sadie. I'm the only thing more powerful than a messiah. The Father. The Creator," he said fiercely.

"The Point of Origin," I said reluctantly. I'd given in to his image of himself before I'd ever even met him.

"Precisely. You will not find a supernatural creature on this earth whose veins don't carry my blood. I cannot say the same for those who humans create unknowingly," he explained.

"Like the *nosferatu* and the *vieczy*?" I asked.

He nodded. "But Survivors are the rarest, strongest kind of supernatural. Though Survivors, too, are capable of inbreeding in such a way that they will create their own version of nosferatu and vieczy," he said matter-of-factly, "as you've seen."

"What makes us different?" I asked.

He ignored me. "I've been looking for you. I've been looking for those damned kids from Salem for three hundred years. And now you've found me," he smiled.

"Lizzie led us here," I said, "because she thought you were good."

"Lizzie didn't lead you here. I guarantee it was *Beowulf*," he said. My eyes widened. "You didn't really think I'd tell pitiful, poor Lizzie who loved me so where to find me? She'd have come for me, before they had produced sufficient offspring. But I knew she'd pass on the book."

So Everett was right. Someone else had marked the passages. "Why did you call yourself the last Survivor? From the sound of it, you're the first of us," I said.

"Quite an astute point. You see, Sadie, many times I've been the last Survivor, though I am — and will always remain — the first. The Alpha and the Omega."

"You do think you're God," I hissed, nauseated by his sacrilege.

"You've got to get over that," he sighed. He was slowly, widely circling me at this point, running his hands over the blank gravestones that he'd formed in his mind. "Let me tell you a story.

"Despite some people's better attempts, everyone's lives involve routine. Even for me. My routine is just more centennial than daily, but it's simple: I build societies all over the world, hotbeds of supernatural activity or places that I want to conquer," he said.

"Like Salem," I offered.

"Exactly. You chose my biggest failure to date."

"Because of how many innocent people died?" I asked.

"What have I told you about mortals? They're dispensable, and it is not for me to feel bad about choosing their time to go," he said.

"It was you who tortured them, wasn't it?" I asked, understanding.

He scoffed at this. "It wasn't exactly torture. I just appeared to them — how they reacted to that was their own fault."

"Are you the man in Black, as they all described?" I asked.

"Don't be ridiculous," he laughed. Raven snapped his fingers theatrically, and suddenly was wearing a Puritan-era suit, shoes, and hat, head to toe in black. "Of course I was the Man in Black."

Tentatively, I asked, "Are you...the Devil?"

Raven laughed. "What is a devil but the opposing force to your God?"

"The Devil is evil," I countered.

"What an abstract term," he sighed. "The Devil, the opposition to God, whomever — that being would be incredibly powerful, above all else. Above the weak, relative forces of good and evil. I'm sure this idea of a Devil stems only from the concern that his power would in any way rival your God's. Yes, you'd hate to think of that, wouldn't you? That someone like me could have that kind of power?"

"It's impossible!" I cried.

Raven rolled his eyes. "Let's dissect this concern you have with my... omnipotence. What makes me any different than a god? I'm immortal. I'm indestructible. I exist whether you believe I do or not, but believing connects you to me in some way, implies you have some reason to believe. And I can control anything, anyone, anywhere, at any time."

This irked me. "Surely you're joking," I said, choking on his arrogance.

He narrowed his eyes at me. "In what way would I be joking?"

"The Alexander Raven that Lizzie told me about was a mentor to her, a quiet, devout Puritan who led her through her times of trouble," I said.

"Ah, Lizzie. My greatest disappointment to date," he sighed. "You know what I envisioned for her…well, there's no comparison. She was so powerful. So dedicated. But she was also naïve, and thus proved to be useless."

"She looked up to you," I said, my throat tight. I hated to hear him talk about her this way.

"Her downfall was her dedication to her faith," he said callously. "I mean, it worked for me initially because she saw me as a part of the faith. But I only adopted the persona of a Puritan in 17th century Massachusetts. She believed it."

"She thought you believed it too," I said.

"Acting the part isn't the same as believing it. You think I actually believed all that Bible-thumping, self-flagellating bullshit?" he asked.

I swallowed hard. That's exactly what I thought.

"I've been a tribal leader in rural Africa, a pharaoh in ancient Egypt, a Buddhist leader in Malaysia, Rabbi to a group of exiled Jews, a Hindi spiritual advisor, a Democrat, a Republican, a Communist, a Marxist, a Nazi. I've been everything it took to connect to people at their most emotionally vulnerable levels. I was a Puritan, and I spoke of their God because they did. I could care less about any of it."

"What about Hannah?" I asked, my voice thick with emotion.

"Who?" he asked.

"Your daughter in Salem. Your only child there. She can see the future like you. You don't remember her?" I asked, my chest tight now.

"I don't care enough to remember," he laughed. "Do you know how many children I have had? One way or the other. Born of a mother or turned into one or created in some way, how many creatures have my blood in them? Sadie, you're worrying me. I agreed to talk to you because I thought I could tell you my story — one of power and of success and unrivaled freedom, of a future in Survival — and you would be hooked. But you're sounding sentimental. What is a family but a distraction, a group of people whose blood you share?"

"A distraction from what?" I asked.

"A distraction from power," he said coolly.

"You just said you create societies — *families* — all over the world. Why would you do that if you didn't want anything to do with them?" I asked.

He stood directly in front of me now, inches from my face, the stillness in his presence unnerving. "For power," he said again. "You have asked the wrong questions so far. Try again: 'Alexander, you create societies all over the world of your kind — why?' and then I'd say, 'For power.' Then, you'd ask, 'But how does that give you power?' and I'd say 'They provide an endless tap from which to acquire new power for yourself.' You see?" he said.

Acquisition. It was all about acquisition. "You create families to kill them," I said, my head feeling light.

"Ah! You *do* understand," he smiled, clapping his hands together.

"And you were looking for me..."

"Because your family is the only one I ever lost," he said.

"B-b-because Lizzie moved us from where we were supposed to be," I said, understanding. Lizzie had thought that by moving us she'd doomed us, but instead this was our salvation. What she saw as her greatest mistake had been the only way our family had survived at all.

And what the Survivors had thought of always as God's work — creating a family, isolating that family to their mountainside — had been the opposite.

"But now you're here. You are the link to what's rightfully mine," he said. "Thank you, my dear, for going through all this trouble to find me."

"When you say take what's yours..." I trailed. "You mean..."

"Their powers," he said.

"Their lives," I croaked.

"What *lives*? What are bodies but holders for powers anyway? I have only the power I started with and the power I acquire. You know that, even though a Survivor is born with a power and houses it, it takes until that Survivor stops aging for the power to take effect. I let them all grow, and each one hones the skill over time. Then, I acquire a fully matured and valuable talent," he explained. The glaring lack of emotion in his voice grated against my bones. "Look, this has worked for me for millennia. I plant the seeds to build families — like your fourteen Salem Survivors — and then I leave, of course. I have to tell you, dear, child-rearing was just never my forte. I let them grow for a hundred years or so, go off and start another family with a few I take along, and then I come back and kill them. It's like growing powers out of nothing, and let me tell you, it absolutely is the best way. Now I'm more powerful than every one of our kind — than every one of *any* kind — that has ever lived!" he shouted, again laughing maniacally.

"You said fourteen Survivors," I said, catching the error, "but there were twenty-six exiled from Salem. How did you erroneously identify a dozen humans as Survivors you'd created?"

"Learn this now: I do nothing *erroneously*. Those were the sorry human offspring of my least favorite peers in Salem. I was doing the world a favor by ending their family trees," he snarled.

"How can you have such disregard for humans?" I asked.

"Oh, I care about humans. That's why I acquire. As I get that much closer to being all-powerful, I save humans while I'm at it," he said.

"How does that save humans?" I asked, heated.

"Well just look at what your siblings have turned into! Ridiculous, murderous leeches if you ask me. And now I can have all of their powers *and* keep them from killing any more humans. It's a win-win!" he laughed.

"But why do you even care about saving humans?" I asked.

"What if, one day, I want them to like me?" he mused. He let the sentence hang there. Why would Alexander Raven need for humans to like him?

"Do you feel no loyalty toward the family you kill?" I asked urgently. "No love toward them?"

"Sadie, do not kid yourself. Your family is weak, burdened by emotion — love, loyalty. And that mixed bag of supernaturals you travel with are just as bad. But that is not the way our kind lives. Haven't you met others like yourself in all your travels? And do they love each other? Do they love anything more than power? More than the kill?" he asked.

I hadn't thought of it that way. I had always accredited this loyalty to God and family as something unique to my *kind*, but it was really just a trait important to my family. I suddenly longed for them. All of them. I wanted peace, and I wanted to be near them, and I wanted this war to be prevented.

"And me coming to you…you are going to kill them now because I'm here? Because you can follow me back to them now?" I asked, my fingertips to my forehead.

"That's the plan," he said casually.

"Then why bring the rogue Survivors into it at all? Why haven't you just killed them?" I asked.

"Well, I hear your family has gotten a little out of control, size-wise. It may be some trouble to take them out all at once," he reasoned. "So your recently vampiric brethren will be very useful. It seems they have something of a score to settle, an angry vengeance to seek against those who — in their eyes — kept them from the euphoria of blood-drinking for centuries. They'll acquire the power for me this time. And then I'll acquire it from them."

"The war. You're entirely responsible for the war," I whispered.

"A war?" he asked.

"Anthony had a vision of a war. Survivors against Survivors. I found you to find a way to defend ourselves against the rogue Survivors. I thought you'd help us. Not lead you back to my family so you could kill them," I said tearfully.

"The last of my kind, alone? Like the last survivor in *Beowulf*? You're such a romantic. And so easy," he mused. He sounded like Sam had in the alley in Salem. Or, rather, Sam had sounded like him.

"Why did you tell Lizzie to keep the Survivors inside the city walls to protect them. What did you care if they became *vieczy*?" I asked.

"All matter of vampiric creatures are the most difficult creatures to deal with. They expose us," he said. "But it doesn't matter. Lizzie didn't listen to me. If she had, there wouldn't be twenty-nine of you in Xox-ocotlán. Thirty if you count the scared kid you brought."

"They didn't leave until I did. It was my fault," I said.

He smiled. "That makes sense," he admitted. "I suppose Lizzie did her part, then. But she couldn't have kept *you* contained." He had wandered away from me now.

"Why?"

"You truly don't know?" he face mystified. Evading, he said, "Ask me another question."

"How do you kill a Survivor?" I asked.

"Now that is a funny story," he said. "I'm not sure you'll believe it if I tell it," he said.

"Try me," I said dryly.

"Did you know that Alexander is one of the oldest names in written history? Its roots are different in different languages, but the name that it stems from is older than I am! In Greek mythology, my name would have been Paris.

"You've heard of the Trojan War?" he asked. I nodded. "So you know the story. Paris wants Helen. Helen is married to the king of Troy, Menelaus. Paris steals Helen, and a war ensues," he explained.

"What does this have to do with killing a Survivor?" I asked.

"Sadie, you ask *how* to kill a Survivor. I ask *why* one can be killed at all. There was a time when our kind could not be killed. It was a glorious time! Do you know what we were called then?" he asked. I shook my head. "They called us gods. All those stories you've read in that book you carry around with you. That was us," he said.

"So what happened?" I asked, not believing him.

"There came a way for us to die, of course. It was my fault. I was careless. In that damn war, I thought I was only fighting humans," he said resentfully.

"What war?" I asked.

"The Trojan War, Sadie! Keep up!" he snapped.

"You were there?" I asked. "History has no memory of you."

"You call it history, I call it I-was-there. I started it for crying out loud. I am Paris of Troy! Who knew that spat would be something the world wouldn't forget?" he laughed. I shook my head. I didn't believe this either. "There was one fighting among them who was supernatural. One who, supposedly, could not die."

"Achilles," I said.

"Good girl. Their superstitions told them Achilles could not die but for that one tiny place his dear mother held him by when she dipped him in the River Styx," he said. "Every warrior has a weakness, Sadie. And every human is stupid. They thought he couldn't die, well I proved them wrong, didn't I?" he shot.

"You're telling me that you killed Achilles? In the Trojan War? That was *you*?" I asked incredulously. "Paris died," I laughed. "Struck by an arrow from Philoctetes in the war. *Keep up.*"

"Like I don't know how to fake my own death. You can laugh all you want, but I take it very seriously. In killing Achilles, I lost my invincibility. Instead of his power, I acquired his greatest weakness, and so, in turn, have all my descendants," he said, his eyes heavy.

"We have an Achilles heel," I said.

"Every one of you," he said. "Which, as it turns out, has worked well for me. That weakness in all of you has led to immeasurable power for me," he grinned.

"It's the heel then?" I asked. Admittedly, I hadn't tried that.

"Oh, come now. Be a little more creative. The *proverbial* heel depends on the individual and his powers. Our greatest weakness is at the source of our greatest power," he said. "Now chew on that, you morbid little girl."

I narrowed my eyes at him. He was playing games. "Why couldn't Lizzie keep me contained in the city? Why can't they keep me contained, even now?" I asked.

"Because of the human in you," he said.

I froze.

He smiled the sly, dark, and invasive smile he'd smiled at the girls with the open wounds. He reached for my covered arms.

"What are you doing?" I asked, fidgeting away, but he grabbed hold tightly, pulling the sleeves back. I fought him.

"Making a point," he said, yanking my arms toward him now. In doing so, he closed the distance between our bodies, intertwining my hand in his as he examined me.

"Please let go!" I cried. Frustrated, he pushed me back against a headstone, and in an instant, I was wearing a completely different gown. I felt my hair lay against my bare back and shoulders then, a sensation so foreign to me I hardly recognized it. When I looked down, I was wearing a much more elaborate couture ballgown in a glowing orange-red persimmon. Its rich layers of tulle encompassed my frame tightly, with huge taffeta ruffled up toward my neck and around my waist. But I was completely exposed.

His eyes lit up at the sight of my bare skin. "Sam told me there were scars, but she didn't do them justice," he said. He ran his hands over all the scars on my arms. Then, cutting through the ghost-fabric, he reached straight through the gown to my stomach, feeling the teeth marks Sam had put there and undoubtedly told him about. "There must be near equal parts in you, human and Survivor, to have scarred — and healed — this much."

"What are you talking about?" I pleaded, praying for the invasive contact to end.

"Simple. You've *healed*," he smiled. "Healing is a particularly human thing, you might say. Something only a living creature can do. The supernatural's body immediately remedies itself with no lasting marks. But healing? Scar tissue? It takes human blood and human skin. The supernatural in you healed the wounds better than a human's would have, let you get away with more, but the human in you healed them and left scars.

"You're the only half-human on this planet. You've got to be. I'm dying to know how it happened," he smiled wickedly.

I forced myself not to believe him. It took every fiber of my being not to believe him — because being human, if even only part — isn't that all I'd ever wanted? And this was Alexander Raven. Someone who lied. Someone who would tell you anything to get you to do what he wanted.

But what if he wasn't lying?

I had always been different. The scars. The looks. The desire to die. Always! Was there an actual reason for this? "I didn't know Survivors and humans could mate," I argued, unwilling to let myself believe a lie.

"They can't," he said.

"Then how could I be half anything?" I asked.

He furrowed his brow, considering this. "That's what I need to find out. You may be a hybrid, even a chimera. I want to see." He stepped in front of me again. "Sadie, I think you are the most important person I have ever met," he said, pulling my body even closer to his. The move was predatory in all the wrong ways. Not like he wanted to kill me. Exactly like he wanted to defile me.

He hadn't called me Daughter since we left Everett and the others behind in the parallel…world. I could see in his eyes that something had changed, and that wasn't how he thought of me anymore.

I struggled against him, but I had no power. His face scraped against mine, and I strained my neck backward to avoid him. I felt him run his thumb down the shimmery new scar on my neck.

He let me go, slamming me backward into a headstone. I had upset him — merely by not reciprocating? I wasn't sure.

"Now you're going to go after my family, aren't you?" I said, knowing an animosity had just formed between us.

"That is my intent," he said. "But you needn't worry about that. Your days of preparing for this war are over. You're free of all that now."

"How?"

"You're coming with me. Join Sam and me. We have a few others waiting for our return to Europe. Though I rather like the mild climate here in Oaxaca."

"I like the cold," I said, crossing my arms across my chest.

"Fine. Europe it is," he said.

"Would you leave my family alone if I came with you?" I asked.

"Darling, their fate is sealed either way," he laughed.

"Then I'm not going anywhere with you," I said.

"You prefer to go back to your family, watch them die, *then* go with me?" he asked.

"I'm not going anywhere with you," I said. "Now or then."

"You don't want to make me torture that poor coven you brought with you, do you?" he said, feigning pity in his voice.

"You are no match for them," I said. "They're stronger than we are."

"I doubt that. *Vieczy* are stronger than all the other vampires, true, but I doubt they are stronger than I am. There is only one kind of vampiric inbreed I'd be concerned about in a fight, and what are the odds that four of those made it here to fight me?" he said. What kind might that be? I wondered. "But, I do not feel like fighting tonight. Perhaps I could charm them into turning on each other? It would be fun to watch. My money is on the cocky young one, who seems even fiercer than the brooding older one. Your boy, of course, wouldn't stand a chance against them," he said lightly.

"I don't care about them," I lied.

"Please, pretty girl, I can feel your feelings as well as you could feel mine if I'd let you. I know how you care for them," he said.

"Kill me, then, and leave them be," I said.

"And give you what you want?" he said gesturing to the scars. "I am not a genie, I do not grant wishes. Besides, why would I kill you? I need you. Can you imagine how interesting it would be if we made some sort of superhumans? If you mated with a human, I wonder what would happen? Or what if you mated with me? What kind of power would we have then? What kind of weakness? And for my finale? Well, you're probably the missing piece."

Finale? I wondered, but I was too distracted to ask him what he meant by that. "Children? You want me to come with you so I can have children for you?" I asked, hostile. He might have had any other purpose for me in mind and I might, I *might* have gone if it would protect my family and the Winters. But procreation?

My stomach tied itself in knots.

"It would be an interesting experiment," he said, clearly not having sensed my disgust. "I would love to have a Visionary like you on my team. You know, I might bring that little blonde along, too. A Mirror is just as rare. But, of course, she can't procreate, so she is not as useful."

My last defense was to find holes in his theory. "Raven, if I'm half-human, wouldn't I be half-dead by now, after trying so hard to die?" I asked, gesturing to my scars.

This troubled him, and by his lack of response, I could tell he didn't know the answer. It gave me reason to think he was lying to me or at least exaggerating. What wouldn't a man like Alexander Raven say to you — however untrue — if it meant getting what he wanted?

"I won't go with you," I said. "I don't believe a word you've said."

He eyed me strangely and put his thin fingers to his chin, tapping. "All right," he said. "You can go. I have a new idea. You know what's fun, Sadie? Making people wait to die. Dragging it out and ruining whatever time they have left. I can do this for your entire family, if you insist. I can let you go," he said. "You'll go and tell them I am coming for them. They'll start preparing furiously. They will not understand that I am indestructible. They won't know that they don't have a chance. They'll have no choice but to sit and wait and worry until they meet their own violent ends. Yes, that is a beautiful plan. Payback for Lizzie's insolence in hiding you from me, in taking you all where I could not find you," he said. "Then every one of your elders' dying memories will be seeing their family torn apart. This is too devious a plan to pass up!" Raven cried. "Come now, Sadie. It's time to take you back to your friends and send you on your way to self-selected torment."

What had I done?

My mind went frantic. Should I tell him I'd go with him? Bargain my soul, my womb, my *anything* to protect my family and the Winters? But how would I even know he'd keep up his end of the deal?

I decided on defiance. "I'll stop you, Raven," I promised. "I'll find a way."

He laughed. "Oh, pretty girl, of course you will." Then he snapped his fingers, and the blackness came and went again. When I came to, I was standing back in the real cemetery at Xoxocotlán with my coat and ripped sweater at my feet. Everything was where I'd left it: Valentin's body on the ground, Ben and the Winters now unbound a few feet from me, the rogue Survivors no longer lain among the flower-covered graves, and Alexander Raven nowhere in sight.

refugee

EVERETT BOLTED TO MY SIDE AND KISSED MY FOREHEAD, PULLING me tight to his chest. "Princess! Oh, my god." He clasped me so tightly I thought I'd break. Electric charges and blurred visions of colors danced in my head. I couldn't make any sense of them. "Don't ever do that again! I just..." he laughed through dry sobs. "I love you so much," he said, crashing his lips against mine, kissing me desperately. He couldn't get close enough to me. I empathized.

"Where did he take you?" Anthony asked.

"To a place inside his mind," I said dryly, dazed. "Where did they go?" I gestured to the empty graves.

"They disappeared — Sam too — when you came back," Ginny explained.

I looked down at Valentin's body again, his lips blue, his white-blonde eyebrows shining in the moonlight, and my stomach tightened again. Ben was sitting on the ground, leaning against a headstone. Knees to his chest. Head in his hands. I was furious with Mark for letting him come.

I knelt next to him. "I'm sorry," I said, reaching out and touching his face.

I could see he'd been crying. "No, I needed to see it," he said, trying to be brave. "It's just…they were right there… Noah was right there…" he choked, tears welling up in his pale blue eyes again.

"I know," I said, and I sat next to him. What could any of us say to Ben, watching his innocence be torn from him in such a violent way? I put my arm around him and tucked his tearful face against my neck.

Oddly, I felt more electric charges, saw colors again. I felt sure this was my reading power, but it meant nothing to me yet.

"What happened?" Patrick asked. "What did Raven want?"

I motioned for Patrick to kneel to me, and I pulled violet wisps with aqua-green in them from my fingertips and put them into his head. My entire conversation with Raven was now in his brain. His eyes widened. "Tell them, Sadie. Tell them what he told you," he urged.

Exhausted, I looked up at the Winters. "He's going to start the war," I said flatly. "He plans to kill us all."

—♦—

ANTHONY AND PATRICK WRAPPED VALENTIN'S BODY IN CLOTH THEY RETRIEVED from the town. "We'll take him back to Narcisa," Anthony said gravely. "The nosferatu bury their dead."

On the jet, my mind began to function again. I hadn't realized how numb I'd felt with Raven until what he'd said started sinking in. What if I was part human? What would that actually mean?

I couldn't even process it. It had been what I wanted all along, only Raven had managed to take this from me too.

Deciding I didn't want to think anymore, I flicked through the pages of applications on my phone, zoning out as best I could. I opened up Twitter and came across a conversation between Corrina and Felix and Ginny and Mark. They'd long since joined Twitter, amused at Corrina and my ramblings. Corrina had slowly warmed up to us on Twitter, though I had still not officially spoken to her since Dallas on her birthday. And on nights when not much was happening, for twenty minutes here and there, we'd all be on there, having one giant conversation. And even among the Winters, I'd feel normal. And I'd be okay.

I often disappeared from these conversations, as if unable to contribute to them because I was too busy to check in on them. Instead, I'd sit and watch as my phone would update, and I'd say nothing. I couldn't bring myself to realize that there were so few things for me to say that sounded normal, that I had a definitive limit on my ability to interact socially. Only none of them ever felt this way. Not even Everett.

It was a Friday night. Felix and Corrina seemed to be home on their couch, and Ginny, *@BlondeLouboutin*, had said she and Mark were with Everett and me. Felix, *@FxWilliams*, made some comment about Everett that seemed uncharacteristically playful.

Mark, *@TheGrnEyedMnstr*, responded to him, "You must have seen some soft-ended side of my brother I've never seen."

To which Corrina replied, speaking of Everett, *@TPWinterB* and me, "Have you missed this? They're in love."

And we were in love. That was true — so true that people who watched us interact in only brief intervals could see it. Why then did it still feel so foreign? Why didn't it feel *good*?

This connection was so intense. And when it was good, it was all-consuming, life-altering good. When we were together we were unstoppable. But we had to be so cautious! Although the 19th century girl in me wanted to hold back, the 21st century girl didn't want to be limited just because further contact might turn me into what he was. So, in being limited, we were trapped.

So was this love? Tension as often as calm? Fighting for our lives and struggling to maintain our beliefs? Anger all the time. Ferocity. Secrets. Lies. Limits. The pain that came with loving him, like Alexander Raven had so astutely pointed out. This was the stuff fairy tales were made of? The passion was rampant, sure. But somehow, the more I loved him, the more afraid I became of it. The more I loved him, the more I wanted out.

Because like in everything else, I wanted freedom. As the plane landed, I wondered if what I wanted now was freedom in the form of keeping my family safe or freedom from my responsibility to the lot of them. And didn't the same question apply to Everett and me? I wondered if my delirious vision of happiness was freedom *with* Everett or freedom *from* him. The beach vision had been Anthony's vision of us. It had never been mine.

In the end, I knew. I wanted to be free from it all.

WE ARRIVED AT THE GATES OF THE SURVIVORS' CITY WALKING SLOWLY. MARK carried Ginny on his back up from the cars, a testament to their use of playful, childlike sibling love as the antidote to the violence that surrounded them. Patrick walked stoically in Anthony's footsteps, carrying Valentin's body. Ben lagged to the side, stumbling as if wounded, which, in so many ways, he was. And Everett held my hand tightly, pulling me close and wrapping my arm around his waist as we approached. He kissed my forehead in just the way I'd seen Patrick kiss Madeline. Now, having thought he'd lost me, he was terrified of losing me for real. Now, all he wanted was his love. A quiet beach somewhere. Warm water. A summer night.

Hannah, Andrew, and Sarah stood at the gates. Lizzie's absence screamed at me like a fire truck siren. Anthony had called ahead and told Adelaide to keep Narcisa in the house so we could tell her alone.

"Did you find my father?" Hannah asked.

"No, Hannah. I didn't," I lied. "But I found the thing that killed him." I would never do her the disservice of telling her what her father was, nor would I tell her that, to him, she was nothing. Not even a memory.

Patrick came up behind us, and as the elders' eyes fell on the wrapped body, they were quieted. Andrew pulled Ben to his chest, and they walked away together, silently, save for Ben's sobs.

When we rounded the corner to the Winters' house, Madeline opened the door and lit up at the sight of her husband. Patrick handed the body off to Anthony so he could hug his wife. His eyes closed as he inhaled her.

Adelaide was next, and she came mournfully, quietly out of the house.

"I'll tell her," I said. "It was my fault. It all is."

"Sadie, we can do it for you," Patrick said, the most tender he'd ever been with me. "We've been down this road before."

But it was too late. "Tell what?" Narcisa asked. "Where's…?" She saw him. "No…" she whispered, her eyes wide in shock. "No," she said more forcefully, her face drained of any color. "No!" she cried now, rushing to the body. "What did you do to him? What'd you do?" she screamed, and beat Anthony's arms.

"It wasn't them," I said. "It was the one we were looking for."

"Let me see him," she said, her voice paper-thin. Anthony laid Valentin's body on the ground and uncovered his face. His lips were pale, and there were deep purple circles under his eyes. Having never seen or known anyone to die, I kept expecting him to open his eyes, to move as if in his sleep. But he was perpetually still.

Tears swelled down from Narcisa's eyes as she pressed her face to his icy chest. Adelaide dropped to her, trying to comfort her to little avail. Narcisa murmured over him in Romanian. "You cannot leave me, my love. I cannot exist without you. I cannot." She was crying so hard she was hiccupping, hiccupping so hard she couldn't breathe. She mumbled more, forcing the words out in soft high pitches between sobs, but I couldn't make most of it out until she started repeating, "I'm a half, not a whole. I'm a half, not a whole."

I'd never seen such a real breakdown. I could feel the dismay hit her and grow as it became real. I could feel warmth drain from her as she lost her breath and her compassion, her heart. I could feel it as she got swept under the tide of grief, pressed under by the weight of loss, ripped apart by the current, by the gravity of her love for him. Oh, that love. Now, that loss.

Everett stood by me, not able even to look at Narcisa. It didn't take my mind-reading powers to know what he was thinking: He never wanted to experience this.

But I already was experiencing it through Narcisa. The pain was so real I felt my airway close. This is where love would get me. This is what I'd have to fear then suffer through. I could see what Raven meant when he said this was weakness. Beautiful, strong, smart Narcisa reduced to a catatonic heap over the body of her lover. Possessed by her own love for him. Doomed to be haunted by the loss forever.

And this kind of loss — the kind you felt for the ones you loved, the kind that split your soul apart — I wouldn't only feel it with Everett. I'd feel it with the loss of each of my family members, my soul ripped into 165 pieces if Raven got his way.

Although I would likely never lose Everett, and he would never lose me, I didn't know how I could ever stand life among mortals if I would have to watch this scene time and time again as they lost each other, as I lost them. And as they lost each other, I would remain.

I couldn't do this. Not right now. Not ever.

Instinctively, I backed away from Everett and the rest of them. My feet were trying to carry me away, hearing the messages from my brain that told me to go, to run.

"Sadie?" Everett finally turned around.

"I…" I tried to speak, frozen there. "I…" I tried again. Now Mark and Ginny had turned around to look at me. Adelaide looked up from her perch next to Narcisa. A few of the elders had gathered, and each of them stared at me in confusion, one more time, Lizzie's face missing from the crowd. "I…can't," I choked.

Everett took two steps toward me, and I flinched.

"I can't," I repeated. "Can't," I said again, dizzy, and hot with fear.

Everett grabbed me. "Sadie, listen to me. Look at me," he said, his strong grasp crushing my shoulder. He didn't mean to do it. He was just terrified. "I know this is hard to watch, but…"

"Everett," I choked. "I can't."

"You can, princess. I love you. You love me, don't you? You feel it. I know you do," he eased, trying to get me to focus, trying to do for me what I'd done for him in the airport in London. To find my senses. Find solace in one another.

But it was too late.

"Can't…" I whispered.

He loosened his grip for one second, dejected. Enough time for me to think he understood. Enough time to run.

I TOOK OFF, SPRINTING FASTER THAN ANY OF THEM COULD CATCH ME. WHEN I broke free of the mountain range, many miles west of the family's city, they were nowhere near. My solitude told me they hadn't come after me.

I SOUGHT REFUGE. IN MORTALITY. IN HUMANITY. IN NEW YORK.

My heart was in the right place. I wasn't running from Everett. I wasn't even running toward Cole. I just needed someone, someone who could understand why what I had seen would make me want to run away from it all. I needed a refuge, and I had only ever had one.

The doorman had gone home for the night, so I entered the code I'd seen him enter on the keypad at his door and in the elevator in his building. When I arrived at his door, my tote bag and traveling pack were in front of it with the plastic wand from Salem sitting on top of them. Mark had projected and brought them here, his way of saying he understood.

I counted to three before I knocked on the door.

When he saw me there, he melted. Thick waves of love surrounded me.

"Sadie," he said, breathless. *Thank God*, he thought.

"Hi," I said. I wasn't sure what I expected to happen. I kept running off on him, kept running out on him, and last time, I had done it in such a way that I threw his offer to give me happiness — to give himself to me — back in his face. So, he could slam the door on me, and I would understand. I knew he would not, but I would understand it if he did.

But he was Cole Hardwick, and so he said, "Come in."

"Thank you," I stood awkwardly in the middle of his living room for a few moments, my arms folded nervously across my body as Cole set my bags aside. The darkness of all I had seen began to consume me.

He stood only inches behind me. *Please tell me you have chosen me. Please tell me you've come here to tell me it's me you've wanted all along instead of that animal.*

I felt guilty. The pang of withdrawal from Everett was real now. It pressed in on me, weighed heavy in my stomach. I *had* chosen Cole, hadn't I? Had chosen to run *from* Everett. Had chosen to run *toward* Cole. I believed Raven when he said there was human in me, even though I tried not to. Believed him that there would be a way out. And so if part of me, the supernatural part of me, could love Everett Winter, then it seemed only fair — fine, maybe it seemed inevitable — that the human part of me could love Cole. Some part of me wanted Everett, sure. The supernatural part I couldn't escape.

All of me wanted to be human.

"No questions?" I asked. "No 'What are you doing here?' or 'You can't keep coming back here like this!' or anything?"

He thought it over. "One question," he said. "Do you want to dance?"

I didn't respond. I didn't know what to say. How could he just accept me in this way? "Come on. You were so calm that time we danced. It will help clear your mind," he said.

He seemed unfazed by my silence, and so he walked to his stereo and put on a song. "We've equally made mistakes this time," he said. "I had no right to give you an ultimatum like that. I once told you I'd listen to absolutely anything you ever had to say, and from the look on your face, you've got a lot to say. You'll tell me when you're ready to. Or you won't." He didn't mean this in any bad way. Instead, he just accepted me. It was the strangest thing about him. He could stand in front of me, love me irrationally, and be completely content with how little he knew about me because he believed — in his beating heart, in his living soul — that he and I would get our chance, that we were meant to be. And so, he would wait for me, just like he'd always said he would. "So," he said, again, "do you want to dance?"

The funny thing was, I did.

I nodded and stepped toward him. He put his hand on my waist and took my hand in his. I felt that electricity again, saw murky colors hit on the tips of my vision, but after a few moments of dancing, all I saw differently were Cole's baby blue eyes glowing brighter in my mind. And in my heart.

We danced for a bit with space between us, just looking at one another.

"I do have one question," he amended.

"Okay," I said cautiously.

"Does that angry boyfriend of yours know you're here?" he asked.

"No," I admitted. "But he could probably guess." I took a step closer to rested my head on his shoulder. He pulled me tightly into him.

I listened to his beating heart, felt the warmth radiating from him, and I had to admit how lovely it all felt. Cole Hardwick was exactly what I wanted.

Just not who.

He bent his head toward mine and inhaled my hair. I had my eyes closed, and I knew he did, too. *I love you, Sadie Matthau.*

I could love someone for what they were, couldn't I?

"Cole?" I said softly.

"Hmm?" he said.

"I'm ready to answer your questions now."

lizzie's prayer

May, 2012
Hills of Romania, West of Suceava

NARCISA CRIED OUT IN PAIN. "WE TRIED!" SHE SCREAMED. "WE DID all we could! Stop!"

Alexander Raven laughed, the nosferatu bodies on the floor of the cave in front of him, heaped together, struggling for breath.

"It was not enough!" he bellowed.

"It was all we could do! Even after we told her what the *vieczy* were capable of, she still traveled with them. They must worship her!" Valentin cried.

"The vieczy travel with her? As if in her coven?" Raven asked, dropping to his knees to grab Narcisa's face in his hand. "Are you sure?"

"We're sure," Narcisa said.

"Her power must be unrivaled," he said, mystified. "You must find her again and travel with her. Then maybe, *maybe* I'll leave you and yours be. But no promises," he smiled slyly.

"Do we have a choice?" Narcisa cried.

"Not really," Raven said, rising to his feet. "I can kill you now, I suppose. But I hate to do that. You could be so useful!"

"We don't fight on the side of evil," Narcisa hissed. This angered Raven. Without touching her, he pulled her body into the air and wrenched it this way and that, until her screams echoed deep in the cave and out into the night.

"You'll fight on whatever side I tell you to. Everyone always does," he said smoothly. "Get to it. I'm sure we'll meet again. I hope for your sake it is with that girl."

⸻◈⸻

May 10, 2012
Survivors' City, Montana

LIZZIE WAITED UNTIL ANDREW AND JOHN FELL INTO A DEEP SLEEP. THEY WERE the last of the elders to do so each night. Neither could bear to let go of their power for long.

She walked directly from her cottage on the square back into the woods, her footsteps careful, silent. When she reached the city wall, she followed it until she hit the break she'd left in the protective barrier she and Rebecca had designed. Though all of the elders could pass over the barrier, the magic also allowed them to trace who came and went. The fourteen eldest Survivors hadn't trusted each other in centuries.

Once safely outside the city wall, she darted higher up the mountain, bounding lightly but swiftly across the melting snow. At the top, she dug in the melting snow until she uncovered the stone cross she'd built there when they first arrived. She lifted the solid stone structure effort-lessly and set it atop a nearby boulder.

She knelt silently before it, inhaled deeply, and steadied herself, making a vain attempt to stop the tears from flowing freely from her eyes. She began quiet, mournful prayers.

"Forgive me, Lord, for the crimes I commit. I did it all to save her from all of this," she said softly, her voice cracking, burdened by grief. Lizzie felt dizzy, unable to focus her emotion clearly on her own guilt or her newfound grief over her dear Sadie. "If I've taken life, it's been justified, though I know You don't condone an eye for an eye. And when I lied, it was to save her! To save her from a father unlike You…one who'd have ended her life mercilessly and without remorse," she choked, trying to justify — to herself and her God — her actions, and Sadie's.

She cleared her throat. "Help me, Savior. She needs You to stay with her. Once she tracks down her answers, I fear she will be all too willing to give her life away. I know that I will be unable to stop her, and this grieves my heart. There is no gift from You more precious than life itself. Why she has never been able to see this, I do not know, but I pray that maybe she will learn this truth before it is too late.

"Lord, I hope she can find a way to love him. She faces forever with him, an eternal bond to him, one that no one, that nothing can stop. And once I'm gone…she'll be his for the taking.

"And I hope she loves You, Lord. I hope she's good. I promise you I did the best I could possibly do with her spirit, with her lineage.

"Oh, Father, I tried to guide her in the right direction. I tried to tell her in time. I tried to save her, but I see now that I am not capable of such a feat. So, please, God, I hoped that you might save her since I cannot," she cried. She dropped her forehead to the ground and could barely contain herself, the sobs racked her small body. "Dear Father, she's just misunderstood."

Lizzie stayed this way for quite some time, searching for the power in her body to stand, to speak, to do anything. She sat back on her heels and wiped the tears from her face, and closed her prayer, "So, forgive me, Lord, for the crimes I commit. I did it all to save her from this."

Weakly, she rose to her feet. Her heart was heavy as she touched her cool fingertips to the cross one more time, her ghostly voice whispering, "Check her name off your list."

acknowledgments

THERE WERE SO MANY PEOPLE WHO WENT INTO THE CREATION AND execution of this book and all the other buzzing pieces of the Survivors world, and to all of you, named and unnamed, I owe my deepest gratitude.

First, my largest thanks. To the readers of and team behind Wattpad. What a gift you have all been. To see the MILLIONS of you who have lined up for *Survivors*, who've sent loving messages, left comments, and shared your own stories with me I THANK YOU. It is all of you, each and every one of you, who makes being a writer one hundred percent worthwhile. Thank you for believing me, for following the story, waiting with a patience I cannot even believe anyone possesses, and most importantly for falling in love with my characters. A special thanks to Nina Lassam for reaching out and everything that's happened since, and to Allen Lau and Maria Cootauco for continuing awesomeness.

To my publisher, Chafie Press, and the over-the-moon wonderful team there: Trish Jones, Erica Erwin, Michael Newman, and Emily Brown. Your patience and dedication with helping bring my insane ideas to life and actually listening to what I have to say have made this a dream process. I cannot thank you enough. To KP Simmon for guidance and friendship and a never-tiring PR mind. To Elizabeth Middlebrooks Steif for all the grammatical First Aid. And, of course, to Jane Cavolina, beloved editor, for continuing to find clarity in my chaos.

A giant hug and thanks to the team at NPG PR — Nicole Pope Gaia, Alexis Tedford, Hayley Frank, and Kiley Kaye — for all the press releases, pitches, hand-holding, ass-busting, traveling, and unbelievable dedication for the PR on my books and the Immersedition app. I can't thank you enough. Truly.

To all my friends who listened as I paced and thought this one out loud, one weird piece of history, fashion, mythology, or insanity at a time, including but certainly not limited to Meghan Hannigan Knoll (we'll always have Salem), Danielle Thienel for telling me when my boys aren't what a girl really wants, Erica Erwin for listening to me ramble and try to make sense of it, and Chelsea Utley for making sure I sort of kind of made sense. To Liz Scofield for pointing out why vieczy can't use iPhones. And of course a GIANT HUGE MEGA thanks to Deanna Walker for seeing in this story what I do, and helping me figure out how to express it when I haven't already. Oh and, for, you know, teaching me how to write songs.

A second (third?) thanks to Deanna for her amazing work on all the Survivors Singles original songs. You've served as collaborator, mentor, muse, and friend, and I cannot thank you enough for your role in all of this. To Rick Beresford and Tiffany Vartanyan for their amazing work on "Who You Are," and to Rick for always having food, wine, and the philosophical piece. To Chris "Lord" Utley/Redbeard for being the single greatest recording engineer on the planet, probably on all the planets. And to his wife Chelsea for letting us borrow him. A great thanks to Ilya Toshinsky for producing the songs with Deanna and bringing us great players. And to the players who bring the songs to life.

Of course a giant debt of gratitude (and awe) to all of the artists who have recorded the original songs: the so-over-the-top-talented Chris

Mann (who is one of my favorite people of all time) for "Pretty Girl" and signing books as Everett, to "Breaking" singer Jess Moskaluke whose voice still continues to blow me away, and to Patrick Thomas and Jenny Gill for making "Who You Are" as beautiful as it is. Thanks also to all the amazingly talented local artists who participated in our soundtrack covers concert series on YouTube, the Survivors Sessions: Minnie Murphy & Sean Weaver, Savannah Grace, Sam Hawksley, Daniel Novick, Sarah Williams, Ashley Nite & Cole Shugart, David Llewellyn & Ida Kristin, Buick Audra, Jeffrey East, Lauren Price, The magical Roberts triplets: Jared, Justin and Jordan, the Granville Automatic girls, Vanessa Olivarez & Elizabeth Elkins, Ryan Thies, and of course the living legend, Pam Tillis since I can still not believe she so kindly agreed to participate. I'll remember each of you always. Every performance has inspired me more than you know, and it's all a part of a dream come true.

And of course, what is music these days without video? To that, I owe Tyler Stein and Gaby Román all the credit. You've both been brilliant to work with, and I appreciate every move you've made. A special thanks to Grant Harling and Tiffany Vartanyan for being Cole and Sadie in our "Who You Are" video. As well as to Mary Stanley, Angelica Smith, and Mel Manson for making everyone so pretty on screen.

Thanks to Tami and Erin at TLC Graphics for taking all the time to listen and making a great cover. And to Meghan McKeighan for a rocking cityscape-and-head-shot.

And to all the bloggers who have contributed in innumerable ways to the success of this series, I cannot thank you enough. Your kindness in sharing your love for the series with your dedicated followers is a gift I can hardly repay. Thank you.

Also for the team at Demibooks who built us the beautiful *Survivors* Immersedition interactive book app and excelled at a massive level of patience with me: Andy Skinner, Waiton Fong, Stacey Williams-Ng, and Rafiq Ahmed.

And I hope it goes without saying, I thank my parents, to whom I owe more than I can count. And to my brother, who calls it like it is and added a contribution or two.

And, finally, to the many sources of inspiration I can't *not* cite here. The soundtrackers: Coldplay, Peter Bjorn and John, The Zombies, Lovers, Florence the Machine, Credence Clearwater Revival, Sara Bareilles, Ingrid Michaelson, Sia, Lykke Li, Missy Higgins, We Were Promised Jetpacks, Franz Ferdinand, Missy Higgins, Denison Witmer, Manchester Orchestra, Grace Potter & the Nocturnals, Old Crow Medicine Show, and Augustana. And to other major listening influences: The Black Keys, Adele, Mumford & Sons, Ray LaMontagne & the Pariah Dogs, Arcade Fire, Fleet Foxes, and a trillion more that would fill up their own book. The designers: from Proenza Schouler to Rebeca Minkoff to Ray-Ban and the million others in-between. And of course, to the biggest of them all, my assumed hometown, Nashville, Tennessee. The people, the places, the music, the food, and the energy radiating up from the streets: You've all been a part of making *The Survivors* what it is and making me what I am. And for that, I owe you everything.

Here's to you all. Or as I should say, all y'all.

A special preview from
the third installment in

.†HE 'SURVIVORS.

the end

A FOG SET IN. ITS MURKY WHITE FINGERTIPS REACHED OUT TO ME, enveloping my body in a careful embrace. Stiff grass bristled against my bare feet, contrasting the fluid movement of silk across my legs. I was wearing a couture gown, green brighter than the grass, so heavy it weighed on me, a train trailing behind me as I crossed the field.

The fog thickened quickly, its grasp tightening around my body until I was consumed by it. Greyness and nothingness filled my senses until I was utterly trapped by the clouds, swept under them as if they were solid. But I remained on my feet. The fog propelled me forward toward an ominous mystery. Somehow, I knew I wasn't alone.

A huddled mass appeared at my feet, and my heart leapt as my mind processed what my eyes had seen.

It was Noah.

His eyes rolled back in his head as his hand twitched. His body was wrenched backwards, and twisted in a way it shouldn't. He was dying.

Then Andrew. His hand appeared at my feet, breaking through the thick fog. Blood ran down his milky skin, obscuring most of a crimson symbol on his wrist. As I stepped closer, the fog ebbed and flowed around him, forming a cavern over him. His body was in a frozen half crawled position, his arms reaching out for help from me. But his eyes were closed, and he was stiff. I knew he was dead.

Then it was Cassie, a young Survivor with burning red eyes and veins so blue-black on her face they looked like cracks in marble. Then Hannah. Then Sarah. Then Lizzie. Sweet, pained, fair-haired Lizzie. Her eyes were open and glassy, perpetually staring into the hopeless oblivion of the scene around her.

Then, one by one, all the Survivors I cared about lay dead at my feet as I walked across the blood-stained plain. I bowed to none of them, though I couldn't say why.

I walked farther and farther across the green landscape, littered with the dead and dying members of my family, trying desperately to escape the fog and the death and the weight it put in my gut. Ahead of me, the fog parted, as if anticipating my arrival, until I reached the final, wispy edges of the air where I could see beyond the clouds. Once in the open clearing of the field, the mangled bodies of every member of my family surrounded me. Bloodied and twisted, some writhing, some still.

They went on for rows and rows this way, until they surrounded me entirely. Then, laid out in a line, arms crossed over their chests, were the six bodies of the human family we'd seen in the house in the hidden city where we'd met Ava Bientrut — Tituba. I thought about them a lot, the Gaulets. Especially of the little girls, tucked into bed with their stuffed animals, the infant alone in the crib, and of the mother who looked as if the baby had been violently ripped from her arms. The massacre of the Gaulets was the strongest, most jarring memory and the purest evidence I could attach to Alexander Raven's evil, and so they haunted me.

I stepped past their bodies, quieted by death, and walked farther into the unending sea of my dead family. The scene was set in such a way that it seemed real — so real that I could taste the smell of blood in the air, the feel of summer wind in the Montana mountains.

Then in front of me stood sweet, soft Cole Hardwick. "It's all right, Sadie," he said in his faint Southern drawl. "Don't be afraid."

"What are you doing here?" I asked him, excited by a living face.

He smiled softly, but as if confused. "I belong here, Sadie. I'm a Survivor, just like you." His eyes were deeper. More purple. His face harder.

"But how?" I asked him.

"In him, all things are possible," he said.

I thought he was referring to God, the parable common. But behind him, Alexander Raven appeared. His menacing eyes and wax-cut face, black walnut hair and hunching statue — they were the embodiments of evil to me now.

"In Raven, all things are possible," Cole repeated.

Raven smiled, one malicious muscle movement at a time. "She knows," he said, his voice the same melodic, misanthropic sound I'd heard in Oaxaca. "Trust me, my son," he eased, placing a bony, ivory hand on Cole's shoulder. "She knows."

Raven kept his eyes on me, that same sick grin on his face, as he produced a dagger and raised it up over his head and in one, driving force, brought it crashing down into the side of Cole's neck.

"No! Cole!"

He fell to the ground. Dead like the rest of them. Dead like them all.

—◆—

I JOLTED AWAKE, SCREAMING HIS NAME. THE BED SHOOK VIOLENTLY AS COLE'S substantial body jumped alongside me.

I saw on his face that he couldn't tell if he was dreaming. I hadn't exactly told him I'd come to lie next to him while he slept in some insane attempt to get to sleep myself, and he had never caught me. In the weeks I'd been in New York, I'd managed to get maybe a couple dozen hours of sleep, none of which happened when I was in his guest room, staring at the ceiling, alone with my thoughts.

"Sadie?" he asked, when he finally gained understanding. "Are...are you okay?" His eyes were half open and his hair was disheveled.

I put my hands on his neck to feel his warmth, his pulse, and his skin intact. This made him question the reality of it even more — me, in his bed, my hands on him. It was something he'd dreamed before.

"I'm fine," I said.

"Was it a nightmare?" he asked tentatively, afraid of what would have made me scream out his name in terror in my sleep.

"Yes," I nodded, looking at my feet. I was dazed by what I'd seen. The images of my family, dead and mangled, more real than anything I'd ever seen in Anthony's visions, gave me the first real understanding I had of what was at stake in this war.

"Do you want to talk about it?" he asked, his eyes searching my face for what he was supposed to do, how he was supposed to react.

He held my gaze just too long. Long enough for me to remember why I wasn't supposed to sleep next to him. Long enough to remember that I had run from Everett Winter to get here. Long enough for me to remember who I was.

"No," I said hurriedly, scrambling to my feet.

"Where are you going?" he asked.

"Go back to sleep," I said, from the foot of his bed.

"No, I'll get up with you," he said, sitting up.

"You don't have to. Please. Just rest," I said, turning to leave his room.

"Sadie, I know I don't have to. I want to," he said tenderly, rising to his feet. "You know I worry about you," he said, but he thought, *You know I love you.*

His eyes were so sincere. They carried the emotion that no eyes I'd ever seen carried. They made promises to you — like he'd love you forever, like he'd make it all go away — and for one second, you believed those eyes. I did, anyway. I suppose I wanted to.

But then, as always, I'd remember it all. The truth. What had become of my reality. What had become of me.

He stepped forward and wrapped his arms around my waist, his movements as gentle, as tentative as they were the day of Corrina's wedding. "Let me be here for you," he said. "I can call out of work. We can just hide out or go out or…whatever you want."

"No. No, Cole, I'm really fine. Just shaken. You and I both know that you can't just miss work. Don't worry about me. Today's the same as any other day. My life is still in shambles, but I'm still intact enough for you to go. Okay?" I asked.

He still had his arms wrapped around me. We realized it at the exact same moment, and he dropped them. "Okay," he relented. He looked at the clock. "Ah, it's too late to go back to bed. I'll go work out instead. I'm never up early enough to. Might as well take advantage," he said. I nodded softly and left him in his room to change, and then he was out the door.

I busied my hands as soon as he left. I didn't want to think about what I'd seen. I needed new sights and sounds to drown out the mind-movie that was currently doing me in. I turned on the TV and watched old *Saved by the Bell* reruns that came on this time of the morning. Corrina used to watch them when she was sleepless, either from drunkenness or missing Felix or both, and so in some weird way it comforted me. Then I pulled out my iPad, flipped to my *Epicurious* app, and found a suitable recipe for a breakfast I thought Cole might like. I dug through his kitchen and found the necessary ingredients and tools to make a frittata. I'd never cooked in my life before these last few weeks, but Cole loved to cook, and it had become a nice way to spend time together. I liked it because it allowed me to occupy my mind fully with something new and nonthreatening. Cole liked it because once my mind was busy, he was more likely to get me to give him honest answers out of convenience. When I was cooking, I didn't have enough mind power to worry about lies, so I just told him the truth.

To be fair, he was running out of questions. I'd answered most of them that night I'd arrived here, disheveled and dirty and exhausted and in fragments after watching Valentin die and feeling Narcisa mourn him and realizing what my life had become.

I'd said, "I'm ready to answer your questions now."

And he took a long breath and didn't say anything for a while. Then finally he'd said, "Let's finish the song first," which was somehow the perfect thing to say. In that moment, he was able to tell me that nothing was more important than the two of us just being there. Happy. Together.

And then, when the song ended, he'd put on more music, a soothing soundtrack to the horror story I was about to tell him. He sat on his couch as I told him everything. At first I paced while I spoke. And then I had to sit down with the weight of it. And then finally, I crumpled against his couch cushions, losing my carefully crafted exterior, and he pulled me toward him, holding me as I hiccupped out the rest of it.

He hadn't said a word the whole time, but I'd had the strength to keep going because I could feel that he believed me. That he knew it made too much sense to be an elaborate lie I had woven. That in some ways, he was relieved. *Who could be normal when they were dealing with this?* he'd asked himself. *Of course*, he'd thought when I'd told him some things. *I just wish I could have been there for you*, he'd thought at other things.

"And then I came here," I'd said. "Because I'm afraid. Because I don't want to go back. Because I can't live that life anymore."

He'd bent forward in his seat, hands folded together, pressed up against his lips. And for the first time in God knows how many hours, Cole had spoken.

"How do we find a way to free you?"

That was all he'd said. *That* was the first question he'd asked. I didn't have to tell him I wanted to be free. He'd heard the story, and he knew that what anyone would want was freedom.

And he'd wanted to know how he could help me find it.

I was replaying this moment in my head when he came back from his workout, all sweaty and human and pink, his pulse working to re-acclimate to its usual pace. He was just so *alive*, and that never got old.

He laughed when he saw the frittata I was making. "I cannot believe you'd never so much as boiled water in a modern kitchen until three weeks ago, and here you are now. A regular Martha Stewart," he smiled as he opened the fridge to get a fresh bottle of water.

"Not Martha Stewart," I corrected. "She can craft too. I can only cook."

This time he laughed out loud, water trickling from the corners of his mouth. "And I *really* cannot believe that you've only lived in this world for going on four years and you can already correct me on the nuances of my pop culture references."

I shrugged, but I was amused. It was kind of fun having a human know my secrets. He seemed to appreciate the skill set I'd amassed in being able to live my life on the outside, considering my original cir-cumstances. And who doesn't like to be appreciated?

"Is that going to be ready before my shower?" he asked.

"Well, on average, it takes you seventeen minutes between the time you walk in there and the time you walk out clean with your suit pants and undershirt on, ready to eat your breakfast. This should be ready in fourteen minutes, if you stop talking to me, and should take me at least ninety seconds to plate and…"

He cut me off. "Got it. Superbrain has already calculated, and now I must go shower quickly so as to effectively play the part of cog in the machine."

"Something like that," I called as he closed the door to his room. I neglected to tell him that Superbrain had made two frittatas as practice while he worked out, and I was hoping this "real" one would actually come out right. If you've only been cooking for three weeks, you lack the proper amount of practice. So I built in my own.

And sure enough, the timing worked out perfectly. I was just pressing down the French press when he emerged.

Cole flipped the channel to *Good Morning America* like he did every morning, ate his breakfast, and said, like he did every morning, that he could get used to this as he tied his tie in the kitchen and shrugged into his suit jacket. He poured himself the last of the coffee into a travel mug, kissed my forehead, and left for work.

◆

FIFTEEN MINUTES LATER, WHEN THE KITCHEN WAS CLEANED, AND I HAD PUT *Good Morning America* on mute because of some talk about a *Real Housewives* show that I really had no patience for, my mind was too idle again. I tried to decide what to do with my day. It would have to be something that had nothing to do with my Survivor life. Not research. Not even reading. Just…something else entirely.

I looked around the room, trying to think of the appropriate distraction. My Moleskine notebook stared back at me from the coffee table. I hated it the most. I tried diligently to ignore the most recent list I'd written in it and pored over every day since I'd arrived in Manhattan. The list of my questions about Raven, all of which arose from our cryptic conversation that night in Xoxocotlán.

A conversation in which Alexander Raven had claimed to be the most powerful creature on earth, with one exception.

Vampiric inbreed. What did he mean?
What could be more powerful than he is?

BOOK THREE

A conversation in which he'd threatened the lives of everyone I knew and loved, a conversation in which he promised to come after us, and so I wanted to know how to come after him first.

How do we find him? HOW? Could we track Sam? (Even though we never have before?)

A conversation in which he revealed to me his plan to kill each of them for his or her powers. Like he apparently had done to all of his families. For the last four thousand years.

And WHY? Why do you need power other than for battle? What is he planning?

A conversation in which he'd claimed I was part human, thereby telling me that I might already be what I'd wanted to be all along. Telling me there might really be a way to die. And telling me of his plans to procreate with me to fill a world with…

Does that make me some kind of half-human hybrid? Why does he care? Why would he want half-humans? And quarter-humans? (What would happen if I was… pregnant? What kind of offspring would I have?)

A conversation in which I learned that he knew too much about me, or had maybe heard of me before in ways I couldn't understand.

He called me "Pretty Girl." Like nosferatu, like eretica, like Sam. What does it mean?

A conversation in which he'd claimed to have inherited the skills, powers, and weaknesses from Achilles in the Trojan War. That's how Survivors got their proverbial Achilles' heel. Because Raven had supposedly received this weakness upon killing Achilles, just like he acquired some of Achilles' other curses.

Who was his Pensilethea?

A conversation in which I began to try to fit pieces together. He never spoke of mothers — of Hannah's mother, of any of the women who raised the creatures he supposedly fathered or created. And in the hidden town in England, we'd found the mother of the Gaulet family particularly brutalized. How did this fit into Alexander Raven's venomous psyche?

His opposition to mothers — like Gaulets?

A conversation in which he'd revealed plenty by what he didn't say.

He mentioned Beowulf, knew it had brought me to him, but he said nothing of Theogony or Macbeth. Why?

A conversation in which he'd alluded to a final, perhaps an ultimate act of evil.

"Finale?" What did he mean by finale?

A conversation that led me to wonder even more about my maternal mentor.

How much of this does Lizzie know?

A conversation in which he'd told me how to kill a Survivor.

"Our greatest weakness is at the source of our greatest power."

His parting words? *Now chew on that, you morbid little girl.*

And so I'd chewed. Over and over and over again. I did not know how to find him or how to escape him. I did not know how to save my family. And so I'd sought refuge — I'd *run* — here. To New York. To the human world. To a life where I didn't have to care about Raven.

But he found me. This morning he'd found me, in Cole's bed, in a couture gown, in my own head, in the place of my greatest fears. I was never out of Alexander Raven's reach.

I looked at the clock. Only twenty minutes since Cole had walked out the door. I was doing an awful job of forgetting. The list infiltrated my mind. The dream pulled at me. I guess now I had to figure out what my final goal was. How long did I plan to stay in New York with Cole? Now that spring had melted into summer, we were well into the months in which the rogue Survivors and Raven's forces could attack at any time. The snow had melted at the elevations where the Survivors' City was. Anthony's vision could come true any day now.

And here I was, hours and hours away from there, even running at my top speed, even if there had been a private jet waiting for me outside Cole's apartment, camped on Spring Street. Had I been so diligent about not thinking that I'd neglected to realize that if the war started right this second, it could be over by the time I arrived there?

This put a knot in my stomach. How I had managed to ignore the logistics was beyond me. Had I abandoned the Survivors and Winters entirely when I'd come here? Or was I just waiting for something? And if I was waiting, what was I waiting for?

My plan to think about anything but this had failed miserably.

Then my phone rang. It rang periodically these days. Cole would call to discuss plans for the evening. Corrina would call to ask about Cole and shopping in New York.

Then the rest of them would call. I had never once answered when that happened. Ginny called constantly and left long, rambling, increasingly angry voicemails. Adelaide called and urged me to come home, and if I wouldn't come home, to at least take care of myself. Anthony left stiff voicemails about strategy and my being the only one who could give our side a fair chance in the impending battle. Patrick did much the same. And on and on and on.

But two of them never called: Mark and Everett. Well, that wasn't true. Everett called at first, when he thought this time was just another day-long need for escape. He called to tell me he loved me. He called to say he understood I wanted space, and so he'd see me soon, when I made it back home to him. But as the days stretched on, his calls thinned out, and his voicemails ended mindlessly, sometimes in the middle of sentences, and without the normally ever-present "I love you."

And Mark hadn't called a single time. He'd been the one who understood, so what was there to say? At first I worried that I'd misinterpreted his original gesture of bringing my bags and the plastic magic wand we'd bought in Salem and leaving them at Cole's door without a word. Maybe that was less of an "I understand" gesture, like I'd thought, and more of a "Good riddance" gesture. But then one night, Cole was texting someone — supposedly Felix — when I read from him that it was Mark. They'd been talking. Mark, unlike the rest of them, wanted to check in on me, but he didn't want me to feel pressured to come home. He always understood me best.

So this morning when I got to my phone and the words MARK WIN-TER lit up across the screen, I didn't know how to feel. Should I do him the service of answering, since he'd done me the service of giving me space when I needed it most?

I debated too long. The phone stopped ringing, and the words MISSED CALL appeared instead. I felt strangely relieved when this happened. Maybe I would call him back. But not today. Today it all felt too close, too real. Today I needed to be Sadie Matthau, born 1990. I needed to feel *human.*

Only the phone rang again. I dismissed the call.

But then it rang again. And again.

Then there were two minutes of silence before the words EVERETT WINTER appeared in their glowing white writing for the first time in weeks. In minutes, my attitude had gone from ambivalent to angry, and now I wanted them to leave me alone.

So I picked up. "I don't want to talk to you, and I only answered to tell you to leave me alone. Not today. I can't talk today."

"Sadie…" he said, his voice soft, broken. What was I doing to poor Everett Winter?

I felt bad about hurting him. But I was hurting too, and I felt it was okay for me to just handle that for once. "I can call you tomorrow, Everett. Or even later today if I get my head clear, I just…"

"Sadie," he said, more forcefully now.

"You're not hearing me," I said, angry again.

"Sadie, shut up."

"Wha—"

"███████ 's dead."

WANT A NEW WAY TO READ

·THE 'SURVIVORS·

DOWNLOAD THE IMMERSEDITION
INTERACTIVE BOOK APP!

Follow Sadie's journey with soundtrack music, historical documents, maps, character profiles, photos, music videos, and more!

**SCAN THE CODE TO
DOWNLOAD NOW!**

Chafie Creative

HAVE YOU HEARD THE SOUNDTRACK?

CHECK OUT THE ORIGINAL SONGS RECORDED JUST FOR *THE SURVIVORS*!

Pretty Girl by Chris Mann
from The Voice Season 2

breaking
by Jess Moskaluke

who you are by Patrick Thomas
& Jenny Gill
from The Voice Season 1

download them now in
iTunes

watch the music videos on
youtube.com/amandahavard